...ills & ... . On her wa...
...to this dream Nina acquired an English degree, a hero of
her own, three gorgeous children and—somehow!—an
...countancy qualification. She lives in Brighton and has
...ed her house with stacks of books—her very own *real*
...ary.

Since 1988, national bestselling author **Rochelle Alers** has
...tten more than eighty books and short stories. She has
...ned numerous honors, including the Zora Neale
...rston Award, the Vivian Stephens Award for Excellence
...Romance Writing and a Career Achievement Award
...m *RT Book Reviews*. She is a member of Zeta Phi
...ta Sorority, Inc., Iota Theta Zeta Chapter. A
...l-time writer, she lives in a charming hamlet on
...ng Island. Rochelle can be contacted through her
...ebsite, www.rochellealers.org

BABY ON THE TYCOON'S DOORSTEP

NINA MILNE

STARTING OVER IN WICKHAM FALLS

ROCHELLE ALERS

MILLS & BOON

First Published in Great Britain 2020
by Mills & Boon, an imprint of HarperCollinsPublishers,
1 London Bridge Street, London, SE1 9GF

Baby On The Tycoon's Doorstep © 2020 Nina Milne
Starting Over in Wickham Falls © 2020 Rochelle Alers

ISBN: 978-0-263-27881-1

0520

MIX
Paper from
responsible sources
FSC™ C007454

This book is produced from independently certified FSC™
paper to ensure responsible forest management.

For more information visit: www.harpercollins.co.uk/green

Printed and bound in Spain
by CPI, Barcelona

BABY ON THE TYCOON'S DOORSTEP

NINA MILNE

To my family,
for putting up with me during the writing of this book!

PROLOGUE

Six years ago

ISOBEL TRIED TO determine which emotion was uppermost, incandescent rage or sheer gut-pounding, rib-squeezing hurt. She opted for the former because she would not succumb to the latter. The thought of breaking down in tears prickled her skin with aversion—she would not give Jake Cartwright the satisfaction.

Instead she watched as Jake paced the room, each stride an angry re-treading of the past hour's conversation, his whole body taut with frustration. Then she hurled words, each one laden with fury.

'How could you do this? And why the hell won't you just admit it?'

'I won't admit it because I didn't do it. How many more times can I tell you this?' He halted in front of her. 'I did not sleep with Anna.' Each word was enunciated with exaggerated emphasis.

'Jeez, Jake. Repetition doesn't make the words true. You must think I'm an A-grade idiot. Fact: I caught Anna sneaking out of your house at one-fifteen in the morning. Fact: she confessed!'

The memory so vivid. Beautiful, blonde, perfect Anna. Supposedly 'just a friend' from Jake's university days.

Anna with her long blonde hair and endless legs and her first-class degree in economics and her brand-new modelling contract. Difficult to know which to be more threatened by.

Long hair tousled, shoes in hand, a cat that's had the cream smile on her face. A smile that had dropped from her lips with almost incongruous speed when she'd seen Isobel approach. 'Isobel? What are you doing here? I... we thought you were at work.'

'My shift finished early. I thought I'd surprise Jake.' The words had fallen from her lips on automatic, her tone ridiculously polite, almost conversational as the full ramifications of the scene pounded her brain. The irony not lost on her. 'Turns out the surprise is on me.'

'Isobel. Listen to me.' Anna's voice was urgent now, those wide blue eyes full of concern.

'There's nothing for you to say.' She sidestepped to get around the willowy model, frowned when Anna reached out and took her arm.

'Wait. Please. Let me explain. Before you see Jake. Please Isobel. Come with me. Hear my side first.' Isobel hesitated; part of her wanted to storm in and confront Jake, part of her recoiled at the idea of seeing him now, fresh from Anna, perhaps still tangled in the sheets... The whole thought shuddered her body with humiliation.

'OK.'

'Thank you.' Anna's grip tightened on her arm. 'We can't talk here. There's an all-night diner round the corner.'

The walk achieved in a dull silence punctuated by the click of Anna's high heels on the pavement; images tormented Isobel's brain as realisation struck. Jake slept with Anna. Jake slept with Anna. Anger began to bubble, anger at him and anger at herself. How could she have been such a fool? Why had she agreed to date him? She should have known this would happen. Jake was gorgeous and rich and fun; used to women falling at his feet, He dated whichever beautiful model or celebrity took his fancy. Now he'd slept with Anna. Jake slept with Anna.

She followed Anna into a small café, redolent with the smell of cooked breakfasts, fried eggs, the whiff of chip fat...

'Sit here,' Anna instructed, placing her handbag on a table as she gestured to Isobel. 'I'll get coffee. Americano right?'

Isobel nodded; it seemed easier than a refusal. Not that she could drink anything purchased by Anna—she'd probably choke. A few minutes later the blonde woman returned, sat down facing Isobel and leant forward.

'You have to forgive Jake. You have to. This was a one-off. I know it is. It's you he cares for and I think I was just a final fling before he commits. To you. I know he will be regretting it and it was my fault—my idea. Jake and I are friends. Nothing more.' Anna put a hand on her arm. 'It meant nothing. To either of us.'

Isobel shook her head. 'But it means something to me.'

'Please. You have to forgive him.'

Isobel rose from the table. 'No Anna. I don't.'

And she still didn't.

After her conversation with Anna she had felt too raw to confront Jake, her insides scorched with sheer humiliation, her brain leaden with the awful knowledge of betrayal. Instead she'd sat, sleepless, by the window of her small rented room until dawn had touched the sky. Sat and thought and soon the mortification had been replaced by a welcome bright bitter light of fury. An anger that didn't allow even the vestige of forgiveness.

Not that Jake was asking for forgiveness—instead he

had the gall to try and turn it on her. Was furious with Isobel for not yielding to his will, for refusing to enter his illusory world where he was innocent. Shades of her childhood. Her stepfather's repeated lies and denials, the excuses that spewed from his mouth, his assertion that it was actually his wife's fault that he had hit her, that he was sorry, that he loved her. And Tanya Brennan always ceded and accepted him back.

No way was Isobel following that pattern—any pattern followed by her mother. Folding her arms now she glared at Jake. 'I have evidence and a confession.'

'You also have my word. I didn't sleep with Anna.'

'Then why was she tiptoeing out of your house at one-fifteen in the morning?'

'I don't know.' Jake gusted a sigh. 'But I can tell you what I think. Anna knew I was out. She still has a key from years ago when she stayed here whilst I was away. I think she used my house last night to entertain a "friend".'

'Then why didn't she tell me that?'

'Because she is seeing a man she has to keep secret— either a politician or someone married—she won't say. When she saw you, my guess is she panicked in case you stormed in and found him.'

'Then why doesn't she tell me now?'

'Because it could compromise him.'

Isobel shook her head. 'You have to admit that sounds sketchy at best. Anyway, if you weren't here, where were you? Prove to me you were somewhere else.'

'I can't. I was out walking.'

'Walking?' She could hear the high-pitched rise of her voice. 'Surely you can come up with something better than that? Walking where?'

'It's the truth. I had a bit of a row with my father.' Isobel stilled. In the months she had known him, Jake had mentioned his father less than a handful of times. 'I decided to go for a drive and then I parked and just walked.'

'So how did Anna even know the house was empty?'

'She called and I told her I was out for the evening. It was risky but Anna has always thrived on risk.' Yet another reason why she and Jake were suited to each other, Isobel thought dully. 'I get it sounds sketchy but it is the truth.'

Isobel stared at him.

She closed her eyes, realising she wanted to believe him. Knew she couldn't. The image of Anna, the way she had walked down the drive, the smile on her face, the urgency of her words—how could she disregard that? Plus, Anna was in Jake's league, beautiful, intelligent, wealthy. She was his type. Isobel wasn't. Isobel had grown up on a barren, desolate estate and then been consigned to the care system; Isobel only had the money she earned herself as a waitress; Isobel had dropped out of school at sixteen. This whole idea of dating Jake had been a mistake of massive proportions and now she was paying for her error in spades, clubs and her own heart.

Now he stepped forward and for a moment, despite herself, she was struck anew by his sheer aura, tried to remind herself that the thick blond hair, the charismatic blue-grey eyes, the strength of feature was a simple genetic chance. 'You have to believe me.'

Wrong choice of words.

That was what her mother had said time and again.

'This time I won't take your stepdad back. You have to believe me.'

Her stepdad talking to her mother. *'I won't hurt you again. I love you. I've changed. You have to believe me.'*

As if the phrase had some sort of hypnotic, magical mesmerism. The power to dictate.

She shook her head. 'No,' she said. 'I don't have to believe you. Not when all the facts tell me the opposite.'

Anger and hurt etched his face. 'Do you truly believe that I would cheat on you and then deny it, lie to you to your face?'

'I don't think you set out to do it, Jake. I think you and Anna got carried away in the moment, you took a risk because you genuinely thought I wouldn't find out.'

'That is not what happened.'

Isobel clenched her hands into fists—she would not believe him simply because she wanted to. Wouldn't repeat her mother's pattern. 'It's over, Jake.'

'Is that really what you want?' His voice was harder now, edged with intensity. 'Because it's not what I want. But it's your call. You either trust me or you don't.'

Be strong. 'I can't trust you. Not after this. And you can't have a relationship without trust.'

'Then I guess it's goodbye.' His voice was pure ice now and she forced herself to turn and leave the room. Refused to acknowledge the ache in her heart, told herself this was for the best. She was better off on her own— she'd always known that.

CHAPTER ONE

Present day

JAKE CARTWRIGHT LEFT the crowded tube station and strode forward through the throng on the pavement. He felt the welcome breeze on his face after the cramped underground journey. Sure, he could afford the chauffeured cars that his father took everywhere—hell, Charles Cartwright had a fleet of limos on tap—and he knew his father despised the fact that his son chose to use public over private transport.

Not that Jake gave a flying fish about his father's opinion. Not any more. He'd spent way too many hours of childhood caring about his father. Wondering why his dad didn't want him, why he lived with his grandfather, only saw his dad once in a blue moon.

Then, when Jake was six and his grandfather died, a limo arrived and Jake was chauffeured to Charles' London mansion. Jake could still remember his searing grief, his burning hope that his dad would be there to comfort him. A hope that had flickered out instantly—Charles hadn't even been home to greet his son. That had been left to Petra, Charles' PA-cum-assistant. It had been a prelude of times to come—Jake had been left to his own devices, his material needs looked after by Petra and the various interchangeable girlfriends and hangers-on that made up his dad's entourage.

Every so often Charles would see him, usually in company, each meeting always edged with awkwardness. Eventually Jake had decided to accept his father's indifference and lock down the emotional turmoil, all the questions, hurt and anger caused. Decided to get on with his life.

But now that Jake held a stake in the Cartwright empire, Charles Cartwright's apathy had turned to antagonism and he seemed dead set on thwarting his son at every boardroom turn.

Jake's pace increased—he would not let his father continue to run the business into the ground with his policy of extracting as much money as possible to spend on his hedonistic lifestyle.

For a moment the image of his grandfather flashed across his brain. *'You are the Cartwright heir, Jake. Never forget it.'*

And he hadn't—his life's ambition was to lead the company into a glorious future. Soon enough he would—in ten days, to be precise. In ten days he would wrest control from his father.

His phone rang and he pulled it from his pocket, noted the identity of the caller—Helen McKenzie, manager of the flagship hotel, Cartwright of Mayfair.

'Jake?' Helen's voice spoke of relief. 'I've been trying to get hold of you.'

'Sorry. I must have lost signal on the tube.' Jake pressed the phone to his ear, striving to block out the noises of the city—the familiar rumble of double-decker buses, the hum of mobile phones, the stream of chatter, the pounding of shoes on the sun-flecked pavements. 'What's wrong?'

'Um… A baby was left at Reception a couple of hours ago.'

Jake frowned. 'Did a guest leave her baby by mistake?' And not noticed for two hours? Unlikely but possible.

'That's what we thought at first. But then—' Helen hesitated. 'When no one came to claim the baby, I gave her to Maria to look after.'

'Good call.' Maria was the hotel's housekeeper, a mother of four with a brood of grandchildren.

'And I was about to call the police. But then Maria found a letter in the carrycot.' Deep breath. 'Addressed to you.'

'Me?'

'Yes. We haven't opened it, but I figured it was best to talk to you.'

Another good call. 'How old is this baby?'

'Maria thinks she is about three, maybe four months.'

'OK. Don't do anything. I'm on my way.'

Jake dropped the phone back in his pocket and moved to the kerb to hail a cab, knowing that would get him to the hotel fastest. His mind raced, told him that, whatever was going on, at least the baby couldn't be his. This past year or so he'd been so caught up in work, in his mission to gain control, he'd had no down time at all. His work hard, play hard ethos had morphed to work hard and work harder.

He took a deep breath as he climbed into the black cab and continued to process the situation, wondering who the baby belonged to and what she had to do with Jake.

Half an hour later he alighted outside the hotel and walked through the revolving glass doors into the opulent marble foyer, rich with exotic greenery, enhanced by the gentle sounds of the water feature to one side and enlivened by the sculptures on display by various London artists. He headed straight for the lift and to Maria's domain. Although Maria didn't live in the hotel she did sometimes stay and a room was available to her at all times.

Jake knocked and then paused on the threshold for a moment when the executive housekeeper called, 'Come in.'

Maria was sitting in her rocking chair by the bed where the baby lay asleep, surrounded by pillows. Both tiny hands curled into fists resting by her head, a head covered in a fine down of wispy brown hair. His breath caught in his throat as he registered the sheer vulnerability of this tiny being who had been deposited in his hotel and he felt a sudden stab of empathy. Left abandoned, unwanted—just like Jake had been.

His father had left within hours of his birth, jaunted off on a nine-month cruise. As for his mother, she'd hung around for a couple of days and then gone on her way and Jake hadn't seen her until he was eighteen. More memories crowded in. His mother's face, streaked with tears as she'd explained, the words tumbling out as though she had stored them up for years. She'd desperately needed money—her younger brother had been dangerously ill, but with the chance of a life-saving operation in the States if they could raise the money. She'd started a charity appeal and Charles Cartwright had contacted her and made a deal: marry him, provide him with a child and leave for a new life in the States—he'd pay for the operation, the aftercare and make a generous settlement.

'I had to do it, Jake.' His mother had dried her eyes, gazed at him with desperate appeal in her blue eyes. *'I had no choice.'*

Irrelevant. What mattered now was *this* baby. Jake was a grown man now, a success—that tiny, vulnerable, abandoned Jake had survived. Thrived. Grown into an uber-successful man with an ideal lifestyle.

'Is she OK?' he asked.

Maria nodded. 'She seems to be fine, an adorable bonny little *bambino*. I have given her a bottle and she went straight to sleep. She was left with a bag full of milk and nappies and clean clothes and a careful list of instructions about her routine. And here is the letter.'

Jake sat down at the small wooden desk and opened the envelope carefully, saw the barely legible scrawl that covered the scrap of paper inside.

Dear Jake

I know this will come as a surprise after all these years but I know I can trust you. Emily is my baby, and I love her very much, but right now I can't keep her safe.

Martin, her dad, is coming out of prison tomorrow. Please, please, don't let Martin anywhere near Emily.

I hope it's OK but I have asked Isobel to come and look after Emily. I know that may be awkward but I trust you both and it will only be for a few days.

Please tell Emily I love her and I will see her soon. I have packed her milk and her teddy and some nappies.

Isobel will explain everything—but please keep Emily safe for me.

Yours sincerely

Caro Ross

Jake stared down at the letter for a long moment as memories streamed back. Caro—Isobel's best friend.

Isobel.

Her image danced up from the cache of memories.

Isobel, with her dark brown hair and hazel eyes that seemed to shift and change colour with her mood. Isobel, his first—his only—disastrous foray into the world of 'real relationships'. Perhaps it had been the folly of youth that had persuaded him to let his guard down, let Isobel in, to allow himself to believe emotions were a good idea.

Well, he'd been proved spectacularly wrong. Emotions had sucked—big-time—and the real relationship had been exposed as based on dust and ashes. *Whoa*—there was no point in a walk down memory lane, not when he knew how the path ended. With him, alone and rejected, stricken with disbelief and hurt as he'd watched Isobel walk away. Just as his mother had, exactly as his father had. Judged and damned as not good enough. Again.

Enough.

At that moment the baby stirred, gave a small whimper and then subsided back into sleep. Emily was the important person here, not Jake and his feelings—feelings that he'd long since got over. Isobel was history, someone who had been a mere fragment of his life. A blip, a mistake never to be repeated, a lesson learnt.

Jake had always known how to move on from the past—and he'd moved on from Isobel. Caro said Isobel would explain everything; ergo he needed to talk to Isobel. That would not be a problem. At all.

Isobel pushed open the door to her room that she rented as part of a flat-share with a couple of other girls.

And breathe.

It had not been a good day. Usually she loved her job,

enjoyed the variety and satisfaction of being an events planner. But today the bride whose wedding she was helping to organise had had an enormous row with her mother, followed by an emotional meltdown on Isobel's shoulder. All over the colour of the bridesmaids' dresses.

On that thought her phone rang and she picked up. 'Hello. Isobel Brennan.'

'Isobel?' For a moment she almost dropped the phone. 'It's Caro.'

'Caro. Is that really you?' Relief and happiness intermingled; she hadn't seen nor heard from Caro for three years, every effort to contact her best friend stonewalled.

'Yes. It's me. It is so good to hear your voice, Isobel, and I'm so sorry for not being in touch for so long. And I'm sorry that I'm calling now because I need a favour. A huge favour.'

'It's OK.' Isobel could hear the break in Caro's voice, the quiet desperation. 'You can ask me anything, Caro.'

'Martin and I had a baby. A little girl called Emily. She's three months old and I love her so much. She is the best thing that has ever happened to me.'

'That's amazing news.' Isobel's head spun at the realisation that Caro had become a mother.

'Yes. But…' Caro took a deep breath. 'I'm scared for her.' Now there was heightened anxiety in Caro's voice, her every word edged with tears. 'Martin has been in prison—he wasn't around for most of my pregnancy or for the birth. But he's coming out tomorrow—I found out he's being released early—I can't let him anywhere near Emily. So I was wondering if…if you would look after Emily for me.'

'Of course I will.' Isobel didn't even need to think

about it. She and Caro went back so far, had seen each other through so many hard times, had survived the care system together. There was nothing she wouldn't do for Caro. 'I'll come and get her.'

'Too risky. Martin has some of his goons watching me. But I gave them the slip. I think. I hope. I took Emily and I've left her with Jake.'

'You've done what?' Isobel could hear the increased volume, the positive screech of decibels in the last syllable and forced herself to breathe deeply. 'Sorry. It just took me by surprise.'

'I figured there is no way Martin would work it out. I slipped into the hotel, left Emily there. It seemed like the safest thing to do. Martin doesn't even know that I know Jake; he does know I would turn to you. Jake has security systems and security personnel and…and, well, he's Jake. I trust him to keep Martin away from Emily. And I trust you to take care of her.'

The desperate certainty in Caro's voice utterly undid her and Isobel closed her eyes, reminded herself that the most important consideration here was Caro and Emily's safety. 'I understand. But what about you? When Martin finds out…' Her voice trailed off. Under his seemingly sophisticated, handsome exterior Martin was a violent psychopathic bully—a replica of Isobel's stepfather. 'You'll be in danger.'

'I know, but I have a plan, somewhere I can go and stay whilst I work out what to do next. But Emily is safer away from me. Just for now. I'm going to get rid of this phone now; that way, if Martin does find me he won't be able to track Emily down. But I'll contact you in a few days, I promise.'

'But…'

'I will be OK. Please promise you'll look after Emily. That's what matters most.'

The plea was so heartfelt that Isobel could feel her own heart ache and she knew she had to assuage the panic and pain in Caro's voice. 'I promise.'

'Thank you, Isobel. With all my heart. And thank Jake as well.'

With that, Caro disconnected. Isobel started to pace the room, tried to get her jumbled thoughts in order— fear for Caro, dread at the prospect of seeing Jake again, wonder at the thought of seeing Emily, a fierce determination to keep her promise to Caro.

Focus.

There was nothing she could do for Caro except do as her friend had asked. Look after Emily. The downside with the steepest of gradients was the fact that Jake was part of the deal. The *idea* of seeing him shivered her whole body with reluctance—she had no wish to come face to face with a reminder of her own stupidity.

Isobel had been a fool to trust him in the first place— should have remembered a truth learnt the hard way in childhood.

Love was an illusory emotion that rendered you weak.

Yet Jake Cartwright had woven a web of deceit so enticing, so beautiful that she had been charmed inside and for a short, magical time she'd believed that maybe, just maybe, fairy tale endings could happen. She couldn't have been more wrong—Jake had turned out to be an untrustworthy snake, a cheat and a liar.

But right now she'd have to pull up her big girl pants and face up to the necessity of seeing Jake the snake again. For Caro's sake.

At that moment her phone buzzed; one look at the

display and the still familiar digits crashed her memory banks.

Before she could bottle it, she answered, 'Isobel speaking.'

'It's Jake.' Despite the fact it wasn't a surprise, his voice sent her tummy into instant freefall and she rolled her eyes in irritation with herself.

'You beat me to it. I was about to call you.'

There was a silence 'So,' he said eventually, 'I didn't see this coming.'

'Me neither. I know it's awkward but Emily and Caro are more important than any personal feelings.' Oh, God—she could only hope he didn't now think she *had* any personal feelings for him. *Moving on...* 'Is Emily OK?'

'She's fine. The hotel housekeeper, a lovely lady with kids and grandchildren, is looking after her in one of our suites. There's a security detail on the door and I'm working in here as well.'

Relief at the arrangements assailed her, forced her to acknowledge that maybe Caro had been right to know Jake would keep Emily safe from harm.

'How's Caro?' he asked.

'It's a long story.'

'Then I'll wait until you get here. I can send a car to get you.'

'No!' Her refusal was instinctive—she had no wish to be beholden to Jake at all. 'It will be quicker by train. I'll leave as soon as I can.'

'We'll be here.'

Once she'd disconnected, she inhaled a deep breath. This was OK—she could do this. No big deal. Moving at speed she packed a bag, then quickly changed into clean blue jeans, a dark grey top and black denim jacket. Boots, a swipe of mascara and a swipe of lipstick to give her a little height and a smidge of confidence and she was good to go. As long as she ignored the swarm of butterflies that swooped and fluttered in her tummy.

Isobel zipped up her bag, took one last look at her reflection and headed for the door.

CHAPTER TWO

JAKE STARED AT his laptop and tried to focus on his work. In the end he gave up, just as his phone buzzed. Isobel.

'I'm here. In the lobby.'

'I'll be right down.'

By dint of an intense effort he kept his body relaxed as he rose and walked over to Maria, who was feeding Emily. 'Isobel is here,' he said. 'I'll bring her up and then you can head home. Thank you so much for this afternoon, Maria—you have been a lifesaver. I don't know one end of a baby from another.' And in truth he had little interest in learning—babies were not his thing. His few encounters with them had rendered him a little bit uneasy, out of his depth.

'It has been a pleasure. This little *bambino* is beautiful.'

Jake nodded and then headed to the door of the luxury penthouse suite he'd moved Maria and Emily into and entered the lift, annoyed to realise that he was... what? Nervous? Edgy? This was no big deal. Isobel had been a blip. A blip he had long since moved on from.

Two minutes later he entered the lobby and scanned the occupants, trying to ignore the accelerated beat of his heart. There she was. Dark brown hair shorter than he remembered, skimming her shoulders in a glossy sweep.

Her stance was the same, graceful yet wary, poised for flight or fight.

As if sensing his gaze, she turned and emotions walloped him.

A flare of anger he'd thought long since extinguished, a visceral punch of desire, his skin sheened with heat and then plunged into goosebumps. His system in overload.

Whoa. Isobel was a blip, remember? His pride demanded he showed her there were no hard feelings—there were no feelings at all. Shouldn't be too hard—he was his father's son after all. Not showing feelings was a walk in the park. He knew exactly how to mould his emotions, squeeze them, constrict them into the shape he needed them to be.

But the key was control and not to let unwanted emotions blindside you. Instead you got rid of them, sloughed them away. His feelings for Isobel were long since dead and buried and he would give them no chance of resurrection. This was just an odd reaction, one that meant nothing.

He moved towards her, a smile on his lips. 'Isobel. It's good to see you.'

Her dark eyebrows rose. 'It is?'

OK. If that was the way she wanted to play it, fine. 'Of course.' He summoned his most charming smile. 'Unexpected but good. Why wouldn't it be?'

Her eyes narrowed and he wondered if she would take up the challenge here and now; God knew he had no wish to replay their final showdown, but if need be he would. The way she had treated him still rankled and for an instant he relived the plummet of incredulous disbelief when she'd accused him of infidelity. The burn of hurt that she'd judged him guilty, that her trust in him was so fragile that she'd believe him capable of sleeping with someone else. That was the type of behaviour his father excelled in and for Isobel to believe he could or would behave like that had been a sucker-punch; it had seared his very soul.

He felt the smile harden on his lips as he held her gaze.

'No reason,' she said. 'Or at least none worth discussing. Especially as my prime, my *only* concern is Emily.'

Ouch. And touché.

'Of course. I'll take you straight to her.' He gestured towards the lift. 'This way.'

He eyed the confines of the space—surely it couldn't have shrunk in the past five minutes? Then Isobel shifted slightly and a flicker of her perfume assailed him, the jasmine scent familiar in its poignancy and a prelude to yet more memories. His senses stirred—the tickle of her hair against his skin, the taste of her lips, the sheen of her skin under his fingers, the touch of her on him.

Hell.

Clearing his throat, he strove for normalcy. Reminded himself that he'd Moved On. Capital M, capital O. This was an aberration—after all, from a purely aesthetic point of view Isobel was beautiful and, like it or not, years before the attraction between them had zinged into instant flame.

'I put Maria and Emily in our topmost suite,' he explained, relieved when the lift arrived at their destination.

He exited and waited as she followed him down a thickly carpeted corridor and stopped outside a door, where he nodded to the security guard posted outside. 'Stefan, this is Isobel, Emily's mum's friend. She's here to look after Emily.'

'Pleased to meet you.' Isobel smiled as Jake knocked

on the door and then pushed it open. He stood back and watched as Isobel entered the enormous, luxuriously furnished room and halted, her gaze riveted to Emily, who was cradled in Maria's arms. The older woman crooned a lullaby and he heard Isobel's breath hitch in her throat as she came to a halt.

'Maria, this is Isobel.'

Maria smiled. 'Hello, Isobel. Your friend's baby is very beautiful and so good. She has had a bath and some milk and we are now having a little cuddle before she goes to bed and I have told her not to worry; all will be well.'

Isobel stepped forward and smiled at Maria. 'Thank you so much for looking after Emily—I know Caro will be very grateful. This isn't her fault. I promise she loves Emily very much.' She reached out and stroked Emily's head and Jake's heart gave a sudden strange lurch at the gentleness, the awe in her touch. 'May I?' she asked.

Maria beamed and rose to her feet, carefully handed Emily across and watched in approval at the ease of transfer, the evident ease of movement as Isobel balanced the baby in the crook of her arm.

'Hey, Emily.' Noiselessly, Jake stepped a little closer, saw the baby's brown eyes widen as she gave a small gummy smile.

'You know what you're doing,' Maria observed. 'Do you have children?'

Now his heart lurched in a completely different way and a small exhalation of dissent or denial escaped his lips. Cue another mental slap-down—what did it matter if Isobel had found someone else, had a family?

'No, I don't. But my boss has a little girl and I've spent a lot of time with her. So I sort of have an idea.'

'You will be fine. Your friend left detailed instructions and enough milk and nappies for another few days. I will leave the two of you to it. All you need to do is put her down in her cot and she should go straight to sleep.'

'Thank you,' Jake said. 'And thank you so much for today.'

'It was my pleasure. You are a good boy. I know you will sort it out.' Jake hoped she was right. 'And if I can help at all you must ask. It is no problem.' With that she headed for the door.

Once it clicked shut behind her Isobel gazed down at Emily, who gave a small yawn, her tiny mouth forming a little oval as she waved her hands in the air. 'Maria is right. I think she is sleepy.' She sighed. 'I almost want to keep her awake, give her a chance to get more used to me, but I guess that would be daft. Probably best if I get her to sleep.' Emily yawned again and Jake nodded.

'I thought you and Emily could sleep in here.' He led the way to a bedroom, themed in gold and red, lush with velvets and dominated by an enormous decadent bed. A travel cot had been set up in the corner of the room.

'Emily will feel like a princess sleeping in here. You didn't need to put us somewhere so swish. Any room would have done.' There was a stiffness in her voice and Jake knew why. Isobel had always had an almost irrational suspicion of his wealth, loathed the thought that anyone would think she was freeloading.

'This suite is easier to secure—it's harder to get access to and no other guests will see the security guard on the door.'

A small sigh but she nodded. 'That does make sense. And on Caro's behalf thank you for all this, Jake. It must have come as something of a shock.'

'It's not every day a baby is left at Reception.' *Or an*

old flame turns up. 'Obviously we need to talk. Once Emily is asleep, I'll sort out a room service dinner and we can figure out what to do next.'

Once Jake had left Isobel closed her eyes and exhaled a sigh, trying to find some kind of inner Zen. Yeah, right. That was so not happening. From the second she'd set eyes on Jake a hot surge of anger and hurt had roiled inside her, made worse by the fact that she had no choice but to feel gratitude to him for the way he was protecting Emily. It was compounded by something else, a latent spark, a frisson of something she was loath to identify.

Whatever it was, she didn't want to feel it—didn't want to feel anything. She'd got over Jake and she was staying over him. Her focus should and would be Emily and she smiled down at the baby.

And now her heart lurched, turned, melted—went through some sort of transformation. As if an instantaneous bond formed, so tangible she could almost see it shimmer into existence and in that moment she knew she would protect Emily with her life if need be. Dramatic perhaps, but also an absolute knowledge. 'I won't let you down,' she promised. 'Or your mum. I'll keep you safe.' And if that meant accepting Jake's help, she'd do it.

Carefully cradling the sleepy baby, she approached the travel cot, laid her down and tucked the blanket round her. Gently she stroked Emily's downy head, watched as the eyelids came down, saw the impossibly long lashes descend and her heart twisted at the baby's complete trust in yet another new person in her life. She waited until she was sure the baby was fast asleep and then she tiptoed from the room.

Isobel braced herself and moved forward, saw Jake

standing at the enormous floor-to-ceiling window that showcased a magnificent view over London.

As she watched him her heart thudded in her chest with the sudden realisation that they were alone—an event she would never have imagined in her wildest dreams. As if he sensed her presence, he turned and she gulped. Why, oh, why was he still so gorgeous? He looked—older. *Well, duh.* He'd filled out; the lankiness of youth had bulked into a body that seemed to be all lithe compact muscle. His blond hair was shorter than it had been, cut close to his head. Grey-blue eyes, rainy day sky with a hint of sun held nothing she could interpret. Her eyes dropped and snagged on the firmness of his mouth and she took a step backwards.

Enough.

Jake might be gorgeous but his handsome exterior was a shallow meaningless shell that housed the soul of the man who had betrayed her.

His lips turned up in a smile but his eyes were wary. 'Is Emily OK?'

'Fast asleep.' She kept the reply short now as he gestured to the table.

'The menu's there.' He gestured to the sleek glass coffee table edged with mahogany.

'Thank you.' She could hardly refuse to eat with him; after all, they were jointly responsible for Emily and they had to come up with a plan of action—one that minimised the need for contact. He could set up the security and she'd provide the hands-on care. Simple. She perused the menu and her stomach gave a low grumble of anticipation. 'This is incredible,' she said, professional appreciation overcoming personal antagonism.

'Thank you. It's a new menu—I've just taken on a new

chef and she's brilliant, if I say so myself. The sample menu she cooked for me was sublime.'

She could well believe it as she chewed her lip and deliberated the choices, eventually deciding. 'I'll have the wild turbot, please.' Casting a sideways glance at him, she asked, 'What are you going to have?'

'The lamb.'

'I nearly went for that. Because of the cocoa beans.'

'We could always go halv—' He broke off and frowned.

A frown she knew she mirrored. Because that was exactly what they'd used to do—pick different dishes and share them. She gave her head a small shake, shocked at how easily they'd fallen into an old habit. Enough. There was a need to be civil—Jake was after all providing Emily with a sanctuary—but there was no need to be friendly. The grim set of his lips implied that this was a conclusion Jake had also come to.

'I'll order,' he said brusquely.

As he did so she walked to the window, marvelled again at the immensity of the glass and the panoramic vista. She turned and studied the surroundings properly, the cool grey walls, the simple yet flowing original artwork—a swoop of charcoal lines that depicted the flight of a flock of birds—the bold fun floral coverings on the sofa and armchairs, the decadent red of the velvet curtains and the eclectic scatter of designer lamps and statues of famous literary personages who had stayed at the hotel over the years, this history echoed by the original cornicing and panelling.

The stunning blend of old and new, the immense proportions were all a reminder of Jake's wealth and status and Isobel felt the old familiar sense steal over her—the same uncomfortable knowledge she'd had as a child—that she was a misfit. The one with fear in her eyes and bruises on her arms, then the 'foster kid' and eventually the ultimate reject, consigned to a care home because no one else would have her.

But now it no longer mattered—Isobel had built her own life, a world where she did fit. Jake's wealth and status were irrelevant and she would not be intimidated by them.

'Would you like a drink?' he asked.

'A soft drink would be great.'

'Elderflower cordial?'

'Perfect. Thank you.' The words emerged both stilted and wary as they eyed each other.

He handed her a glass and sat down opposite her. 'I'd like to know what is going on,' he said. 'Caro said you'd explain. I assume you and she came up with this plan together. But what I don't understand is why you didn't tell me first. There was no need for Caro to simply dump Emily at Reception and leave.'

There was definite anger in his voice and Isobel could see his point. 'I didn't know Caro was going to do that. I didn't know anything about this plan until a few hours ago. I didn't even know Caro *had* a baby until a few hours ago.'

'Excuse me?' Jake stared at her and inhaled deeply. 'I'm not getting any of this.'

'What did Caro tell you?'

He reached into his jeans pocket and pulled out a folded piece of paper. 'See for yourself.'

Isobel accepted the letter, perused it and tried to put herself in her friend's shoes. 'I think Caro had to come up with a plan fast and she came up with this. She may have been worried that you wouldn't agree to have Emily, she may have decided it was too dangerous to try to contact you first… I don't know. I haven't seen or spoken to Caro in three years.'

His eyebrows rose in surprise. 'But you and Caro were like family.'

'We were,' Isobel said softly and now sadness and guilt intermeshed inside her. 'But then she met Martin. And everything changed. At first he seemed perfect for Caro, appeared to worship the ground she walked on. But then, slowly, he started to change.' The change had been so gradual, so insidious that Isobel had told herself she was being paranoid. 'He became more possessive, started to control what Caro wore, started to put her down. Then he persuaded her to quit her job so he could look after her. Isolated her. Then one day he hit her.'

Jake flinched and his eyes hardened. 'Go on,' he said.

'Caro forgave him, said she knew he wouldn't do it again, that he was under a lot of stress at work and she'd provoked him. That he was truly sorry.' Isobel twisted her hands together, remembered her own clutch of fear as Caro had spoken. 'I told her to leave him, told her that this was the start. But all I did was antagonise her. And him. The violence got worse but she wouldn't leave him. Soon she was making excuses not to meet me. Then she told me she couldn't see me any more.'

The scene replayed in her mind, Caro's soft voice. *'I can't leave Martin—he'd never let me go. And I need him. I love him and he does love me. I know he is sorry whenever he hurts me. He and I will work it out, but he's right. It's better if it's just the two of us.'* The fervency in her voice, the desperate need to believe tore Isobel's heart. Her mother had said the same.

'I can't leave...'

'Simon loves me...'

'He's going to change this time...'

'I know he's sorry...'

She'd wanted to weep, to pound her fists against the

walls, to do something—anything to save her friend. But she hadn't been able to, just as she hadn't been able to save her mother. The taste of another failure, the realisation that she'd let someone else down was bitter in her mouth.

Now she looked at Jake. 'I haven't seen or heard from her since. I tried. Texted, called, wrote… Maybe I should have tried harder.'

'There was nothing you could do. If someone doesn't want to see you, they don't want to see you. You can't force them to.' Isobel glanced at him, heard the harsh note of experience in his voice and wondered at it. He rose and started to pace the room, a frown grooved on his forehead, his lips set in a grim line. 'This changes things.'

'Why?' Foreboding touched Isobel.

'What you have told me, what Caro has gone through appals me. Truly. And if I can do anything to help her I will. But right now Emily is my priority. I haven't set eyes on Caro for over six years and you haven't spoken to her in three. How do you know she is going to come back?'

The idea shocked her. 'Of course she will come back. Emily is her daughter. She won't abandon her.'

'You don't know that.' She glanced at him, saw the grim set to his lips. 'You don't know her any more. Can we contact her? Do we even know where she is?'

Isobel shook her head. 'She's going to call me in a few days.'

He drummed his fingers on his thigh. 'I think we should call the police.'

'No.' Her reaction was straight from her gut, born of visceral fear. 'You can't do that.' Isobel forced herself to remain still, to project calm. 'If we call the police, they will call social services.'

'Maybe social services need to be involved—maybe they can help.'

Now panic spiralled and she reminded herself that Jake didn't know how the system worked, didn't even know that Isobel had been in care. Because she'd never told him. She hadn't wanted his pity, hadn't wanted to further highlight the stark contrasts between their different backgrounds. 'How do you work that out?'

'Martin could persuade Caro that he is a changed man; she could get Emily and go straight back to him. You said it yourself. She has forgiven him time and again.'

'She won't do that to Emily.' Her voice was low as she tried to inject optimism into it, but she knew it was misplaced; Isobel's mother had loved Isobel, but that love hadn't been strong enough to withstand her dependence on Simon, nor had it enabled her to protect Isobel.

'You can't know that and the most important thing is Emily's safety.' His voice was inexorable.

Safe. Isobel knew what it felt like to not be safe; it was a knowledge wired into her very being, her bones, her soul and she never wanted Emily to have to feel that. Images crowded in on her. Herself as a small child, huddled under her bedclothes, sounds through the walls, raised voices, the thud of fist on flesh, her mother's cry. Isobel's hand stuffed in her mouth to keep silent, the taste of her own fear, the weight in her gut at her own cowardice, that stopped her from flying into the other room to claw and fight and kick to protect her mother. The knowledge of what would happen if she did, the thud of the fist in her stomach, the shove, the twist of the arm. The loom of her stepfather's face before her, flushed and mottled, the words in her face, spittle flying.

Her own terror, the knowledge that she was defenceless. Just as Emily was now.

A conflict of emotions battled inside her but she knew her priority. 'I swear to you that I would never hand Emily back if Martin is in the picture. But please let's give Caro a few days. If there is any chance that she and Emily can be safe together we owe her that. Owe them that.' There was silence as he continued to pace. 'Right now, Emily *is* safe. Here.'

'That we can agree on. I will keep a full security detail on the suite; we have surveillance cameras here and there's me. I won't let Martin anywhere near Emily. That's a promise. I hope he turns up. Trust me, I'll enjoy meeting him.'

His voice was hard and as she looked at him she knew he meant every word. Her gaze lingered on the ripple of muscle in his arms, the sheer bulk and strength of him and a funny little thrill shot straight through her and warmed her veins.

Stop right there.

Yes, Jake was big and strong, but surely she could accept that without this daft, *stupid* reaction.

'Then Emily can stay with us? No police?'

There was a long silence and she could see the shadows chase themselves across his grey eyes, wondered what dark thoughts streamed through his mind. Then he nodded. 'OK. Let's give Caro a chance. You're right— she does deserve that.'

'Thank you.' Relief ran through her, along with reluctant gratitude. Enough to make her smile at him. 'Really.'

'That's OK. As long as we are clear that I will change my mind if circumstance dictates.'

Before she could answer, a knock on the door heralded the arrival of their food.

CHAPTER THREE

JAKE MOVED TO the door, relieved to have a little space to process their conversation. Anger at what Caro had gone through, an ache for Emily, so innocent of the turmoil around her and the difficulties to come. But uppermost swirled thoughts of Isobel, her fear so palpable, her hazel eyes shadowed with darkness. Followed by her smile when he'd agreed not to call the police; its radiance had touched him. Which was not good. He had no wish to be affected by Isobel at all.

Pulling open the door, he smiled at the waiter. 'Thank you, Rashid. I'll take it from here.'

'No problem, boss.'

Jake wheeled the trolley into the room and Isobel moved over to help set the table, transferring the aromatic dishes onto the sleek cherry wood dining table. Jake froze momentarily, pushing down the urge to tell her not to bother, to please just sit down. Because, dammit, she was way too close. Which was causing reactions of a different and equally unwelcome type. Her scent tickled his nostrils and when her arm brushed his, his lungs hitched as desire tugged in his gut. A glance at her face showed her hazel eyes widen in mirrored reaction.

Now he did speak. 'Sit down. I've got the rest of this.'

Once seated, she looked down at her plate, studied its

contents and he did the same, hoped that if he focused on the food it would ground him—remind him what was really important here. He tasted a piece of lamb, watched as she cut off a morsel of fish and followed suit. 'Fabulous,' she said. 'My compliments to the chef.' Another mouthful and then she met his gaze. 'So I guess we should figure out the logistics of the next few days.' She glanced round the suite. 'I can look after Emily here. If I need to take her out for some fresh air or to the shops maybe Stefan can come with me? You can get on with your normal life.'

Was she for real? Jake stared at her. 'That's not the way it will work. I'm staying with Emily too. In person. Caro made me responsible for her safety—that's not something I'm willing to delegate.'

'But wouldn't you prefer to be working?'

'I'll juggle it. Move a few appointments. It's only for a few days.' And right now, in the prelude to the board meeting, there wasn't anything urgent that needed his attention. Nothing he couldn't delegate or manage via email or conference call. 'After all, what about *your* work?'

'I spoke to my boss on the way down here and she is completely fine with me taking the time off.'

'Then it looks like we will be looking after Emily together.' He topped up their glasses, watching as she took another mouthful, and he sensed that her mind was still working on a way out. 'And I don't think we should remain here.'

That got her attention. 'Why not?'

'It's possible Martin will persuade Caro to tell him where Emily is. So, much as I would like to take Martin on myself, I'd rather Emily is completely safe, especially if he has hired muscle at his disposal. It makes sense to take Emily somewhere Martin can't find us. I was thinking about the Cotswolds. Near Oxford.' He had lived and worked there for a while and knew the area well. 'It's beautiful there and I think it would be a lot better for Emily not to be cooped up in a hotel suite for days. What do you think? If he does turn up here, Stefan and his security team will deal with it.'

Isobel looked considerably more cheerful. 'That does make sense but, given that it is truly impossible for Martin to find Emily if we go somewhere new, I may as well take Emily on my own. Or, to be completely safe, Stefan could come with me.'

An irrational feeling of hurt prickled his skin—it seemed clear that Isobel truly couldn't stand breathing the same air as him. 'So if I said to you that Maria could look after Emily, would you agree?'

'That's different. You are fulfilling your responsibility to Caro by finding a safe house for Emily, by providing a security guard.'

'Maria would provide Emily with love and care.'

'I am not leaving Emily.'

'Neither am I.'

She glared at him, picked up her fork, put it down again. 'I get you feel a personal responsibility but…'

And now his hurt solidified into anger.

'How about you tell me exactly what the problem is? Because I thought this was about putting Emily first and doing what Caro has asked. I thought it was about a small vulnerable baby who we both want to help.'

Heat flushed her face. 'That is exactly what this is about. But if we can figure out a way to minimise spending time together, I'd appreciate that. I thought you would too.'

'It's been six years. We have both moved on.'

'Yes, we have. But that doesn't mean I want to spend

time with a man who betrayed me. Even if it was six years ago. Even if I am grateful that you are helping Caro.'

'I don't want your gratitude and I did not betray you.' Frustration seethed inside him at her obdurate belief.

She let a huff out and raised her hand in the air. 'Six years on and you still can't admit it. Why the hell not?'

'Six years on, why can't *you* just believe that I didn't do it?' It was a question he'd asked and asked himself in the aftermath of their break-up. He did understand how damning the evidence had seemed but Isobel should have trusted him. Why couldn't she? In the end he'd decided it didn't matter.

After all, for years he'd never understood how his parents could behave as they had either. What mattered was accepting it and moving on. Same thing with Isobel. Accept it and move on. And learn from it. He'd been a fool to open himself up to hurt, the possibility of being abandoned *again*. By anyone. So never again.

'This is getting us nowhere,' she said finally. 'But you're right. This is about Emily. She is why we are here and I will do my best to look after her. But I'm pretty sure it will be bad for her to have us at each other's throats the whole time we are looking after her.'

'What would you suggest we do? I can't admit to something I didn't do to make you feel better.'

'It's not about making me feel better.' Her forehead creased into a small frown. 'It's about closure. I want you to tell the truth. I want to know why you did it.'

Again the question hit him. 'Do you really have not a single doubt in your mind that I am guilty?' Remembered hurt bubbled and seethed underneath the barriers he'd erected.

Her chin tilted upwards. 'Nope. The facts speak for themselves.'

For a long moment they glared at each other, her hazel eyes hard with exasperation, frustration and amber glints of anger. And…hurt. All emotions he suspected he was reflecting right back at her.

He tried one last time. 'I didn't do it, Isobel. I swear it.'

And now, for the first time, he saw just a glimmer of doubt cross her face, the faintest crease of doubt imprint her forehead, and he knew what they had to do. 'Give me a chance to prove it.'

'I don't understand.'

'We both want to do what is best for Emily, to look after her and keep her safe. I suggest we focus on that, but also use this time for closure. Six years ago we were both too angry for that. Now we can look at it with cooler heads.'

'The only way I'll get closure is if you admit the truth.'

'I have admitted the truth. Maybe the only way you'll get closure is if you actually believe me.'

'So you want to spend the next few days convincing me you were innocent all those years ago.' Every word was dusted with scorn.

'Yup. That is exactly what I want to do.' This was a chance for vindication, a chance to challenge and figure out her lack of faith in him. 'What do you think?'

What did she think? Isobel looked down at her near empty plate, her mind in tumult. She realised the conversation had absorbed her so completely that she had barely noticed eating the food, apart from vaguely registering that it truly was sublime. For a moment she focused on the last few mouthfuls and savoured each one, the hint of wild garlic, the tang of the chervil, and tried to concentrate her mind.

Then she looked up from her plate and studied his quizzical expression. She knew that he'd thrown down a challenge, a gauntlet.

'Do you really have not a single doubt in your mind that I am guilty?'

The impact jarred—all the stifled doubts from the past crowded back, hustled and jostled. Had she been wrong? No! She'd had evidence and a confession. Jake had been guilty as charged.

Then why was he continuing to lie? Was this some sort of game to him, a power thing? A need to trick her, a way to pass the time. Perhaps he quite simply had to win. Well, fine. Pushing her plate away from her, she smiled at him slowly, accepting his challenge. 'Bring it on.' He could spin it any way he liked; if he hadn't been able to convince her six years ago, there was no way he could do so now. But a discussion, a cool-headed debate would bring complete closure.

'Excellent.' Jake leant back and smiled right back at her and, to her consternation, her tummy did a funny little flip and a sudden sense of caution reared its head. Ever since she'd got here, set eyes on him, her body had kept reacting to him, almost as if their raw, visceral attraction still smouldered. Time for her hormones to catch up with the plot—this was all about closure.

'I suggest we agree to some ground rules. First, Emily is our priority—we need to make sure she is safe and happy. Any arguments or discussions about the past are kept to times that she is asleep. When we are looking after her, we focus on Emily and are civil to each other.'

'Agreed. It's a deal.'

It was far from the deal she had intended to make. Yet closure was a good idea. So why did she feel as if she'd made a deal with the devil?

* * *

Jake opened his eyes, aware that a completely unfamiliar noise had awoken him. It took his sleep befuddled mind a couple of seconds to orientate himself. Then he clocked the sound. It was a baby crying. Emily.

Instinct propelled him out of bed and into a pair of jeans. Shoving his arms into a shirt, he pushed open the door and raced into the living area.

He came to a halt as he saw Isobel standing by the window cradling Emily in her arms, making soothing sounds. She looked up as she saw Jake, her expression calm, no sign of the panic that cascaded inside him.

'What shall I do?' he asked. 'Is she OK?'

'She's fine. Just hungry. I'm waiting for the formula milk to cool down. Caro's instructions said she usually wakes up needing a feed about two and, right like clockwork, here she is, up and ready. Aren't you, sweetheart?'

'You should have woken me up. I could have helped.'

'It's fine, I can manage—you go back to bed.'

He shook his head. 'I'm awake now. I'll give you a hand.' After all, he was the one who'd insisted on looking after Emily together.

'OK.' Isobel moved towards him and his breath caught in his chest. She looked beautiful—dark hair tousled, hazel eyes bright but still flecked with a hint of sleep and dressed in a pair of flannel pyjamas with a fluffy robe pulled over them. Her cheeks were flushed and for a fleeting second her gaze lingered on his bare chest. Then her eyes hardened and she gave her head a small shake, the gesture dispelling the moment.

Looking down at Emily, she stepped closer to him. 'Why don't you take Emily and I'll get her bottle?'

Take Emily.

Panic surged. There was no way on this earth he could be trusted with so fragile and vulnerable a being.

'Better if she stays with you. I'll get the milk.'

He moved over to the kitchenette and picked up the bottle, wondering how on earth to check it.

'Dribble a few drops onto your wrist and see if it's room temperature,' Isobel instructed.

He did as she said and then, satisfied it was right, he handed the bottle to her and watched as she sat down, positioned Emily carefully and started to feed her, the baby guzzling happily, her tiny hands on the bottle. The surreal domesticity of the scene filled him with awe. The tenderness in Isobel's stance, the curve of her body as she bent over Emily, the dapple of moonlight on her dark brown hair all combined to unravel a strange rush of emotion inside him.

Perhaps it was sadness at the knowledge that his mother had never sat with him like this—he wasn't sure that anyone had, had no idea who had looked after him in the first nine months of his life, before his grandfather had stepped in. Whoever it was, he was grateful.

Isobel looked up. 'You're a natural,' he said.

'Not really. I only know what I'm doing because of Natalie.'

'Your boss's daughter?' She nodded. 'So tell me what you're doing now. Not still waitressing?' Six years before, when he'd met her, Isobel had been working as a waitress in a high-street pizza chain. The memory of their first meeting was crystal-clear even now. He'd been at a school reunion, their booking at a different restaurant had gone awry and they'd ended up at a pizza place. Fine by Jake, but less appreciated by others in the group.

Isobel had placed a pizza in front of one such person, Hugo Fairley, who Jake had despised even when he was a small boy. Hugo had turned and snarled at her, 'I'm not eating this pigswill.' He'd flung out his hand in emphasis and upended a jug of water and he'd lost the plot, stood up and stepped right into her face.

Jake could still remember Isobel's expression—a flash of fear as she'd instinctively stepped back, but then she'd held her ground—and in that moment a mix of admiration and a desire to protect the slender brown-haired waitress had surged within him. He'd risen to his feet and moved between Hugo and the woman.

Blinking away the memory, he focused on Isobel in the here and now, waiting for her answer.

'No, I'm an events planner now and I love it. I'm part of a small company, a two-woman band, and we organise weddings, corporate parties... Any and all events, really.'

'How did you get into that?' Against his own will he could feel curiosity rise. He liked the lilt of enthusiasm in her voice, the way her face lit up, the spark in her hazel eyes.

'After you and I broke up, I moved from the pizza place to working in a hotel. Waitressing again, but then I moved across to the catering team and from there to the events desk. I worked there for a few years, helping organise weddings, corporate parties, conferences, all sorts. Then Clara, one of the brides who held her reception in the hotel, someone I'd got on with really well, approached me. She was setting up an events management company and wanted to offer me a job. I took it.'

'Good for you. It sounds like a brilliant opportunity.'

He knew she would have more than deserved that opportunity. He remembered Isobel's work ethic—she was loyal, committed and worked her socks off in pursuit of her main goal—security. She'd not said much about her family, simply that her parents were dead and she was on her own.

'It was. Clara really knows what she is doing. She'd been in events for years but once she got married she wanted to work out a way to juggle a job and being a mum. So she started her own business. That way she could bring Nat to work with her and I pitched in and helped. Natalie has been to meetings, weddings, corporate parties… You name it, Nat's done it.'

'Sounds a bit like my grandfather and me. He took me everywhere with him; my earliest memories are of all the Cartwright hotels.' As always when he remembered Joseph Cartwright, his emotions were conflicted. Joseph Cartwright, the man who had looked after him for the first six years of his life, the man Jake had loved and had believed loved him back. The man he had mourned, only to discover years later that love had nothing to do with it. Because his mother had explained to him exactly why Charles Cartwright had wanted an heir. Turned out Joseph Cartwright had issued an ultimatum to his son.

'Provide me with an heir or I'll disinherit you, cut you off without a penny.'

So Charles had supplied Jake and Joseph had taken him in, not because he loved him—but because he wanted an heir to mould in his own image as his legacy. And that was why he'd taken Jake to work with him.

'I'd make dens in his office, if we visited the hotels I used to play in the kitchens and in the housekeeping rooms. The staff were all amazing to me. The kitchen staff used to sneak me food and the porters let me play on the trolleys and help them with the luggage.' Perhaps, though, the supreme irony was that it had worked—the seed Joseph had sown flourished and thrived, at first because Jake thought he owed it to his grandfather's memory, and then because Cartwright was in his blood.

'I didn't know that.'

There was so much he hadn't told Isobel back then; he had been too intent on a demonstration of strength, all his assets and none of his weaknesses. So he'd kept his family out of it—hadn't wanted her pity. Now he contented himself with, 'I had a lot of fun.'

'So do Clara and Nat. We all do. I've been really lucky—building up the business together has been incredibly positive.'

'Sounds more like a partnership.'

'I hope one day it will be—that one day I can buy my way in. That's my medium-term plan. Along with getting a house. As soon as I can get a deposit together, I'll buy a student house. That way, I can live in it but also let the other rooms out.'

'You'll cover your mortgage payments and you can still save towards the partnership.' It was a good, well thought out plan. Clearly Isobel was still as goal-oriented—as he was.

'Yes.' Then a shake of her head. 'Listen to me. Telling you all this—there is no need for you to be interested.'

'I am interested.'

She looked down at Emily, but not before he saw scepticism flash in her hazel eyes.

'Did I say something so unbelievable?'

'Well, yes, actually. Why would you be interested? The amounts I am talking about are chicken feed in your world. You think in millions where I think in thousands. Plus I am talking about a two-person partnership; you deal with a global empire, make decisions that affect hundreds of employees. Compared to that, my plans pale into tiny insignificance.'

'It doesn't work like that.' Now she made no attempt to mask the sceptical raise of an eyebrow and his frown deepened. 'The amounts of money at stake aren't relevant. It's about your individual hopes and dreams—that's what's important.'

'But when you deal with the bigger global picture, surely individuals all blur a bit, become like ants.'

'Nope. Because people are the most important thing, people are what make global empires tick. I've seen that.' Her hazel eyes studied his expression, her face animated in the low lights of the room as she listened. 'I spent four years working my way through all the different roles in the hotel industry.'

Her turn to frown. 'I thought your plan, your dream was to get a management role at Cartwright.'

'It was.' It was what he'd worked towards his whole life, the moment when he could start to make a difference, begin his quest to take Cartwright into the glorious future. 'Unfortunately, my father had other ideas. I went to see him, requested an undergraduate trainee post and he turned me down flat.'

Though he still didn't get why. To that date his father's attention to his activities had been negligible. Whatever Jake had asked for he'd acquiesced to without so much as a flicker of interest. But that time…

'Don't be daft, boy,' he'd said. *'What do you want to get involved for? Go and have fun. Party, live it up. Buy a yacht. Or two.'*

'I can have fun and work,' Jake had said. Swallowing the obvious additional words. *Unlike you.*

His father turned up to board meetings when absolutely necessary, and otherwise spent his whole life in pursuit of pleasure, accompanied by an interchangeable array of trophy girlfriends and a ragtag crew of various so-called friends and hangers-on.

'*No.*'

Jake had waited, but that had appeared to be the sum total of what his father was going to say. Charles had headed to the door, picking up a jacket on his way.

'*Forget it, Jake. I say no and I'm the boss.*'

Isobel's voice pulled him into the present. 'So you went and worked for a different hotel?'

'Yup. A small chain based in the Cotswolds, owned by an amazing bloke called Marcus Elderflower. He took me on but said the best way to understand the business was to work in every role. I spent four years doing exactly that. I was a waiter, a porter, dishwasher, chauffeur, parking attendant, maintenance man, housekeeper, maid. I learnt that people are the most important part of an enterprise, each and every individual one of them.'

'And what about now? You clearly work for Cartwright now.'

'Yes. Once I reached twenty-five I came into my inheritance proper—an actual shareholding in Cartwright. That gave me automatic entry to the board.' And there had been zip his father could do about it. Though the fuss he'd made, you'd think Jake was the devil himself, not his only son. As always, thoughts of his relationship with his father brought a bitter taste with them.

'And being management hasn't changed your perspective?'

'No, I see people as individuals. Like Maria, like Stefan.'

'But they are also your employees, cogs in the Cartwright wheel. When you make big decisions you can't just think about Maria and Stefan's needs.'

'Sure. But I owe every Cartwright employee the right

to be a cog in a functioning, lucrative wheel, with fair wages and job security. To do that I do have to see each individual cog.'

Now she smiled. '*Touché*. Excellent answer.'

Jake realised he'd missed this—the exhilaration of conversation and debate with Isobel. Years before, it had been underlain with a frisson of desire, the spark of debate leading to the spark of desire. The animation on her face, the glitter in her hazel eyes, the vibrancy of her voice had always heated his veins.

Hell and damnation.

It still did and suddenly the atmosphere ratcheted as they looked at each other and he sensed Isobel's thoughts had veered down the same bit of memory lane. The discussions and debates from years before that had ended in laughter, or mock pillow fights or him sweeping her into his arms.

Her face flushed in the dappled moonlight that flooded the room, and he saw the tell-tale sign of awareness as her eyes darkened to a coppery hue he remembered so well. Now his gut tightened in an intense twist of desire, a yearning so deep it shocked him, almost rocked him back in his chair.

Emily gave a sudden small whimper and the moment was broken. Isobel blinked, looked down at the sleeping Emily and the spell broke. 'I… I need to get her to her cot.' She almost leapt to her feet as Jake nodded until his neck almost popped.

'Good plan. I'll see you at breakfast.'

CHAPTER FOUR

ISOBEL OPENED HER eyes to the sound of Emily's gurgle and checked the time. Six-thirty and Emily must be hungry again, though for now at least the baby seemed content to wave her fists in the air and chat to herself. Swiftly, Isobel climbed out of bed and tiptoed to the bathroom, taking a moment to marvel anew at its proportions. The white-veined marble was cool and soothing, the enormous shower area boasted a double rainwater shower and as for the bath tub—she suspected she could swim in it. Large white candles, huge fluffy towels and two wicker chairs with towelling cushions added a sense of decadence.

Quickly, she availed herself of the facilities and returned to the bedroom, leaned over the cot and smiled as Emily cooed up at her. A quick nappy change and she placed the baby gently down on the plush velvet bed that dominated the room. Emily kicked her legs, her eyes seemingly focused on the hand-painted tropical-themed wallpaper as Isobel changed into jeans and a dark grey T-shirt.

'OK, sweetheart. Let's go.' Isobel picked Emily up and headed towards the lounge, telling herself that strange moment in the early hours of the morning had been imaginary, nothing more, brought about by lack of sleep and the surreal situation.

She saw Jake sitting at the table, netbook open. Short blond hair, shower-damp, T-shirt that showed off the swell of muscle—her tummy lurched slightly.

For real, Iz?

Irritation sparked inside her at her body's reaction. Again. This had to stop. But her brain seemed powerless to intervene, to prevent her gaze from lingering on the sculpted shape of his arms, the masculine beauty of his forearms, the strength of his wrists.

He turned and smiled. 'Morning.'

'Morning.'

He rose and went to the fridge, got out the milk she'd prepared the night before and popped it into a bottle warmer.

'Where did that come from?'

'Maria brought it round, along with some toys, and Stefan brought a sling. Apparently, it truly is the best contraption ever invented for transporting a baby.'

'That's a brilliant idea, actually—it will mean Emily is always attached to one of us, so if Martin turns up he won't be able to snatch her. I'll make sure I thank Stefan.' She glanced around the luxurious living area, the sumptuous furniture and plush rugs sprinkled now with toys and a play mat. 'And Maria as well. That's lovely of them both.' It was and it occurred to Isobel that perhaps they had done it because they liked Jake. That when he had said he did see his employees as real individuals he had meant it. Had she been unfair to him the previous night?

He handed her the bottle and she glanced at him. 'Would you like to feed her?' she offered. His head shake was a little too quick and, like the previous night, she'd swear she saw a flash of panic cross his eyes. She wondered why he was so worried about holding Emily. Was

he worried that he'd drop her, hurt her or was there something more to it?

'Nope. I'm good. I'll make coffee. Breakfast is on
the way.'

A few minutes later there was a knock on the door
and Isobel went to sit at the table with Emily whilst he
went and wheeled the trolley in, quickly set the table
and served her.

Isobel inhaled the scent of coffee with gratitude, re-
garding her heaped plate with approval. Scrambled eggs,
hash browns and bacon.

Heaven!

Once Emily had finished, she burped her, dropped a
kiss on her head and then carefully placed her on the play
mat on the floor. Emily instantly kicked her legs with
glee, her tiny fingers reaching up to touch the brightly
coloured hanging items. She smiled down at the baby.
'She is a happy little soul,' she said. 'I'm not sure if this
is the right thing to say or not, but thank God Martin
did go to prison when he did. It must have made such a
difference to Caro's pregnancy and it allowed Emily to
have a happy first few months.'

Like her own had been. Her mother had told her the
story. How happy they had been as a family, poor but full
of dreams and ambitions. Then it had all gone wrong. Her
father, desperate to earn money, had engaged in a get-
rich-quick scheme, agreeing to transport some 'stuff' for
a 'friend'. Turned out it had been contraband, he'd got
caught in inter-gang rivalry and in the crossfire he'd died.

Soon after, her mum had met Simon and any chance
of happiness was gone.

It would not be like that for Emily or Caro, Isobel
vowed. This time she would pull off a happy ending.

'Isobel?' She blinked, realising that Jake was looking at her with concern in his grey eyes. 'You OK?'

'Yes, I was just hoping it all works out for Emily— that she stays happy. She's so vulnerable and small and trusting.'

Jake's gaze rested on the baby for a moment and then flickered away and again she could see shadows in his eyes. 'I hope so too,' he said. 'Now, are you all packed? I thought we'd head off after breakfast.'

'Works for me.'

A few hours later, and 'Nearly there,' Jake said as he ex- ited the motorway.

Isobel leant her head back and simply gazed at the scenery as it rolled past, savouring the winding country lanes, bordered by rolling fields and hills of every hue of verdant green and russet brown, splashed with bright yellow crops. Occasionally they passed through pictur- esque hamlets with honey-coloured cottages that seemed to come from a bygone era.

Jake turned onto a gravelled driveway and parked. 'Here we are.'

A small huff of appreciation escaped her lips. The cot- tage was like something out of a fairy tale, made of stone, with blue windows and a white front door, surrounded by a splash of vivid red poppies. As she climbed out of the car she inhaled the glorious fragrance of spring flowers that pervaded the air. 'It's magical,' she said.

'Let's go see inside.'

For a moment as he hefted their bags out of the boot and Isobel took Emily out of her car seat she realised that to any passer-by they would look like a young family on holiday. The idea was strange—the realisation that this facsimile of family life might well be the closest she got to the real thing. If she and Jake had stayed together, this could be for real, perhaps they would have had a baby, perhaps—

Enough.

Perhaps meant nothing, the game of what-if a dangerous one to play as it excluded reality. Yet it seemed to her that regret tinged the air.

She followed Jake up the flagged path, through the trimmed hedges to the front door, where he opened the key box with the required code, pulled out the key and opened the front door.

They toured the cottage together. The interior was bright and light and airy, with a well fitted pine-themed kitchen, a cosy lounge with comfortable furniture and a large sliding glass door that opened out onto a magnificent garden. Upstairs showed two double bedrooms with en suite bathrooms; one of the bedrooms had a travel cot already set up in it.

They both laughed when Emily kicked her legs enthusiastically. 'She's right,' Isobel said. 'Actually, it's time for her nap. Though she did sleep for a while in the car.' She thought for a moment. 'I'll try it and if she doesn't sleep I'll get her up.'

'How about I go and make us a cup of coffee—we can drink it in the garden? With or without Emily.'

'That sounds good.'

Fifteen minutes later she joined him, sitting next to him on the slatted wooden bench that overlooked the myriad flowers and trees.

'Is Emily OK?'

'Amazingly, she went out like the proverbial light.' She sipped her coffee and then shifted slightly. 'You need to tell me how much I owe you.' No way could she let Jake pay for all this. In truth, however beautiful it was, a part of her wished he'd chosen somewhere more utilitarian, less…romantic.

'For what?'

'For this place. Also we need to keep tabs on what we spend on food and stuff.'

'You don't owe me anything. I'm doing this for Caro and Emily.'

'I understand that but I would like to contribute—Caro asked us both for help with Emily. This is a partnership. I'd like it to be an equal one.'

'An equal partnership has nothing to do with money.'

'It has everything to do with money.'

'But you can't base equality on money—that's wrong. Surely you don't think you aren't my equal just because I have a bigger bank balance than you.'

'Of course not, but in a partnership money is important. That's why I'm buying into a partnership with Clara.'

'But it doesn't always work like that. People can bring different things to a partnership. Two people can go into a partnership because one has money and the other has talent or connections. Clara may ask you to be a partner and waive a capital contribution because she values you and doesn't want you to be lured away by the competition, or set up on your own in the future. Or maybe she would prefer to have a partner, someone to share the risk with.' He raised an eyebrow. 'Do I need to go on? It's not all about money.'

Isobel's eyes narrowed as she recognised the validity of his words and yet… 'That sounds great in theory but if I let Clara gift me a partnership I would always feel like the junior partner, the one who hadn't contributed my fair share.'

'Is that how you felt about us? Did my money make

you feel like the junior partner in our relationship, our partnership?'

The unexpectedness of the question threw her for a moment. 'Your money did bother me.' A lot.

'I gathered. That's why you never let me pay for anything or take you to any fancy restaurants. We could only go to places we could both afford. Because you wanted to pay your way and pull your weight and not freeload.'

She narrowed her eyes, trying to gauge his expression and saw a flash of remembered exasperation. 'Yes, I did. What's wrong with that? I'm sorry if I didn't want to play Cinderella to your Prince or the Beggar Maid to your King Cophetua.'

'Excuse me?'

Isobel turned to face him, meeting his gaze full on, and saw that his exasperation had hardened to anger, but she was damned if she would back down. 'You heard me. Paying my way mattered to me.'

'And I understood that and I respected it. I had no wish to be your benefactor—I never saw you as Cinderella or a beggar girl. But at the end of the day I do have money and I'm damned if I'll apologise for wanting to spend some of it on taking my girlfriend to a posh restaurant. It's not a sin to be rich. That's part of who I am—suck it up.'

There was a silence and Isobel turned to look at him. 'Maybe we should have said all that six years ago.'

'Maybe we should have.'

She replayed his words and, almost against her will, she gave a small gurgle of laughter. Their gazes met, his eyes still dark with anger. 'Something funny?'

'Suck it up?' she asked.

Now his eyes softened and she saw the small tell-tale tug of his lips as he tried not to smile. Then, 'You're right. I shouldn't have said that. I should have said, Suck it up, Cinderella.'

Now they both began to laugh, and she could feel the tension dissipate and fly away on the spring breeze. Turning to him, her breath caught. He looked so—*gorgeous*, and he was a man who could laugh at himself, who could see the funny side of a fraught situation. The idea churned her up inside—it was suddenly hard to see this man as the villain of the piece. And yet she had to. Because the alternative was—what? Leaning over and brushing a kiss on his cheek? Accepting that he had been innocent six years before? Neither option was possible.

Jake looked at her. 'But clearly we should have talked about the money thing more. I had no idea it bothered you so much.'

'That's because you are the one with the millions in the bank. But try to imagine that you haven't, picture an empty bank account. Then along comes a woman with shedloads of money, and you start dating. She wants to eat in fancy restaurants where she foots the bill, buys you clothes so you can conform to the dress code, she buys you diamond cufflinks and designer clothes... How would you feel?'

'I'd feel uncomfortable.' Her eyebrows practically reached her hairline in mute challenge. 'OK. I'd hate it,' he admitted. '*But* if the relationship was worth it, I'd figure out a way round it.'

'Exactly. And I did. I figured the only way to make it work was if we only went to places I could afford, places where I would fit in.' She regretted the last words as soon as they left her lips, as his grey eyes turned to lasers.

'What do you mean, fit in?' he asked.

'I—it doesn't matter.'

'Yes, it does. Because this is what we agreed—to

talk, to aim for closure, to try and figure out what went wrong.'

Jake was right and if she wanted him to tell her the truth about Anna, then she needed to be truthful too. That way, maybe she'd get why he had strayed. Maybe her attitude to money had exasperated him more than she'd known—it made sense that he'd missed his usual lifestyle, the expensive venues.

'It wasn't only about the money side of it or being able to pay for my half of the bill. I didn't feel comfortable in fancy restaurants. I didn't know how to behave. I didn't fit in.' In truth, she had never felt she fitted in anywhere, still wouldn't feel comfortable in his milieu. 'I didn't have the right clothes. The right background.'

'None of that mattered. You could wear a bin bag and you would still behave with grace and politeness.'

His words touched her and she smiled at him; without thought, she reached out to touch his arm. The contact was electric and for a split second she froze in shock—the feel of his skin, the swell of his forearm under her fingers sent a sharp tingle through her body. She pulled her hand back in attempted nonchalance, looking away from him at the beauty of the landscaped garden, the riot of flowers, the neatly trimmed green of the hedges. Tried to refocus on the conversation.

'Thank you. That's kind, but it's not true. Everyone in those restaurants, everyone at the glamorous yacht parties you asked me to—they would all have known I didn't fit.' The very idea had made her soul shudder with horror. 'I didn't know what to say, how to act around the rich and famous, the glamorous—your crowd, in other words.'

'All you had to do was be you. You had nothing to be ashamed of or worried about.'

She could hear the bafflement in his voice. 'I wasn't

ashamed. It felt as though you were slumming it with me and everyone knew it. All your previous relationships were with glamorous celebrities who meshed with your lifestyle. Your friends were all wealthy or university graduates with posh backgrounds.'

Bafflement morphed into concern and he turned on the bench, placing his coffee cup on the ground. 'Look at me. Whatever our differences, I swear to you I never once felt I was slumming it with you. Education and background don't define you. That would never make any difference to me.'

Isobel shook her head. 'But it made a difference to me. You had a private education, went to uni, could buy anything you wanted. One day you will run a huge global empire. It made me feel…inadequate, a fish out of water. Maybe that's why it was so easy for you to sleep with Anna—she was your type, your natural fit, someone who would go to glamorous shindigs, would enjoy being seen at fashionable restaurants.'

'Anna was a friend, or at least I thought she was at the time. I didn't sleep with her. Why would I have, Iz? Because you're forgetting something important here, something we had. Something that had nothing to do with background or education.' Now his eyes were like lasers again, watching her, daring her to ask.

'What?' she almost whispered, even though she knew the answer.

'Attraction, desire—the tingle in your veins when you want to kiss someone and you know it's mutual. When you can't keep your eyes off each other, when the lightest touch—' and now he glanced down at his arm where she had touched him earlier '—causes a cascade of yearning, when you look for any excuse to be close, when you want the other person so much it burns. That was us.'

His words slid over her skin, leaving a layer of goose-bumps and an insidious prickle of desire. Now yearning did cascade; it shivered through her, igniting a stream of memories of the pull of attraction that had drawn them together—had caused need and fulfilment and joy. It took her back to a time when a simple glance had made her skin heat, when the brush of an arm had sent delicious flutters of sensation through her—a giddy, dizzy sense of promise and anticipation.

Without even meaning to she'd edged closer to him as awareness permeated the air with a siren lure of temptation. One kiss wouldn't matter…

Then Emily's wail emerged from the baby monitor at her waist, shattering the spell. Isobel leapt to her feet, striving for composure. 'That's Emily,' she said unnecessarily. 'I'll go and get her. I think we should take her out this afternoon.' That way they could avoid a resumption of this conversation. They were skating perilously close to the edge of doubt, the chasm of attraction, both black holes she must not fall into.

He nodded. 'Agreed.' He gave her a glance and she wondered if he was as shaken as she was at how close they had come there. 'Why don't we go boating? In Oxford.'

'That sounds perfect.' They couldn't get up close and personal in a boat.

CHAPTER FIVE

AN HOUR LATER, with Emily safely strapped in her sling and securely attached to Isobel, they approached a brightly coloured red-striped gondola-shaped paddle boat, watching as it bobbed jauntily up and down on the water next to the jetty.

Jake climbed in first and then he reached out a hand to steady Isobel as she followed suit. Gingerly, she placed her hand in his and he told himself that a simply friendly gesture shouldn't impact him any more. But it did; the feel of her fingers in his was stupidly evocative, ridiculously provocative, and each fleeting touch seemed to add another drop of fuel to the slow burn of desire building up. Isobel had always had this effect on him, been able to conjure up desire with the most ephemeral of touches or the simple beauty of her expression. He'd assumed that reaction would be nullified by the bitterness of their break-up, by the elapse of time. Clearly not. Their spark was still smoking and he knew reigniting the flames would be disastrous—would distort and blur closure.

So he would block it, guard against the insidious tendrils that were trying to pull him back into a web he had no intention of entering. Isobel had rejected him, judged him and found him wanting. Game over with no chance of a replay.

Yet this time her accusation about Anna hadn't delivered the same sucker punch of anger and hurt as before. Because, for the first time, Jake could see the glimmer of a reason why Isobel *might* have found it so easy to believe. If she truly thought Anna was his type, if she'd spent months thinking she didn't fit into his life... So now he had to make her see that her reasoning was at fault. As the man who had persuaded most of the Cartwright board to his way of thinking, he could do this. He could make Isobel see the truth, in the same way he'd shown the board that his plan could and would work.

He blinked, seeing that Isobel had narrowed her eyes, suspicion etched on her expression. 'You're looking very pleased with yourself.'

'No reason not to be. The sun is shining, we're on this beautiful river, teeming with wildlife.' And indeed it was a timeless setting—sun motes dappled the blue-green of the water, the riverbank abounded in shades of green and a warm breeze carried the hum of insects.

He leant back and studied the pedals in the centre of the boat. 'Probably best if I pedal and you look after Emily.'

'Works for me.' She adjusted the sling so that the baby could see the ripple of the water. 'I think she likes movement and colour—she was fascinated by the wallpaper in the hotel suite.'

'She's got taste—that is hand-painted wallpaper.'

Jake started to pedal, enjoying the feel of the small blue boat cleaving the water, yet his eyes returned again and again to Isobel; she was relaxed, her dark brown hair ruffled by the breeze, a smile on her face as she chatted to Emily. He watched the way she looked at the baby, her focus absolute as she talked, pointed out the sky and the water, tickled her under the chin and elicited a small gurgling chuckle. The way she held her, the utter vibe of safety and caring and love she exuded—it filled him with awe.

'Oh, look.' Jake followed her line of vision and brought the boat to a halt as he spotted a brood of ducklings followed by their mother swimming into their path. 'Ducks, Emily. They go quack-quack.' The baby smiled a gummy smile and Jake couldn't help but smile as well.

'We may spot some swans as well, and keep an eye out for kingfishers. If we get close enough to the bank you should see dragonflies and there are lots of butterflies here as well.'

'You sound like you've done this a lot.'

'When I was working at Elderflower Hotels Marcus liked his staff to be able to talk knowledgeably about local activities so I came on a few boat trips for research. Then sometimes I'd come out because I like it—it's peaceful out here on the water.'

'Was it strange working for a different hotel?'

'It wasn't what I had planned to do but it was the best thing I could have done. Marcus was right—it's the best way to learn the business, a chance to appreciate how a hotel works and what makes it tick. It gave me the basis for a business plan—reward your staff. They make or break a hotel, so pay them fairly, include loyalty bonuses. I want Cartwright to be authentic, individual, environmentally aware, fun, an escape or a home away from home, something for all guests.' He stopped and rolled his eyes. 'Jeez, I sound like a politician addressing a rally. Sorry!'

'Don't apologise. It's a fantastic ethos.'

If only his father agreed. Jake's jaw hardened. In a week or so his father's agreement wouldn't be necessary, would be an irrelevance and Jake would have control. He felt a sudden qualm and he pushed it away. His vision for Cartwright was the right one—he knew it and he'd spent the past four years slowly convincing the other minority holders of it. But all attempts to persuade Charles Cartwright had been stonewalled. At the board meetings his father had sat, an unreadable expression on his face, and simply voted against any proposal Jake put forward. If asked for a reason he simply said, 'We want to maintain the status quo.' That was his vote—end of.

Jake assumed his father was worried the money would dry up, that his lifestyle would be at risk, that Jake wasn't capable of taking control. Each time frustration welled inside Jake, each vote against him the equivalent of another kick of rejection from the man who had fathered a son to avoid disinheritance and who'd handed that son over as a commodity.

But soon enough his father's wishes would be irrelevant. Next week the rest of the board would give Jake their formal support and his father would have no choice but to comply—because he would be outvoted.

Emily made a sudden noise, tugging him from his reverie, and he watched as she kicked her chubby legs happily, her tiny hands reaching out as if she wanted to trail them in the water. Awe touched him at this tiny happy life—mixed again with a sadness that he had never engendered such feelings.

Isobel too was watching Emily, her expression soft as she stroked Emily's hair, and then she glanced at him. 'Do you think you'll do this for real some day? Come here, or somewhere like it, on a real family day out?'

'No.' Easy to give an unequivocal answer. 'I'm not interested in marriage or children. I've figured out a great work/relationship balance and a lifestyle that suits me down to the ground.'

'So how does that work?' Her voice was a tad over-casual.

'Right now, work is my priority so I haven't even dated for the past couple of years. And that suits me—a long-term relationship wouldn't be fair, even if I wanted one. Which I don't. When work calms down I will start dating again, but I like my relationships to be short and sweet.'

He couldn't help but note that the temperature in the boat had sunk to chilly.

'And how does *that* work?'

Jake kept pedalling, resisting the urge to let a defensive note creep into his voice. He had no problem with how he handled relationships.

'I'm upfront with any woman I date that I'm not looking for anything serious. Just a few weeks of fun. For both of us.'

'So you take a woman out for dinner and over the caviar and champagne you explain you only want to see her for a few weeks but don't worry, it will be fun?'

'Yes. It's honest and upfront. If she's looking for more then we enjoy dinner and go our separate ways.'

'Define fun.'

'Depends on the woman.' The one thing he would never do was what his father excelled in—treating women like a generic set of trophies. His father used gifts to buy people; he had a closet full of jewellery, designer clothes, expensive watches that he'd use to woo his succession of trophy girlfriends. Or to apologise for his numerous infidelities. Jake had vowed never to be like that; any relationship he had would be tailor-made to the individual. 'Some women prefer to jet off for a skiing holiday, others prefer a more tropical location, some prefer seclusion, others prefer glamorous yacht parties.'

'So they tell you what they want and you buy it for

them?' Her outrage was clear from her expression, though she was careful to keep her voice even and low so as not to upset Emily. 'It sounds like an all-expenses-paid holiday. With a bonus available if they perform well.'

Anger surfaced and he forced himself to keep the boat on an even keel, aware of Emily, who was happily engaged in trying to get her toes into her mouth, oblivious to the increasing heat of the exchange above her. 'If I take a woman on an all-expenses-paid holiday what is actually wrong with that?'

'Because you are buying them.'

'Some women are willing to be bought.' His voice was hard. Just as his own mother had been bought. 'But those aren't the type of women I'm interested in. I don't take them on holiday in return for their sexual favours. I date women I like and who like me back. We enjoy each other's company and we're both honest enough to say what we want. A non-messy, uncomplicated time together.'

'It just seems a bit shallow.'

Jake shrugged. 'Then shallow works for me. There's no chance of anyone getting hurt and it leaves me free to focus on work.' That was what drove him—the desire to take Cartwright into the future, make it larger, more global. He would not be like his father, simply living off his grandfather's spoils; he wanted to earn his living, deserve his wealth.

'So you see a relationship as a hindrance to your work.'

'Hindrance is a strong word. But I think it would be unfair to commit to a relationship where I would always put work first as a priority. That's why my work/relationship balance works for me.'

'You didn't see us as short and sweet.'

'No, I didn't.' His relationship strategy had been devised after Isobel. No one could say he didn't learn from his mistakes. With Isobel he hadn't planned, or calculated or thought. From the moment he'd intervened in the pizza place all he'd wanted was to be with her. It had been nothing like his previous relationships, all quick flings with celebrities or other wealthy socialites. Isobel had been different—he'd let his guard down, allowed himself to care, succumbed to the foolish possibility of love. And ended up hurt and disillusioned. Par for the course. Once he'd believed his grandfather loved him, only to discover that to the old man he had been a commodity, a prize, the coveted heir, a tool to further his own ambitions. When he'd gone to live with his father he'd longed for love so hard he could still feel the ache of remembered hope in his gut now. All he'd met was indifference, not dislike, but he'd sensed he discomfited his father, made him almost squirm with discomfort. It had certainly not been love, though his father denied him no material thing.

The outlines of a pub appeared around the curve of the river and he pointed to it. 'How about we moor the boat and grab something to eat?' he suggested. And once there he would definitely change the subject.

Twenty minutes later they were seated in the outdoor garden of the riverside pub, Emily in a baby bouncer provided by the friendly waiting staff. A weeping willow draped its branches into the water and the lazy drone of the river life hummed in the air. The pretty rustic tables were scattered over the newly mown grass, the scent of which tinged the air.

A waiter brought their food to them—steak and kidney pie for Jake whilst Isobel had opted for the king prawn, crab and chorizo linguine. A tantalising aroma arose from both dishes and she gave a small murmur of appreciation.

That was until Jake looked across at her. 'So what about you?'

'What about me?' Isobel twirled some linguine carefully around her fork.

'Are you in a relationship?'

Isobel hesitated, gently touching the baby bouncer as she saw Emily's eyes starting to close. She realised she could hardly refuse to reciprocate in giving information. 'No.'

Was it her imagination or did some tension drop from his powerful shoulders; did his jaw seem to relax a smidge?

'Like you, I'm very focused on work and—' she shrugged '—I like being on my own. For now, at least. Maybe for ever. But definitely until I have security, a house of my own, money in the bank.' Free and clear of any sort of dependence on another, be it for money or happiness. 'Then—who knows?'

His expression was quizzical now. 'What if you meet someone now? You can hardly ask them to wait until you have security. Why not buy a house together?'

'Because that's not what I want to do. If I did that it wouldn't be my home and I'd have to—'

'Compromise? Share?'

'Yes. No...' She glared at him, realised how hard it was to explain. But Isobel knew she wanted to own her own house, needed it to be hers and hers alone. One of the worst things about foster care had been not having *anything* of her own. Having to live in bedrooms decorated by other people, bedrooms used by other foster kids. Knowing any minute she could be moved on without warning. No way would she risk having her home taken away from her. Having a joint mortgage, it reeked of being in someone else's power. 'It's too risky. If you buy a house with someone and you split up then where does that leave you?'

Now surprise flickered across his face. 'So you don't believe in the fairy tale ending or the happy ever after of marriage?'

'No.' This time there was no hesitation. 'Not enough to bet my house on it.' Isobel's mother's relationship with her stepfather had run the gamut of negativity—destructive, violent, rife with his infidelities and her mother's forgiveness of everything in the name of love. A love that created debilitating dependency and gave Simon power. Isobel would never be dependent on anyone, never cede power. Love made you weak; independence made you strong. Simple.

'You're saying you'd rather have ownership of bricks and mortar than a relationship.'

'Yup.' No question in her mind. 'Then, once I have that, have security, I'd consider a relationship. With an equal, with security of their own, who will enhance my life.' But not someone she needed. 'I'd prefer we lived separately, had our own lives as well.'

He hesitated and then said, 'He sounds a bit like a wind-up toy.'

'Excuse me? He sounds nice and kind and he'll be there for me...'

'Whenever you want him. Someone who you choose to bring out whenever you feel like it. Someone with a prescribed amount of money in his bank account, not too little and not too much. A customised wind-up toy.'

Isobel shrugged. 'Then a wind-up toy works for me,' she said. 'Just like shallow works for you.'

'And what about kids? How do they factor into this separate house, equal partnership?'

'They don't.' Isobel looked down at Emily and for a moment regret shivered through her, that she would never have a baby of her own.

Now his eyebrows jolted up in surprise. 'You don't want children?'

Again she wondered, as she had done so many times, if her decision was foolish. But then all her reasons resurfaced, the ones she had been over time and again since she'd split with Jake, and she shook her head. 'No, I don't.' The idea was too scary, the responsibility too much, the risk too great. For a moment she recalled an overheard conversation between two social workers, after yet another of her foster placements had broken down.

It's tragic, what her mother has done to her, what the system has done. And at this rate the cycle will continue, like it always does.'

The words had stuck with her and, whilst she knew it wasn't always the case, statistics did show that patterns often repeated. What if she was a rubbish mother—what if she let her child down, the way her mother had let her down time and again? Or, come to that, the way she had let her own mother down. The thought made her feel clammy inside.

'No, I don't,' she said firmly. 'I love Natalie but I am happy to hand her back at the end of the day.'

The words were not wholly true and she could see the look of puzzlement on his face—could see more than that. His blue-grey eyes studied her for a long moment. 'I'm not buying it,' he said eventually. He gestured towards the sleeping Emily. 'I've seen you with Emily. You're a natural and you're amazing with her. I can see how caring you are and I can't believe you don't want a baby of your own.' Now his gaze met hers. 'Years ago I got the distinct impression you wanted them. We even discussed what our hypothetical children would look like.'

The conversation was still fresh in her memory, played itself out in her mind, so clear she almost felt she could reach out and touch their younger selves, hear words murmured as dawn had streaked its first light through the open bedroom window.

They'd been sitting up in bed, hand in hand, leg against leg, backs against the headboard, draped in the silken cotton of his expensive sheets—a moment of intimacy, of closeness, where words could be spoken without thought or censure.

She'd looked up at him, studied his eyes, the length of his eyelashes. 'If we have a baby I hope she gets your eyelashes.'

'And your eyes,' he'd said. 'And your hair and your smile and—'

'No! Definitely your hair.'

He'd turned then and something sad had flashed across his eyes. Then he'd shaken his head and reached out to her. 'And perhaps right now we should put in a little practice in how babies are made.'

'Hmm…they say practice makes perfect.'

And then conversation had been forgotten as they'd slid into each other's arms, the sense of desire familiar and yet achingly, intensely precious…

Isobel blinked the memory away, caught his gaze, saw his pupils darken and knew he'd replayed the same memory reel. 'We both said a lot of things back then,' she said flatly. 'Any baby discussed was strictly hypothetical.' As well as foolish—the idea of having Jake's baby had been mooted when she'd been living an illusion, not knowing that the curtain had been about to fall, exposing the sham for reality. After Jake she'd toughened up her stance on relationships and children, relearnt the lessons first absorbed in childhood. 'Anyway, what about you? How do kids fit in with short and sweet relationships?'

'They don't,' he said, echoing her own cadence and phrase. 'They can't. It wouldn't be fair to father a child if I'm not willing to commit to its mother. And if I had a child I wouldn't leave them.' His voice was filled with determination and she recalled that his own parents had split when he was young, that he'd ended up with his father.

'But don't you want a child to leave the Cartwright empire to?'

It was clearly the wrong question; he physically flinched and his eyes were shadowed with anger. 'That is not a reason to have a child.' His voice was harsh and, as if he realised it, he inhaled deeply, his voice calmer when he resumed. 'Anyway, I may have a child who loathes the hotel industry.' He looked across at Emily again and she saw a sudden sadness in his face as his gaze rested on the baby, her eyes closed, her hands curled into tiny fists. Now curiosity touched her. Years before had he ended their hypothetical baby conversation because he knew even then he didn't want kids?

'Fair enough—then let me rephrase the question. Don't you think one day you may want to move on from "short and sweet"? You can't want to work all your life. So maybe one day you will want to settle down.'

'Nope. But even if, hypothetically speaking, I did change my mind—let's say I meet someone and we get together—there is no absolute guarantee that we would want to stay together. Odds are I wouldn't get custody and anyway I wouldn't want to take a child from his or her mother.'

'Then you share custody. You would still be your child's father—you would still play a huge part in your child's life. Lots of couples manage it.'

'And kudos to them. It's not something I could "manage"—especially if my ex decided to move abroad, or remarry.'

'But you may not break up.'

'There is a huge possibility. Think of the divorce statistics.'

'But—' She was sure there was a flaw in his argument—she just couldn't seem to spot it. Because he was right—there were no guarantees. Yet she *knew*, whatever Jake was telling himself, there was more to his decision to eschew parenthood.

He glanced at his watch. 'We'd better head back.' It was a clear signal that the conversation was over.

By the time they got back to the cottage Emily was more than ready for bed and Isobel decided to skip the baby's bath and get her straight down before she got over-tired. Emily was asleep almost before she had been lowered into her cot after her night-time bottle. Isobel tiptoed to the door and exited.

She paused on the threshold as she saw Jake standing in the kitchenette, studying the carton of formula milk powder, and watched as he carefully spooned formula into a bottle and then moved to the kettle and poured the water into the bottle.

Again her heart thudded with a strange sense of warmth—brought about by the intense look of concentration on his face that brought a smile to her own. A man who was such a success in the boardroom, a multimillionaire who whisked women off to tropical islands, doing something so domestic made her smile.

It brought a question to her lips. 'Out of interest, do you do domestic? I mean, do you hoover your house, clean your own bath?'

He looked up. 'Actually, yes, I do. I even have a duster.'

Was he telling the truth? His deadpan expression gave her no clue.

He screwed the teat back on the bottle and made an attempt to shake it to mix the powder in. A spray of milk emerged, straight onto his shirt and hair. He cursed and Isobel couldn't help it; she giggled. The slapstick moment on top of the idea of Jake wielding a duster was too much.

'Sorry,' she said. 'I truly didn't mean to laugh but—'

He glanced down at himself ruefully. 'It's OK.' And then he chuckled. 'I was trying to be helpful.'

'And I appreciate that. I really do.' And she did. 'I'll show you how to do it if you like? There's a technique. First time I tried it with Natalie's bottle I had a similar accident.'

'I'd like that.'

Isobel headed to the kitchenette, scooped powder into another bottle and handed it to Jake, waiting whilst he poured the water in from the kettle.

She took it from him and stepped closer to demonstrate. Too close—way too close.

Focus. But not on his body, the sculpted forearms, the swell of his upper arms, the strong thighs. Not on his smell, not on the way his hair spikes up—

This was a bad idea but, for the life of her, she couldn't figure a way out of it.

'Put your thumb over the top of the teat, so you're blocking the hole. Then you shake. Like this.'

Her voice emerged squeaky…breathless…*ridiculous*.

He'd moved even closer to her now and his eyes held a wicked glint that ripped the breath from her lungs.

'So it's all in the wrist action,' he said straight faced and her gaze flew to meet his, in shock at the double entendre.

'I—'

Then he grinned and wiggled his eyebrows. 'Sorry, I couldn't resist. Puerile but—'

'Yes,' she said, trying to keep a straight face. 'Definitely puerile.' But she succumbed to a giggle, which morphed into a full-blown laugh. And in seconds he had joined in.

Now their gazes locked and she could feel the shift in the atmosphere, the swirl of desire, the fugue of need. They were even closer now. His scent tantalised her, the warm smell of baby milk mixed with a hint of citrus-sharp shower gel and a whiff of bergamot. Her head whirled and there was an utter inevitability about what happened next. She wasn't sure afterwards who initiated it, who made the fatal decision or whether it was a completely synchronised movement.

But one step took them closer and then she was in his arms and her lips met his and oh, God, it felt so good. His lips were so familiar and yet so new, and her lips tingled as tremors of raw desire shuddered through her body. Gentle, hesitant at first as if they both feared rejection and then the kiss deepened, intensified, searing through her veins. His fingers tangled in her hair, she pressed her body against his, wanting more, her pulse rate accelerated at his taste, his scent, the way his kiss could drive her to the edge of desperate need for more. Her body was alight and craving more of him—of Jake—

she wanted his touch, wanted the satisfaction her body knew and remembered.

Then an image of Anna penetrated the haze of desire, her cat-that-got-the-cream expression as she'd exited Jake's house. What the hell was she doing? She pulled away and they sprang apart, staring at each other for one appalled instant. How could she have been so stupid? This was the man who had cheated on her, splintered her heart.

Humiliation roiled inside her, clashed with the still present desire and doused it. She swiped her hands across her lips and saw emotion shadow his eyes, a glimmer of hurt.

It didn't matter. Nothing mattered. Sheer mortification started a slow burn as she stumbled backwards, trying to process what she'd just done.

Fool!

An urge to run nearly overcame her but then she realised there was nowhere to run to; she was stuck here, in this perfect cottage, with the man she'd kissed as though her life depended on it.

Well, if she couldn't run she'd have to stand and face the music, accept that she had orchestrated it herself. 'I'm sorry. That shouldn't have happened.'

Jake's expression was neutral, completely unreadable as he leant back against the counter. Until she looked more closely, saw the clench of his jaw, the tautness of the folded arms.

'No. It shouldn't. But it did.' He dropped his arms to his sides. 'All we can do is make sure it doesn't happen again. Put it down to a moment of stupidity.'

'Utter stupidity.'

'Stupid, yes. Surprising, no.'

'How do you figure that? I am plenty surprised.'

'Really?' He held her gaze now and she felt heat creep up her cheekbones. 'We always had a spark, straight from the get-go, and I guess that's hardwired into us.'

'That spark was six years ago and was well and truly eradicated when you cheated on me!'

'Then explain what just happened. I wasn't the only person involved.'

She'd love to be able to claim exactly that, but she couldn't. 'That kiss was a throwback—an aberration.'

'Or your body knows something that your mind won't accept. It knows I didn't cheat on you. Knows I had no reason to.'

The intensity of his voice rocked her, her body and mind still caught up in that kiss, her whole being still seared with sensation and desire and need as she sought an answer.

He stepped towards her and then back again, his gaze never leaving hers. 'I have never felt this level of attraction to any other woman. There was no way on the planet I would have slept with anyone else.'

Now there was a longer silence. In the burning aftermath of that kiss his words rang with truth; the knowledge of how completely physically attuned they had been strummed her body. Isobel stared at him, heard nothing but truth in his voice, saw only sincerity in his eyes. And yet…anyone could lie. So many people had lied to her. Social workers who had promised her that her mother would turn up to see her, foster carers who had told her this was her 'for ever place', told her they 'loved her'. Words meant nothing, could be spun and used. Sincere gazes could be practised in front of the mirror.

And yet this time her gut told her that Jake was not speaking falsely. Had she been wrong? Or did she want to believe him? Perhaps the physical attraction had messed with her head. Instincts warred inside her—her gut rolled, racked with indecision.

As her mind whirled it took a while to register the buzz of her mobile phone. She pulled it out of her pocket, looked down at the familiar number with relief and quickly accepted the call. 'Hey, Clara.'

'Hi, Isobel. Can you talk for a minute?'

'Of course.'

CHAPTER SIX

JAKE WATCHED AS Isobel moved away from the kitchenette to the living area, silhouetted against the vast window as she spoke to her business partner.

Relief vied with irritation at the timing of the call. Relief that he had some time out—that kiss had felt like a reboot of a connection and he knew that the only way forward was to pull the plug. He wouldn't open up his heart to a woman who had already crushed it once. He didn't want to open up his heart to anyone, full stop. But he *had* wanted to continue the conversation because he'd seen doubt in her hazel eyes—doubt about his guilt—sensed he'd verged on a breakthrough.

He looked back at Isobel and saw by her frown and the way she was gesturing as she spoke that there was a problem.

'Clara, I'll figure something out and call you back. Just hold tight.'

'What's wrong?' he asked.

'One of my clients, Lucy—a bride-to-be—is having a bit of a meltdown. It's a tricky wedding to co-ordinate. There's a lot of family wrangling because they all have different opinions. They keep changing their minds about everything—venue, food, clothes, colours, flowers. Anyway, it's the wedding rehearsal the day after tomorrow;

it's all falling apart a bit and they want me to go. But that's not the only problem.'

'Go ahead.'

'We've got a new client who wants to book us for a big event. She's been let down by someone else so wants to meet Clara ASAP. Preferably the day after tomorrow. It could be a really lucrative ongoing relationship.'

'Where's the rehearsal?'

'Cheltenham.'

'That's only a bit over an hour away.' Jake considered the problem; the solution seemed easy enough. 'Then you need to go.'

'I can't go. What about Emily? I can't take her with me. Not on my own.'

'I get that. I'll come as well. I'll look after Emily whilst you look after the client. You said you and Clara used to take Nat to things.'

'This is different. I promised Caro *I* would look after Emily—so that is what I need to do.'

'Caro asked both of us to look after Emily. I don't think Caro would object, especially when you're in the vicinity.'

'Nope. It wouldn't feel right. You're the security detail. I'm the hands-on one.'

'That's not set in stone. I'm sure you would do your best to protect Emily and I can be hands-on…' He broke off as he saw her small frown, sensing her hesitation. 'What?'

She shrugged and her forehead scrunched in question. 'Can you? I mean, you haven't shown any interest in Emily at all so far.'

That stung. 'That's not fair. Or true.'

She shook her head. 'Sorry. That came out wrong. I totally believe if anyone threatened her you would step in. I believe you care intensely about her safety. I meant you haven't shown any hands-on interest in her. As an individual. You haven't interacted with her. You haven't even held her.'

A quick search of his memory showed him that Isobel was right and a funny little knot of unease tugged inside him. 'Only because I have no experience with babies so it made more sense for you to look after her. It doesn't mean I can't look after her.'

'It's not that easy.'

'I get that and I'm not suggesting you simply hand her over. We have a whole day tomorrow where you can show me the ropes. Plus you'll be around on rehearsal day.'

Isobel chewed her bottom lip and he could sense her reluctance, guessing it went against the grain to accept a favour from him. But this wasn't only about her; this was about her business, about Clara, about Lucy, and he wasn't surprised when she gave a small nod.

'If you're sure, then let's give it a try. Starting tomorrow morning, you're in charge. But I'll be right next to you.'

'I'll look forward to it.' The words fell so easily from his lips, yet the after-effects rippled through the air, shimmered into the elephant in the room that had been banished by Clara's phone call. That kiss.

Isobel sighed. 'Look. About what happened earlier. The kiss—can we just forget it? It shouldn't have happened—it won't happen again. Let's delete it from our memory banks.'

'I'll try, but I don't think it's that easy. Think about what I said, Isobel. I don't think you could kiss me like that if you truly believe I cheated on you. I'm telling the truth about Anna.'

She said nothing, looking away from him out into the darkness of the night, illuminated by moonbeams. 'Let's just focus on Emily for now.'

The following morning Jake opened his eyes and identified a knot of anxiety in his stomach. He swung himself out of bed and frowned. He didn't do anxiety—not since he was a child, when he'd figured out the best way to control anxiety was to control his own destiny. Instead of living in his father's chaotic house, where he had no idea what was happening from one minute to the next, he'd asked to go to boarding school.

His father's relief had matched his own. 'Sure. Which one do you want?' had been Charles Cartwright's response.

From then on Jake hadn't looked back, and now he was on the cusp of control of Cartwright itself.

So there was no need for anxiety now. Looking after Emily wouldn't be a problem—it was simply a matter of learning how to do it. A quick shower, pulling on jeans and a top, and he emerged into the living area just as Isobel entered, Emily in her arms.

'You ready?' she asked.

'Um…' He could feel his already tenuous confidence desert him as he saw how Isobel held Emily—the baby looked so snug and cosy and safe and loved. How was he going to give Emily those same vibes? He was pretty sure he'd never received them—maybe he quite simply wasn't wired to do this. Maybe that was why he hadn't instinctively wanted to interact with Emily.

'Jake?' She moved towards him, clearly ready to hand Emily over.

'Yup.' Jeez. He could feel a bead of moisture on his temple. 'Though maybe you should feed her first—if she's hungry that may be best.'

'I think she'll be fine.' She met his gaze. 'Question is, are you?'

'Of course I am.'

'You look like you've seen a ghost or something. What's wrong?'

'Noth—' He broke off. 'I don't know.' He gave a half laugh. 'I didn't expect it to be so…scary. I mean, she's so tiny. What if I drop her?' After all, being in control of your own destiny was all very well—being responsible for someone else was different. Suddenly, all the things that could go wrong crowded into his mind. 'What if I hold her and she starts to cry?'

'Then it won't be personal.' Now he flinched as a locked-down memory suddenly shot free and impacted him so hard he nearly faltered.

Nothing personal. That was what his mother had said. She'd begun to cry, silent tears snaking down her cheeks.

'I'm sorry. So sorry. But I had to save my brother. I swear to you, Jake, it was nothing personal.'

'Are you OK?' Isobel's hazel eyes glinted with concern now. 'You look like you've seen a ghost.'

'I'm fine.' He forced a smile. 'Maybe a little nervous.' But the words sounded stilted and as he looked at Emily something stirred in him, something he didn't understand. Emotions conflicted inside him—the desire to hold the baby and a sudden…sadness.

'Then let's take it slowly.' Isobel carefully held Emily towards him. 'You ready?' she asked.

'I'm ready.'

'Here.'

Heart pounding, Jake accepted Emily, careful to support her head.

Deep breaths.

He looked down at Emily, held her safe and close; he

could smell the warm, milky baby smell, powder and baby shampoo. Emily flailed her hands, grabbed his finger and he would swear something shifted in his chest; a strange heat enveloped him, awe that this baby was so trusting, so dependent, so vulnerable. And it did twist his heart, made him wonder how his mother could have walked away from him, then stayed away.

'I signed an agreement saying I'd give you up. How could I have fought the Cartwright family against that? I told myself that you would have your own life, a happy life. And—' She'd made a helpless gesture around the room. *'Then I met my husband.'*

He'd got it—she'd made herself a new life—one she wanted to protect, he'd realised as he saw her furtive glance at her watch, then at the door. So he'd left.

The memories stabbed into him one by one and he forced himself to remain still, feeling Isobel's gaze on him. He had to lock this down; he despised the feeling that somehow, without his permission, emotions had crept up on him, caught him unaware. Emotions did not control him, he controlled them.

This must stop now.

'Jake?'

He looked up at Isobel. 'She's lovely,' he said. 'And I would have happily looked after her.' The words rang hollow in his ears. 'But I've had a better idea, better for Emily and easier for you. I'll ask Maria to come down for the day and come with us. It makes more sense. You will be more relaxed because you'll be more confident that Emily is being properly looked after.' He forced himself to smile, an easy practised smile. 'So you're off the hook—having to show me how to look after Emily. You may as well feed her whilst I call Maria.'

He stood up carefully, took one last look at Emily.

Sorry, little one, he thought. *It's not your fault you simply trigger too much emotion inside me.* She made him feel weak and vulnerable, as he must have been nigh on thirty years ago.

'Here you go,' he said and looked at Isobel expectantly.

There was a pause and then she shook her head. 'Actually, would you hold onto her whilst I go and get her milk?'

And with that she headed to the kitchenette, quite literally leaving him holding the baby.

As Isobel took the milk out of the fridge and warmed it up, her mind raced. The rational, logical part of her brain told her to leave it—if Jake didn't want to look after Emily that was none of her business. The idea of asking Maria was a good one and did solve the problem—provided Lucy didn't mind Isobel arriving accompanied by two companions and a baby. Which she wouldn't.

So it was all good, right? But it wasn't—Isobel had enough demons on her own back and she could recognise the symptoms. Whatever had happened to Jake just then, as he'd held Emily, had been important—his grey eyes had held the darkest of shadows, his expression haunted. He had been a man in pain.

Picking up the milk, she made her decision and headed back to Jake, who was standing exactly where she'd left him, Emily still safely enclosed in his arms, and for a moment she stilled, watched him. She saw how carefully he held the baby, and warmth touched her chest. Then Emily whimpered, a precursor to a full cry as she waited for her milk.

Jake's lips tightened and she sensed his tension, recognised it as panic. Wordlessly, she held the bottle out. 'She's just hungry. Why don't you feed her?'

Now he frowned. 'I thought I explained—I am going to call Maria.'

'I get that. But that doesn't mean you can't feed Emily.'

'I know that.'

His gaze met hers and she held it steadily. 'I think you're scared. Are you?'

He hesitated and she felt her heart twist at the expression in his eyes—a look of almost bemusement as he looked down at Emily. 'I'll take her,' she offered. 'But I'd like to know what's going on.' As she took Emily from him she sensed his relief and his withdrawal. 'I'd like to help.'

'I don't need help.'

'OK then. But I'd still like to know. We agreed that this time together would be used for closure, for talking through what went wrong with us.'

'This has nothing to do with what went wrong with us.'

'Maybe, maybe not. But I think it's something important to you, something important in your life.'

He shook his head. 'I've dealt with it and moved on.'

'You admit there is an "it". If you've dealt with it, then prove it. Feed Emily. If you've moved on from it you may as well tell me what it is.'

To her surprise, and perhaps to his, a small smile quirked his lips and for a second amusement glinted through the clouds in his grey eyes. 'What?' she asked.

'It's you. I'd forgotten how tenacious you are and how earnest.'

Tenacious and earnest—the two words pricked her feminine pride even as she nodded acknowledgement. 'I'll take that as a compliment and an admission I'm right.'

Jake's shoulders lifted in a shrug. 'Fine. I had a reaction to Emily.' Again the smile, but this time there was no amusement. 'I made it sound like an allergy. Maybe it is like that—she triggered something inside me.' He shifted from foot to foot, his discomfort at this conversation more than evident.

'I don't understand.'

'I'm not sure I do either. I think Emily reminded me of my own past. My mother left me when I was a baby. Not like Caro left Emily. I mean she packed her bags and left me in the hospital. I was only a couple of days old.'

Isobel could feel her skin go cold as her brain struggled to understand the words.

'I didn't see her again until I was eighteen. Someone presumably took me home from the hospital, but I don't know who it was.'

'Your father?'

'No. It couldn't have been him because he took off on a nine-month cruise.'

'But who looked after you?' Unconsciously, she realised her hold on Emily had tightened and she relaxed, saw that Emily had finished her bottle.

'I don't know. I do know that my grandfather stepped in when I was nine months old. I lived with him after that.'

Isobel burped Emily, dropped a kiss on her head and then carefully placed her down on her play mat, making sure she was happy and seemingly intent on whacking the cloth animals that dangled from the bar. Then she turned her full attention to Jake. 'But those first nine months?'

'Well, obviously, someone looked after me, maybe a nanny, maybe some well-wishing friend. Who knows?' Jake frowned. 'In the end, who cares?'

'I do.' Isobel's voice was low and without thinking she reached out and took his hand, interlaced her fingers with his, her whole being heated with sheer outrage on Jake's behalf. Because she did care—of course she did—she would care about any baby abandoned by the person who was meant to nurture them. Even her own mother had kept her, done her best. Imperceptibly, she shifted closer to Jake and in that moment she knew that whilst all abandoned babies mattered, this was personal. It was Jake she was thinking of, imagining him as a small defenceless baby, handed over to an anonymous carer.

'It doesn't really matter. It happened. I survived. I moved on.'

'It does matter.' Her hand gripped his so hard he glanced down involuntarily and she relaxed. 'Sorry. I am just so livid on your behalf. How could they?'

He shrugged, but he kept his hand in hers and she hoped the connection gave him the comfort that she sensed he would take as unwanted pity if she put it in words. 'They did what they did, but in the end I had food, clothes, a roof over my head, an expensive education and plenty of money in the bank. It all worked out. No big deal.'

'It is a huge deal and you know it. Or at least your body does. Isn't that what you said to me yesterday— you told me to listen to my body. Maybe right now your body is telling you that it does matter and maybe you haven't dealt with it.'

'I have dealt with it.'

'Then why won't you feed Emily? Or interact with her?'

'Maybe I'm not a baby person.'

'Maybe you aren't. But perhaps you should give yourself a chance to find out. What your parents did to you sucks and it is holding you back from bonding with this gorgeous small, innocent being. You can change that. If you want to. Yes, it means you may have to face some emotions but surely it's worth it.'

There was a long silence. 'I'm not really an emotional kind of guy,' he said eventually.

And she couldn't blame him—no wonder he didn't want to think about what his parents had done. She truly couldn't comprehend how his mother could have walked away and how rejected that must make him feel. But for his father to have acted in the same way was a double whammy that must have put salt in the wound.

'There is nothing wrong with emotion.' Jake raised an eyebrow and she knew that he thought there was everything wrong with emotion. 'Not when you get the chance to bond with Emily.'

Another silence as he looked down at Emily. 'I guess I can try,' he said finally.

'Then let's take her out for the morning,' Isobel suggested. 'Just to the park to feed the ducks. She seemed to like the ducks yesterday. I'll get her stuff together and you keep an eye on her. All you have to do is watch her and if she cries pick her up. Or sing to her. Or wave one of her toys—she likes that.'

'OK. Got it.'

Isobel turned round before she left the room, saw how intently he was looking at Emily, saw him tentatively reach out and stroke the baby's downy head and something melted inside her, made her feel gooey and warm.

Whoa. Careful here, Iz.

Gooey warmth was great when it came to chocolate brownies—not when it came to feelings, especially for Jake. She'd got her life on track, made a niche for herself where she fitted in, where she was happy. Most important of all, she was heading towards security and independence and safety. No way would she forget that.

CHAPTER SEVEN

JAKE WAVED A brightly coloured, crinkly-sounding toy that he thought might be an elephant at Emily and she kicked her legs and smiled as if he had performed the most amazing feat in the universe. And in truth he felt as if he'd done just that. The door opened and he looked up as Isobel re-entered briskly, holding up the sling.

'Let's get you buckled up,' she said cheerfully.

He rose, oh, so careful not to let his feet anywhere near Emily, and Isobel moved towards him until she was so close he could smell the tantalising apple scent of her shampoo and he had to resist the urge to lean in and inhale her, to run his hand through the silken tresses. Quickly, he took the sling from her, unsure whether the fleeting brush of their hands was deliberate or accidental. All he did know was that the touch impacted him out of all proportion. That her closeness dizzied him.

Enough.

He seemed to be losing his grip on *all* his emotions at an alarming rate—and it would stop now. Stepping back, he studied the sling.

'You need to slip your arms in and then adjust the straps. You can carry Emily forward-facing—that way she can see what's going on, but she's close to you so she feels reassured and cared for.'

'How's this?'

Now she did step forward, stood on tiptoe and tugged on the straps, quickly ran her hands round his waist to check the sling was correctly secured. Her hair tickled his chin and he bit back a small moan, knew he must not unravel now.

'Looking good,' she said and he noted her quickened breathing.

'I aim to please.' For Pete's sake. What had that been? Banter? Had he been flirting? Teasing? Panicking? That was it. Nerves over Emily had somehow affected his sanity.

Isobel picked Emily up and carefully placed her in the sling as he stood stock still. He felt his lips curve into a smile as Emily kicked her chubby legs as if inciting him to get a move on.

The walk to the park had a surreal feel, the birdsong louder, the flowers brighter, the clouds whiter. 'It's almost as if I'm seeing the world through Emily's eyes,' he realised.

Isobel nodded. 'That's exactly it.'

They continued in comfortable silence until they got to the park and approached the lake. A few more steps and she looked up at him. 'How are you feeling?'

He considered the question. 'Part of me is terrified that I'll mess it up but most of me is feeling great.' It was true; this moment was a happy one and the realisation gave him a momentary qualm. He, Jake Cartwright, on the cusp of pulling off the coup he'd worked towards for all his adult life, was walking through a park to feed the ducks with a baby and a woman he'd believed he'd exorcised from his life and he was…happy.

Some of that happiness was brought about by the closeness of the baby—her utterly new and innocent perceptions of the world, her trust and belief that that world held safety and love and—milk and ducks and hugs and wellbeing. The knowledge that right now she trusted him to provide that was huge.

'I'm glad because you're doing great,' Isobel said with the sweetest of smiles that encompassed both Jake *and* Emily.

'It's made me think as well that the nanny, or whoever it was who looked after me, maybe she was OK. I mean, Emily only just met us and she seems happy, right?'

Isobel nodded. 'Definitely,' she said as Emily gave a little gurgle that truly did seem to indicate joy with the world.

They whiled away an hour throwing bread to the ducks and walking, letting the sun warm their faces, watching children playing on the swings, building sandcastles in the sandpits.

'I brought a picnic,' she said after a while. 'You can feed Emily and then she can have her nap on a blanket in the shade whilst we eat.'

'Good thinking.' So that was what he did. He settled himself against the trunk of a shady willow tree and under Isobel's instruction put the bottle to Emily's lips. Emotion rocked him again. This act of providing sustenance brought home the fact that Emily could not do this for herself, was dependent on them.

The baby guzzled happily, so trusting and peaceful, her tiny hands reaching up to touch the bottle, her eyes already closing, her satisfaction so evident it touched his heart with warmth.

'What now?' he whispered.

'You have to burp her. Just hold her up and pat her back gently.'

It should have been simple but it flummoxed him and

Isobel moved next to him, her warmth giving him confidence as she showed him, his feeling of achievement as Emily emitted a belch ridiculously strong. 'You're a natural,' Isobel said and the words gave him a buzz, a glow. 'I think she'll sleep now. Pop her down on the blanket.' He lowered Emily gently and watched as the baby gave a small murmur and then closed her eyes.

Isobel unpacked her rucksack. 'I've got cheese sandwiches.'

'Sounds great. I'm ravenous.'

As they ate he watched her for a moment, looked at Emily and hauled in a breath. 'Do you think I could look after her tomorrow? At the rehearsal?'

'Absolutely I do.' Her smile was wide and contagious and he returned it as his gaze absorbed her beauty.

'Thank you for persuading me to take a chance with Emily.'

'I'm so glad you did. You have truly been brilliant with her. Calm and nurturing and gentle and—safe.' Her emphasis on the word told him that there were different ways of keeping a baby safe and that he'd fulfilled them all. 'And thank you for telling me about your parents. I know that must have been hard and, for the record, they missed out. Big time.' Then she leaned forward and kissed his cheek; for a second his body froze, the scent of jasmine, the nearness of her jolted him and he revelled in the tickle of her silky hair against his skin.

Then he moved, shifted so that his gaze met hers and he saw a spark ignite as her hazel eyes darkened. And then she tumbled into his arms, and oh, so slowly, so very tantalisingly slowly, he cupped her face in his hands, his palms against her cheeks feeling so sensuous, and his eyes met hers directly, wanting to make sure this was what she wanted too, that this was their choice, their decision.

And she didn't hesitate—she leaned towards him and brushed her lips against his, the touch ephemeral, and yet the sensation that rushed inside him was exquisite in its intensity. Now he couldn't stop the momentum of this instant of time and he didn't even want to try.

Then he kissed her, plundered her lips, unleashing a riot of sensation. He tasted the traces of chocolate, as desire rocketed and surged through his veins.

The moment felt timeless and it was only the sudden disappearance of the sun behind the clouds that pulled them from the fugue of desire. The sudden morph from hot to cold shadowed his skin as she pulled away from him, her hazel eyes wide, still fogged with desire.

He leant back against the solid reality of the tree trunk as she rocked back on her haunches, their breathing ragged, and he stared at her, knew he was in trouble. That had been too intense, too overwhelming; it had left his body tied in knots of desire, aching with frustration.

'We shouldn't have done that, should we?' she asked.

'Probably not. But I don't care.' Because, despite the knowledge that it had been both reckless and foolhardy, right now he couldn't bring himself to regret it. And that was more troublesome than anything else. It was time to get a grip.

'Well, I do.' She closed her eyes. 'I don't know what's going on here but we have to stop it. It's not…what I want. It's all confusing enough as it is. I don't know what to think any more—about Anna and you, about the truth, about what's going on here. And kissing you—I'm scared it's messing with my head, my judgement.'

Hope spiked inside him that maybe she was beginning to believe she'd got it wrong all those years ago.

'I'm sorry,' he said. 'I didn't mean to muddy the water or blur the lines. You're right. We're looking for closure—reigniting our physical connection isn't going to achieve that.' He managed a smile. 'However tempting it may be.'

'No, it isn't.' Her hazel eyes were troubled now. 'No more kisses.'

'No more kisses,' he agreed.

The next morning Isobel watched as Jake strapped Emily into her car seat, saw the deft movements and felt a glow of satisfaction, of happiness at his confidence and the way he had bonded with Emily. However confused she was right now, and inner turmoil had kept her awake most of the night, she was glad that Jake had shared some of his past with her, thrilled he'd connected with Emily.

But now she had to think of herself—events were swerving out of her control. The idea had been to gain an insight into why he had betrayed her and get closure. Instead of insight, all she had were doubts—the more she heard, the more she saw, the more she believed he had told her the truth all those years ago. That Anna had lied. As for closure, she was pretty damned sure kissing was not on the closure agenda. Let alone kissing him twice.

But now she needed to focus on work, on the rehearsal. Not Jake.

So, once they were on the way, she was relieved when he said, 'Tell me about the wedding rehearsal.'

'We're heading to Lucy's mum's house. It will be a bit chaotic. Lucy will be there, so will her mum, her two sisters and the chief bridesmaid. I'm going to have a catch-up, make sure she's happy with everything, and then we'll head to the church for the rehearsal.'

'Right, so what do I do?'

'I've explained you're coming with Emily and they

are fine with that. So just hover in the background and try to radiate calm and goodwill and hopefully that will rub off on everyone else.'

'Got it.'

An hour later he pulled into a driveway that fronted a large Georgian house. 'Right. Let's do this.'

They reached the front door, where Isobel took a deep breath, focused and then knocked. Seconds later the door was pulled open.

'Isobel.'

'Hello, Natasha.' Isobel smiled at the mother of the bride, a woman in her early sixties, made-up to perfection, her hair a perfect honey-ash bob, pale pink lipstick on a thin-lipped smile and blue eyes that were harder than ice.

'Thank heavens you're here. Clara has been acceptable but we need you. You can manage Lucy.'

Isobel smiled. 'It's always hard to come into a wedding plan halfway through but I know Clara has enjoyed working with you and we really appreciate that you've accommodated us.' It was diplomatic and made it very clear that she and Clara were a team. 'But I'm also really pleased to be here for the rehearsal and thank you so much for saying Jake and Emily can come too.' She turned to Jake. 'Jake, this is Natasha Redwood, mother of the bride.'

Natasha looked at Emily. 'So sweet,' she said in a tone of voice that didn't indicate any such thing. 'Please come through.'

They stepped onto a polished wooden floor and Isobel grinned as Lucy hurtled down the stairs. 'Isobel!' the redhead shrieked. 'I am *so* glad to see you. Everything is a mess, my hair looks like straw and I've eaten my own weight in chocolate—and I don't know if the dress is right, and—'

'Lucy, it's all going to be fine, I promise. You look fantastic and anyway, Jim would love you even if you were quadruple your weight with no hair.' She hugged the other woman. 'And today will be fun and our opportunity to make sure you're all happy with everything. And if you aren't happy I'll fix it.'

'Well, actually, I do have some things to talk to you about—' The words were synchronised as both mother and daughter said the same thing, and then both launched into a litany of problems and counter problems.

'OK. It sounds like we need a good catch-up. Would it be possible for Jake to perhaps take Emily into the garden or—?'

Now Lucy turned to Jake. 'I am so sorry. You must think I'm rude or mad or both! I'm not, honestly—I'm just afflicted by wedding fever and Isobel here is the only person who can bring my temperature down. In real life, I am completely normal—I work in an art gallery, I'm good with people and I have an eye for colour which has completely deserted me. And I'm talking too much.'

'Yes, you are,' her mum intervened. 'Honestly, Lucy, sometimes you're no different from when you were six. No matter how hard I've tried. Anyway—' Natasha sighed '—Jake, if you would like to take the baby into the conservatory, that would be fine.'

'I'm happy to look after him,' purred a voice suddenly and a tall, svelte blonde entered the room and glided towards him. 'I'm Julia; I'm a bridesmaid. Here to be helpful.' She smiled at Jake. 'I love being helpful.'

Isobel froze in mid-sentence and turned, watching as Julia sashayed over to Jake. How had she not noticed before how stunning the blonde woman was? Her hair fell down her back, she was tall, slim, elegant, with endless legs and a plummy voice redolent of a private education.

Not that it mattered, yet a stab of sheer envy knifed Isobel.

Envy? Of what, for Pete's sake? The other woman's gorgeousness? The fact that she had headed straight for Jake? The fact that Julia was in the Anna mould? So bloody what? Just hours ago, she'd questioned whether Jake had even slept with Anna. But that wasn't the point—the point was that Anna had been Jake's type.

'That would be wonderful, Julia,' Natasha said. 'You show Jake the conservatory and we'll all head to the church after our pow-wow.'

For a treacherous second Isobel was tempted to request that Julia join the 'pow-wow' and pressed her lips together to stop the suggestion from emerging. That way lay madness—she must not, should not, would not walk that road. She had no stake in Jake's love life—perhaps Julia would be perfect for one of his short and sweet relationships. The thought caused another tinge of green and she knew this had to stop.

'Great,' she said. 'Shall we convene in the dining room?'

Out of the corner of her eye she saw Julia usher Jake out of the room. 'What an adorable baby.'

Again negativity twisted her tummy and she forced a smile to her lips. 'OK, let's get started.'

Jake watched as Isobel left the room, with only the most fleeting of backward glances. There was a smile on her lips but he would swear something flashed across her hazel eyes—an expression that he'd seen before, though he couldn't quite place it.

He turned his attention to Julia, who had moved forward in a gust of perfume to tickle Emily's cheek. 'Such a sweet little baby,' she gushed at Emily, who stared wide-eyed at her for a few seconds and then emitted a wail that propelled the blonde woman backwards. 'Babies usually love me,' she said.

'She's probably hungry, or not used to a new person,' Jake said diplomatically, aware of Isobel's instruction to radiate goodwill.

'I'll show you to the conservatory. Would you like tea or coffee? Anything at all.'

'I'm fine, thank you.'

Jake was aware of a wish that Julia would go and join the others—give him time to focus on Emily, make sure he was doing everything right, but instead she seemed far more interested in making conversation and he duly complied until Natasha appeared in the doorway.

'Julia, we need you—come and try to talk some sense into Lucy about her hair.'

'Hope to see you later.' Julia blew a kiss and sashayed from the room.

'Peace at last,' Jake said to Emily, who was lying on the floor studying her toes as if they held the answer to the universe. 'In here, anyway. Goodness knows what is happening with Isobel.'

He took the baby's gurgle to be a sympathetic response and sat down next to her until she started to grizzle. Quickly, he picked her up and started to feed her.

Isobel entered as Emily emitted an enormous burp.

'You wouldn't think someone so tiny could make such a loud noise,' he commented.

'No.' The syllable was clipped and he couldn't see so much as a hint of a smile on her face.

'Tough pow-wow?' he asked sympathetically.

'It was fine. Is Emily OK?' Now she did smile as she

headed to the baby and stroked her cheek. 'Hello, poppet,' she cooed.

'Everything is fine. What's happening now?'

'We're headed to the church. Natasha says you can stay here if you like.' Her hazel eyes studied him, almost as if this were some sort of test.

'I'm happy to take you.'

Her eyes narrowed and he sensed that had been the wrong answer though, for the life of him, he couldn't figure out why. 'Why?'

'I thought you may want a bit of a break in the car. And I assumed you'd want to be near Emily.'

That wrong-footed her, though again he was at sea. 'Oh. OK. Then that would be great. Thank you.'

In the car he tried again to instigate a conversation, but gave up when she answered in monosyllables. Perhaps Isobel needed quiet to regroup, yet the silence was edged with discomfort.

Once they arrived at the church Isobel turned and gave him a quick perfunctory smile. 'Thank you. Feel free to come inside and watch...proceedings.' An emphasis on the last word. With that she slipped from the car and headed towards the pretty stone church, where it looked as though an argument had broken out, both Lucy and Natasha gesticulating, the sound of raised voices carried on the still spring air.

Jake decided to wait before exiting the car. He watched as Isobel approached the mother and daughter, spoke to them both, clearly restoring calm before they entered the picturesque church.

He frowned, trying to work out what on earth was going on, aware of a sense of both bewilderment and hurt and a nagging sense that he should be able to figure this out. They'd been getting on—getting on too well if anything—so it didn't make sense for Isobel to suddenly turn a cold shoulder. Unless it was her way of trying to reverse the damage done, offset the heat and smoulder and warmth. Perhaps it was a good strategy. Yet instinct told him it was something else.

A noise from Emily jolted him from his thoughts and he turned to soothe her before climbing out of the car. A few minutes later, Emily in his arms, Jake slipped in the back of the church and stood in one of the pews.

He watched as Lucy walked down the aisle, saw Jim waiting for her, saw the goofy smile on the soon-to-be groom's face and realised that perhaps he wasn't to be pitied that much. In truth, there was something beautiful about the rehearsal.

He stepped further in the shadows as Lucy and Jim walked back down the aisle hand in hand, the bride-to-be smiling up at her chosen partner in life with a smile so full of happiness that for an instant he nearly bought into the whole wedding malarkey.

Then he shook his head at his own idiocy—marriage wasn't about the walk up and down an aisle—it was about being able to pull together as a partnership for years and years.

Before he could exit the church Julia headed towards him. 'Hello, Tiger.'

For a moment he wondered if she was speaking to Emily then realised this was directed at him.

'Hey,' he said warily.

'Did you enjoy it?'

Before he could answer, Emily began to grizzle. Jake decided that it could be Julia's perfume the baby disliked, the musky scent a little too heavy and cloying.

'It was sweet enough, I suppose.' She answered her own question. 'But I won't be lining up to catch the bouquet.'

There was a pause that Jake realised he was supposed to fill.

'Why's that?' he asked.

'I'm fresh out of a relationship and I'm looking for some fun. And you look like a fun guy. I'm not usually so forward but what the heck. Here's my number.' She pushed a piece of paper into his hand and then turned and walked away before he could say anything at all.

Jake contemplated the paper and then he slipped it into his back pocket; in truth, he wasn't sure what to do next. He could hardly follow her out and explain he wasn't interested. And he definitely wasn't. Julia may be up for short and sweet but he felt nothing for her; there hadn't been even a glimmer of—anything. How could there be when Isobel was in the picture?

A warning bell began to clang at the back of his mind; he and Isobel were pursuing closure. In a few days she would no longer be in the picture and he would be preparing to walk into the most important meeting of his life—the board meeting that would bring him what he had striven for over the past four years. Control of the Cartwright business.

A quick scan showed no bin in the vicinity so he shrugged, shoved the note in his pocket, exited the church and headed towards Isobel.

'I need to chat to the photographer, then we're good to go.'

'We're ready when you are.'

There was now a definite coolness to her voice as, she took Emily from him. 'Hello, sweetheart. I missed you.' Now her gaze softened as she held the tiny baby to her.

But when she turned her eyes back to him he could see glaciers in her eyes. Jake frowned slightly as his mind raced, running over the day's events, trying to see them through Isobel's eyes, and suddenly the penny dropped. But now wasn't the time to discuss it, not whilst Emily was awake.

Isobel stared at the pasta dish Jake had made, telling herself it would be childish to refuse to eat it. She had to get a grip. So what if Julia liked Jake? Come to that, so what if Jake liked Julia? Isobel certainly had no hold on Jake at all—a couple of kisses, a couple of *mistakes* didn't mean anything. Yet…it rankled, goddamn it, it *hurt* that those kisses clearly hadn't rocked his world the way they had hers. Otherwise how could he be interested in Julia? And he must be interested—they'd spent long enough together in the church. Plus, the woman was gorgeous, smart, fun, wealthy… On and on rolled the list.

'That looks delicious,' she managed, even as her appetite left the table. 'Thank you.'

Jake raised an eyebrow as she served herself a fraction of her usual portion.

'Is it OK?' he asked.

'It looks delicious.' And it did. The sauce was simple yet aromatic, the ingredients all favourites of hers—tomatoes, basil, olives and capers.

'I thought you'd like it. And you definitely deserve it. You did an amazing job today. From Chaos to Calm—that could be your slogan.'

'Thank you.' This was better. Normal conversation. 'You did brilliantly with Emily. Was it all right?'

'It was fine. Great. I enjoyed it; she's a very edifying conversationalist.'

'She liked Julia.'

Really, Isobel? Really?

Aware of his grey eyes studying her expression, she forced herself to relax.

He shook his head. 'Not really. I don't think she liked her perfume. Bit too cloying.'

'Julia's nice, though, Lots of fun, according to Lucy.'

Stop it, Isobel.

But she couldn't. 'What did you think of her?' The attempt at casual fell flatter than flatbread.

'Why do you ask?'

'No reason. Just curious. Making conversation. She seemed interested in you.'

'Is that a problem?'

'Of course not.' Once the lie escaped her lips she knew she had to back it up; somehow she had to make it into the truth. She loathed the fact that she did mind, that she detested the idea of Jake and Julia together. 'I—' she jutted her chin '—I just thought…if you were interested in her maybe I could…tell you more about her.' This was getting worse and worse; the idea of helping Jake get together with Julia was excruciating. That realisation itself made her want to kick herself round the cottage.

'Isobel—' he raised a hand '—you don't have to do that. I am not interested in Julia. At all.'

'You aren't?' Her voice came out ridiculously small and she shook her head in annoyance.

'Nope.' His frown deepened as he studied her face and she dropped her gaze to her plate, forked up a mouthful of pasta. 'Iz? Look at me. Why is that so hard to believe?'

There was a question she could answer. 'Oh, come on! The woman is beautiful. Blonde hair, legs to her armpits; she could be a model. In case you hadn't noticed, she is also super intelligent, with an excellent background. I think she even has a first-class degree from Oxford.' A replica of Anna, though she didn't say it. 'Julia is the sort of woman you could easily take to yacht parties or jet off to the Bahamas with.'

'That's all great. Problem is, I don't want to take her. I'm not interested. If I were I'd tell you.'

Isobel closed her eyes, trying hard to separate irrational feelings from genuine ones. Trying to figure out the best thing to say or do. She opened her eyes and studied his face, the fine mix of strength and masculine beauty of his features—the squareness of his jaw, the jut of his nose, even the strong curve of his brows. It occurred to her that this was a man you could trust, he had no reason to lie to her and he wouldn't even if he did.

Looking at him, she gave a small nod. 'OK. I believe you.'

'Good.' Now he smiled at her and she smiled back. The moment seemed to stretch into a timeless chasm, and then her phone rang.

It was an unfamiliar number and she grabbed it, heard the caller's voice. 'Isobel?'

'Caro? It's me.'

CHAPTER EIGHT

JAKE STILLED, INSTANTLY clearing his mind of their conversation, and watched Isobel's expression.

'Caro, are you OK…? Yes, Emily is fine. Super-fine and absolutely adorable… What's happening…? Jake's here. I'm going to put you on loudspeaker.'

She suited action to word, placing the phone on the table, and they both leaned forward slightly.

'I'm going to meet with Martin tomorrow.'

He and Isobel exchanged glances. 'Is that a good plan?' he asked.

'I have to meet him. I can't run and hide for ever. I'm going to get him to agree to leave us alone.'

'How?' Isobel asked as her face creased with worry.

'I'll explain I'll get a legal injunction, that if he comes anywhere near me he'll end up back in jail. I've got a lawyer.'

'Then maybe the lawyer should handle this,' Jake suggested.

'Where are you meeting him?' Isobel asked.

There was a hesitation. 'At his house.'

'Why not at the lawyer's office?' Jake asked.

'Because Martin refused to do that.'

'Caro—' Isobel's voice held a plea now '—it's not safe to go and meet Martin alone.'

'I haven't got a choice.'

'Yes, you do. Meet somewhere else. In a public space.'

'He won't do that. And I have to see him. I have to get him to promise to leave us alone. Otherwise—'

'I know, Caro. I know. But you have to take someone with you.'

'It will be OK. I have to do this my way. I'll let you know how it goes and then I'll come for Emily. Please give her a huge hug from me and tell her I will see her soon. And thank you, both of you, for looking after her.'

With that she was gone.

Isobel's face had paled to chalk; she placed her hand in a protective curve over her tummy and stared at him wide-eyed. 'I can't let her go in there alone. It's not safe…'

'I don't get it.' Jake started to pace. 'Why is she seeing him at his house? Why won't she take the lawyer with her? Why doesn't she insist he—?'

'Because it doesn't work like that!' Isobel's voice was taut; her words whipped through the air and halted him in his tracks. 'She can't.'

'Why not?' Frustration laced his tone—he knew Caro, she was smart, funny, a bit quiet but definitely not stupid. And this was stupid—to go and meet a violent man in his house, alone. Isobel must see that.

'You don't understand what it's like, Jake.' Now she was pacing too, each step nervy and terrified and scared.

'Then tell me. Tell me why she is walking into danger.' Frustration fuelled his anger. 'It's a stupid thing to do.'

'Don't be so judgemental. It's not that easy for Caro.'

He studied the fear in her hazel eyes and saw its depth, but also saw an understanding that he knew was born of experience.

Now he ceased his strides, stood and leant back on

the kitchen counter and instinct made his voice gentle. 'OK. Explain.' He sensed Isobel's fear for Caro had sent her to the edge of a personal hell.

She halted in front of him. 'Caro is scared of him and she is trying to confront that fear. But she is also trying to please him, to set a scene where he won't hurt her. It's what abusers do—they induce this strange double-stranded reaction of fear and hope. Caro knows what it's like to be hurt and she knows what Martin is capable of, but she also hopes that this time he'll be nice, that he'll give her what she wants. But he won't. We have to stop her.'

Reaching out, he took her hands in his. 'You've experienced this, haven't you?' The thought imploded in his brain and he hoped that he was wrong, knew that he wasn't.

Isobel hesitated and then she nodded. 'My dad died when I was a baby. A year later my mum met Simon and he charmed her, made her believe he'd look after her and me. Turned out his methods of looking after people left a lot to be desired. I grew up in fear. That's what he thrived on, because fear gave him power. We never knew when he would flip, and all I cared about was not triggering his rage because he would take it out on Mum. Every time he hit her, my heart would break a little more and my fear would notch a little higher.' Jake could see that remembered pain and fear etched on her face and anger and sadness tightened his chest. 'My mother tried so hard to please him, lived in hope that somehow he would change. And that's how he messed with her head—because there were times when he would be loving and kind and then suddenly, wham, out of the blue he'd lose his rag.'

Each and every word, the vivid picture she painted, chilled his blood, hurt his very soul and he wished he knew what to say, wished he could go back in time and protect Isobel. 'What about you? Did he hurt you?'

'Yes, but mostly just bruises, not like he hurt Mum.' Her matter-of-fact tone was even worse than if she'd bemoaned her fate. 'But he would shout in my face, insult me… Worst of all, he would tell me it was my fault he had to hurt Mum. If I ever tried to protect her or stand up to him, he'd take it out on her and make me watch. He told me that if I went to the police he'd kill her. And I believed him.'

'Why didn't she leave?' He heard the anger in his own words and shook his head. 'Sorry.' Anger was the last thing she needed to hear right now, even if it wasn't directed at her. Yet the idea of Isobel, small and vulnerable and scared and hurt, rocked him with rage, twisted his chest with an ache of sadness.

'I'd beg her to leave. When I was older I found details of refuges and gave them to her—there were so many times when I told her we should just run and hide. But she couldn't. It's difficult to explain the hold he had over her; she was in thrall to him because he had her life in his hand. And somehow he made her believe that he loved her.' She spat out the last words with contempt.

His chest constricted as he imagined how appalling her childhood must have been. 'I know that nothing I say can change what happened to you, but I am so truly sorry that it did.'

She inhaled a deep breath. 'It's OK. I didn't tell you because I want pity.'

'That's good because I'm not offering pity. I'm offering admiration for the person you've become, for the bravery you must have shown to survive, and I'm offering compassion because no child should have to go through that.'

'Thank you.' But he could see she didn't believe his words, that her childhood had caused wounds that it would take way more than a few words to heal. He wondered if a part of her did believe Simon's words, that she blamed herself. So, because he didn't know what else to do or say, he moved forward and, hesitantly at first, wanting to give her the chance to move away, he put his arms around her.

For a moment she stiffened but then she relaxed into his hold and leant her cheek against his chest. So they stood for a few minutes whilst he tried to somehow convey sympathy and support and regret.

After a while she gently disengaged and looked up at him with a mixture of shyness and defensiveness on her face. 'Truly I didn't tell you that for sympathy. I told you because I wanted to explain why Caro is behaving how she is and how important it is that she doesn't go back to Martin. That she doesn't talk to him on her own.'

Compassion deepened as he realised how terrified Isobel must be for Caro, because she knew first-hand exactly how much damage Martin could do, both physically and mentally, to Caro. She knew too how Caro's actions could impact on Emily; Isobel must see herself in Emily, must want to protect the baby from growing up in fear as she had. He could only imagine the anguished tangle of her feelings and Jake couldn't help himself. Gently he cupped her face in his hands, felt the smooth silk of her skin, saw the tiny birthmark that dotted the top of one angular cheekbone, the length of her lashes.

'Whatever your reasons, I'm glad you told me. Now we need to figure out how to protect Caro.' For Caro's sake, but also for Isobel. He wanted—*needed*—to alleviate the fear in her hazel eyes. 'I'll go with her to Martin's, with Stefan and three other security guards. And a lawyer.'

'Caro won't let you.'

'Yes, she will. Because if she doesn't I will take Emily to social services. Full stop.'

'But—'

There aren't any buts. I'm not bluffing—I will not risk Caro going back to Martin and trying to take Emily back. But I don't think it will come to that. I'm pretty sure Caro will agree. Hopefully, Martin will be intimidated, see that Caro has real protection now. Perhaps if she sees him back down it will help break his hold over her.'

Now Isobel smiled and he saw the relief in her stance. 'Thank you. And I agree—Caro won't risk Emily going into care. But it doesn't solve the problem long-term. You can't keep a security detail with her for ever.' Isobel frowned. 'We need somewhere safe for her to stay. Like a refuge. I couldn't persuade my mum but I will do my best to persuade Caro. I'll start researching now. Then I'll call Caro.' She moved closer to him. 'Thank you for doing this.'

'There is no need to thank me. I want to do this. For Emily. For Caro.' But also for Isobel; now he knew about her childhood he understood how deeply this must be affecting her. How desperate she must be to prevent a repeat, how badly she must want to save both Emily and her best friend.

The following morning Isobel threw the duvet off, pulled it back on again, tried to snatch a few more minutes of elusive sleep. Uneasy dreams had agitated her night—fear for Caro and for Emily.

Enough. Far better to muster positive thoughts. Caro had agreed that Jake could come with her, had promised to bring her own lawyer. Jake would keep Caro safe. As long as Caro didn't go back to Martin. Because then she would lose Emily and that would send her friend spiralling downward, extinguish all hope and light. Without Emily, Caro would fall, give up, like Isobel's mum had when Isobel was taken into care. Guilt seeped through her being—she should have done *something* to stay with her mother, hidden the abuse better, not slipped up…

Pushing the dark thoughts away, she got up and fifteen minutes later she emerged into the living area where Jake sat and an additional fear twisted within her. 'You will take care?'

'Of course. I don't think Martin will try anything. He's just out of prison. There will be a lawyer present. And plenty of witnesses. All we need to do is deliver Caro's message—that he needs to stay away from Emily.'

Isobel nodded. 'And I have details of the refuge—Caro has agreed to talk about it. It was set up specifically to help mothers like Caro; it's a residential clinic for mothers and babies or young children. She'd be with other people in similar situations, women getting away from violent partners. The result is the clinic is very hot on security. But, most important, they offer counselling and support them after they leave, help them find a home, a job. And they have a vacancy coming up.'

She pressed her lips together, knew she was talking too much because she didn't want him to go. Her imagination went into overdrive—what if he got shot, like her father? But she knew he had to go, knew he would never send Stefan or any of his employees to face a danger he was unwilling to face himself.

'Isobel, it's going to be OK. I won't let Caro get hurt.'

'I'm not just worried about Caro. I'm worried about you.' The idea that something could happen to him weighted her limbs—fear he might get hurt, frustration that she couldn't go with him, the knowledge that life had no guarantees, could change irrevocably in a moment. Her mother's life, her own life had changed in the moment her father had made his fatal decision to get involved in a crime. 'Take care, OK? And I know it's not the time or place, but I do believe you. I believe that you didn't sleep with Anna.' She couldn't let him go into danger without telling him that.

'You don't have to say that.'

'I know. I'm saying it because I want you to know.' In truth, she wasn't even sure where the certainty came from, just knew that over the past days it had seemed increasingly impossible to believe that Jake would have behaved so dishonourably. A small voice in the back of her head questioned the wisdom of this leap of faith, pointed out that the evidence and the confession still stood. But Isobel dismissed them. Giving Jake the benefit of the doubt felt—right. Without hesitation, she stood on tiptoe and brushed her lips against his. Sensation shivered through her, a sweetness so potent she caught her breath. 'Good luck.'

His hand stroked her cheek and then, 'I'll see you later, I promise. And thank you for believing me. We'll talk later.'

Isobel watched him leave, knew the next few hours would be interminable and, despite her best efforts to remain busy and not give Emily bad vibes, that was exactly what those hours were. Minutes stretched and pulled as if time itself had morphed and slowed. Her thoughts jumbled and whirled as she wondered what was happening, whether everyone was safe, whether somehow Martin would prevail. Just as she'd always believed Simon could and would. Until finally her phone buzzed and she snatched it up, saw Jake's number.

'We're all safe. And on our way home.'

Isobel dropped the phone and picked Emily up for a cuddle. 'They did it,' she said. 'You are going to see your mummy.' Quickly, she raced to give Emily a bath, dressed her in her prettiest outfit, white with little pink flowers, and waited impatiently until she heard the front door open. She heard the pound of footsteps and then Caro tore into the room.

Isobel stepped forward to hand Emily over. Her friend looked tired but radiant as she smiled down at her daughter, even as tears glinted on her cheeks. 'I'm back, sweetheart. Mummy has missed you so much.' She looked up at Isobel. 'I was so scared, Isobel. So terrified I'd never see her again. Thank you. And I am so sorry. And it's so good to see you too.'

'And you Caro. Now, tell me what happened.' Isobel broke off as Jake entered the room, accompanied by a tall, lanky dark-haired man.

Caro blushed. 'This is Theo. He's my lawyer. We were studying together before I dropped out and I went to him to help me with Martin. He was fabulous.'

'It was easy to be fabulous flanked by Jake and Stefan,' he said modestly and Isobel studied him. He had a kind face and eyes that also held a glint of humour—she liked him, she decided.

Jake grinned. 'We made a good team. Martin didn't know what hit him. Figuratively speaking,' he added.

Caro sat down, Emily still held close to her body.

'He was so…shocked; he couldn't believe I hadn't listened to him. He blustered a bit and made some threats but as soon as Jake stepped up to him he just deflated. Agreed to leave us alone, agreed he wouldn't come near

Emily.' Worry touched her expression and she hugged Emily closer, lifted her to her shoulder. 'But I know he won't let us go that easy. I called the refuge and they sound incredible. I can move in in a few days.'

'And until then you can stay with me,' Isobel said firmly.

Caro shook her head. 'No. That's too dangerous. I'm going to stay at Theo's—Martin won't be able to find me there and Jake has assigned Stefan to stay with me until I get to the refuge.'

Isobel opened her mouth to argue and then she saw the glance Theo gave Caro; it held affection, kindness, strength and something else and she decided to hold her peace.

They spent the rest of the day catching up. Isobel and Caro sat in the garden and talked, rekindling a friendship that Isobel knew could never die completely. Until finally in the early evening Caro rose to her feet.

'Time to go. Thank you again, Isobel, and I won't ever lose touch with you again.' One final hug, a handshake with Theo and a final goodbye with Emily.

Isobel stood next to Jake on the driveway, waving until the car's tail-lights disappeared.

'It feels odd,' she said. 'I know we've only had Emily a few days but… I miss her. It's as though something is physically missing.'

'Our lives have revolved around Emily for the past few days—bottles, naptimes, nappies; it's amazing how quickly the human mind and body adapt.'

It was. It occurred to Isobel that it wasn't only Emily she'd got used to—it was Jake as well. Now it was time to move on and she was aware of a reluctance, a dip in her stomach, an unwillingness to say goodbye. How had that happened? Somehow he'd got under her skin and now she questioned whether the quest for closure had been a good one. In her head, she'd expected answers that would explain why Jake had betrayed her. Instead, all she had now was the belief that he hadn't, that she'd condemned him unjustly. Which opened up a vista of what-ifs and buts she didn't want to contemplate.

'It's natural to miss her,' Jake continued. 'But you should also be proud of yourself.'

'Proud?' She looked at him, a question in her eyes as he nodded emphatically.

'Yes. Caro is safe and with Emily and a lot of that is down to you as well as her.'

'And to you,' she said.

'We made a pretty good team.'

'We did.'

'But it's not over yet.'

Isobel looked at him. 'What do you mean?'

'It's like Caro said. I don't think that Martin will take this lying down. He was taken by surprise earlier and he knew he didn't stand a chance, but he was humiliated and he'll want revenge.'

'Then he'll go after Caro and Emily.' Panic caused the questions to emerge staccato. 'Will he be able to trace them? Does he have Theo's details?'

'Agreed and possibly and yes.' A tidal wave of fear rolled inside her, washing away her previous relief and pride, and Jake quickly took her hand in his. 'Whoa. It's OK. Theo and I came up with a plan. He isn't taking Caro and Emily back to his house—he's taking them to Wales, a farmhouse belonging to friends of his. There is no way Martin will find them there but, as an added precaution, Stefan has gone too.'

Relief touched her again and she squeezed his hand. 'Thank you. Again.'

'No thanks needed. It was Theo's idea and Stefan volunteered. He's very taken with Emily and he definitely did not like Martin.' Jake watched her for a moment. 'But that brings me to you.'

'Me?'

'Yes. If Martin can't find Caro or Theo he may turn his attention to you. And me. So I think we should stay here for a few more days. Give him a chance to cool down. What do you think?'

Isobel stared at him. What *did* she think? Conflicting thoughts jostled and head-butted each other in her brain. A part of her wanted to stay. Anticipation unfurled inside her at the thought of spending time with Jake, of exploring where they went from here, now they had closure. Another part told her that now they had closure there was nothing to discuss—the sensible option was to go.

CHAPTER NINE

JAKE TRIED TO focus on anything except Isobel's answer; he looked around the front garden at the vibrancy of the flowers in the early evening light, the deep green of the hedges, the hue of the sky. His shoulders tautened, his breath caught in his lungs and he forced himself to breathe properly. Realised that he wanted her to stay. Too much. Her face was scrunched in indecision and he decided, to hell with it. 'If you decide to go home I'll assign a security guard to you, but I'd like you to stay.'

'Why? I mean I'd like to stay but I don't know if it's a good idea.'

'Neither do I. But I'd still like you to stay.' He tried to gather his thoughts into coherence. 'If you stay maybe we can figure out if it's a good idea or not. If you go we'll never know.'

'That makes sense. I think.' Her face was still creased in indecision and he had the impression she was trying to both reassure and convince herself.

'Exactly,' he said. 'And things are different now—we need to talk about what you said earlier.' He hesitated. 'Did you mean it? Do you believe I told the truth about Anna?'

'Yes.' Her answer was unequivocal. 'I do believe you now. Six years ago I couldn't, because I was terrified

I'd follow Mum's pattern. She allowed herself to believe Simon again and again. She believed his lies, believed he'd change, set herself up again and again. And I wished so much that the first time he hit her she'd walked out then.'

Jake reached out and placed a hand over hers. So much made sense now. 'I get that. Back then you thought you'd set a pattern for our relationship where I'd be unfaithful, lie, you'd believe me and I'd do it again.' And again and again. Just as Simon had abused her mother again and again.

Isobel nodded.

'I understand that.' He truly did, saw now how all her doubts and insecurities that he hadn't even known existed would have fed her belief that he could commit infidelity. Once confronted with a confession and the evidence, she couldn't let herself believe him; the risk had been too great. 'Thank you for believing me now.'

He realised he had a big smile on his face, not of triumph or vindication—more of happiness that she knew him to be innocent, that those hazel eyes no longer looked at him in judgement or doubt. But also because now Isobel knew that he hadn't cheated on her, that she hadn't been judged inferior to Anna, that he'd been happy with her.

Then he realised she wasn't smiling back, that worry still creased her brow.

'What's wrong?' he asked.

She shrugged. 'I messed up,' she said. 'If I'd believed you back then, what do you think would have happened to us?'

Jake inhaled a deep breath, watching a last flicker of sunlight highlight her chestnut hair with a pattern of blonde highlights. 'I think *I'd* have messed it up—I'm not cut out for a relationship. Work is too important to me; I don't think I could have balanced that with a relationship. And that wouldn't have been fair to you.'

'I haven't seen that side of you in the past few days,' she said.

'These past days have been an exception.' The lull before the boardroom storm—he'd done all the hard work in the past four years. 'This isn't who I really am.' A man who played with babies, fed the ducks, babysat at wedding rehearsals. 'My life is my work and I think that would have driven you away, would drive any woman away.' Soon enough he would be completely wedded to work, to implementing his plan. And he wanted that; the idea filled him with both excitement and anticipation.

And then it occurred to him that Isobel actually shared his work ethos, had an equal determination to succeed in her career. Could mutual ambition have worked for them rather than driven them apart? It wasn't a question he knew the answer to. 'But there's no point playing the what-if game.' He'd learnt that long ago too. You had to play the cards you were dealt, deal with the chips as they fell. 'This is where we are now and it's up to us where we go from here. Why don't you stay for the weekend and maybe we can figure that out?'

A long silence and then she nodded. 'OK. I'd like that.'

The smile broke out on his face again. 'Then I think we should go and celebrate. I've heard there's a great piano bar recently opened in Oxford, with amazing musicians and incredible cocktails as well. The clientele ranges from students to OAPs, a real mix.'

'It sounds perfect.' Her smile illuminated her face, alleviated his realisation that he had no idea what he was doing. 'I'll go and change.' Yet as he watched her go a warning bell clamoured at the back of his brain, asked him whether this was a good idea. Events seemed to have overtaken him, their connection had crashed through the gears, evolved without his control or consent. Battened down emotions had escaped and right now Jake wasn't sure what to do about them.

Perhaps the answer was to think about work; he checked his messages and frowned at the sudden realisation he hadn't heard anything from the other board members for the past few days. And he hadn't contacted them either—had been so caught up in events that he hadn't given it much thought. That was a mistake and one he knew he needed to rectify. Quickly, he called his PA, left a message for her to call him back. He couldn't let the prize slip now, not when there was so much at stake.

The thoughts derailed as Isobel entered the room; his breath hitched in his throat as he absorbed her sheer beauty. Her chestnut hair fell in loose waves to frame her face, her hazel eyes were bright. She wore black jeans, topped by a strapless red vest top and a denim jacket.

'Let's go. I've ordered a taxi and it should be here—' his phone rang on cue '—right now.'

Minutes later they were en route to Oxford and Jake directed the driver to stop in the centre. Together they walked through the historic city. The shops were closed now but their displays still enticed. Further on, they walked past the facades of many of Oxford's most ancient buildings—the reason why it was dubbed the 'city of dreaming spires'—the Ashmolean Museum with its stunning architecture, the university colleges that had featured in so many blockbuster films, the oldest library in Europe and so very many literary places, pubs where authors had drunk.

'It's so strange, isn't it? To imagine Thomas Hardy sat in there,' Isobel said as they walked. 'He couldn't have known that so many years later people would still read his works. That people would study them.'

He nodded, suddenly aware that somehow they were hand in hand, her palm secure against his, and it felt—good. So he wasn't going to question it—after all, she'd told him she no longer believed Anna's confession, had absolved him. And tonight was about celebration of their teamwork.

'We turn down here,' he said.

'Have you been here before?' she asked and he shook his head.

'No. But someone told me about it and I was thinking about maybe introducing the idea into the hotels. A piano bar, and maybe focus on cocktails.'

'So this is all about work,' she said, her tone tragic, and he turned to her with a startled look.

'No, I didn't mean it like that. I meant it came up in my research and I thought of it and—' He broke off as she grinned at him.

'Gotcha.' She squeezed his hand gently. 'I don't mind if it is about work. I'm happy to be your research partner. Lead me to the cocktails.'

They entered the dim interior of the low-ceilinged bar; brick walls showed posters of jazz greats and piano notes strummed the air, mixed with the buzz of conversation. A waiter approached, casually dressed in stone-washed jeans and a T-shirt imprinted with an image from one of the posters that decked the walls. 'I booked a table for two,' Jake said.

'Cool. This way.' He led them to a small round table tucked into an alcove, handed them both menus and left.

'Wow.' Isobel regarded the list. 'It may take me half the night to decide.'

He knew he should be focused on his own choice but

he preferred to watch Isobel, the small cleft in her fore-head as she studied the menu. 'You look as though the fate of the world hangs on your choice.'

'Ha ha! Not the fate of the world. But I don't drink often so I'd like to make sure I make the right choice. I can't decide whether I should play it safe or take a risk.'

Silence followed and an arrested look widened her hazel eyes before she quickly looked back down at the menu. The aftermath of her words rippled. Play it safe—keep their attraction contained? Or play with fire—flirt, banter, encourage the flames and hope they would dance to his tune?

The waiter returned and she gave a sigh that could indicate relief or regret. 'I'll play it safe. I'll have a Cos-mopolitan, please. I know I like those.'

Jake looked at her and then back at the menu; he closed his eyes and jabbed a finger down. 'I'll have this one. Take a risk.'

The waiter nodded. 'Cool. They won't be long. Would you like to order food?'

Jake glanced down at the menu. 'I'll have the steak sandwich with fries.'

'Make that two,' Isobel said.

'Sure you don't want to try the katsu chicken burger with blue cheese? Take a risk?'

'I'm sure. And I can't afford to always take risks,' she said primly. 'I can't afford to discard my cocktail and just buy another if I don't like it.'

'I don't believe that had anything to do with your de-cision. And you don't either.' He grinned at her. 'In fact, admit it. You're annoyed you didn't take a risk.'

Her eyes narrowed, but he saw her lips quirk.

'Gotcha,' he said.

'OK, OK. But it will serve you right if you have ordered something revolting.'

The waiter arrived with their drinks and he looked at his doubtfully, noted the vivid blue colouring and the pineapple pieces.

'Looks good,' Isobel said, and she began to laugh, the low chuckle infectious, and he grinned at her.

'Want to go halves?' he offered.

'I'm good, thanks. With my nice safe Cosmopolitan.'

Jake sighed and sipped the vivid blue concoction. 'Actually, it's not that bad. I'm broadening my horizons.'

'Sure, sure.' She took another sip of hers and made an exaggerated sigh of appreciation. 'I think I'll stick with playing it safe.'

He held his glass up. 'To Caro and Emily.'

She clinked against his and smiled, thought for a moment. 'What did you think of Theo?'

'I liked him. He was calm under pressure and he wasn't scared of Martin. I almost got the feeling he would have stood up to him without Stefan and me being there. I was chatting to him earlier, whilst you were with Caro, and he's definitely got a good head on his shoulders and he cares about Caro.' He watched her face, saw the conflict of expression. 'Didn't you like him?'

'I did. It's just… At the very start I liked Martin. And there is a theory that people follow patterns in life.' He watched as she traced a pattern on the table in a drop of liquid.

'You think Caro may be attracted to violent men?'

'Possibly, though I hope not.'

'Do you believe your life is following a pattern?'

Now she shrugged. 'It's hard to know, isn't it? I do know that a lot of children who suffer domestic violence can go on to abuse others. I *know* I won't do that. I couldn't imagine ever hurting someone else, let alone a child. I also know, though, that sadly often women do go from one abusive relationship to another. I believe that your past shapes you and you can't undo that.'

Jake shook his head. 'I disagree. Your past is part of you but it doesn't have to shape you. You shape yourself, control your own destiny.'

'To a point, of course you do. We all have choices but I'm not sure how free those choices are. Maybe you don't want children because of what happened to you as a baby.'

'No.' His denial was vehement. 'I don't want children because I recognise I couldn't give them a family life they'd deserve.' Yet even he could sense that his tone was over-emphatic.

Now she raised her eyebrows. 'But perhaps you couldn't give them a family life because you didn't experience one. Maybe the same goes for me.'

He considered the idea for a moment. 'So you're saying if we both had experienced conventional childhoods, with two happy parents, a pet and a picket fence we'd want to repeat the pattern ourselves.'

'Yes. And a bit of me is sad that I don't think I can do it. When I think of Emily a part of me does want a baby of my own. Surely you felt the same way? I saw you with her—you bonded, you were a natural.'

The question jolted him, projecting a sudden image of himself looking down at his own baby, a tiny being with chestnut hair and hazel eyes. The sheer idea pierced him with a strange emotion, gave rise to a debate he didn't want to have—did he actually want a child, despite acknowledging the impossibility of fatherhood? For a moment a sense of discomfort probed at the decision he had made long ago—that Cartwright came first, that it would be irresponsible to have a baby when he had no wish to commit to a relationship, when he knew that relationships had no guarantee.

The thought of Cartwright steadied him—that was his future, his legacy. His decision was correct and he refused to be saddened by it. He shook his head. 'I'm good with my life choices. That's the important thing. To have no regrets.' Yet despite the clarity of his words the image of that baby still lingered and he met Isobel's gaze. 'That's why, if you have regrets about your choice, don't be afraid to change your mind. I can only imagine how difficult your childhood was but I don't believe that means you can't be a brilliant parent yourself. In fact I know you would be.'

'Thank you.' He heard the sincerity in her words but suspected she didn't believe him. 'So would you. I hope you believe that.' Her hazel eyes studied him with way too much discernment and to his own annoyance his gaze dropped to his nearly finished drink, studied the final piece of pineapple. In truth, he didn't believe that at all; he knew he would never abandon a child or treat them with indifference but he knew he would be unable to balance his love for his job with the needs of a child. And he would not contemplate being an absentee parent—that would make him no better than his own father. Neither would he take his child to work—would never place a mantle of expectation on them, make them believe all he wanted was a successor—that would make him no better than his grandfather.

Isobel reached out, placing a hand over his. 'Listen to me,' she said. 'I get it's hard for either of us to believe we could be good parents, but I think there's something we should both remember. We did a fabulous job over the past few days with Emily.' Now she smiled. 'And we're meant to be celebrating!' She raised her glass and they both drank the final gulp of their drinks.

'One more?' he asked.

'Just the one. Hopefully, the food will absorb the alcohol and we haven't really had a chance to listen to the music. It would be great to sit here for a little longer and soak it in.'

'What would you like?'

Now she smiled at him, a huge sunny smile. 'I'll have the seventh one on the second page. Whatever it is.' She paused. 'As long as it isn't your blue one!' Another smile. 'I'll take the risk.'

He grinned back. 'You've got it.'

As he approached the bar his phone buzzed—his PA, returning his call of earlier. Quickly he put the phone to his ear. 'Hi, Bethany.'

CHAPTER TEN

ISOBEL LOOKED UP as Jake returned and handed her a vivid orange drink. A Mai Tai,' he said, and smiled. 'Rum, pineapple juice and almond liqueur.'

But his smile was edged with preoccupation and she frowned. 'You OK?'

'Fine.'

Doubts suddenly assailed her. 'Look, if you don't want me to stay, I don't have to.'

He held up a hand. 'It's not that. At all. I do want you to stay. I got a call—a work-related one, that's all.'

'Bad news?'

'Not exactly. More a bit of a wake-up call. I have an important board meeting next week and I need to do some work.'

'That's fine—really. I get work is important.' Yet irrational disappointment surfaced that this weekend would be impinged on. 'Truly I don't mind going home tomorrow morning. Or—'

'There is no need for you to go home. In fact I was wondering if you'd like to go to a ball tomorrow night? The work I had in mind is networking.'

'A ball?'

'Yes. It's a charity gala bash, held annually in London at the Milton Park Hotel. The guests will be a mixture of businessmen and celebrities. Cartwright usually takes a table and I and some of the other board members attend. I'd planned to go, but I cancelled as I thought we'd be with Emily. But now I could go and it would give me a chance to chat with the other board members.'

Isobel shook her head. 'That's really not my sort of thing.' Understatement of the year—the thought of mingling with high-flying executives and celebrities at a star-studded event made anxiety flutter her nerves into agitation. The thought of going with Jake sent the panic into the stratosphere. 'It's not my style.'

He shook his head, his grey eyes glittering with bemusement. 'I don't get it. You organise events like this charity gala.'

'Exactly. I'm an organiser; it gives me status, a reason to be there. I'm not being judged for myself but for the job I do and I don't have a problem with that. I'm good at what I do.'

'You're also good at being you. You would easily hold your own in a crowd like that.'

Isobel shook her head, wondering how to make him understand. 'Not in that context. I wouldn't know what to say or how to behave, or what to wear or—'

Jake sipped his drink, studying her for a moment. 'How about we do it this way? You think about it as work, come in your professional capacity. Come to network. The place will be full of people who could help promote your business, people who use events companies a lot.' He leant back and smiled at her, a smile that curled her toes and spoke of his satisfaction at finding an argument he knew to be unassailable.

A smile he was entitled to—he had her. Clara would be thrilled and Isobel knew this was too big an opportunity to be missed. If she could get even a single contact it would be gold.

'You in?' he asked.

'I'm in.'

'Then it's a date.'

The simple phrase rolled through the air as if carried by the notes of the piano, changing the tempo of the evening. A date with Jake? The idea sent a funny little thrill through her veins. 'Is it?' she asked before she could stop herself.

'Do you want it to be?' he countered.

Isobel looked down at her drink, took a small sip on the brightly coloured straw. The tang of pineapple contrasted with the hint of almond, the overall effect both refreshing and a hint sinful because of the kick from the rum. His question whirled in her head: did she want it to be a date? To risk a cocktail choice was one thing—to hazard a date was a whole new strata of jeopardy. She made her decision.

'No. This ball is about work—you said you need to talk to the board and I want to try and network to make contacts. So let's not blur those lines.'

'Fair enough. But I want you to know that I'd be proud to take you as my date. You are courageous and intelligent and professional and loyal. And beautiful and poised and graceful.'

The sincerity in his voice touched her; she knew he believed the words even if she couldn't.

'Got it?' he asked.

'Got it,' she replied, mesmerised by his voice, his gaze, the way he was looking at her.

'And you will wow every single one of those guests tomorrow night.'

'OK.' Now she did smile. 'If you're ever out of a job

you could have a whole new career as a coach. You give a mean pep talk.'

'Thank you.'

She glanced at him, aware of a daft shyness. 'You really think I'm all those things?'

'I really do.' Now his voice was husky. 'I meant every word. I want you to be able to see it—to see yourself like I see you. The ugliness of your childhood isn't you; you're like a beam of light that shines through it.'

The beauty of his words overwhelmed her and she leant forward and oh, so gently brushed his lips with her own, tasting the fruit juice, the slight tang of alcohol. She raised her hand to his cheek, lingered on the roughness of his six o'clock shadow, closed her eyes and let the strains of the music envelop her.

Hearing his small groan, she threw caution to the wind. She simply lost herself in the moment, in the kiss, in the soaring sensations he aroused in her, in the gentleness and the depth of passion, unsure what this meant, whether it was a symbol of closure or a way of showing her gratitude for his words.

The change of song as the pianist morphed into something more rock 'n' roll pulled her out of the spell and she sat back, stared at him. 'No regrets,' she said instantly. The feeling liberated her. She had no idea where this weekend would take them, but she'd wanted that kiss. A kiss, now she knew he wasn't a philanderer, wasn't a liar, hadn't betrayed her. She'd deserved one guilt-free kiss. And it had been a humdinger.

'No regrets,' he echoed.

For a moment the urge to kiss him again threatened but that, she knew, would be a mistake. Time for practicalities.

'So what time will we need to leave tomorrow? Because I need to go shopping.'

'That's fine. We'll get a train up to London in the afternoon, stop at mine to change and then Roberto can drive us to the event. Then we can either stay in London or come back here.'

'Come back here.' The words left her lips without hesitation; she knew she didn't want to stay in a fancy hotel, she wanted this weekend to be spent in the cottage where they had shared so much and found closure.

'Then we'll head into Oxford in the morning, shop and we could visit the cathedral if you like?'

'It's a plan.'

CHAPTER ELEVEN

THE FOLLOWING MORNING Isobel stood in the changing room of a small boutique in the centre of Oxford and looked at the two dresses hanging on the peg in front of her.

Two dresses. One choice.

The two were completely different—both were professional, but there it ended. Dress number one was demure, black, fitted, high neckline, it contoured her body and wearing it she looked svelte and elegant. She'd look good, but she wouldn't stand out. It was the play it safe dress…

Then there was dress number two, which was more shadowy, more shimmery—a dress that skirted with danger. Nude underlay with a chiffon overlay patterned with a black flower and leaf pattern, a V-necked front that tantalised without revelation, and then the material shimmered to the floor in a waterfall of perfect folds. But it was what the dress lacked that made it stand out—in short, it left her back bare.

Isobel had never worn anything like it, but it made her feel—different. Sexy, alluring—perhaps the likes of Anna and Julia always felt like this. The idea was a strange one. And she wanted Jake to see her in this, wanted to knock his socks off, wanted to live up to his words.

Beautiful, poised and graceful.

She wanted to add to that list. Even if she sensed the dress represented danger, a skirmish with risk.

She stared at the dresses. Two dresses. One choice.

Jake stood outside the cathedral, spotting Isobel with unerring accuracy as she threaded her way through the twisty, windy streets that spoke of so much history, watched the grace of her movement, the sway of her chestnut hair in the breeze.

As she approached, he smiled at her. 'Successful shop?'

'Yes.' The word was said with emphasis and he raised an eyebrow.

'Good.' He looked at her, hoping that last night he'd made her see herself as she truly was. For a moment their kiss haunted him; it had held an intensity he couldn't explain, it had avowed something. Dammit. Forget the kiss—his focus needed to be on his meeting with the board members later on. Bethany had reported that in the few days of his absence Charles Cartwright had actually been seen in the office, had met with the other board members individually. It was possible that his father was going to try and make a fight of it.

'Shall we go in?'

She looked up at the exterior. 'I thought it would be bigger.'

'It's one of the smallest cathedrals in England, but it's like a slice of history.'

They entered and next to him Isobel gave a small gasp of wonder as she took in the rich vaulted ceiling in its splendour, the glory of the stained-glass windows.

'It's awe-inspiring.'

'So is the story behind it,' he said. 'Originally this was a church that grew up around the shrine of a saint—a woman called Frideswide. She was an important noblewoman who founded a priory in Oxford. But she caught the eye of a Mercian king who didn't care about her vows of celibacy—he wanted to marry her anyway. She fled, he chased her and was struck down. Frideswide went on to live to a ripe old age as an abbess in a nunnery; she is also said to have created a well with healing powers. She died in about 750 AD.'

Isobel gave a small shiver. 'And we're still talking about her nearly ten centuries after her death. And she might have stood here on this very spot at some point in her life. The idea is so…immense.'

It was the perfect word and again he felt that sense of connection, of being attuned with her as they continued through the cathedral and entered the chapel.

Isobel paused to read the memorials. 'So many Cavaliers were buried here as well. All those men who believed in their king and ended up dead.'

'Soldiers who fought bravely for an ideal, those who believed it was Charles I's right, his divine destiny to be King.' Destiny—those soldiers had fought and lost their lives to protect the destiny of one man. Had it been choice or simply fear of the repercussions if they didn't? Or a simple need to earn money? He recalled Isobel's assertion of the previous evening—that people had choices but they weren't always as free as you might believe they were. What about his own choices? His choice to wrest control of Cartwright. His destiny or his choice? 'And then the Roundheads, who believed no one should be given that right just because of their birthright. They fought equally as bravely and their victory in the end was short-lived.'

'But their actions had huge repercussions,' she said. 'Future monarchs had less power and then still less and eventually they lost the power to rule. Yet their destiny is still to be royal.' There was little choice to be had there.

They stood for a moment and then she looked up at him. 'I get the feeling this place is important to you.'

'It is.' He met her gaze squarely, knowing he wanted to share this with her, in the same way she had shared with him the previous day. 'I came here soon after I met my mother.'

'When you were eighteen, you said?'

'Yes, I went to find her when I was eighteen. I wanted some answers. Until then I'd always bottled it; at eighteen it seemed the right time. I traced her to California, arrived unannounced. She was…shocked.' At the time he'd been unable to figure if that shock had been born of sadness or horror or happiness. Perhaps a mixture of them all. 'But she explained why she'd left. Explained it all. It turned out that my grandfather delivered my father with an ultimatum. Told him if he didn't get married and produce an heir he would disown him. My father obeyed the letter of the law—he paid my mother to marry him and produce a child. She agreed because she was desperate. Her younger brother needed an operation, one he could only get in America if someone paid for it. My dad offered to do that. In return my mother had to give me up. So that's what she did. To save her brother. My dad gave me up so that he could save his lifestyle. My grandfather instigated my birth in order to mould an heir.'

Her hazel eyes were wide, full of compassion. 'I cannot believe any of them acted like that, without any thought for you. And you, at eighteen, if you didn't know any of this it must have been a cataclysmic shock.'

It had been exactly that—the facts had torpedoed his beliefs. Until then he'd believed his grandfather had stepped in out of love; now he realised that in fact his grandfather had orchestrated his creation—had demanded an heir and been presented with one. It hadn't been love; it had been a man's desire to live on through his legacy.

'That's what I came here to think about,' he said. 'My mother's explanation at least gave me clarity, explained the way they'd behaved. At least my mother had some excuse; as for my father, I have always known how important his lifestyle is to him. The real whammy was my grandfather—I knew he had always wanted me to be the Cartwright heir but I had always believed he took me in out of love. I wanted to do as he wished because I loved him too and I felt I owed it to him.' He shrugged. 'But once I knew the truth I realised I owed him nothing.'

She had moved close to him now. 'You must have had so much to think about; it must have made you question your whole life.'

He nodded. 'I could renounce my inheritance, build my own empire, I could become a doctor or a blacksmith. And I looked at all these people here.' He gestured to the gravestones. 'It made me think about the decisions they made. St Frideswide—maybe she didn't even want to become a nun, maybe her parents decided that for her. Maybe it tore families apart when some declared for the king and others for Cromwell. I thought about my grandfather and I realised that I wanted to lead Cartwright, not because it was my destiny but because it was what I wanted to do.' He'd known that he couldn't abandon the business; to him the empire was too real, almost like a live entity.

'Have you ever regretted it?'

'Not once.'

'What about today? Have you come here today to make a decision?' she asked.

Had he? It was an astute question. Had he come here to question his current course—a course that set him

on a collision path with his father. A fight for control of
the board. A fight he would win—he'd put the work in,
proved his worth and now it was time for his vision to
take the company forward. The decision had been made
and there was no way he'd back down now. He hadn't
come here to decide but to seek some sort of validation.

Perhaps men had come here in previous centuries to
decide where their allegiances lay—come to ask for advice or guidance, hoping that St Frideswide would guide
them on the righteous path. In the here and now he knew
he had no choice—he needed to wrest power or watch
the business stagnate and crumble and he wouldn't—
couldn't do that. Charles Cartwright had opposed Jake's
every effort to take Cartwright into the future. Jake believed that his father was worried that the new plan was
too risky, might jeopardise his income stream and lifestyle. He didn't trust Jake to take the helm. In which
case, now was the time to be ruthless, to continue his
efforts to unseat the man who had never wanted him in
the first place.

'My decision is already made,' he said and glanced at
his watch. 'Now, we need to get back. We have a ball to
prepare for.' He was looking forward to it, though a small
niggle accosted him, a worry that somehow his father had
undermined him, somehow turned the other members.
Hell, it would only take one of the others to vote against
Jake and with Charles—and Jake would lose.

A few hours later they arrived at his home, a terraced
three-bedroom house that his grandfather had left him.
He had let it out until he'd inherited his shares and decided it would be sensible to have a base in London. He
saw Isobel glance around, tried to see how his home
must look through her eyes. The décor was neutral, cool

greys and stone colours, the furniture chosen for comfort and ease.

'I like it,' Isobel said and he felt a sense of pleasure at her approval.

'You can change in the spare room,' he said. 'It has an en suite bathroom—if there is anything you need, just shout. I'll be through there.' He pointed down the hallway to his room.

Isobel nodded. 'Thank you. I'll try not to be too long.'

'No problem. Roberto is picking us up at seven so we've got plenty of time.'

Enough that he settled down to do some work before quickly showering and donning his tux. He exited the room and made his way to the lounge. 'Ready to…' The words died on his lips, his brain froze as he halted and simply stared at Isobel. 'I… You…' There simply weren't words for how she looked—the dictionary didn't cover it. The best he could do was, 'You look stunning.' The dress could have been made for her, the bold black pattern eye-catching, the material moulded to her figure and swept in regal folds to the floor. Her hairstyle was simple, falling to her shoulders in sleek chestnut waves, her make-up discreet, yet it emphasised the hazel of her eyes and the generous curve of her lips. Political correctness be damned, he couldn't take his eyes off her, couldn't help but let his eyes rove her body.

'Thank you. I wanted to live up to the occasion.' Her hazel eyes sparkled and her cheeks flushed slightly.

'Truly, you look sensational.' He gestured towards the door. 'The car awaits.' Isobel walked past him and now Jake nearly swallowed his tongue as he clocked her bare back, smooth creamy skin, her slender waist accentuated by the cut of the dress, and he closed his eyes. Heaven help him.

Roberto climbed out of the car to open the back door and they slid onto the smooth leather seats. 'Well, I'm quite happy to sit here and look at you for the whole journey,' he said.

'You don't scrub up so badly yourself.'

She smiled but as the car ate up the miles he could sense a proportionate growth in the tension in her body, saw her hands clench. 'You don't need to be nervous.'

'I'm not nervous. I'm bricking it.' She closed her eyes. 'Oh, God. What if I say something like that to someone important?'

'You won't—and it wouldn't matter if you did. You will fit in, Iz. And you look incredible.'

'Yes, but I've realised that doesn't make any difference. I used to try to dress the part as a child. It wasn't easy but sometimes Mum and I would manage a shopping day out, buy new clothes, and I'd try to wear what the popular girls wore. I'd go into school and hope, really hope they would include me. But they never did. They knew where I came from, knew I was the weird kid.' He could hear the bitter-tinged resignation in her voice. 'People can tell and they will be able to tell now, that I don't fit.' Her foot tapped the floor. 'Who did you take last year?'

'Hayley Jensen.'

'The supermodel?' Her voice was tauter than a fixed crossbow and Jake knew that words wouldn't cut it, knew that nothing he said would take away her gut belief that she was still the weird kid, about to be ridiculed by celebrities and executives alike. 'Turn round,' he instructed.

'Why?'

'You'll see. Nothing sinister, I promise.'

She did as he asked and he inhaled silently, looking at the bare skin of her back, the curve of her shoulder blades.

Then carefully he lifted his hands, brushing her hair out of the way, feeling a shiver ripple across her skin. He began to massage her shoulders, felt the tautness, the knots and realised exactly how tense she was. Gently he kneaded and worked, heard her small moan as he began to dissolve the tightness.

'That's amazing,' she murmured when he decided that any more would be too much. For her and for him. The urge to kiss the nape of her neck, to turn her round and capture her lips was almost too strong to withstand. 'Thank you.'

'You're welcome.' His attempt to keep his voice even was a spectacular fail and he cleared his throat. 'I hope it helped.'

'It did, thank you.' Her breathing had quickened slightly, heat tinged her cheekbones and he knew she was as affected as he was.

This had to stop; he needed to focus. This ball was about work. He couldn't afford the slightest risk to his plans—plans he had made over the past four years. His mission was so nearly achieved—he couldn't let himself be distracted.

'Good. Now, I just need to get a bit of work done, if that's OK.'

'Me too,' she said and he saw his own guilt mirrored on her expression. 'I've got a list of people I should try and approach,' she explained. 'And a few facts about them. I need to make sure I've memorised them.'

CHAPTER TWELVE

ISOBEL SMILED AT Roberto as he opened the door for her and she climbed out, felt the welcome evening breeze on her face. Welcome because she'd got herself all hot and bothered or, rather, Jake had. Her skin still tingled from the brand of his hands, the slow sensuous massage imprinted as his fingers had wielded their magic, ratcheted up her body's need for him.

Whoa.

Not need. She didn't need him; she would never need anyone. Never give that power. Now his hand touched the small of her back and she nearly yelped. She forced herself to focus on their destination, the lavish exterior of the Milton Park Hotel, lit up now by an array of twinkling lights that shone on a deep red carpet, upon which milled an assortment of celebrities and a stream of photographers and TV crew. Cameras abounded and Isobel blinked at how utterly surreal it was for her to be here.

Oh, God, what was she doing here? Her eyes widened as she recognised people hitherto only seen on TV or glimpsed on the covers of celebrity gossip magazines At least no one would want to take a picture of her. And now, as she looked at the dresses of the other guests, doubts hustled her.

Then Jake took her hand. 'Walk tall,' he whispered. 'You deserve to be here.'

The feel of his hand steadied her and she glanced up at him with a quick grateful smile. Just as, from nowhere, there was a cry of, 'Jakey!' and a tall blonde woman glided into their path.

Hayley Jensen. Of course it was. Isobel looked up at the stunning model and felt herself pale into insignificance.

'Hayley.'

'Jakey! I hoped you'd be here. I want you to meet Matt.' The slender blonde waved her left hand at them. 'We're engaged! Matt's a surgeon. Let's get a picture.' Hayley waved and almost immediately she and her fiancé were surrounded by photographers.

Before even a stray reporter could home in on them, Jake moved towards the hotel entrance and they entered the lobby, ushered in by the magnificent moustached porter stood at the revolving door.

Once inside, they were asked to sign the guest register and after a discreet security check they entered the ballroom, which glittered from the lights of four ornate chandeliers that dipped from the high vaulted ceilings. Round tables were beautifully decorated with white and pink floral centrepieces and matching helium balloons floated above silver champagne buckets. Isobel forced herself not to shrink backwards, stayed close to Jake as a silver-haired man made his way through the throng towards them. 'Jake! Glad you could make it.'

'Good to see you, Dillon. This is Isobel, an old friend of mine. Isobel this is Dillon, a board member at Cartwright.'

'Rumour had it you wouldn't be here.' Dillon's eyes

narrowed. 'Especially as you've missed a couple of meetings recently.'

'Yes. It was unavoidable, I'm afraid.'

'Hmm. Not the best timing. Clarissa and I were wondering if you'd bottled it. Or simply changed your mind. As your father says, you're still young, maybe you'd rather have a more relaxed lifestyle.' Now his gaze went to Isobel and she knew that he believed her to be part of the relaxation package.

Isobel felt Jake tense beside her, saw his jaw clench. 'I'm sure my father would prefer it if I did exactly that,' he said smoothly. 'However, that is not my intention. I'm sorry that I've been away from the office for a few days. I agree that it was unfortunate timing, but I'm around now and happy to go over any points you would like to discuss. Either this evening or any time that's convenient to you.'

The man looked mollified. 'Good, I know that Angela and Jonathan have a few doubts as well. They are here too. And Clarissa. Perhaps we could all have a chat. You're asking us to put our faith in you.'

'I know that, but I'm confident that my plan is the right way forward and that I can allay your concerns. In fact I'd welcome the chance—I want us to be agreed on this.'

'I'll go and tell the others you're here and up for a talk.'

Isobel watched as Dillon walked away.

'Everything OK?'

'It will be.' Now his tension was palpable. 'It's my fault—I should have kept better tabs on them the past few days, seen them in person.'

'Has looking after Emily affected your work in some way?'

'No.' He shook his head. 'It's nothing to do with Emily.

I just made a small miscalculation, took my eye off the ball. I'll sort it out.'

But there was a trace of frustration in his voice, the tiniest hint of worry, and Isobel shook her head, knowing it wouldn't help if Dillon believed Jake had been on a short and sweet romance with her.

She glanced round the seething mass of people and took a deep breath, tugging her hand from Jake's. 'I'll be right back. Nature calls.'

But, as she left him, her eyes scanned the room for Dillon, finally pinpointed him in conversation with three others, no doubt the other board members. Isobel cleaved a way through the crowd towards them.

'Hi,' she said.

Dillon looked round. 'Hi—Isobel, was it?'

'Yes, I'm Jake's friend and as his friend I wanted to clear something up with you. The past days—Jake's absence—he has been helping a friend of ours and what he's done has genuinely changed a child's life.'

Dillon frowned. 'Jake's whereabouts are his business—he doesn't have to explain it to us.'

'He isn't,' the red-haired woman pointed out, 'this young lady is. Please go on, Isobel. I'm Clarissa, by the way.'

'Earlier, I got the impression that you believe that Jake was spending his time on holiday. He wasn't. A mutual friend of ours is a subject of domestic abuse; Jake stepped in to help look after her baby and help her. I am quite sure that you want to be led by a man with principles. I wanted you to know that Jake has those.'

Clarissa nodded. 'Thank you, Isobel,' she said. 'I doubt Jake would have shared that with us. And it is worth taking into account.' As she turned away, Isobel heard her say, 'It seems as though Charles was wrong in his assessment of the situation.'

As she headed back through the crowd Jake approached her. 'Is everything Ok?'

'Yes.' Isobel hesitated, then decided it would be better to tell Jake the truth—he needed to know the exact score. 'I spoke to Dillon to explain that you haven't been skiving off the past days, that you've been doing something good.'

His gaze softened as he stared into her eyes and her insides started to go gooey. 'You didn't have to go to bat for me.'

'Yes, I did. I don't know exactly what is going on but I know how much Cartwright means to you. My assumption is you need their support for something important.'

His hand came up and he gently brushed a strand of hair off her face, the gesture so soft, so gentle, so sensual that she closed her eyes.

'So now you go and talk to them. I'll be fine.'

'I'm not going to abandon you.'

'You aren't. I'm here to network.' She tried to keep the wobble from her voice, knew damn well she was going to go and hide in the toilet rather than introduce herself to anyone.

'Nope.' Jake glanced around and, before she could stop him, he waved at Hayley.

'No, I don't want—'

'She's a nice person, Isobel, and she and I were never an item. Truly.'

Before she could speak, Hayley had reached them. 'Hayley, could you help me out? Isobel here is an events planner and a damned good one. I was hoping to introduce her to a few people but—'

'Don't tell me, work calls.' Hayley shook her head.

'This is just what he was like last year,' she said. 'I barely saw him—he was so busy working.'

'Go.' Isobel made a shooing gesture and after a second's hesitation Jake turned and headed towards the board members.

Isobel smiled weakly at Hayley. 'Look, you don't have to babysit me. I know there are plenty of other things you'd rather be doing and—'

'Nope, I'm more than happy to help. I only come to these things because it's for a good cause and my agent tells me to. Parties aren't really my thing.'

'Oh.'

Hayley watched Jake for another moment. 'It's probably the last we'll see of him,' she prophesied. 'One of the many reasons why he and I could never have worked. But he's a nice guy. Upfront, you know?' She took a couple of glasses of champagne from a passing waiter and passed one to Isobel. 'We figured on our first date that we were not going to work. I want the real thing—love, kids, a farm in the countryside. I love modelling, for sure, but I'll be happy to retire in a few years. I've invested my money well and I want to settle down and have loads of children. And chickens.'

'Chickens?'

'Yup. And a horse and dogs—and Matt wants that too. And I'll live in wellies and old clothes and no make-up.'

Isobel blinked—this was not how she'd pictured the conversation going.

'Anyway, let's start introducing you.'

Her nerves still strummed but Hayley's easy confidence, the knowledge that underneath the glamour the model wanted nothing more than to muck out pigs whilst dressed in wellies imbued Isobel with a strange confidence.

And, to her surprise, most of the people Hayley introduced her to were easy to talk to; the ability to hide behind a professional persona was a huge help and soon Isobel relaxed and the next hour glided past until she sensed rather than saw Jake approach.

'How's it going?' He came up beside her, where she was standing watching the dance floor being set up, a glass of juice in her hand. 'I'm sorry I was so long.'

'It's truly fine. Hayley was great—she wants us to plan her engagement party—I've made some really good contacts and I have a whole list of follow-ups and a couple of meetings. Clara is going to go ballistic with joy. How did it go for you?'

Jake exhaled. 'Good. I'll make sure I stay on them until next week but I think they're back on board, pardon the pun. Thank you for what you did. It was kind.'

'I told the truth.' She'd known that Jake wouldn't have wanted to sound as though he were making excuses.

He looked to where the orchestra were preparing to start.

'It was still kind and it made a difference. May I have the honour of the first dance?'

The seriousness of his voice made her skin shiver in anticipation, as if it were in truth an honour. It's a dance, she told herself. No big deal. But her body wasn't buying that. Because she'd be in his arms, up close and personal, and that was a massive deal. Even if she wasn't sure of the terms.

'You may,' she said softly and it felt as though she were committing to something far more.

Just a dance, she tried again.

He took her hand, the grasp so firm and right, and he led her onto the floor, where the orchestra had started to play. One arm encircled her waist and now his hand was on her bare back and his touch felt decadent, glorious, like a brand, and she knew that it would be impossible for her to dance with anyone else. The thought of another hand on her felt wrong.

And this felt so right; her body seemed made for his. She pressed against him with a small sigh of relief, her cheek against the solid breadth of his chest, her hand on the muscular strength of his shoulder. She swayed with him to the music, lost in a world of pure sensation—the lilting, melodic notes that touched and wove through the air, the soft cloth of his tuxedo, the muffled beat of his heart, the scent of his soap, the feel of the skin on the nape of his neck against her fingers—his small gasp when she placed her fingers there. And then the tune danced its way to a close.

'And now for something a little more lively, ladies and gents. Are you ready now?'

She stepped back as the music morphed into a faster beat, the drums and the trumpets mixed it up and jolted her out of her near trancelike state.

'You up for this?' he asked and she nodded, hoped that the segue from slow and romantic to this would shake the dreamy languor from her mind and body.

And it did—but now her whole body pulsed to a different type of dream; this was about passion and movement and as he twirled her away from him and then back hard and fast into the strength of his body, desire changed its tempo from languor to sharp and edgy and needy. Until the final notes and then he caught her, laughing and breathless and wanting, yearning him.

'You didn't tell me you were such an expert,' he said, but she could sense the words were an attempt to impose normality. Because his grey eyes had darkened with desire; his body told her that his need matched hers, that the same burn of longing lashed his body too.

'I'm not. It's you.' Their bodies were attuned on the dance floor, as they had been in the bedroom, a reminder she so did not need right now. She knew she should step back, from their proximity, from the rush that cascaded her body, from the signals that threatened to overload her brain, which was telling her the desire had to be doused. Her biggest problem now was that she no longer remembered why. 'Just you.' Now she knew that no level of argument, of logic, could stem this. And she no longer wanted to. If it was a bad idea so be it; she'd take the consequences. 'Jake?'

'Yes?' His deep voice was low with desire.

'I… When this is over, I want… I want…you.'

Just him.

'Are you sure?'

'Yes. What do you think?' She stared now at the buttons on his tux, focused on the material until she felt dizzy.

Then, 'Look at me.'

She did. 'I don't think, I *know* that I want you. So much it hurts.'

Afterwards, Isobel had no idea how she got through the rest of the ball, knew she must have, hoped she managed it with professional courtesy and calm. Knew she must have eaten, knew too that the food must have been gorgeously, meltingly good. But all she could think about was the night ahead. Then finally, eventually they had said their goodbyes and were heading for the car. He slid in after her and took her hand, held it in a cool firm grasp, his thumb circling her palm. The rhythm, the movement was poignantly sensual and desire built, burned inside her as the car ate up the miles until finally, finally they were back at the cottage.

A farewell to Roberto, who was driving back to London, and then they half ran up the pathway to the front door. The keys—why was it taking so long?—his fingers made clumsy by a need for haste. Then he swung the door open and they bundled in, laughing as they nearly got stuck in the doorway.

'I can't slow down,' she said. 'I want you so very badly.'

He swept her up into his arms and headed for the stairs, then straight up and into his bedroom, where he placed her gently down so she faced him. 'Here I am. However you want me.'

Now she smiled and it was a slow languorous smile as if now they were finally at this point she could slow down, take her time. 'Naked would be a good start.'

'That can be arranged.'

'Allow me.' She stepped forward and her fingers deftly undid the buttons of his shirt; she placed her hand on his chest and she could feel his heartbeat accelerate under her fingers.

'I lied earlier,' she said. 'I didn't buy this dress for the occasion; I bought it for you. Just you.'

'For my eyes only.' Another pulse of desire jolted through her and he gently turned her round, dropped the lightest of kisses on the nape of her neck, trailed his fingers over her bare back and the shiver of her response shuddered her body. Deftly he unhooked the dress and she felt the silky folds slither down and pool on the floor. She heard his groan and then she turned round, stepped forward into his arms and they tumbled backwards onto the bed.

CHAPTER THIRTEEN

ISOBEL OPENED HER EYES, aware of a dreamy, wonderful sense of joy, happiness, release… Memories of the past hours tumbled over her and she turned to look at Jake, who still lay asleep, one arm flung over her in a protective embrace.

The glorious realisation that she was allowed to study him filled her with a warm gooey sense of happiness—the nape of his neck, the breadth of his bare back, the tangle of the duvet round their legs all brought a goofy smile to her face. Unable to help herself, still amazed that she could, she gently trailed her fingers down his back and he rolled over and smiled a big lazy grin.

'Morning.'

'Morning.'

He shifted so that she could snuggle into the crook of his arm. 'Sleep well?' he asked.

'Yup. I feel incredibly refreshed and—' Her tummy gave a small rumble. 'And incredibly hungry.'

'I'll rustle us up some breakfast. Stay right where you are. I'll be back with breakfast in bed.'

'You are…amazing,' she said. 'In more ways than one,' she added as she watched him climb out of bed, completely unselfconscious in his nakedness. He pulled on a pair of jeans and a T-shirt and smiled down at her. 'Hold that thought,' he said.

Once he had left the room Isobel scrambled out of bed and used the bathroom, glanced around the room in search of clothing and oh, so daring, pulled open a drawer and took out one of Jake's T-shirts. She pulled it over her head and revelled in the feel of it, the smell of it; the sheer intimacy of wearing his clothes sent her giddy.

Slow down, Isobel.

An inner voice tried to insert a word of caution and she shut it down. Consequences be damned; whatever happened, the next days would be conducted without analysis or regret.

Jake entered carrying a laden tray and brought it over to the chest of drawers. 'Help yourself.'

'Where did you get these from?'

'I made a quick run down to the local bakery.'

Pastries, toast, butter, scones, jam… Isobel heaped her plate and carried it back to the bed and soon they were sitting cross-legged, facing each other and eating with gusto.

'This is perfect,' she said. Before he could respond his phone rang. Placing his plate down, he reached for it, glanced at the number and then rose lithely to his feet and put the phone to his ear.

'Good morning, Clarissa.' He listened for a minute and then smiled. 'That's great to hear and thank you. Any questions at all, just call.'

As he returned to the bed, Isobel pushed her empty plate away. 'Good news?'

'Yes. That was Clarissa, confirming she's still happy and it was good to talk last night.'

'What *was* all that about last night?'

He shook his head. 'It doesn't matter.'

'Yes, it does. Clearly it's important to you—and I'd genuinely like to know. I feel part of it now.'

'I'm planning on taking control of Cartwright's future. To do that I need the support of the minority board members, including Dillon and Clarissa.'

Isobel frowned. 'How does that work? Surely as a Cartwright you have enough clout to be able to do what you want.'

'It's more complicated than that.' He took a bite of his croissant.

'Go on.'

Seeing him hesitate, she felt a sudden stab of hurt. 'You can trust me.'

'I know that. I don't want to bore you.'

'You won't.' Swiftly, she put her plate on the floor and leant back against the headboard. 'Honestly.'

He shifted to sit beside her, leant back against the headboard and stretched his legs out against her's. 'Basically, my father owns forty-nine per cent of the shares, and I now own twenty per cent. The remaining thirty-one per cent is held by Dillon, Clarissa and two others. Until I was twenty-five my shares were held in trust and my father was able to use them to vote so he has been able to do whatever he wants to do.'

'And now you want to do things differently and your father doesn't agree.'

'Got it in one. When I first came into my shares at twenty-five, whatever I suggested he vetoed and the rest of the board agreed with him. But over the past four years I've won the board round, because they can see the validity of my ideas. I've also worked damned hard and they can't question my commitment any more. I've put together a five-year plan and called a board meeting to vote on it.'

'Wouldn't it be easier to try and persuade your father that your ideas are good? Get his support?'

'That's not going to happen.'

'Why not?' Charles Cartwright didn't sound like an ideal parent, but surely he'd want his company to prosper.

'Because he's made it clear he doesn't want change, and he's not prepared to consider any of the proposals. That's his stand and he's told every one of the board members that. As far as I can tell, he wants to maintain the status quo; he thinks my plans are too risky and could affect his income and lifestyle. He also believes I won't have the staying power, that I'll give up at the first hint of trouble.' His body tensed next to hers. 'Forcing a vote is the only way I can do this, the only way to save Cartwright.'

'Have you spoken with him?'

'No.' He shrugged. 'There isn't any point. He doesn't do conversation with me.' His tone was flat. 'He never has.'

Isobel frowned, trying to connect all the events of his childhood. 'What happened after your grandfather took you in? Did you see your dad?'

'Occasionally, my grandfather took me to visit him. But it never really worked. I ended up being looked after by one of my father's friends in another room and all I could hear was them yelling. I hated it. But then my grandfather died when I was six and I was devastated. I can remember the grief mixed with the sheer funk of not knowing what was going to happen to me.' Isobel reached out and interlaced her fingers through his; she knew that feeling all too well, the uncertainty and the fear of the future. 'But then someone turned up in a limo and drove me to my dad's. A huge mansion in London, full of bedrooms and people. I thought it was a party but after a while I realised that that's how my dad lives all the time.' He shook his head. 'I hardly ever saw him on his own. He was always with someone else.'

'Who looked after you?'

'Whoever was around. It was kind of a communal thing. Thankfully, he also employed an assistant, a kind of PA called Petra. She made sure there was always chilled champagne available and the right type of caviar and she also looked out for me, made sure I was fed, watered, clothed, enrolled at school.'

'But where was your father?'

'Sometimes he was around, sometimes he wasn't. There were times when he and his entourage would pack up and go to Nice for three months. Every so often he'd ruffle my hair, or ask me if I needed anything. One day when I was about eight, I told him yes, and I asked if I could go to boarding school. He shrugged and said, "Sure. Which one?" So that was that. After that I saw him occasionally; he'd always ask if I needed anything or tell me some anecdote about his latest conquest. That's it.'

'It doesn't sound like he spent a lot of time in the boardroom.'

'No. That's why I was surprised with how he reacted after I graduated. His refusal to give me a role at Cartwright.'

'And that's the first time he refused you anything?'

'Yup.'

'Which doesn't make sense. I still think you should talk to him. Ask him why.'

Jake sighed and her heart tugged at the sudden weariness in it. 'It wouldn't work, Iz. He and I don't work like that. In truth, we don't work at all. I've accepted that and moved on.'

Who was to say he was wrong? And yet it didn't make sense.

'It's just—' She hesitated and then decided to go on. 'There are so many things I wish I'd had the chance to talk to my mum about. So many unanswered questions, so many things, small and big. I didn't even have the chance to say goodbye.'

He shifted closer to her now, took her hand in his. 'What happened?'

'When I was ten I was taken into care.' The fact sounded so clinical. 'Teachers realised that my home life wasn't great. I'd become agitated at school, was bunking off and a teacher spotted the bruises. So I was taken into care. Entirely against my will, I might add. I kicked and screamed and they pretty much had to drag me out.'

He frowned. 'But…surely you wanted to get away.'

'I didn't want to leave Mum. I knew that, without me, everything would be so much worse for her. At least we had each other.' Guilt still rippled through her. 'I still wish I'd done things differently, hidden it better, figured out a way to stay with her.'

'But what about you? If you'd stayed—' He released her hand and put his arm around her instead, pulled her in close and safe, and she watched the emotions shadow his face.

'I know. And my head understands that social services had to step in. But I hated foster care—with all my heart. Being in care made me feel like a charity case, made me feel beholden, to the state and to the carers. As if I had moved out of Simon's power into the hands of social workers. Don't get me wrong, some of those people were good people—I know that. But, at the end of the day, to most carers I was a commodity, a job—a means of paying their bills. And when I became too much trouble they moved me on.'

Isobel gave a sudden smile and Jake studied her expression. 'I'm guessing you were a lot of trouble.'

'Yes, I was. My master plan was to be so bad I'd get

sent back to Mum. Of course it didn't work out like that. All that happened was I ended up in a care home.'

'Where was your mum all this time? Did you see her?'

'Yes. But they were often supervised meetings or held in awful office buildings. I did try and sneak off and see her and we texted, but she didn't always turn up. Simon would stop her and I soon realised that her seeing me infuriated him, which meant he'd hurt her. So I stopped the visits, told her it was OK, that I'd got a plan. That as soon as I became sixteen I'd get a job, get myself together and I'd rescue her. Make her leave Simon and we'd live happily ever. That was my happy ever after dream.'

'What happened?' But she sensed he knew, just wanted to delay the inevitable conclusion.

'Ten days before my sixteenth birthday I found out my mum died of pneumonia.' The memory was a dark cloud of grief, disbelief. 'Due to an "administrative error" I only learnt of her death three months after it happened. She'd already been cremated. I wasn't even there. A friend, a woman I'd never heard of, sprinkled her ashes out to sea at Bournemouth. I don't even know why.'

Jake's arm was around her shoulders now, the weight the equivalent of a comfort blanket, and she turned to face him. His grey eyes were so full of concern. For her. The feeling was novel and wonderful, but she needed to get her point across.

'So you see I never got a chance to talk to her, I'll never know why Bournemouth; there are so many things I'll never know. So maybe, just maybe, you should think about talking to your dad.'

'I'll think about it. But first, I am so sorry for your loss.' His gaze was so full of sympathy, his focus entirely on her, and that sent a trickle of warmth through her; the sense that he genuinely cared made emotions swell and cascade inside her and she snuggled in even closer to the strength and comfort of his body. The sense of having shared these memories gave the moment an intimacy she'd never experienced before and it both moved and scared her. Enough that she shifted slightly away from him, needed to lighten the moment.

'Me too. But hey…' she smiled at him now '…it happened a long time ago and I've come to terms with it all. I just wish I could have said goodbye.' She shifted on the bed and looked at him again. 'Promise me you'll think about talking to your dad.'

He sighed. 'You don't give up.'

'Not easily.' A pause. 'So you promise?'

Now he chuckled and nodded. 'I promise.'

But sadness lingered in his eyes and she wanted to dispel it, wanted to clear memories of their parents from the room. 'Thank you. And then go for what you believe to be right.' She shifted to face him. 'But, in the meantime, I think *we've* talked enough.'

Now he smiled, the kind of smile that made her look down at her toes to see if they were actually curling in response.

'Sounds like you're looking for some action.'

'Action sounds like an excellent idea.'

'Got any suggestions?'

'Hmm. We could go for a run.' She kept her tone utterly serious and his expression fell in a ludicrous mix of puzzlement and disappointment and she couldn't keep it up.

She chuckled. 'Gotcha,' she crowed, and gave a squeal as he growled in mock anger.

'I have a way better idea than that.'

A few hours later Jake smiled across at Isobel; they were both seated in a local café tackling plates of lasagne and chips. God, she looked beautiful. Her hazel eyes were luminous, her skin glowed and warmth touched him at her closeness. The past hours had brought an intimacy he'd never experienced before, both physical and emotional—he'd shared experiences, opened up for the first time, and it felt both good and terrifying.

An alarm bell pealed in the back of his brain, warned him that he'd opened up and by definition that left him vulnerable. He shut it down, told himself that it was too late to worry, that maybe he and Isobel could figure something out—a way to stay connected, stay close. After all, Isobel wanted an independent relationship, one where she and her partner lived separate lives. Maybe that would work—maybe somehow he could manage to work every hour of the day and still see Isobel—maybe he'd think about this later.

Because there was something else he wanted to talk to Isobel about. 'I've had an idea.'

'Another one? Already?' She raised an eyebrow and he grinned.

'Not that sort of idea.' Now his expression sobered. 'And if you don't want to do it I won't be offended.'

'Go ahead.'

'I wondered if you'd like to go to Bournemouth. Maybe sit on the beach and you can say goodbye to your mum. We could take a balloon—' He stopped, realising how stupid that sounded. 'I did some research and apparently letting go of a balloon in memory of someone is a good way to say goodbye.' Still she said nothing and he shifted uncomfortably, wondering if he'd got this wrong. It was just that her story had touched him—her love and understanding for her mother, despite her mother's shortcomings, the weight of responsibility and guilt she carried. The tragedy of her childhood. All of it made him want to lighten her load. 'Sorry. This was a bad idea. I didn't mean to overstep, or intrude or try to understand your grief. I—'

'Stop.' Her voice was low and as she looked at him he thought he saw a tear gleam in her eye. 'It's a beautiful idea. Thank you and yes, I'd love to do that.'

And so a few hours later they arrived at Bournemouth beach, Isobel clutching a helium-filled gold heart shaped balloon.

They sat down on the sand in a secluded spot and looked out at the waves, slightly choppy in the late afternoon breeze; clouds scudded across the sun, though the sand was still warm beneath them. She sat close to him, looking absurdly young and vulnerable as she stared out to sea.

'Mum loved gold things. I made her a picture once using a whole tube of gold glitter. I always hoped that one day I'd be able to buy her a real gold necklace. That's what makes death so sad—it takes away all those opportunities and dreams. When my dad died, my mum said what broke her heart most was all the things he'd miss.'

'What happened to your dad?' Isobel had never mentioned him, just that he'd died.

'He wanted to make a better life for his family, so he broke his own rules. He'd been made redundant, he was desperate so he took on a dodgy job, told my mum it was a one-off. It all went wrong and he ended up caught in a gang shoot-out. He died. I was still a baby so I have no memories of him at all, only a couple of photos. I used to think about him a lot, wonder what life would have been like if he hadn't made that one stupid choice. But, as you said, there is no point playing the what-if game. But it's tough not having any memories of someone.' She gave a small inhalation. 'I'm sorry, Jake. You know how that feels.' She shifted even closer to him. 'Have you seen your mum again since the first time?'

He shook his head. 'No. She's married with three kids, two boys and a girl. None of them know about me, even her husband doesn't, and she wants to keep it that way. I'll respect that.' Though he had thought about that long and hard—the idea that he had siblings out there who knew nothing about him and never would had imploded his world.

'That must be hard for you.'

'Yes.' He would always carry the sadness that his mother had stayed with them, brought them up, loved them but had walked away from him. Whatever the reasons. 'But it isn't something I can change. Perhaps one day she'll change her mind and tell them. Who knows?' He smiled at her. 'But this isn't about me. It's about you and your memories. You don't have any of your dad but you do remember your mum. Maybe the important thing is to remember the good times.'

'You're right. We used to love reading together. And we both loved ice cream. Mint choc chip. That was one of our favourite treats. If it had been a bad day or a rough night, if we knew Simon would be out we'd sneak out to the park and sit on a bench with our ice creams. Sometimes we'd go on the swings and Mum would swing so high, as if she were trying to escape to freedom.'

'Hold that thought,' he said. 'We passed an ice cream van on our way down. I'll be back.'

He returned within minutes and handed her a cone and she smiled her thanks. 'I feel as though she is here, that somehow her spirit is watching. Does that sound daft?'

'No, it doesn't. I hope she can see you now, see how wonderfully you've turned out. I know she would be really proud of you—of everything you've achieved and the person you've become.'

'Even though I let her down? Failed to rescue her like I promised I would.'

'That wasn't your fault.' Somehow he needed to make her see that, believe it. 'You tried and she knew that. I'm sure that brought her happiness. You did everything you could to save her.'

'I know. I wish I could have saved her from herself, protected her from her own demons. But I couldn't. And sometimes she couldn't protect me. But the most important thing is that I know she loved me and I loved her.' Isobel looked up at the sky. 'Goodbye, Mum. I wish it could have been different. But I love you. I hope you knew that.'

Jake caught his breath as she let the balloon go, watched Isobel's face as she watched it drift upwards, saw the tears shine in her eyes and he tightened his arm around her, wished he could take the pain away.

They watched as the balloon floated upwards; caught by the breeze, it glittered in the sunlight as it bobbed and weaved its way. Buoyed by the wind, it dipped down and then up again, floated higher and higher until finally it was a tiny gold dot in the distance.

'Thank you.' She wiped away a tear and snuggled against him. 'Truly, thank you. That felt cleansing. As if I've made my peace. I will always wish her life could have been better, wish I could have had a happy ever after with her, but I know she did love me. And I can't change the past.' She shifted and she met his gaze. 'But if I could I would never have accused you six years ago. I should have known you are a good man.'

Happiness welled inside him and as she looked out to sea for the first time he did wonder whether if they had stayed together—could they, would they have made it? But, if they had, would he have still been on the verge of winning Cartwright?

The question chimed discord in his brain—the chips had fallen and now Cartwright was his priority. But, here and now, he wanted to simply enjoy this moment, this time with Isobel.

'How does a fish and chip dinner on the beach sound?'

'It sounds perfect.'

The next morning Isobel caught herself whistling as she cleared the breakfast dishes into the dishwasher, felt a hum of happiness in her veins as she tried to come up with a plan for the day. Perhaps they could laze the day away watching films and eating popcorn. The sheer cosiness of the idea made her smile. She clicked the dishwasher on and then looked round. Jake was in the lounge on a conference call to two of the board members.

Isobel glanced at the washing machine and decided she might as well put a wash on—the domesticity felt in keeping with her mood.

As she climbed the stairs and went over to the laundry basket, the idea of their clothes being mixed up seemed significant—ridiculously intimate—fuelling the growing part of her that couldn't help but wonder if maybe, just maybe, they could make this work. Yes, Jake was focused on work but so was she. Wouldn't it be better to see each other occasionally than never see each other again? It wouldn't be a 'short and sweet' contract, but perhaps they could negotiate different terms that suited them both. Or perhaps they could simply see what happened...

She pulled the washing out of the basket, automatically checked his jeans pockets for coins and her fingers found a twist of paper and she pulled it out, was about to put it on his side of the bed when she caught a glimpse of a scrawl of writing. A name she recognised. Before she could question the wisdom of it her fingers untwisted the paper and she read the words.

Hey, Tiger. Here you go! Call me.

This was followed by the digits of a mobile phone number.

Can't wait to have that fun!
Julia xxx

Isobel stared down at it. Read the words again. And again. She sank down onto the bed as the impact of the words crashed into her brain. Julia, Lucy's chief brides-maid. Beautiful, svelte, blonde Julia. How could she have been such a fool? Julia even looked like bloody Anna; she'd known that.
Slow down, Isobel.
Jake had said, categorically said, he wasn't interested in her. And she'd believed him.
But if he wasn't interested why would he have her number? Why would she have felt it was OK to give him her number? Why had he even kept her number? Panic began to swirl inside her—panic that she'd got this oh, so very, very wrong.
She spun round as she heard the door open and saw Jake enter, a smile on his face—a smile that vanished when he saw her expression.
'Iz? What's wrong? What's happened?'
'This. This is what is wrong.' She couldn't even shout; all she could feel was an icy coldness inside her, as if her body was trying to protect her, ice her feelings.

'What is it?' He frowned and stepped forward as she handed him the paper. He read it and then looked at her, his eyebrows raised in query. 'I'm not getting this.'

'You can't see the problem?'

'No, I can't. I forgot I even had this.'

'You forgot you had a beautiful blonde's number in your pocket?' The high pitch of her voice echoed the shrill scream inside her, the tide of realisation that she'd been suckered.

'That is what I said, yes.' Now his voice had hardened slightly and her anxiety escalated and caused her skin to become clammy.

'OK. Well, now I've reminded you, perhaps you can tell me what it's doing in there.'

'Julia gave it to me at the wedding rehearsal.'

'Why?'

'You'd have to ask her. I assume it's because she wanted me to call her. I haven't even read it.'

'Then why did you take it?'

'What was I supposed to do?'

The question made her pause. Technically, at the wedding rehearsal Jake had been a free agent. But that wasn't the point. The point was that Jake had claimed not to be interested in Julia, had omitted to mention this note. He'd lied to her. She'd asked him time and again, given every opportunity for him to tell her, had even offered to further his cause. Yet all the time he'd kept Julia's number.

'You could have refused to take it. You could have told her you weren't interested. You could have thrown it away. So many options.'

'I didn't want to be rude to your problematic client's chief bridesmaid.'

'Then why did you keep it?'

'It would have been hurtful to chuck it away before

her eyes and anyway there was a distinct lack of dustbins in the church. After that I forgot about it.' Anger sparked in his eyes. 'I'm not interested in Julia. We've been through this.'

A small part of her knew she had gone into fully fledged panic mode; she had to slow down, re-evaluate. Crossing her arms across her chest, she went to the window, her back to Jake whilst she tried to think, tried to impose some sort of order and logic despite the tornado of fear and hurt that swept through her. Fact: she'd suspected that Jake had an interest in Julia and vice versa. Fact: she'd asked Jake and he'd denied the interest. Fact: Jake had kept a note from Julia with her number. Conclusion: Jake could have lied.

Isobel closed her eyes in silent turmoil, opened them as she sensed Jake's approach. 'Isobel… Don't do this. There is nothing between Julia and me. You have to believe that.'

Oh, God. The mantra of *You have to believe me*, as espoused by Simon and her mother—and various foster carers. None of whom had been speaking the truth, however much she'd hoped they were.

But Jake wasn't Simon, wasn't any of those people and yet—how could she ignore the facts again? A second time. She'd decided to believe him about Anna, but now insidious doubts began to make tendrils into her brain, into her very heart. Had she been taken for a fool?

Had she believed what she wanted to believe? Been sidelined, distracted by his positive points—and there were many of those. Jake was nothing like her stepfather and she'd taken that to be enough. Jake was a good man—he'd helped Caro, would have protected Emily with his life, he'd shown Isobel care and support. But he was also a man who had told her himself that he kept his romances short and sweet, had no wish for commitment, a man who'd been brought up in an environment where fidelity was unimportant, lies a commonplace.

'I don't have to believe anything, Jake. For all I know, you were saving her details for your next short and sweet "romance". I suppose I should be pleased that this time you weren't going to sleep with her on my watch.'

She stood her ground as anger flared in his eyes and now she could almost hear the past echo into the room. The years spun backwards and they were back to that impasse again. The silence reverberated, rebounded, ricocheted around the room as they both absorbed her words—words she couldn't unsay even if she wanted to. And now she didn't know what she wanted, didn't know how it had come to this. From the joyous awakening that morning, the tangle of limbs, the kisses, the laughter, the safety of being cocooned in his arms—and now this.

This ugliness.

This reality.

He ran a hand over his face and she could see his attempt to contain anger, an anger that was palpable in the hardness of his jaw.

'I thought that chapter was closed. I thought you trusted me.'

'It was. I did. But now…' She faltered.

'Iz, I forgot I had the piece of paper in my pocket. I can barely remember what Julia looks like. I only took the damn thing out of politeness. It's the truth.'

So much of her wanted to agree, make this whole nightmare scenario go away, try to claw back to the happy day of watching films. But she couldn't. What if she was wrong, what if she was setting herself up again? As her mother had, again and again.

Yet Jake was nothing like Simon. *Could* this man who

had taken her to Bournemouth to say goodbye to her mother, who had held Emily, stood up for Caro, taken her for cocktails, held her, listened to her, shared his own childhood with her, now be standing there lying to her?

Fact: yes, he could.

'You either trust me or you don't,' he said now. 'Your choice.'

'I want to,' she said softly.

'That's not enough.' The sadness in his eyes was palpable.

What to do? Twisting her hands together, she stared out of the window at the garden. Her choice. If you wanted to be with someone you believed in them. Only it didn't work like that, did it? If you *needed* to be with someone you conned yourself into believing them. When they lied to you, you deluded yourself, coated the words with glitter and gold to hide the ugly truth. You gave them power. You gave them control. She'd spent too long not in control, had known that Simon could do as he wished and she had no recourse or comeback. Same with social workers, foster carers. All she had known back then was that one day she and she alone would control her life. If you loved someone you became dependent on them, became weak, let them make a fool out of you. All because you were dependent on them.

Love.

This wasn't love—she wouldn't let it be.

Love was an illusory emotion that rendered you weak.

It was time to get out now, play it safe—maybe Jake was telling the truth, maybe he wasn't. The point was she didn't know, couldn't risk the latter. Or she'd be in too deep, on the verge, the edge of ceding control, handing over power.

'No, it's not enough,' she agreed.

The words tore at her heart and she could feel the hot prickle of tears threaten. This time there would be no comfort to be had from Jake, no arm round her shoulder, no kisses, no sympathy.

She stared at the cold, hard set of his face and waited for his reaction.

Jake felt rooted to the spot. The events of the past twenty minutes had come out of nowhere. A curve ball he'd not seen coming. How could he have stopped it? He didn't know, but he wished he could find a rewind button, wished he could see a way out of this.

But there wasn't one, not a gleam of light at the end of the midnight darkness of the metaphorical tunnel. Isobel didn't believe him. Again. She didn't believe him and there truly wasn't a damn thing he could do about that. Yet for a moment he wanted to try, to rant and rave. To yell and shout and make Isobel believe in him. Make her stay.

Dear God, would he never learn his lesson? You couldn't make people stay—he certainly couldn't. The cold, hard pain of rejection solidified inside him and all his defence mechanisms, learnt and honed over a lifetime, sprang into place—took the pain, the hurt, the dull ache of dismissal, the icy knowledge that she'd judged him unworthy—and converted the emotion into something he could use.

Aged eight, when he'd figured out nothing he could do would make his father notice him, let alone love him, he'd taken that realisation—he'd used it, moulded it to take him forward, figuring that boarding school was the best route. At eighteen, when he'd realised his mother still wanted nothing to do with him, that his grandfather hadn't loved him, he'd taken that, used it to fuel his ambition. All his life he'd stood firm; Isobel had hurt him once and he'd used that hurt and channelled it and he could do it again.

He would use it to propel himself forward at work, would use it to ensure he focused his energies where they should have been all along. On Cartwright.

Yet as he looked at her, saw the pain on her face, for one mad moment the urge to take her into his arms persisted. But what could he say? Isobel didn't trust him and she clearly never would. This time was different—they'd both shared so much and he'd believed that the bond they had formed was stronger. Instead it had crumbled at the first test.

And still he oh, so nearly took that step forward. But he stopped himself. He wouldn't expose himself to that humiliation, that rejection—wishing for love that couldn't be given. He couldn't force love, couldn't force trust. He couldn't fight to win it, like knights of old. He knew that.

End of. It was time to roll with the punches, minimise the hurt and move on.

A repeat of six years ago, only this time the hurt was infinitely more; this time she *knew* him and had judged him. There could be no comeback from that.

'Then there is nothing more to say. Except goodbye.'

'Goodbye.' Her voice was a whisper as she turned and left the room.

How had he let this happen? Again.

Three days later

Isobel entered the park, looked round and saw Caro seated on a blanket, Emily by her side, surrounded by toys. She strode across the grass in a half run. 'So it's really true?'

'It's really true.' Caro's expression was a mix of relief and guilt. 'I feel absolutely awful for the poor man he assaulted but I'm so relieved that Martin is back behind bars and this time for a long time, I hope.'

'What happened?'

'The police turned up at the refuge to tell me. Martin got blind drunk and went on a tear. He smashed cars, windows, stole a car and then marched into Theo's offices. The security guard tried to stop him and Martin assaulted him. Badly. He was about to turn his rage on the receptionist when Theo got there.' Caro gave a small smile. 'It turns out Theo is a martial arts expert. He had Martin down in three minutes. He will also make sure the guard gets compensation. I went to visit him in hospital; he was so sweet. He said he'd rather Martin got him than me or the receptionist.'

'So you're free—' Isobel hugged her friend '—at least of Martin's presence.'

'Yes. It may take a while for the nightmares to stop. Or for me to trust anyone again.' Caro looked troubled.

'Theo?' Isobel guessed.

'Yes, I like him and I know he cares for me but I'm worried about so many things. Trusting him… Whether I can trust him, whether it would be foolish to rush in, whether if I ask him to wait I'll lose him, whether—'

'Take your time, Caro. It's early days yet. If he truly cares for you he will understand.'

'I know, and I also think that I need some time on my own, figuring what it's like to be independent, be just me…and Emily…without the fear of Martin overshadowing us. That's what I want—to live my life without fear. And if Theo sticks around, I'll give him a chance.' Caro tickled Emily's toes and then turned to her friend. 'But enough of me. What about you?'

'What about me?'

'You and Jake?'

'I told you. That ship has sailed.' It was a shame it had taken her broken heart with it. Because this time was so very much worse than the last time. This time she couldn't banish his image from her mind. Or her dreams.

Caro opened her mouth and then closed it again.

'What?'

'I just… It's hard to believe Jake lied like that. Again.'

I know that, she wanted to scream. Instead she shook her head. 'I will always be grateful to him for what he did for you and Emily, but I have to face the facts—I messed up.'

'You sure?'

Of course she wasn't sure. The doubts jumped and danced through her mind day and night, taunted her, urged her to call Jake. To give in. And she loathed herself for this dependency, this weakness, this need that she couldn't rid herself of. But she would.

'I'm sure enough,' she stated and leant forward to give Emily a kiss, avoiding the question in Caro's eyes.

Jake looked around his office and inhaled deeply. In an hour's time the board would convene. He'd present his proposal and put it to the vote and, barring any last-minute hitches, he'd win. This was what he wanted. This was more important than anything else. So why did he feel so—flat? The suspicion it was due to the constant ache of missing Isobel was an unwelcome one. But he did miss her, more than he would have believed possible. Her scent, her smile, her touch, the tickle of her hair, the way she snuggled into him.

Focus. On this meeting.

This was the meeting where he would bring his father

down; he'd been working towards this goal for years—all his life. Jake frowned; discomfort edged his thoughts. Was that his goal—to vanquish his father? No. His aim was to do right by Cartwright, the company he loved and felt such a responsibility for. It was *nothing personal*.

Hell and damnation. Those were the words his mother had used and they sucked.

Now Isobel's voice echoed in his head. *'I still think you should talk to him.'*

An image of Isobel as she'd let go of the balloon, told her mother she loved her despite the things she'd done wrong. Her forgiveness, her understanding for her mother whilst accepting her flaws. The way Isobel had fought for Caro, even when Caro cut off contact with her.

'Promise me you'll think about talking to your dad.'

He'd promised he'd think about it, not actually do it. His father had paid a woman to have his baby, not because he wanted a child but because he didn't want to lose his lifestyle. His father had abandoned him as a tiny baby, let his grandfather have him.

But his father had at least chosen a woman who wanted the money for an altruistic reason, he had taken him in, he might not have shown him love but he had provided him with all material comforts, had agreed to his choice of school, of university—had denied him nothing. Except the thing he wanted most—a role in Cartwright. Why? Isobel was right—it didn't make sense.

Dammit.

Jake picked up the report and left the room, walked down to Charles Cartwright's lavish and largely unused office. Before he could change his mind, unsure even of what he meant to say, he knocked on the door.

'Come in.'

He entered and saw Charles' look of surprise. 'Jake.'

'Yes.' He approached the desk and Charles waved at the seat opposite. He sat, still wondered what to say.

After a while Charles cleared his throat. 'How can I help?'

'You can tell me why you are so opposed to this proposal.'

'Because I have no interest in growth. After I'm gone you can do what you like.'

'But why don't you have any interest in growth—in making the company more successful now?'

'I don't need a reason. I will vote against it.'

'Then why won't you give me a chance?'

'Why does that matter to you? You're going to try and take it, regardless of my reasons.'

There was little point in denial. 'Yes.'

Charles leant back and gave a mirthless laugh. 'You really are a chip off the old block. I'm sure your grandfather's spirit will attend the board meeting, will be there applauding you.'

His father's words brought a vivid image to mind and for a moment Jake could almost see Joseph Cartwright standing in the room, watching them with approval. Watching Jake, his coveted chosen heir, with approval as he tried to take Charles down. Suddenly the idea didn't sit well with him.

'This isn't personal. I'm doing this for Cartwright.'

Nothing personal. His mother's words. Again.

'Don't kid yourself. This is personal. Cartwright is personal. This company has dominated my life and it ruined my mother's. Your grandfather was obsessed with Cartwright and he was obsessed with the need for an heir. My mother was a kind, gentle, quiet woman and he treated her appallingly because she suffered miscarriage after miscarriage—until eventually they had me.'

Shame flushed Jake's face, heated his body with guilt—he'd never asked, never wondered about his grandmother, never questioned why the relationship between his grandfather and his father had gone wrong—had assumed the blame lay with his father.

'Surely that must have made him happy.'

'Nope. I was a perennial disappointment to him—a "namby-pamby mummy's boy", with no interest in his precious company or running it. I wanted to be an artist.' His bark of laughter was both self-derisory and mocking.

'Why didn't you?'

'Because if I had he would have thrown me out and I'd never have seen my mother again. So I decided to give up, to enjoy the money and the lifestyle and by the time my mother died I didn't want to give it up. I was enjoying myself too much.'

Yet Jake wondered now if he truly had.

'So when dear old Dad gave me the ultimatum about an heir I provided him with you—a worthy successor.'

Jake could hear the bitterness. 'But why didn't you look after me yourself?'

Now he saw genuine pain in his father's eyes. 'I miscalculated. When your grandfather gave me that ultimatum I should have decided to have a child in the right way, be a good father. But I was so consumed by my hatred of him, I decided to take him at his word, and so I turned you into a commodity. Then you were born; I took one look at you, so small, so vulnerable and I realised the enormity, the stupidity of what I'd done. I'd doomed you to a life without a mother and I panicked and then I did something I'll regret for the rest of my life. I ran, convinced myself that was for the best. I left Petra to arrange a nanny; I knew my dad would come to claim his own soon enough. I told myself you'd be better off with him. I left because I was too weak to fight for you, because the battle was over before it began. I had nothing to give you. That decision has haunted me ever since.'

The anguish in his father's eyes was genuine and Jake could sense, could feel his emotion. Yet he still didn't understand. 'But when he died why didn't you try to bond with me then?'

'It was too late and I didn't know how. Plus, how could you ever forgive me for what I had done? I couldn't expect that of you. I did what I could, gave you whatever you wanted.'

'Except Cartwright.'

Charles nodded. 'I wanted to allow you to go your own way, not to have to tie yourself to Cartwright. I want you to have the chance to have a different life, be what you want to be. Not be consumed by Cartwright like your grandfather was.'

Jake hesitated. Was he consumed?

His dad continued. 'I've watched you the past four years and all you have done has been focus on Cartwright. Everything. Tell me what is the most important thing in your life.'

The answer was automatic. 'Isobel.'

For a long moment father and son stared at each other and then, for the first time, Charles smiled, a genuine smile. 'Then there is hope for you yet.'

Isobel opened the door of the flat and blinked. 'Roberto?' Not that there was a need for the question. It was definitely Jake's driver.

The man smiled at her. 'Jake asked me to deliver this.'

Isobel looked down at the invitation, complete with embossed writing.

Mr Jake Cartwright
invites
Ms Isobel Brennan
to a meeting at
Cartwright of Mayfair
at 8:00 p.m. on Friday

She looked at her watch. 'It's nearly 6:00 p.m. now,' she pointed out.

'Yes. If you agree to attend the meeting, I can take you straight there.'

'But…' Isobel looked down at her clothes—on the plus side she wasn't in her pyjamas. On the down side her jeans and oversized checked flannel shirt weren't a whole load better.

'What to do? What to do?' Oh, God. She'd said the words out loud.

Roberto cleared his throat. 'Um… I know it's not my place but we—that's Maria, Stefan and me—we think you should come and see him. He's—'

'He's what?'

'He hasn't been himself since the two of you…since… you left. I'm not trying to force you to do anything. But Jake is a good man.'

Isobel sighed, knowing she couldn't send Roberto on his way. In truth, she was relieved for the excuse to go— she would go for Roberto, for Stefan, for Maria. Not because her whole being craved the sight of Jake.

'Let's go,' she said. If Jake wanted to meet her at Cartwright he'd have to accept her as she was. It occurred to her suddenly that he always had. It had been Isobel who worried and agonised over whether she would fit. He'd never cared. Not six years ago and not ten days ago.

The drive passed in easy conversation and she was

grateful to Roberto for initiating simple topics; she learnt about his family, that he was in fact Maria's son-in-law, how much he enjoyed his job, his love of cars.

Once they approached Cartwright he smiled and dropped her at the entrance. 'Good luck.'

Her heart pounded against her ribcage and she considered turning around and running as fast as her trainers could carry her. Knowing that would be the coward's way out, instead she stepped through the revolving door and into the marbled lobby, looked around and there he was.

Jake.

Isobel halted, tamed the urge to move closer to him. Bad enough she now knew how a parched plant must feel when the first raindrops scattered down in nourishment. But she couldn't help the need to look, to absorb his image—the warm strength of him, the spikiness of his blond hair, the set of his jaw, the mesmerising grey eyes. An image she put onto the lock screen of her brain.

It occurred to her that as she'd stood rooted to the spot he too had been looking at her and she wondered what thoughts crossed his mind. He stepped forward. 'Thank you for coming. I wasn't sure if you would. Come through.'

Belatedly, it occurred to her that the lobby should have been busier on a Friday night. She shrugged the knowledge off as unimportant as they walked down the richly carpeted corridor, followed discreet signage to the hotel's signature restaurant.

Great. He was taking her to dinner in a Michelin-starred restaurant full of rich designer-clad people and she was in her Cowboys 'r' Us outfit. Well, tough—if he was trying to prove a point, whatever that was, so be it. She'd walk in and be herself.

But as he pushed the door to the restaurant open she frowned, her senses on alert. Something was off, missing, not how it should be. Then she realised—there was no hum of chatter, no clatter of knives and forks, none of the noises you'd associate with a busy restaurant on a Friday evening.

As she entered it became clear why. The room was empty, dimly lit, apart from a table in the centre. As she stepped closer she gave a small gasp of appreciation. An array of candles flickered and dappled the flower-strewn surface. Snowy white linen napkins, silver cutlery, crystal glasses.

And as Jake held out her chair, piano music filled the air. Isobel looked across the room to where the grand piano stood in its glory, recognised the same pianist they had listened to in Oxford.

She looked around the room. 'What's going on?' she asked.

'We're having dinner. I figured you'd prefer it without an audience. The pianist can't hear us.'

'You've closed the restaurant? What about all the guests?'

'They have been suitably compensated. No one is missing out; I've made sure of that.' Before he could say any more a waiter appeared and placed two plates in front of them.

Isobel looked down at a beautifully presented dish of scallops, with crispy pancetta, complete with a circle of butter flecked with green and slices of— 'Apple?' she asked.

'Pickled apple,' Jake said.

'And what have you got?'

'Lemon sole with samphire and bacon and sweet potato fries. I thought we could go halves.'

Isobel took a deep breath. 'Jake, the food is lovely, the table is lovely, but what the hell is going on?' It was a question she could well ask herself. This man had lied to her, splintered her heart, yet she was here.

'I thought we should try and get closure now, rather than wait six years and hope fate gives us another shot. I don't want a repeat of six years ago, where you decide I'm a lying bastard, I defend myself, you walk out and I let you go.'

'Which bit do you want to change?'

'Pretty much all of it. But, most of all, the bit where you leave. Six years ago I didn't fight. I figured you can't make people love you, you can't make them stay, just like I couldn't make my mother or my father love me. Or stay. That's still true. You can't force someone to love you. But there is something I can do. I can't force you to love me but I can tell you the truth. That I love you.'

Her fork clattered into the scallops, tumbled onto the linen tablecloth. He loved her?

Isobel sat frozen, her whole body in shock, her brain in conflict. Every instinct informed her that Jake was genuine, but all she could do was listen.

'Six years ago I was too hurt and angry and scared to say it. I'm still hurt and angry and, yes, I'm still scared but this time I want you to know you are loved.'

Isobel stared at him, opened her mouth to shout that she loved him back. But something stopped her.

What was it? Then realisation crashed in on her. It was fear. What had Caro said to her? That she didn't want to live her life with the fear of Martin overshadowing her. Wasn't that what Isobel was doing—still living in fear? Fear of a relationship, fear of sharing, fear of letting love into her life.

The knowledge was absolute and tears prickled the

back of her eyelids in a bid to escape and she heard Jake's curse.

'Iz? I didn't mean to make you cry. I won't say another word. I wasn't trying to put pressure on you. I—'

She summoned a smile, swiped her eyes with the back of her hand. 'Stop. It's OK. I love you too.' The words liberated her as the shadow of fear receded. 'I love you,' she repeated. 'I've just been too scared to admit it.' She'd been caught in Simon's thrall of fear: fear of love or trust. 'Scared to let it in. Because I thought love bred fear, equalled weakness and gave power. But it doesn't.' It all seemed so much clearer now, as if lit up by the light of real love. Because the bond between her mum and Simon hadn't been love—it was a travesty of love. The knowledge seemed so obvious now, but it hadn't been. It had taken Jake's love and understanding and his actions over the past week to make her see it.

She came to a stop. Saw the shell-shocked look in Jake's grey eyes.

'You love me?' There was a whisper of disbelief in his voice and that hint of vulnerability from this strong man tore her heart as she realised that she might be the first person to say the words to him in his life.

'Yes, I love you.' She took his hand in hers, wanting, needing a physical connection. 'I loved you six years ago but I needed to believe Anna, because the alternative was to trust you, trust myself. A week ago I still couldn't take that leap—it was still easier to walk away than to trust you. I'm sorry I doubted you, when I know you are honourable and good and truthful.

'I love you for your strength and your understanding and your capacity to listen. You have never tried to browbeat me or make me agree with you. You have listened, really heard me. And you have accepted me—who

I am, whether it's in a designer dress or jeans and a T-shirt. You took me to Bournemouth and a glamorous ball. You've made me realise that you can love someone and you can rely on them but that doesn't make you needy or dependent. I can still strive to be the best at what I do with you by my side.'

Now Jake's smile had hit beam status as he raised a hand. 'My turn. I love you because you're caring, kind, loyal, fierce in your determination, so courageous to have overcome everything you had to face in your childhood. Yet you have come out a good, beautiful person who can see the good in people. You made me see that there are things and people that are worth fighting for. That there is more to life than work. Thanks to you, I spoke to my dad.

'And I get being scared. I was too scared of being abandoned, rejected again. When you left six years ago it hurt. So very much…but I couldn't fight because I thought there was no point. I thought it would intensify the pain to try and fail. But now I know that the risk is worth it—that there was every reason, even if I only got the chance to tell you I love you.' His arm tightened around her. 'But I much prefer this ending,' he said. 'The one where we love each other. For ever,' he added firmly. 'I know there are no guarantees but I'm damn sure this is a lifetime partnership. Of two equals.'

'Yes.' Her voice was serious now. 'That's something else you've shown me. It doesn't matter how much money you have or what your background is. You and I work. As a team. We fit.' The concept brought a smile to her face. And then the meaning of his words sank in. 'You talked to your dad? What happened?'

He exhaled a small sigh and she squeezed his hand gently. 'It turns out that it's more complicated than I thought. He's not the terrible person I thought he was.' As she listened to what had taken place, hope surged in her heart that maybe something could be salvaged, some sort of relationship be forged.

'So what happened at the meeting?'

'I withdrew my proposal. I explained that I would prefer to get it through with my father's support, if at all possible. And my father and I—we've decided to talk. If I can show him this is truly what I want I think he'll give me his backing, but I understand that for him Cartwright is a monster, whereas for me it's something beautiful. But, whatever happens, I will not get consumed—you will always be more important. And if we have children so will they.'

'Children?'

'Only as and when we both agree it's right. But, yes, I would love to have children with you. Not hypothetical ones but real ones. Because I don't believe we will repeat our parents' patterns—I know you will be an amazing mum.'

'And I know you will be an amazing dad.' That belief was heartfelt. Jake had been abandoned, treated with a confusing indifference and yet his inherent goodness, his honour and his principles shone through in all his actions. And he would give his child all the love and attention he had been starved of. Just as she would ensure her child was safe, secure and loved and she would always put her child first. There was no reason to fear the repeat of a pattern, no reason to live in the shadow of fear any more.

'And I know our children are going to be incredibly amazing,' Jake said. 'But not until you're ready. I know how important your work is to you as well and I respect that.'

Isobel nodded—the idea of a family, of having children with this man swelled her heart with love and joy.

Jake gestured to the plates. 'But in the meantime I think it's time for dessert.'

Isobel nodded, her head spinning, giddy with joy, and a few minutes later she smiled up at the waiter as he placed a plate in front of her. 'It's beautiful,' she exclaimed.

The waiter gave a small bow. 'Enjoy,' he said and left, just as the pianist struck up a gorgeous blues song; the notes strummed the air evocatively, seemed to complement the happiness that bubbled inside her.

She studied the spun sugar confection, a beautiful delicate cage that topped a golden egg. Carefully she removed it.

'Allow me,' Jake said and he rose, moved to her side and unscrewed the egg.

Isobel eyes widened and she gave the smallest of gasps. Inside were beautiful colourful sugar roses, pink, red, and white, each one exquisite in its detail. And nestled amongst them was a ring—a classic single solitaire diamond glittered and glinted in the candlelight.

Jake reached in and took it out and dropped to one knee.

'Isobel, will you marry me? So that we can walk together through life. I promise I will be there for you through good times and bad, I want to hold you and love you and be by your side for the rest of my days.' Now he gave the smallest and wickedest of smiles. 'And nights. You are my life, my soul, my love, my balance.'

Tears of joy tickled the back of her eyes as she rose and pulled him to his feet. 'I will marry you—I want to spend my life with you. You have my full trust and I give you my love without reserve or condition for ever.'

And as he slipped the ring onto her finger she knew that she had found the one place she would always fit, would always be loved for herself and would always be safe.

* * * * *

STARTING OVER IN
WICKHAM FALLS

ROCHELLE ALERS

Chapter One

Georgina Powell stared at her reflection in the full-length mirror, shocked and saddened at the same time with her transformation. The last time she'd taken special care with her appearance was for her high school prom. And that had been more than a decade ago. What, she asked herself, had she been doing for the past fourteen years? But she knew the answer; she hadn't been living but just existing.

Her dream of enrolling in art school to become an illustrator had vanished completely with the unexpected death of her thirteen-year-old brother from meningitis. Her parents had been planning for Kevin to take over running the store once they retired, but their plans were transferred to her.

Kevin's death changed their family's dynamics. Her mother appeared emotionally unable to recover from losing a child; her father threw himself into running the business as if it was a startup instead of one that had been well established for generations. And it had taken Georgina a very long time to come to the realization that her brother, whom she'd nicknamed Shadow because he followed her around as if he feared she would disappear, was gone and wasn't coming back.

Tonight signaled a change in Georgina's life. Not only did she look different outwardly, but she'd also changed inwardly. The body-hugging black gown and matching four-inch, silk-covered stilettos had replaced the ubiquitous navy blue smock with Powell's Department Store stitched over the back she wore over dark slacks. Her face with smoky shadows on her lids and a vibrant vermilion lip color, curly hair flat-ironed and tucked into a twist behind her ear completed her outward makeover. But it was her determination to move out of the house where she'd lived for the past thirty-two years that would alter her life.

Once her father downsized, and then eliminated the arts and crafts area of the store in order to expand the sporting goods section, it sparked an idea that had nagged at her for weeks. Georgina boxed up the stock and dropped it off at a storage facility with the intent of establishing her own business in the same town where she'd spent her entire life.

Picking up a black silk-lined cashmere shawl trimmed in faux fox, to ward off the chill of the mid-March night air, an envelope with the invitation and a beaded evening bag, Georgina walked out of the bedroom and down the back staircase to the garage located behind the two-story house. She managed to leave without encountering her mother. This was to become her first Wickham Falls Chamber of Commerce fund-raiser, an event that had been supported by both parents over the years, and then by only her father following Kevin's passing.

Georgina was shocked one night when after closing, Bruce Powell informed her that he wouldn't be attending and that she should take his place to represent the business. And when she'd asked her father why, his comeback was that it was time for her to prepare to take complete control of the department store once he retired. She'd wanted to tell him that she had no intention of managing the store because if she was going to assume that type of responsibility then it would be her own business enterprise.

She slipped behind the wheel of her late-model Nissan Rogue, an SUV she'd purchased to celebrate her thirty-second birthday. And at the beginning of the year, she'd made a New Year's resolution to cross off at least three of the remaining nine notations on her to-do list. The first had been to trade in the Mini

Cooper for the Rogue because she needed more room to transport the items needed to stock her new store.

Georgina started up the vehicle that still claimed a new-car smell and headed for the venue in Wickham Falls where the fund-raiser would be held for the first time. In the past the members of the Chamber had contracted with a hotel off the interstate to hold the annual event in one of their ballrooms.

A shiver of excitement rippled through Georgina when she thought about the plans she'd made for her future. She was aware that she had to work hard and probably make unforeseen sacrifices to realize her dream to become an independent business owner. But the knowledge that she would join a small number of women owning and operating their own businesses in Wickham Falls, West Virginia, was heady indeed.

Fifteen minutes later she maneuvered into a space between a Ram 1500 and a Ford F-150. *You can take the boy out of the country, but you can't take the country out of the boy*, she mused. Whether attending the local sports bar or a semiformal affair, pickups were the preferred modes of transportation in the town where the population still hovered below five thousand.

Thankfully, the Gibsons, who owned the Wolf Den, when they erected a barn at the rear of the property for larger gatherings, had paved the parking lot.

Georgina gathered her belongings off the passenger seat and alighted from the SUV.

A small crowd had gathered at the entrance to the barn and as she waited in line, she recognized several customers who patronized the department store. Powell's, as the locals called it, had survived despite big-box stores going up in neighboring towns because the Falls' town officials insisted if its citizenry lived local, then they should shop local. The town council had repeatedly voted down any developer's bid to put up strip malls with fast food restaurants and variety shops because they would impact and threaten the viability of Wickham Falls' mom-and-pop stores.

She finally made her way to the reception desk where the wives of several members were checking off names against ticket numbers. The woman glanced at her ticket, and then up at Georgina, her eyes widening in shock.

"Oh, my dear," she whispered. "I almost didn't recognize you, Georgina."

She gave the elderly woman with stylishly salt-and-pepper coiffed hair a sweet smile. "There are occasions when we're forced to clean up, Mrs. Bachmann."

The woman, whose husband was the Chamber's treasurer, nodded. "And I must say you clean up very well. I'm sorry your father can't attend, but I'm glad you're here to represent Powell's. By the way, you're at table number seven with others who will attend without a plus-one. You'll find your place card there."

"Thank you."

She wanted to tell the woman that Bruce Powell was upset that he'd had to attend another social event without his wife, which led to rumors that he and Evelyn were having marital issues. There wasn't an issue but that Evelyn Powell had become a social recluse. She was rarely seen in the store and had resigned from all the town's civic organizations. Even after sixteen years, Evelyn still mourned the loss of her son. Georgina would occasionally remind her that she did have a daughter, but the older woman ignored her as if she hadn't spoken.

She glanced around the barn that was reminiscent of a bygone era with strings of tiny white lights around the perimeter of the ceiling while gaslight-inspired chandeliers and hanging fixtures cast a warm, golden glow over round tables with seating for six. And in keeping with the theme of the time period of the early twentieth century, the glass, flatware and ornately carved mahogany bar added to the venue's rustic ambiance. White-jacketed waitstaff circulated with trays of hors d'oeuvres and flutes of champagne. Georgina draped her shawl over the back of one of the chairs at table seven.

"Georgi Powell, long time no see."

She turned to find Langston Cooper standing a

few feet away, holding a glass with an amber liquid, the color an exact match for his eyes, grinning at her. The orbs in a light brown complexion reminded her of champagne diamonds. Her attention was drawn to the minute lines fanning out around the eyes of the man who wasn't much older than she was. Langston had left Wickham Falls to attend college and had spent most of his career as a foreign journalist covering wars in Africa and the Middle East. She'd always thought of him as good-looking with his balanced features and a hint of a cleft in his strong chin, but there was something about Langston's body language that communicated he was so tightly coiled that people had to walk on eggshells in his presence.

"I could say the same about you," she countered, smiling. "Are you here as a member or as a reporter for the paper?"

Langston's eyebrows lifted slightly. "Both. Well, as editor-in-chief of *The Sentinel*, I'm expected to attend this soiree. What I don't remember is you coming last year."

"That's because this is my first year."

To say he was surprised to see Georgina at the event did not match his shock in seeing her wearing something other than the smock that identified her as an employee of Powell's Department Store. But then he had to remember she wasn't an employee but the daughter of the owner. He knew staring was rude, yet he couldn't pull his gaze away from her beautiful face with a subtle hint of makeup. However, it was the décolletage on the black halter gown that made it almost impossible for him not to stare at the soft swell of breasts each time she took a breath.

Mixed-race Georgina had inherited the best physical attributes from her Scotch-Irish father and African American mother. She'd concealed the faint sprinkling of freckles with makeup that was perfect for her light brown complexion. The brown curly hair with glints of copper were missing, and in its place was a sleek hairstyle that made her appear quite the sophisticate. When he'd returned to Wickham Falls the year before to purchase the failing periodical and encountered Georgina, the first thing he'd noticed was she no longer had the noticeable gap between her front teeth. He had always thought her pretty, but tonight she was stunning!

"Is there something I can get for you from the bar?"

She glanced at the waiters with the bubbly wine. "I'll have champagne. Meanwhile, I'm going to see what they're serving at the carving station, because if I'm going to drink, then I need to eat something."

Langston pulled out the chair with her shawl. "Please sit and I'll get you something to eat and your wine. How do you like your meat cooked?" He removed his suit jacket and placed it over the back of the chair next to hers.

She sat, smiling up at him. "Medium-well. Thank you, sir."

He returned her smile. "You're welcome, ma'am."

Langston approached a waiter. Reaching into the pocket of his suit trousers, he took out a money clip and handed the man a bill. "Can you please leave a couple of flutes at table seven?"

The young man pocketed the money, nodding. "Of course. And thank you, sir."

He wended his way through the crowd to the carving station, chiding himself for not telling Georgina that she looked incredible but did not want to come on too strong, because he didn't know if she was involved with someone. Just because she'd come unescorted, it did not translate into her being unencumbered. After all, she was a beautiful woman and heir to a successful business that had survived for decades despite the Great Depression and several recessions to remain viable.

Langston expertly balanced plates along his arm, a skill he'd learned when waiting tables as a college student. When he'd asked the waiter to leave a couple of flutes at the table, he hadn't meant a couple each for him and Georgina.

She pointed to the quartet of glasses. "He must have assumed we were thirsty," she teased.

He set down small plates with thinly sliced roast beef and horseradish, pasta with a vodka sauce, prawns with an Asian-inspired dipping sauce, and filo tartlets filled with spicy cilantro shrimp. "I'm willing to bet we'll need them because what I've selected for us definitely isn't bland."

Unfolding her napkin, Georgina spread it over her lap. "Spicy is good."

Langston gave her a sidelong glance. "So you like it hot?"

She nodded. "I enjoy a little heat," she admitted, spreading a smidgen of horseradish on the roast beef. "Do you cook?"

Her question caught him completely off guard. "I can. Why did you ask?"

Georgina shrugged bare shoulders. "Just curious."

Langston waited for her to chew and swallow a mouthful of meat. "What else are you curious about?"

"How is the paper doing since you took over?"

He successfully concealed his disappointment because he'd expected her to ask him something more personal—perhaps why he had come without a date. "It's taken a while, but we've managed to increase the circulation and advertising revenue."

"There was a time before you bought the paper that we thought it was going to fold. We've always relied on *The Sentinel* to advertise the store's daily and weekly specials."

"Powell's has advertised with the paper from its inaugural issue."

"It's the only way we can get the word out when we put items on sale."

Langston speared a prawn, dipped it into the piquant sauce and popped it into his mouth. "Do you find it odd that the Gibsons would offer an eclectic menu for the cocktail hour when they're known for barbecuing meat?"

The owners of the Wolf Den had established a reputation over several generations of serving the best grilled, barbecue and smoked meats in Johnson County. Longtime residents had whispered about the Gibsons keeping them supplied with illegal moonshine during Prohibition, and that revenue agents couldn't offer anyone enough money to snitch on their supplier. What went on in Wickham Falls stayed in Wickham Falls, and it was the reason he'd come back to his hometown to start over rather than remain in Washington, DC.

"They are full of surprises," Georgina said. "I suppose for catered affairs they like to change it up a bit."

"I really like the change."

"So do I," she agreed. "If this place had been up when we had prom, then we probably wouldn't have had to pay as much for our tickets or to contend with a power outage and a malfunctioning generator."

"My parents told me about that fiasco when they came up to New York for my college graduation."

"Some of the kids were talking about wrecking

the place when we were told we weren't getting a refund because the contract stated the owners weren't responsible for power outages or acts of God."

Langston shook his head. "I don't believe that would've gone over well with their parents who would've had to pay for the damages."

"My folks would have grounded me for life if that had happened."

"Speaking of your folks, how's your mother?"

Langston asking about Evelyn Powell was another reminder for Georgina to move out of her parents' house. "She's well."

What she wanted to tell him was that her mother had elevated manipulation to an art form. She'd feigned not feeling well whenever Georgina mentioned going out because Evelyn feared she would meet someone and possibly have a future with him.

"Tell her I asked about her."

"I will," she promised. Evelyn always perked up when someone asked about her. "How are your parents enjoying their retirement in Key West?"

"What can I say, Georgina. Dad just bought a boat that sleeps four. He, Mom and another couple sail down to different islands in the Caribbean to fish and shop, while using the boat as their hotel. I did ask them why they bought a bungalow when they spend most of their time on the water, and they couldn't give me an answer."

"Don't begrudge them, Langston. It sounds as if they're having the time of their lives."

He affected a half smile. "I suppose I'm a little jealous because they're having so much fun."

"Have you planned what you want to do once you retire?"

"No. I haven't thought that far ahead." He took a sip of champagne. "What about you, Georgi? Have you figured out your future?"

Langston shifted slightly to give her a direct stare, and Georgina sucked in an audible breath when she realized there was something in the way that he was looking at her, which made her feel slightly uncomfortable. Worldly and erudite, she wondered if he could see under the veneer of sophistication she'd affected for the fund-raiser to glimpse a girl in a woman's body struggling to control her destiny.

"Yes, but first I have to find someplace to live."

A frown appeared between his eyes. "Don't you live with your parents?"

When she'd met with Sasha Manning, her best friend from high school, to discuss her future, the pastry chef who'd recently opened Sasha's Sweet Shoppe on Main Street had advised her that in order to grasp a modicum of independence, she had to move out of her parents' house.

"Yes. I've made the decision to move out and get my own place."

"Where?"

"I'd prefer Wickham Falls, but if I can find something in Mineral Springs, I'll take it."

Langston gave her a *you've got to be kidding me* look when he said, "How can a girl who grew up in the Falls actually consider moving to the Springs? It just isn't done."

Georgina laughed, the sound carrying easily to a nearby table as several people turned to stare at her and Langston. The rivalry between the two towns had begun years ago during a high school football game when several players from Mineral Springs were charged with unnecessary roughness. The incident ended a player from the Falls the opportunity to take advantage of an athletic scholarship when his leg was so severely injured that he would never be able to compete again. Students from the Falls who dated people in the Springs were socially ostracized. It had become the modern-day version of the Hatfields and McCoys, with students in neighboring towns rather than families as archrivals.

"I know that, Langston, but I don't have a choice if I can't find something here in the Falls." Mineral Springs was larger, more populated, and there were several properties that were available for rent or purchase.

"Do you want to rent or buy?" he asked.

"It doesn't matter." Georgina had saved enough money for a sizable down payment on a house that would suit her tastes, but she was also willing to rent until she found a property where she hoped to spend the rest of her life. "You run a newspaper, so you must know just about everything that happens in Wickham Falls."

Langston affected a sly grin. "There are things I'm aware of and would rather not know. Have you checked with Viviana Remington? Correction. She's now Viviana Wainwright, and her husband is the developer who's building the new single-family homes on the Remington property. I would suggest you check with her before talking to a real-estate agent."

"Thanks for the tip. I'll let you know if I find something."

Georgina knew Viviana Remington was a direct descendant of the infamous Wolfe family who'd owned most of the coal mines in the county and were reviled for how they'd made their fortune taking advantage of their workers. And they preferred closing the mines rather than upgrade to meet the government's safety regulations. She was grateful to be seated at the table with Langston, because he'd given her the lead she needed to find somewhere to live before she sought out Miss Reilly, the local real estate agent.

He leaned close enough for their shoulders to touch. "I need a favor from you."

She went completely still. The last man who'd asked her for a favor needed fifteen thousand dollars to cover his gambling debts. He'd been siphoning money from the sale of cars at his father's used-car dealership to gamble, and when the accountant called to say he was coming to go over the books in order to file the corporate tax return, he panicked. Although they'd dated for almost eight months and Georgina thought she was in love with him, she ended their relationship and blocked his phone number.

She'd wanted to believe he was different because he worked for his father who had one of the most successful used-car dealerships in Beckley, but it was apparent he was no different from the men in the Falls who equated her to dollar signs. Boys in high school vied for her attention not because they'd thought her pretty, smart, or even talented, but because she was now sole heir to a business that had earned the reputation as the longest-running family-owned business in the town's history.

Georgina swallowed to relieve the constriction in her throat. "What do you want?"

Langston placed his hand over her fisted one. "Why do you make it sound as if I'm asking you to give up your firstborn?"

"That would be easy, because I don't have any children."

He angled his head. "Do you want children?"

His question gave her pause. It had been too many years since she had been involved with a man to even consider marriage and children. "I suppose I'd like one or two somewhere down the road."

Langston chuckled. "Just how long is that road, Georgi?"

She smiled. It was the second time he'd called her by the nickname kids in the Falls gave her to distinguish between her and another girl named Georgiana. "I really don't know, because I have a few requisites before I can even consider motherhood."

"Does finding a husband figure in your requisites?"

"That helps, but it's not mandatory."

"So," he drawled, "it wouldn't bother you to be an unwed mother?"

She scrunched up her nose. "I prefer the term *single mother*. If I decide to adopt a baby and not marry, I would be a single, not an unwed, mother."

Langston inclined his head. "Point taken."

"Now that we've settled that," she said after a pregnant pause, "what favor do you want from me?"

He leaned even closer, his nose brushing her ear. "Save a dance for me."

Georgina was shocked and relieved that all he wanted was a dance. The invitation indicated there would be music and dancing. "What if I save you two?"

Langston chuckled. "If I'd known you were that generous, then I would've asked for three or maybe even four."

"Don't push it, Langston."

He held up both hands. "Okay. Two it is."

Georgina didn't know Langston well, had had very little interaction with him in the past, yet she wanted to think of him as a friend. And she'd had very few close friends in the Falls other than Sasha Manning. She and Sasha had shared many of the same classes and confided in each other as to what they wanted once they graduated school. And now that Sasha had returned to town as a former contestant in a televised bakeoff, and the ex-wife of an A-list country singer, she'd sought her out to solicit her advice as to the steps she should take to realize her dream to become an independent businesswoman that did not include the department store.

Pushing back her chair, she rose to her feet, Langston rising with her. "Please excuse me, but Sasha just walked in and I need to talk to her."

Chapter Two

Langston watched Georgina walk, and felt as if he was able to breathe normally for the first time. He didn't know what it was about Georgina Powell that made him less confident in her presence than he was with other women he'd known or grown up with. The only other woman to have a similar effect on him he married. However, his ex-wife proved to be the opposite of Georgina, but he hadn't known that until after they were married. And, although he found it odd that as a thirty-something young woman Georgina still lived at home with her parents, he was curious to know the reason for her wanting to change residences.

He'd traveled the world, lived abroad for more

years than he could count and had interacted with people he wasn't certain were friend or foe. All of which served to hone and heighten his acuity when perceiving a situation. Langston did not want to relate to Georgina as a journalist, watching and waiting for a clue behind what she said, but as a man who'd found himself pleasantly enthralled with the very grown-up Georgina Powell.

She was at least three, or maybe even four, years his junior, which meant they did not share the same classes or friends, although they'd grown up in the same neighborhood. What they had in common was their parents were business owners. His parents, both pharmacists, owned the local pharmacy, and the Powells, the department store. By Wickham Falls' economic standards, the Coopers and Powells were considered well-to-do, but their social standing was of no import when they enrolled their children in the Johnson County Public School system. Every student was treated equally, which fostered an environment of one school, one team.

Langston was aware that despite its seemingly picture-postcard appearance with one- and two-story homes, and two traffic lights, and being touted as one of the best little towns in the state, Wickham Falls did have a history of labor unrest that came close to rivaling Matewan's coal-mining strikes, with months-long battles between union and nonunion workers. After the owners closed the mines, it taught the residents to depend on one another to ensure survival because of labor solidarity. And it was in the Falls that he felt more relaxed and able to recapture the peace he'd known and felt when growing up.

The decision to resign from the cable news station, where he'd worked as a foreign correspondent, sell his Washington, DC, condo and purchase the house in Wickham Falls from his parents after they'd retired and planned to live in their vacation home on Key West was an easy one for Langston. His contemplating buying a biweekly with a dwindling circulation was much more difficult. Despite becoming an award-winning journalist, and a *New York Times* bestselling nonfiction writer, he wasn't certain whether to invest in a newspaper when local papers had folded, and popular magazines were going from print to an electronic format.

He'd approached the owner of *The Sentinel* with an offer and after several weeks of negotiations, Langston had become the publisher and editor-in-chief of a failing paper. He'd thrown his experience and energies into revamping the biweekly's format, meeting several times a week with the staff to solicit their input for new ideas that would resurrect what had been a popular and necessary medium to disseminate information to the community. It had taken a year to realize an increase in circulation, and the paper's new design, columns and highlighting of individuals and businesses seemed to resonate with many subscribers.

Langston's focus shifted to Georgina as she laughed at something Sasha Manning said. He hadn't had any direct contact with her since returning. He'd caught glimpses of her whenever he went into the department store if she was summoned from the office to assist a customer or an employee. And he never would've suspected she had been hiding a magnificent figure under the loose-fitting smock and slacks. The generous slit in the body-hugging gown revealed a pair of slender, shapely legs and ankles in the sexy heels.

She's like Cinderella, he mused. During the day she went about with a bare face, shapeless clothes and her hair fashioned in a single braid; however, tonight she'd transformed into a seductress that had him and other men taking furtive glances at her.

Langston hadn't come back home to become involved with a woman; he'd come back to hopefully recover and heal from recurring episodes of PTSD, which had plagued him when he least expected. Spending too many years covering wars in two African countries and the Middle East had affected him psychologically. He'd gone into therapy to help cope with the nightmares, and it was only after he resigned his position as a correspondent had the macabre images decreased in frequency.

He stood up when Georgina returned to the table.

He pulled out her chair, seating her. Langston retook his seat and turned to look at the well-dressed elderly woman with bluish hair next to him when she rested a hand on his arm. Bessie Daniels had become a fixture in the town as the proprietress of Perfect Tresses hair salon. She'd begun using a blue rinse once she grayed prematurely and had earned the moniker of The Blue Lady.

"Langston, I wanted to tell you that I like what you've done with the newspaper. Eddie Miller ran *The Sentinel* into the ground after he took over from his father. What had been a fine newspaper was filled with reprinted articles no one cared about. Trust me, Langston, we don't mind reading about events that occurred a long time ago, but in my opinion, he was just too damn lazy to go out and gather current news to print."

"I'm glad you like the new format," he said. There was no way he was going to bash the former owner of the newspaper because not only did he still live in the Falls, but Bessie was an incurable gossip and whatever he said to her would no doubt be repeated and get back to Eddie.

"Your folks must be very proud of you, Langston."

He smiled. "I'd like to think they are."

"Please send them my best whenever you talk to or see them again."

"I will."

"By the way," Bessie continued, seemingly without taking a breath, "do you know why Bruce sent his daughter when he usually comes every year?"

Langston smothered a groan. He didn't know why the woman was interrogating him about something she probably knew, but just needed confirmation on. "I do not know." The four words were pregnant with a finality that he hoped she understood.

"Ladies and gentlemen, please be seated," came an announcement over the PA system. "Our mayor and the officers of the Chamber would like to say a few words before dinner is served."

"Nice timing," Georgina whispered in his ear.

Langston shared a knowing smile with her. It was apparent she'd overheard his conversation with Bessie Daniels. "Do you want to switch seats?" he teased, sotto voce.

"You're a big boy, Langston. Please don't tell me you're afraid of a harmless little lady."

He wanted to tell Georgina that the little lady was not harmless, and if the paper had a gossip column then he would've hired her. He'd added two new columns. "Sound Off", in which residents could anonymously voice their concerns about any or everything they felt strongly about, had replaced the "Letters to the Editor," and "Who's Who" to highlight residents who have made a difference. Langston blew out an audible breath when he realized Mrs. Daniels had turned her attention to the woman on her left. He had been given a pass from the chatty woman—for now.

* * *

The speakers droned on, and Georgina knew why her father had tired of attending the fund-raiser; there were too many speeches, which were much too long. She realized she had to get used to it because once she became a business owner it was incumbent she support the Chamber.

She lowered her head, hiding a smile when she saw Sasha roll her eyes upward while shaking her head. Her friend had turned heads in a chocolate-brown, off-the-shoulder dress with a revealing neckline. Georgina assumed it wasn't only the pastry chef's attire that had garnered attention, but also who she'd come with. Her date was the town's resident dentist and single father, Dr. Dwight Adams. Sasha had insisted her part-time employee's father was only a friend, and Georgina wondered, noticing the couple's entrancement with each other, how long they would remain friends. Even given the dearth of romance in her own life, Georgina was a romantic at heart, and she silently cheered for her friend to be given a second chance at love.

Now that she was focused on opening a craft shop, the notion of dating was not on her agenda and it nagged at her that she'd had to use subterfuge because she feared her father would use his influence to block her signing a lease on the vacant store around the corner from Main Street. Georgina had planned carefully when she directed an attorney to set up an LLC for her and gave them power of attorney to negotiate the terms of the lease on her behalf. With the executed lease, she'd applied to the town's housing department for a permit to operate a business and was currently awaiting their approval. The clerk at the town council told her there was a minimum two-month wait before her application would come up for review.

There had been a time when she resented her parents once they'd withdrawn their offer to pay the tuition for her to attend college because they expected her to assume complete control of Powell's once they retired. Georgina had argued they were nowhere near retirement age and her leaving home for four years would not negatively impact the viability of the store. As a recent high school graduate, she hadn't been aware of her mother's emotional instability. One moment she could be laughing, and then without warning she would dissolve into tears about losing her baby. Seeing her mother cry achieved the result Evelyn sought when Georgina promised she would stay. And she'd stayed for fourteen years while feeling as if she was losing a bit of herself day by day, hour by hour and minute by minute if she did not take control of her life and destiny.

Living with her parents and adhering to their rules had taken its toll on her own emotional well-being. She loved her mother and father, respected them as her parents, but she didn't want to turn into someone angry and resentful with the hand she'd been dealt because she had surrendered her will to others who had their own agenda.

"A penny for your thoughts, Georgi."

Langston's voice broke into her musings. "I can't believe how long these speeches are," she lied smoothly. Being deceitful did not come easily for Georgina, yet lately she'd become very closemouthed about her plans because she didn't want anything to come up that would delay or derail them.

"My folks told me when they first joined there wasn't a cocktail hour and the speeches went on for what appeared to be hours before dinner was served. That changed after some of the members threatened to leave the organization if the officers did not change the fund-raiser format."

"It's apparent they listened," she said, smiling.

"They didn't have a choice," Langston countered. "But there was a trade off. Membership dues and the price of the dinner tickets were increased to offset the cost of a cocktail hour. This year they've projected realizing a larger profit from the fund-raiser because they didn't have to rent space at the hotel because the Gibsons decided to donate this venue."

Georgina liked talking with Langston because he was a wealth of information about the goings-on in the town. The store had become her world, isolating her from everything outside the doors of Powell's Department Store.

She'd spend most of the day in the office, checking invoices, inventory, and managing payroll, while
her father passed the time on the floor, interacting
with customers and meeting with various vendors
and deliverymen. And whenever she felt as if she
was going stir-crazy, Georgina would leave the office to exchange pleasantries with customers, walk
down to the bank to deposit receipts, or go across
the street to Ruthie's for lunch. Working at the store
since graduating high school had become a good
and bad experience. Good because she'd learned the
inner workings of to how to operate a business, and
bad because after spending so many hours at the
store she had little or no energy to do much more
than take a long soak in the tub and go to bed, just
to get up the next day and do it all over again.

She had already established hours for her own
shop so she wouldn't work seven days a week, or
ten hours a day, and it would be the first time when
she would be able to balance work with possibly a
future social life.

The speeches ended to rousing applause, and
within minutes the waitstaff began serving those on
the dais, town officials and then the assembly, while
the DJ increased the volume on the music, but not
so loud that one had to shout to be heard. Georgina
had to admit her choice of roast capon with rose-
mary cider gravy, roasted cauliflower with scallion
and lemon, and rice pilaf was not only appealing in

presentation but also scrumptious. Meanwhile, bartenders wheeled carts around the room, filling beverage orders.

The man on her right, the owner of the laundromat/dry cleaner, talked incessantly about missing his wife of more than thirty years who'd died earlier in the year, and that running his business wasn't the same without her presence. The cheerful woman who'd manned the laundromat had greeted everyone with a smile, and most of the residents in the Falls turned out for her funeral.

Georgina had to admit, aside from the long-winded speeches, she was enjoying herself. Various floating conversations had her smiling when someone let it slip that a woman was cheating on her husband with their neighbor. She hadn't been to a social event since prom, so she did not have a frame of reference from which to ascertain whether the fund-raiser was an overwhelming success. The silent voice in her head chided her for not experiencing normal events a twenty- and thirty-something single woman would or should have. She'd become the good daughter in every sense of the word, but to her emotional detriment, which threatened to make her as socially reclusive as her mother.

She coveted what little free time she had occasionally watching her favorite TV shows, knitting or crocheting, and she had to thank her grandmother for teaching her the handicrafts passed down through generations of Reed women. Grandmother Doro-thea, or Dot, insisted she pay close attention when she taught her to cast on stitches to knit her first garment. Georgina proudly wore the scarf and then began her next project—a crocheted ski cap. By the time she'd celebrated her twelfth birthday she was able to follow and complete difficult patterns uti-lizing multiple colors, needles and hand or machine quilting. Although Powell's had stocked fat quarters for those who still pieced quilts, it had been years since Georgina had made a quilt.

She had inherited a prized collection of antique quilts hand sewn by her great-great-great-grand-mother she had wrapped in tissue paper and stored in moisture-free plastic containers on a top shelf of her bedroom's walk-in closet.

Georgina shifted her attention to Langston. "How's your fish?" He'd selected broiled flounder stuffed with lump crab and topped with shrimp in a béarnaise sauce.

"It's delicious. The Gibsons have outdone them-selves tonight. I'm so used to their smoked brisket, ribs and chicken that I had no idea they could get hoity-toity on us."

Georgina laughed at Langston's description of the dinner choices of roast prime rib with an herbed horseradish crust, fish and chicken. "They had to change it up if they want repeat business."

Langston draped his right arm over the back of her chair. "Do you ever go to the Den?"

"Hardly ever. Once I come home, I veg out."

"Are you saying it's all work and no play for you?" he asked.

"Just about. I work six days a week, and alternate Sundays with my father."

"That's a heavy schedule."

"It is. But I'm used to it." Georgina was used to it and she was counting down to the time when she would log a forty-hour workweek instead of an average of sixty-five. "How about you, Langston? Do you put in long hours?"

"It all depends. If I must cover a town council meeting in the evening, then I come in later in the day."

Georgina met his eyes, silently admiring the length of his lashes. It had been a while since she'd taken out her sketch pad to draw, but there was something about Langston's face that made her want to capture his image on paper. "Do you like working for yourself?" He smiled, bringing her gaze to linger on his mouth and still lower to the slight cleft in his strong chin.

"What I like is the flexibility. I have an incredible office manager who doesn't need me to be there to supervise her. She's been with the paper for years and she's not shy about telling me what our subscribers don't want. I trust her instincts because I've been away for almost twenty years."

Many young people left the Falls to go to college or enlist in the military, but Georgina had become the exception. "You left and I stayed." Georgina had spoken her musings aloud.

Langston leaned closer. "Did you ever think about leaving?"

Georgina lowered her eyes. "More times than I can count."

"What about now, Georgi?"

"I can't now."

"Are you engaged?"

A slow smile parted Georgina's lips. "No. I don't have time for a boyfriend. And if a man did ask me out, he'd have to have me home before midnight because I'm up at six and in the store at eight to get everything ready to open at nine."

"What about tonight? This event is scheduled to end sometime around one. Last year it wasn't over until after two."

"I'm not scheduled to work tomorrow." The store's Sunday hours were twelve noon to six.

"So Cinderella can stay out beyond midnight," Langston teased.

"She can stay out all night if she chooses."

Georgina could not remember the last time she'd stayed out all night. When she'd dated a man from Beckley, she would occasionally spend the night at his house even though she had to get up early the next morning to drive back to Wickham Falls. Her father knew she was sleeping with a man, but never broached the subject with her. After all, she was an adult and responsible for her own actions and behavior.

"Now if we were in DC or New York we could leave here and hang out at a jazz club and listen to music until the sun comes up. Then we would go to an all-night diner for breakfast."

She was intrigued by his supposition. "What would we do the next day?"

"Sleep in late. I'd also make dinner for you before taking you home."

Georgina laughed softly. "So you do cook."

A smile ruffled Langston's mouth. "I do all right."

"How much is all right?" she questioned.

"It depends on which type of cuisine you'd want. I'm partial to Middle Eastern and Mediterranean dishes."

Georgina slumped back in her chair, then sat straight when Langston's fingers grazed her exposed skin. His touch raised goose bumps on her arms as shivers eddied down her celibate body. And not for an instant could she forget that Langston Cooper was a very attractive man and eligible bachelor.

Langston had become a hometown celebrity after he was hired by a major all-news cable station where he was assigned to cover wars and skirmishes on the other side of the world. When his first book depicting his experience as a foreign correspondent was released it was as if every resident in Wickham Falls was reading it at the same time. The follow-up to his first book proved to be controversial when he was summoned to appear before a congressional committee where some members had accused him of being a spy or collaborating with enemy forces because of his knowledge of classified information. The charges proved unfounded. Langston resigned from the news station and returned home with superstar status.

"I'm really impressed," Georgina said after a noticeable pause. "I love Italian food."

"Do you have a preference?"

"Shrimp scampi and ravioli filled with any meat, cheese or vegetable."

"One of these days when you're free for dinner, I'll cook for you, always keeping in mind that you have to be home before midnight."

Georgina sobered quickly. She didn't want Langston to believe that she was flirting with him or soliciting a date. "You don't have to cook for me, Langston."

"Why are you sending me mixed messages?"

She went completely still. "Is that what I'm doing?"

"That's precisely what you're doing, Georgi. You tell me you love Italian food and when I offer to cook for you, you do a complete one-eighty. I can assure you that I don't have a dungeon in my home where I imprison unsuspecting young women in a modern-day Château d'If."

Georgina turned her head and bit her lip to keep from laughing in Langston's face. "Why are you being so melodramatic?"

"Is that what you believe? That I'm melodramatic?"

She shifted to face him again, putting her thumb and forefinger together. "Just a wee bit."

He smiled. "Maybe you're right. But I have to admit that you're the first woman since I've been back that I've invited to my home."

"Why me, Langston?" The instant the question rolled off her tongue Georgina chided herself for asking it. Why couldn't she just accept that he wanted to spend some time with her.

"Why not you, Georgi?"

Georgina did not have an answer for him. However, she couldn't help thinking he could be comparing her to the worldly, sophisticated women he'd met since leaving Wickham Falls, and found her gauche and gullible. Well, she was neither and she intended to prove it to him.

"I'll call you at your office to let you know when I'm available to come for dinner."

Reaching into the breast pocket of his jacket, he removed his cell phone and handed it to her. "Give me your cell number and I'll call you."

She wagged a finger. "Not yet. I'll give you my number but only after our first date." Langston's expression of surprise was priceless. It was apparent he wasn't used to women establishing the rules even before they had gone out together.

"Okay," he conceded. "I'll wait for your call. If I'm not in the office, then just leave a message with the receptionist."

Georgina felt as if she'd won a small victory, because she'd sworn after breaking up with her ex that she would never want another man to believe she was *that* grateful because he'd asked her out. She may not have had a lot of dates, but that did not make her feel diminished.

The tempo of the musician changed again, this time with more upbeat tunes as coffee and desserts were served. Several couples were already up on the dance floor, and minutes later others joined them. Pushing back his chair, Langston stood and offered Georgina his hand.

"May I please have this dance?"

She placed her hand on his outstretched palm, smiling as he eased her to stand. The music selection was a slow, romantic tune. He led her to the dance floor, and her body molded against his when his arm curved around her waist. Georgina closed her eyes as she lost herself in the smell of his cologne, the warmth of his breath in her ear and his protective embrace that allowed her to temporarily forget why she'd refused to date a man from her hometown. And if she did share dinner with Langston in his home, he would become the first. However, unlike other men from Wickham Falls, she wasn't concerned that his interest in her was wholly financial. Not only was he a business owner, but he was also a bestselling writer. Georgina wasn't looking for a boyfriend, or even a committed relationship, and for her, cultivating a friendship with the editor-in-chief of the local newspaper would be a plus.

The song ended and she kissed Langston's jaw. "Thank you for the dance and I owe you another one, but I have to leave because I just remembered I have to meet someone early tomorrow morning."

Nodding, Langston escorted her back to their table, waited for her to retrieve her shawl and evening bag, and then walked her out to the parking lot. "Get home safely."

She gave him a warm smile. "Thank you. And you get home safely yourself." Georgina started up her vehicle and maneuvered out of the crowded lot. Although she wasn't scheduled to work the next day, she needed to get up in time to drive to the town's only bed-and-breakfast to confer with Noah Wainwright about his construction project. The sooner she initiated her plan to move, the sooner she would be able to tackle the next item on her journey to achieve independence.

Chapter Three

Georgina walked into the kitchen early Sunday morning to find her parents sitting in the breakfast nook. "You guys are up early."

"So are you," Evelyn countered. "I thought you would've slept in this morning."

She picked up a mug and popped a coffee pod into the single-serve coffeemaker. "I would've if I didn't have to meet someone."

"Does your someone have a name?"

Georgina stared at her mother. Evelyn Reed Powell had lost at least twenty pounds following her son's death and had never regained it, leaving her to appear emaciated. Her dark brown complexion appeared unhealthy, while her once-thick black hair was now sparse, graying wisps. The extremely attractive woman who had become the envy of most young women in the Falls when she got Bruce Powell to not only profess his love for her but also claim her as his wife. Once she became aware of her mother's depression, Georgina begged her to seek treatment, but Evelyn refused, declaring there was nothing wrong with her.

Bruce frowned at his wife. "Let it go, Evelyn. Have you forgotten Georgina is a grown woman and entitled to her own privacy?"

·Evelyn rounded on him. "As long as she lives under my roof, I have a right to know where she's going and who she's seeing."

The fragile rein Georgina had on her temper when interacting with her mother snapped. "That's not going to be much longer," she spat out. She hadn't planned to inform her parents she was moving until she found a place to live.

Evelyn looked as if she was going to faint. "What!"

Georgina pressed the button on the coffeemaker harder than necessary. "I said I'm moving out."

"What about the store?" Bruce questioned.

She smiled at her easygoing father. He'd lost most of his bright red hair and now at fifty-nine was left with a fringe on the crown of his head. There were times when she wondered how he had put up with his controlling wife, but it was apparent he was either used to or ignored most of her complaints.

"I'll still be working in the store."

Georgina didn't have the heart to tell him that she wasn't certain how long that would be. She'd contacted her first cousin, Sutton Reed, who had not renewed his contract with a Major League Baseball team after he'd suffered a season-ending injury. He had promised to let her know when he would return to Wickham Falls to help his uncle manage the store for a year while he contemplated life after baseball. Other than Sasha, only Sutton knew she wanted to leave the department store to go into business for herself.

Bruce exhaled an audible breath. "That's good to know."

"But she can't leave!" Evelyn screamed.

"Yes, she can, Evelyn. Have you forgotten that our daughter is thirty-two years old and she should've lived on her own years ago? It's you who doesn't want her to leave."

"I lost my son and now I can't bear to lose my daughter."

Georgina rolled her eyes upward as she ignored her mother's forced tears. "You're not losing me, Mom. I'm moving out, not away."

"I'm still losing you."

She'd had enough of the theatrics. Georgina poured the coffee into a travel mug, added a splash of cream, secured the top and walked out of the kitchen. She wasn't about to get into an argument with her mother because there would be no winners, only losers. And while she'd always bitten her tongue or walked away before she said something that would completely fracture her relationship with the older woman, Georgina knew she was through being diplomatic. Come hell or high water, she was moving.

Georgina parked her car in the space designated for guest parking at the antebellum-designed B and B. It was the largest and most impressive house in the town and had been known as the Wolfe House, the Falls House and now currently the Wickham Falls Bed-and-Breakfast.

Her contact with Viviana and her brother Leland was nearly nonexistent when growing up because they'd attended a private boarding school. When Viviana married New York City-based developer and real-estate mogul, Noah Wainwright, some of the locals were grumbling that money begat money. There were three other cars in the lot beside hers, and she hoped Noah would be available to talk to her.

After walking up the front steps to the mansion, Georgina opened the front door as a chime signaled someone had come in. Viviana appeared as if out of nowhere, and Georgina smiled at the tall, slender woman with a wealth of black, curly hair framing her face and cascading down her back.

She extended her hand. "I'm Georgina and—"

"I know who you are," Viviana said, cutting her off and taking the proffered hand. "Even though we live in the same town I rarely get a chance to leave this place. Is there something I can help you with?"

Viviana was right, because she'd had very little interaction with the woman who'd occasionally come into the store to buy yarn or fabric. She noticed the circle of diamonds in the eternity band on Viviana's left hand. "First, congratulations on your marriage."

Clear, toffee-brown eyes in a flawless golden-brown complexion crinkled when she smiled. "Thank you. I'm still attempting to get used to introducing myself as Wainwright rather than Remington."

"I'm certain a lot of newlywed brides have the same problem," Georgina said.

"Even though all of the guests haven't come down for breakfast I could get the cook to fix you a plate."

"Please, no. I came to ask your husband about the homes that are being built on your land."

"Noah's in New York, but maybe I can help you. Come into my office so we can talk in private."

Georgina followed Viviana through the grand entryway to a room where the proprietress had set up her office. "This place is magnificent."

Viviana waited for her to sit before taking a

matching needlepoint chair opposite her. "You wouldn't have said that if you'd been here almost two years ago. Thanks to my brother, I was able to make repairs and restore the furnishings to where they are almost new. This place was a boardinghouse before I converted it to a B and B. Half the bedroom suites are set aside for the business and the other half for personal living. I know I've been running off at the mouth when you want to know about the houses that are under construction."

"Yes. I'd like to know if any are completed and up for sale."

"Only the model homes are completed. It will be at least another six to eight months before the rest of the structures will be ready for sale and occupancy."

Georgina schooled her expression not to show her disappointment. "I'm planning to move out of my parents' home, and I was looking for something here in the Falls either to buy or rent until I decide on something permanent."

"I have two vacant fully furnished guesthouses on the property you can rent."

How much Viviana was going to charge her to rent the guesthouse wasn't a deal breaker because Georgina preferred living in the Falls. And the last time she went through the classified ads in *The Sentinel* there was one house for sale and listed as a fixer-upper. She had no intention of investing her money in a property that needed extensive repairs even before she could move in.

"Is this a good time for you to show them to me?"

Viviana smiled. "It's perfect."

When Viviana tapped the key card and opened the door, Georgina couldn't stop grinning. Her eyes lit up like a child's on Christmas morning when seeing piles of gaily wrapped gifts under the decorated tree. The guesthouses were far enough away from each other and the main house to ensure complete privacy, and the interior claimed two bedrooms with sitting areas, flat-screen TVs, and there was a loft with a king-size bed overlooking the living/dining area. It also had a galley kitchen and full bathroom with a freestanding shower. A stackable washer/dryer unit was concealed in a closet off the bathroom.

The furniture was contemporary, upholstered in red, brown and green, and was a colorful contrast to the lemon-yellow walls. A desk, worktable and chair positioned in a corner under a window was the perfect spot for her to set up a computer program for her business. She could use the extra bedroom to store her inventory rather than continue to pay a storage company. A wall of French doors spanned the rear of the house, allowing for unlimited light during the day.

"As a guest you're entitled to a buffet breakfast from seven to ten. Cordials and desserts are served in the parlor at 8:00 pm, and the entire property is wired with cable and Wi-Fi. You're entitled to daily housekeeping services, and if you need clean linen then leave the placard on the bed."

"It's perfect for my needs," Georgina told Viviana. "Is it possible for me to rent it until the houses are completed?"

"Yes. The rental rates vary for month-to-month, or three, six, nine and twelve months. If you decide to rent for six months, then you will get a twenty percent discount than if you decide for three."

She thought about the projected two-month minimum wait for the approval of the permit to open her shop. "What if I rent the guesthouse for three months with an option for an additional three?"

A pregnant silence ensued as Viviana appeared to be deep in thought. "If that's the case then I'll charge you the six-month rate, which should allow you a greater discount. And if you move out before six months, then I'll prorate the difference. I can't have folks who live in the Falls talk about me cheating them. Even though Leland and I are Remingtons, people seem to get a kick out of reminding us that our mama was a Wolfe and Daddy was a junkie."

Georgina had grown up eavesdropping on conversations between her mother and other women whispering about Emory Remington. His military career ended when he was wounded during a deployment, and his dependence on prescribed meds segued into addiction to heroin and subsequent imprisonment for armed robbery to get money to support his habit. And anyone claiming Wolfe blood was reviled because of their corrupt, immoral ancestors.

"And the same hypocrites have so many skeletons in their closets that if you open them, they would rattle like dice."

"I agree with you," Viviana said. "It's always the ones with the most to hide who are always beating their gums about something. Let's go back to the house and I'll review the rates with you."

An hour after Georgina walked into the B and B, she left with a rental agreement and a key card for her new residence. The moment she handed Viviana her credit card she realized although she'd lived in Wickham Falls all her life, it was if she was starting over.

Renting a fully furnished house was convenient, because she didn't have to buy furniture or kitchen items. All she had to do was pack her clothes and personal items and shop for groceries to stock the fridge and pantry. Although she could take advantage of the B and B's buffet breakfast, Georgina planned to prepare her own meals.

Her father's car wasn't in the driveway, which meant he was probably at the store. She went into the house and found her mother in the family room watching her favorite televangelist. The Sundays she was off, Georgina had invited Evelyn to attend church services with her, but when her mother appeared to be mute, she'd stopped asking. Georgina knew it wasn't healthy for her mother to stay indoors for weeks on end and had stopped attempting to devise scenarios to get Evelyn to leave the house.

"Mom, did you eat breakfast?"

Evelyn glanced at her. "I had toast and coffee."

"I'm making an omelet. Do you want one?"

"No, thank you."

"What about fruit? There's still some cantaloupe and honeydew left."

"I'll have fruit."

Georgina found it hard to believe Evelyn had agreed to eat more than her usual toast and coffee. Perhaps announcing that she was moving out had penetrated her mother's shroud of self-pity, and awakened the reality that she could no longer depend on her daughter for companionship when she had a husband who loved her unconditionally.

"Do you want to eat in the family room or in the kitchen with me?"

"As soon as my show is over, I'll join you in the kitchen."

She went into the kitchen to make her Sunday breakfast favorite—an omelet, fresh fruit and wheat toast. Sundays she didn't work, she usually cooked different meats and side dishes to last for several days. Georgina had defrosted pork chops, a couple of pounds of large shrimp and a roasting chicken.

She'd also planned to make a black bean soup with andouille sausage, baked macaroni and cheese, corn muffins and cranberry bread pudding with bourbon custard and cranberry sauce.

Whenever she cooked, Georgina felt as if she was paying homage to her Grandma Dot. Growing up, she'd believed there wasn't anything her grandmother did not do well. She was an incredible cook and was disappointed that her daughters were less than enthusiastic about following in her footsteps. However, Dot's faith was restored when her only granddaughter inherited her love of cooking and needlework. And once Georgina exhibited a talent for drawing it was Grandma Dot who'd encouraged her to become an artist. She missed her grandmother but knew she would be proud of her once she opened the shop that she planned to call A Stitch at a Time.

Georgina had just finished chopping the ingredients for the omelets when she noticed Evelyn standing at the entrance to the kitchen. "Please come in, Mom, and sit down."

"So you're really serious about moving out?" Evelyn asked as she entered the kitchen and sat on a stool at the cooking island.

"Yes."

"When?"

"Sometime this week. I'll start loading up my car in a few days to begin moving my clothes and other personal items."

Closing the storage unit and storing the boxes in the smaller of the two bedrooms in the guesthouse had become Georgina's priority. And although she had to wait for the town's building department to approve the permit for her to open the craft shop, she felt confident it would become a reality. The landlord had renovated the space and added a bathroom after the last tenant vacated, brought everything up to code, and it was now turnkey ready.

She had also ordered shelving, reception-area furniture and chairs and loveseats for an area she'd planned to set aside for her customers to relax while working on their handmade projects. There would also be a refreshment station with water, coffee, tea and baked goods from Sasha's Sweet Shoppe.

"You've found a place." Evelyn's query was a statement.

"Yes, Mom. I'm renting one of the guesthouses on the Remington property."

"Do you really want to get involved with *those* people?"

Georgina glared at her mother. "When are you going to let it go that Viviana and her brother aren't responsible for how the Wolfes treated folks who worked in their mines?"

"Never," Evelyn said, frowning. "The Wolfes fired my grandfather after he was diagnosed with black lung disease. They claimed it had come from his smoking cigarettes, and I still remember his having to drag around an oxygen canister to help him breathe. He died cursing the Wolfes once they'd begun closing the mines one by one because the bastards didn't want to comply with the government's safety regulations."

"Mom, you have to forgive what happened over which you had no control, even if you choose not to forget."

"Like that boy who tried to extort you for money to pay his gambling debts?"

Georgina regretted telling her mother why she'd stopped dating Sean Bostic despite promising him she wouldn't tell anyone, yet she hadn't wanted to lie about why she'd abruptly ended their eight-month relationship. Instead of being supportive that a man had attempted to take advantage of her daughter, Evelyn appeared to celebrate the breakup because it meant Georgina wasn't going to get married and leave her.

"There's nothing to forgive because I didn't give Sean any money. But I did learn a lesson about not ignoring the signs whenever a man talks about money, whether it's his or mine."

"You have to know that a lot of men these days are looking for a woman to take care of them. A prime example is my sister Michelle. Once Sutton's father discovered she'd inherited some money from our Daddy's life insurance he latched on to her like a leech, while sweet-talking her into buying him a new car and whatever else he wanted. And, when the money ran out, he also ran out, leaving her practically barefoot and pregnant."

Georgina remembered her aunt Michelle cackling like a hen laying an egg when she'd revealed to her sister that Sutton's father came skulking back like a whipped dog after the news that his son, whom he'd never met, after graduating college had become a first-round draft pick for a major league baseball team. The first-base, homerun-hitting phenom who'd signed a multimillion-dollar, four-year contract wanted nothing to do with the man who'd deserted his mother when she'd needed him most.

"Aunt Michelle may have had to raise her son as a single mother, but in the end, she came out the winner and her baby daddy the loser. What was one of Grandma Dot's favorite sayings?"

Evelyn's eyebrows lifted questioningly. "Which one? She had so many that I couldn't keep track of them. Like 'what doesn't come out in the wash will come out in the rinse.' Or 'she took the rag off the bush.'"

"It's the one about getting by but not getting away. In other words, karma is always waiting at the end of the road before she decides to punch your expiration ticket."

Evelyn flashed a rare smile. "I've lived long enough to see folks reap what they've sown, and most times it's not a good deed."

"You're only fifty-nine, so you're not that old."

"There are times when I feel so much older," Evelyn admitted.

"That's because you spend so much time alone in the house. You should ask Dad to take some time off and go somewhere exotic where the most strenuous thing you'd have to do is raise your hand to get the attention of the resort employee to bring you something to eat or drink."

"I can't do that."

"And why not, Mom?"

"What about the store?"

Georgina narrowed her eyes at her mother at the same time she pressed her lips together to stop the acerbic words from coming out. Evelyn was the queen of excuses. And if she said it, then she tended to believe it. "Do you really think the store is going to close its doors if Dad isn't there for a week? Remember when he came down with the flu a couple of years ago, and I took care of everything? Powell's may not be as large as other department stores, but we've been in business for more than one hundred years, and chances are it will continue long after we're gone."

"You know there's an unwritten rule that the store has to be managed by a family member, so what's going to happen if you don't get married and have children?"

"I don't have to be married to have children,

Mom. I could always adopt. And don't forget I'm not the only Powell. Dad still has a brother and sister who both have kids."

"Paul just retired from the army after twenty-five years, and there's no way he's going to give up living in Hawaii to come back to the Falls. And forget about Donna. She's never going to leave Alaska, her husband, children, grandchildren and her beloved sled dogs."

"Not to worry, Mom. Dad's not ready to retire, so that's something we don't have to think about until years from now."

Georgina talking to Evelyn while she cooked felt like old times before Kevin passed away. She wasn't certain whether her mother had accepted what she couldn't change—her moving out or realizing that her inability to solicit her husband as an ally was futile.

"Maybe I'll ask your father if he would like to take a few days off and go away."

"Do you have an idea of where you would like to go?"

"Definitely someplace warm. Maybe we can go to Hawaii to visit Paul."

Georgina flashed a smug grin. Getting her parents to go away for a week or two would be good for both of them. She'd proven in the past that she could manage the store without her father's presence, and during their absence she would stay at the house.

"Make certain to take a lot of pictures."

"Your father can do that. I can't take a decent picture if my life depended on it. Speaking of pictures, did you take any at the fund-raiser?"

"No, but Jonas Harper was there representing the town and the newspaper. I'm certain there will be a lot of pictures in the next issue."

"Was Langston there to cover it for the paper?"

"Yes. In fact, we shared a table."

"It's a shame his wife cheated on him with that so-called actor while he'd risked life and limb covering wars on the other side of the world."

Georgina did not understand how her mother was privy to so much gossip when she hardly ventured outside the house. Did she keep in touch with someone who kept her abreast of the goings-on in town, or had she pumped her husband for information and then drew her own conclusions?

She set the table in the breakfast nook with bowls of sliced melon and quickly made two Western omelets. Evelyn devoured it, saying it was delicious, and Georgina didn't want to declare an early victory in getting her mother to eat, but it was a start.

Evelyn retreated to the family room to watch television, while Georgina cleaned up the kitchen before taking out the ingredients she needed to prepare Sunday dinner.

It was Monday morning and minutes before seven when Georgina pulled into her reserved parking space behind the department store an hour before her normal arrival time. Most of the businesses along Main Street were still closed; the lights coming from the popular restaurant Ruthie's indicated they were preparing for their all-you-can-eat buffet. She noticed a car from the sheriff's department parked at the far end of the lot. Since being elected and sworn in as sheriff, Seth Collier had increased patrols of the downtown business district after an attempted break-in at the pharmacy. He'd suspected the burglar or burglars were looking for drugs. Residents of Wickham Falls were not exempt from the opioid epidemic sweeping the country.

She unlocked the rear door, disarmed the security system and then closed and locked it behind her. Before her father closed at night, he had made it a practice to leave a few lights on so if the sheriff or his deputies checked stores in the downtown business district, they were able to view the interiors to detect possible intruders.

She punched in the code to the office and walked in. Last year the space had undergone a complete renovation with a new coat of paint, ceiling tiles, carpeting and recessed lighting. A glazer had installed one-way windows, which allowed her to observe all activity on the sales floor. Security cameras were installed throughout the building to deter shoplifting. Her father had also updated the employees' break room and bathrooms.

After placing a container with her lunch from the dishes she'd prepared the day before in the office's mini fridge, she picked up the telephone and dialed the number to *The Sentinel*, listening for the prompts on the voice mail messaging. It wasn't the recorded message that greeted her, but a familiar male's voice.

"Langston?"

"All day and all night."

Georgina smiled. She hadn't expected Langston to answer the phone at this hour in the morning. "Good morning, Langston. Do you usually begin working this early?"

"No. The office doesn't open until nine. I'm here because I didn't go home last night."

"You spent the night there?"

"Yes. I began writing a piece on the Chamber fund-raiser and lost track of time. I should finish it in a couple of hours, then I'll go home and crash."

"I'm not going to keep you. I just called to thank you for recommending the Wainwrights, because I'll be renting one of their guesthouses. The new homes are still under construction, and probably won't be ready for sale until the end of the year."

"I'm glad you found something in Wickham Falls."

"Me, too," Georgina said in agreement. She was more than glad and had to tamp down feelings of euphoria whenever she thought about moving into the guesthouse.

"Once you're settled in, we have to get together so I can make my butternut squash ravioli for you."

She smiled again. "Okay. I'll call and let you know when I can come up for air."

"Take down my cell number. If you can't reach me here, then you can always send me a text."

Reaching for a pen, Georgina wrote down the ten digits, and then repeated it to Langston. "I'm going to give you my number, so you won't have to call me here at the store."

A low chuckle caressed her ear. "What's so funny?"

"You, Georgi. First you claim you won't give me your number until after we have our first date, and now you've reneged."

"Have you ever changed your mind about something?"

"Yeah."

"There you go. Now, take down my number before I change my mind again."

"Talk to me, Cinderella."

She gave him the number to her cell phone. "If I'm Cinderella, then who are you?"

A beat passed. "I haven't yet decided whether I'm the prince from *Sleeping Beauty* or *Cinderella*."

"You can't mix fairy-tale princes, Langston. And, how do you know so much about princes and princesses?"

"My mother used to read them over and over to my sister."

"By the way, how is your sister doing?"

"Jackie's well. She's left teaching for a while to become a stay-at-home mom and she loves it."

Jacklyn Cooper, who'd been in Georgina's graduating class, left the Falls to enroll in Howard University as an English major. "Give her my regards when you talk to her. I'm going to hang up now so you can finish your article, go home and get some sleep."

"Okay. Later."

"Later, Langston."

Georgina ended the call and then leaned back in the desk chair. Langston said inviting her to his house for dinner was a date. And he'd also revealed that she would be the first woman he would invite to his home since his return. He'd been back a little more than a year and she wondered why her and not some other woman.

Cinderella. Had he likened her to the fairy-tale princess because she'd informed him that she had to be home before midnight; or did he view her as the young woman who hadn't been permitted to leave home until she met her prince who'd freed her from a life of monotony? And, she mused, did she need rescuing? Or did she want Langston to become her prince?

If she was truthful, then she would have to give Sasha Manning credit for hearing her out and suggesting she move out of her parents' home for the first step in establishing her independence. Sasha had left the Falls within months of graduation, while Georgina had given up her dream of leaving and attending art school. Whenever she heard that another of her classmates had gone to college, enlisted in the military, or even accepted employment outside Johnson County, she sank further into a morass of helplessness until she'd accepted her plight. She would live at home and work for the family-owned business.

Once her father began downsizing the arts and craft section the lightbulb in her head was suddenly illuminated. Bruce claimed he wanted to expand the sporting goods area and had contacted the vendor selling yarn and fabric to cancel all future orders. She'd stayed after hours to box up the entire craft materials section and took it to a storage company in Mineral Springs. Yards of yarn and bolts of fabric had become her one-way ticket to a life she never would've imagined if her father hadn't decided to scale back the inventory.

Smiling, Georgina booted up the store's computer and clicked on the app for accounts payable. She'd computerized all vendors, paid them electronically and direct-deposited payroll checks into employees' bank accounts. Her father oversaw the front of the store and monitored the clerks checking out customers and would periodically empty the registers of cash and store it in the office safe.

Powell's had had two burglaries in the past, and an armed robbery several years ago. Unfortunately for the perpetrator, he was unaware that a plain-clothes deputy on loan from Mineral Springs was at checkout and managed to disarm and apprehend him before he could escape. The incident prompted her father to install panic buttons under the counters at checkout, which were wired directly to the sheriff's office.

The office door opened, and Bruce walked in. "I can't believe you got here before me."

Georgina smiled at her father. He'd shaved his head. She'd suggested he get rid of the circle of fading red hair a long time ago like so many men who were balding. "How handsome you look."

Attractive lines fanned out around Bruce's dark-blue eyes when he smiled. "I know you've been after me to shave my head, and I must admit it's really liberating. I'm certain Joe's Barber is going to miss me, but I'll still go there for a professional shave every couple of weeks. Now, why did you get up before the chickens?"

"I want to get most of my paperwork done so I can leave a little early to go home and start packing."

Bruce sat on a chair next to the workstation. "I'm glad you decided to move out."

"What!"

"I'd wanted to tell you a long time ago that you should live on your own. But I didn't want to start up with your mother. Speaking of your mother," he continued without taking a breath, "she suggested we go to Hawaii to visit Paul and his family."

Georgina studied her father's face, realizing for the first time that she was a softer, more feminine version of the man. Whenever he came to her school, kids would announce loudly that her father was there to see her. Grandma Dot used to say that Bruce Powell had figuratively spit her out.

"Are you going?"

"I'm seriously thinking about it. When I called Paul, he said he was looking forward to having us come. But if I do go, then you're going to have to spend most of your time on the floor."

"Don't worry, Dad. I'll ask Dan Jackson if he's willing to work security until you get back." Dan had become a lifer in the corps, and after separating worked security for private social events.

Bruce's pale eyebrow lifted. "I guess that settles it. You call Dan while I research flights."

"How long do you plan to stay?"

"Probably a week to ten days." He placed his hand over Georgina's and gave her fingers a gentle squeeze. "Thank you, baby girl."

A slight frown creased her forehead. "For what, Dad?"

"I believe you telling your mother you were moving out made her aware that she didn't have to depend on you for companionship. I told her she would never be alone if I'm alive, because I'd made a vow to be with her through the good times and the bad ones. I love her just that much."

"Why did it take her this long to come to the realization that she does have a loving and supportive husband?" Georgina asked.

"I'm not complaining about how long it took, because I've been given a second chance to get my wife back."

Georgina did not want to ask, but she wondered if her mother had even spurned her husband's attempt to make love to her. "You can think of it as a second honeymoon."

Bruce smiled. "That's what I'm hoping."

"If Mom comes back pregnant, I'm going to disown both of you," she teased.

He jerked back his hand as if hers had burned him as blood drained from his face, leaving it a sickly yellowish shade. "Your mama had a difficult delivery with Kevin, and the doctor couldn't stop the bleeding, and subsequently she had a hysterectomy that made it impossible for her to have another child. That's part of the reason she was so devastated when he died."

Georgina covered her mouth with her hand and closed her eyes. She had no idea that her mother had undergone a hysterectomy. She'd believed Evelyn had spent a lot of time in bed because she'd had a Cesarean.

"I'm sorry, Daddy. Why didn't you tell me?"

Bruce's expression softened. "Your mother made me swear never to tell anyone. Are you aware that it's been years since you've called me *Daddy*?"

Rising slightly, she leaned over and kissed his smooth-shaven jaw. "Is that what you want me to call you?"

Bruce ran a hand over her curly hair. "No. I'm waiting for the day when you'll call me Grandpa."

Georgina hadn't missed the longing tone in her father's voice. "Give me time to get my life together, and one of these days I'll hope to make you a grandfather."

"Don't wait too long, sweetie, or I'll be too old to toss my grandbaby in the air and catch them."

She cut her eyes at her father. "You will not toss my babies."

"Have one or two, then we'll see." Bruce stood up. "It's time I get the register drawers."

Georgina focused her attention on the computer screen while Bruce opened the safe and removed the drawers to the registers. He'd made it a practice to fill them the night before, which eliminated the need to count out bills and coins before the clerks arrived.

The weekend had been full of surprises. She'd attended a social affair and was seated with a man who'd invited her to his home for a dinner date; she'd revealed to her parents that she was moving out; had rented a house that would fulfill her current needs;

her father and mother were going on vacation for the first time in years, and he'd revealed the underlying cause for his wife's depression.

Georgina was annoyed with her father because if he'd told her about Evelyn's inability to have more children, she wouldn't have spent so many years resenting her mother's need to cling to her surviving child because she feared losing her, too. She also faulted him because he should've tried harder to help his wife deal with her grief and not sanction her emotional manipulation of their daughter.

Her father wanted grandchildren, but that could not become a reality until Georgina was able to cross off several more items on her wish list.

Chapter Four

Langston studied the gallery of photographs that were taken two weeks ago at the Chamber dinner on the computer monitor. While Jonas Harper was Wickham Falls' official photographer, he also freelanced for the paper. The man truly was an artistic genius. He'd photographed every table, and his lens had captured expressions ranging from stoic to ebullient.

A smile tilted the corners of his mouth. The lens had captured an image of him and Georgina smiling at each other as if sharing a secret. When he'd left the Falls to attend college, Georgi was a cute teenage girl. Fast-forward more than a decade and she was now a stunning woman.

Her sensual voice, the way in which she glanced up at him through her lashes, and her fluid body language were traits that had him thinking about her days later. And he hadn't lied when he revealed she would become the first woman he'd invited to his home. The house where he'd grown up had become his sanctuary, a place filled with warm and happy memories of his childhood.

His parents were protective, and affectionate with one hard and fast rule that he and his sister do well in school because without an education he would never be able to realize his dream to become a journalist. Langston struggled to balance sports with academics when he joined the baseball team as a pitcher, and during his junior year when his grades began to slip he had to decide which he craved more—the roar of the crowd when he struck out someone on the opposing team, or getting into the college of his choice. In the end it was the latter.

His private line rang, and he tapped the speaker feature when he saw the name on the console. "I got them, Jonas."

"What do you think, Lang?"

"They're incredible. Your lens is pure magic."

Jonas laughed. "I had to use a long lens so not to be obtrusive. Folks tend not to be so candid when you put a camera in their face. You look really cozy with Powell's daughter."

"We had fun."

"No doubt. Did you find the one where you were dancing together?"

"Not yet."

"Keep scrolling and you'll see what I'm talking about. You told me you wanted to include a two-page spread in the upcoming edition, so if you want me to include it you should be ready when folks talk about you hooking up with Powell's girl."

"She happens to have a name, Jonas."

"I know, but everyone refers to her as Powell's girl."

Langston scrolled through the photos until he came to the one with him dancing with Georgina. She'd closed her eyes, her head resting on his shoulder. And his expression said it all. He was enjoying having her in his arms.

"Let them talk, Jonas." He'd witnessed too much death and dying up close and personal to concern himself with gossip. He'd survived being embedded with troops in war zones and had been absolved of being a spy and/or traitor after the publication of his second book by a congressional committee, so chitchat or innuendos were inconsequential to his well-being.

"I hear you, man. I've numbered each of the captions to correspond with the photos and I'm now uploading them to you."

"Thanks, Jonas. Don't forget to send me an invoice so I can pay you."

"You bet."

Langston ended the call, propped his feet on the edge of the desk and stared at the rain sluicing down the windows. The temperatures hinting of an early spring had dropped drastically and it felt more like December than early April.

A light tapping on the door garnered his attention, and lowering his feet, he swiveled in the executive chair to see the middle-aged man who was responsible for advertising. Within days of purchasing the paper, Langston called a staff meeting and advised everyone their position was at risk if the circulation and the number of ads continued to decrease. Randall Stone had become the focus of the meeting because he headed advertising.

"Yes, Randall?

"When do you plan to send the paper to the printer?"

Langston stared at the pale, slender man who'd relocated to London to live with a widow he'd met on the internet. He spent eight years there before deciding that he missed the States *and* Wickham Falls. He returned home, married a divorcée with two adult sons and claimed he was living his best life.

"I'd like to deliver it Wednesday. Why?" If he didn't get the issue to the printer before midnight on Thursdays, then it would be too late to print the paper.

"I'm still waiting for Powell's Easter sale ad. Do you want me to go there in person to pick it up?"

"No, Randall. I'll contact Bruce to find out about the delay." The owner of the department store usually took out a full-page ad for most major holidays.

Randall affected a snappy salute. "Okay."

Langston waited until he was alone to buzz the receptionist. "I'll be out for a while. Please take my messages."

Pulling on a rain poncho he covered his head with a baseball cap and headed for the back staircase to the street level. He didn't mind the cold, heat, or even snow. But there was something about getting drenched that annoyed him. His mother used to tease him saying he was part feline.

He sprinted down the street to Powell's and waited for the automatic doors to open. Other than Ruthie's, the department store was Langston's favorite place to shop. It was stocked with countless items including housewares, party goods, CDs and DVDs, candy, sporting goods, cleaning, beauty and school supplies. Many of the discs in his permanent music and movie collection he'd purchased from Powell's. There weren't many customers in the store, and he attributed that to the weather.

Langston approached a clerk near the checkout counter. "Is Mr. Powell around?"

"No, sir. Mr. Powell is on vacation. His daughter is in the office. Do you want me to page her?"

"Please."

He exchanged a nod of recognition with Dan Jackson as the man slowly walked up and down aisles. The highly trained ex-military sniper had begun a second career when he opened a security and protection business, only hiring former military.

Langston could not stop staring when he saw Georgina make her way to the front of the store. It wasn't the first time he'd observed her not wearing makeup; however, he was shocked to see the bluish circles under her clear brown eyes that made it impossible for him to look away. Even her face was thinner, and she looked as if she hadn't slept in days. He wondered if she wasn't feeling well.

"Are you all right?"

"What happened to good afternoon, Georgi?"

Langston clamped his jaw tightly. She wanted to engage in pleasantries when he wanted answers. He knew he had no right to be concerned about her physical well-being, yet he was. Talking and dancing with Georgina at the fund-raiser was a blatant reminder of what he'd been missing even before his marriage ended. It had taken a while for him to forgive his ex-wife for her duplicity but he eventually realized he'd contributed to her seeking companionship with another man. He'd known of her unresolved childhood issues surrounding abandonment, when they were separated for months, and there were times when she hadn't known whether he was dead or alive.

"Good afternoon," he said between clenched

teeth. "I came to see your father because Randall needs your ad for this week's issue."

Georgina groaned. Her father was responsible for determining which items would go on sale, and then they would sit together to work out the design.

"I'm sorry, Langston, but my father is on vacation and he's not expected back until the end of the week. And that means I'm going to have to select the sale items and design the ad. How soon do you need it?"

"The final copy will have to be at the printer before nine Wednesday night."

She groaned again. "I'll stay after the store closes and work up one for you."

"Are you sure that's what you want to do?"

Georgina stared at Langston as if he'd suddenly taken leave of his senses. He'd come asking for the ad because he was on deadline, while in the same breath was questioning her. "Do you or don't you need the ad?"

"Yes, but not at the expense of you falling on your face. When was the last time you had a restful night's sleep?"

"I don't remember," she said truthfully. "I've been burning the candles at both ends running the store and packing up what I need to move into my new place."

Cupping her elbow, Langston steered her over to a rack with snacks, candy bars and mints. "Are you eating regularly?" he whispered.

"I do when I can."

"I'm coming over after you close to bring you something to eat and to help you with the ad."

"You don't have to do that, Langston. I can get something from Ruthie's."

"I'll get something from Ruthie's or the Den. The choice is yours," he said. There was a hint of finality in his voice.

Georgina glared up at him. "I don't need you taking care of me."

"Someone should, because if you continue burning the candles at both ends you're never going to survive long enough to enjoy your new home. You'll end up in the hospital from exhaustion."

"Why are you so concerned about my health?"

"I'm concerned, Georgi, because I like you. A lot," he added.

She didn't want to believe their spending a few hours together more than two weeks ago had elicited feelings in Langston that had him inviting her to his home and concerned for her well-being. A hint of a smile flitted over her expression of uncertainty. And despite her limited experience with the opposite sex, he was the first man, other than her father, who appeared genuinely interested in her welfare.

"Do you feed all the women you like?" she teased.

"Nah, because there aren't too many women that I like as much as you."

"Why me, Langston?"

He blinked. "Why not you? Do you believe you're unworthy for a man to care about you?"

"Of course not!" Her protest came out much too quickly for Georgina to even believe what she'd just confessed. She was aware she had a lot to offer a man but only if he would take the time to get to know and understand her and not relate to her as Powell's girl or daughter. She also wondered if they would get to see her differently once she left the department store to start up her own business.

"Good. Now, let me know what you'd like to eat, and I'll bring it by after seven."

Georgina knew it was futile to argue with Langston. Not when anyone within earshot could overhear them. "Surprise me. Send me a text and I'll come and open the back door."

He smiled, bringing her gaze to linger on his mouth. "Now, that wasn't so difficult, was it?"

She smiled when she didn't want to. "Now, go so I can finish some paperwork before I decide what to put on sale."

Langston sobered. "Do you feel safe staying here alone after the store closes?"

"Yes. I'll arm the alarm, which is wired directly to the sheriff's office."

"That's good to know."

Georgina stared at Langston's departing figure and when she looked at the two women at checkout she realized they also had been staring at him.

Girls in their neighborhood had always flirted with him, but to their disappointment he related to them like he had his sister. There was little or no interaction between her and Langston because he was older than she was. She and his sister Jacklyn shared a few classes but somehow, they never connected. Georgina had become fast friends with Sasha Manning, where they trusted each other with their heartfelt secrets.

She'd looked forward to leaving Wickham Falls to attend art school, while Sasha couldn't wait to graduate to escape her parents' dysfunctional relationship. Her friend left and returned as a successful pastry chef to open her own bakeshop, while Georgina had stayed and was now looking forward to opening her craft shop.

She walked up and down aisles searching for items to discount for sale. Easter was late this year and while they traditionally discounted Easter-themed candy after the holiday, Georgina decided to advertise them as pre-holiday items. She would further cut the price of chocolate bunnies, jellybeans and Peeps until they exhausted their inventory.

The success of the store came from the dedication of longtime employees. Many were hired within days of graduating high school, and elected to stay because of paid vacation and sick leave, and merit-based raises. Bruce had a policy that if you treated people well, then they would become loyal workers. The store opened at nine and closed at seven Monday through Saturday, and from noon to six on Sundays. And in keeping with the town's tradition that everyone should be given the opportunity to participate in the three-day Fourth of July celebration, shopkeepers were given the option of closing one day out of the three. Last year Bruce had closed for all three because the Fourth fell on a Friday, and reopened on Monday.

The Fourth of July and the Fall Frolic festivities were her favorite holidays, and even if she'd moved away, Georgina knew she would return to the Falls year after year to celebrate with her townspeople. She took out her phone from the pocket of her smock and snapped photos of the sale items, and went back to her office to finish what she'd been working on before Langston arrived.

She consciously tried not to think about him, because when she did she'd found herself distracted as she recalled what it felt like to be in his arms when they'd danced together. Then there was the way that he stared at her as if he could see beyond the fragile veneer of confidence she worked hard to project whenever she found herself in the presence of a man to whom she was attracted.

Georgina had convinced herself that becoming involved with Langston would prove detrimental to her emotional stability because she couldn't afford to be distracted by romantic notions, and he was much too attractive and virile to ignore for long periods of time. He was the total package: looks, intelligence and professionally successful.

She knew he was interested in her, but if she could keep him at bay until she felt confident that her business was viable, then she would be more than willing to become involved with him.

Georgina met the stockroom boy as he handed her a packing slip for a shipment of paper goods. "I checked off everything, Miss Powell."

"Thank you, Justin." Her father had hired the high school senior to work from three to closing. He proved to be a reliable employee, arriving on time to unpack boxes and stock shelves.

Every barcode was scanned into the computerized cash registers, and twice a week Georgina checked the inventory to determine which items needed to be reordered. Now that she looked back, she realized working full-time at the store for fourteen years had given her the experience and acumen needed to operate her own enterprise.

A ringtone on her cell phone indicated Georgina had a text message. Langston was at the back door. Everyone left minutes before seven and she'd locked the automatic front doors and activated the security gate that protected the interior of the property from intruders, and then set the alarm. There had been a time when the janitorial service arrived once the store closed, but Bruce had arranged for them to come between the hours of eight and nine to clean up because he hadn't wanted to stay behind to monitor them. They were bonded by their employer but that hadn't stopped the theft of housewares and small appliances. He canceled his contract with the company and hired a local man who'd retired as a custodian for the school system who now came in every morning to sweep the floors, clean the bathrooms and bag the trash and garbage.

Georgina punched in the code for the alarm and opened the door. Langston's slicker was drenched. It hadn't stopped raining. "Come in and dry off."

"I don't like getting wet."

She waited for him to walk in to close the door and rearm the system. "Why? Because you're so sweet you might melt like brown sugar?" she teased.

Langston set two shopping bags stamped with Ruthie's logo on the floor, then lowered his head and brushed his mouth over hers, deepening the kiss until she pushed against his chest. "Tell me, Sleepy Beauty. Am I sweet enough?"

Laughing, Georgina swatted at him as if he were an annoying insect. He reached for her again and she managed to sidestep him. "It's not Sleepy, but Sleeping Beauty. What happened to me being Cinderella?"

Winking at her, he picked up the bags. "You're that, too. You admit that you haven't had much sleep, so the prince thought he'd wake you up with a kiss."

He wanted to continue to kiss her, and she'd stopped him because she wasn't ready for whatever Langston would want from her. Would kisses be enough for him or would he want more? And if he did, then she wasn't ready for the more, which to her translated into them perhaps sleeping together.

She gave him a sidelong glance as she led the way to the break room. "But he only kisses her to wake her from the spell in which she would sleep for a hundred years."

"You really know your fairy tales, don't you?"

Georgina flashed a sexy smile. "You're not the only one whose mother read them fairy tales. But as I got older, I realized some of them were very scary with wolves attempting to eat little pigs, Red Riding Hood, and they are also filled with wicked witches and jealous stepmothers."

"I never thought of them like that." Langston paused. "Are you saying that if you have children you won't read fairy tales to them?"

Having children was something Georgina did not consciously think about. First, she had to get her life together before bringing another one into the world. "I probably will because kids nowadays aren't frightened of too many things. There are animated movies about friendly monsters, so I doubt if the characters from fairy tales will bother them. What I really like are nursery rhymes and stories from the Little Golden Books." Georgina smiled when she recalled happier days before she'd started school when her mother would allow her to crawl into bed with her, and she would beg Evelyn to read to her. "By the way, how much did you order?" she asked, deftly changing the topic from children.

Langston rested the bags on a folding chair and then removed his slicker and cap, hanging both on hooks attached to the wall. "Enough for tonight and leftovers for several days."

Georgina opened an overhead cabinet and took out plates, glasses and two bottles of water from the refrigerator. By the time she'd set the table, Langston had removed containers with roast chicken, steamed green beans, broccoli, carrots, rice, mashed potatoes, pickled beets, caprese and fried shrimp.

His head popped up. "There's chicken pot pie, beef stew, fried chicken and corn on the cob in the other bag."

"There's no way I'm going to be able to eat all this food even if I have it for breakfast, lunch and dinner. You're going to have to take some home with you."

"Are you going to come over and share it with me?" he asked.

Georgina bit her lip to smother a smile. "What's with you trying to get me to come to your house?"

Langston sobered. "I don't like eating alone."

"You need a girlfriend." The suggestion was out before Georgina could censor herself.

Langston lowered his eyes. Georgina had just verbalized what he'd been contemplating for several months now. He hadn't had a girlfriend since coming back to Wickham Falls, even though he'd dated a few women since his divorce yet hadn't felt at the time that he was ready for a relationship because his life wasn't exactly stable. He hadn't been certain whether he would continue to work for the television station but once he was subpoenaed to meet behind closed doors with a congressional committee about his book, Langston had had enough of reporting on wars, navigating DC rush-hour traffic and repeated requests to name his sources.

"You're probably right," he said after a pregnant pause. "Do you know any candidates?"

"Nope. But if I think of someone, I'll let you know. Should she have any particular qualities?"

Langston waited for Georgina to serve herself, then he served himself. "I prefer she be between the ages of thirty and forty. Her physical appearance isn't a deal breaker, but I would like her to be able to hold an intelligent conversation without her repeating the word *like* ten times in a sentence."

Georgina laughed. She knew exactly what he was talking about, because she'd noticed people peppering their speech with the word when making comparisons. "Anything else?"

"She should prefer men."

"What about dogs and kids?"

"I like dogs and kids, but not particularly in that

order," he said. "I'm less enthusiastic when it comes to cats. I have a friend who has the cat from hell. Every time I'd visit his house, that little furry sucker would come up behind me and rake a paw over the back of my head. I'm certain if I shave my head you'd see scars from her claws."

"What did you do to him?"

"It was a queen, and her name is Precious. But she was anything but precious, and I didn't do anything to her. She just didn't like me."

"That's where we differ, Langston. I happen to like cats because they are quiet and independent."

He speared a forkful of beets. "You like cats and I prefer dogs. Does this mean you are not in the running?"

"That's exactly what I'm saying, Mr. Cooper."

"What if I decide to take a liking to cats?"

Georgina shook her head. "Oh no, Langston. You're not going to pretend to like cats on my account. And besides, I don't have time for a boyfriend."

"Why not, Georgi?"

"Because right now I have much too much on my plate. I work seven days every other week, I'm moving and I'm working on samples to exhibit once I open my shop." Georgina closed her eyes, groaning. "Oops! I shouldn't have said that," she whispered.

Langston realized she'd made a faux pas, but it was too late for her to retract it. "You're going into business for yourself." The question was a statement. She opened her eyes, nodding. "Do you want to tell me about it?"

She exhaled a breath. "Only if it doesn't go beyond this room."

He gave her a long stare. "Any and everything you tell me is off the record."

Chapter Five

Georgina didn't want to believe a slip of the tongue would result in her revealing her plans to a man who made a living disseminating information. But she had to trust him, because he'd given his word. He would keep her secret.

"I decided to go into business for myself once my father downsized and then eliminated the store's arts and crafts section. I boxed up all of the merchandise and rented a storage unit."

"You're that proficient that you'll be able to give instructions?"

"Yes. My grandmother taught me to knit, crochet, quilt and the rudiments of embroidery and needle-point."

Langston's expression brightened. "I remember visiting my maternal grandmother in South Carolina during the summer recess and at the end of the day she'd sit on the porch and knit sweaters for me and my sister. Every Christmas she would send us knitted socks, gloves and scarfs."

"Handmade garments are a dying art, so that's why I want to open a shop catering to those who want to learn, and others that still knit, crochet and quilt."

"Will it be here in the Falls?" Langston asked, and she appeared startled by his query.

"Yes. I discovered there were a few vacant storefronts on Sheridan Street. I've already signed a lease with the landlord and submitted an application to the town's housing department for a permit for occupancy."

"How long do you project you'll have to wait for their approval?"

"I was told two months. What I don't understand, Langston, is why it takes so long for the town council to approve startups."

"There's a lot of bureaucratic red tape involved with a new company because of an intensive background investigation. I went through the same thing when I offered to buy the paper. What the council doesn't want is for someone to use a business as a front for illegal activity. Before I left for college I'd overheard my parents talking about the guy who'd opened the shoe store to launder money for a cousin who was trafficking in drugs and needed somewhere to hide his money. The IRS caught up with him when it was apparent he was depositing a lot more money than his reported income, and that alerted the mayor and the members of the town council so they decided not to fast-forward any future applications for new businesses."

Georgina angled her head. "I do remember the notice posted on his door because of a tax lien, but I can assure you I will not be laundering money for anyone."

"Do you feel confident running your own business?"

Georgina gave him a death stare. Did he believe because she was a woman she would fail? "What do you think I've been doing the past fourteen years? I can tell you off the top of my head every piece of merchandise we stock in this store. I'm also familiar with accounts payable and receivables, payroll and employee benefits. Every item has been scanned digitally with a barcode and I've developed a computerized inventory program with alerts when to reorder. So to answer your question, yes, Langston. I feel very confident running my own business."

He held up both hands in supplication. "I'm sorry it came out like that. What I meant to ask is do you think you'll get enough customers for it to remain viable?"

Her attitude changed, becoming more conciliatory. "Yes. When we had the arts and crafts section in the store they sold well, but then my dad decided to expand sporting goods with the increasing popularity of soccer. And there's talk the school's athletics department is forming a soccer team."

"How does he feel about you leaving Powell's?"

"He doesn't know yet."

"What!"

Georgina bit back a smile. Langston looked as if he'd been stabbed by a sharp object. "I'll let him know once my permit is approved."

"But doesn't he depend on you to help him manage the store?"

"Yes, but I'm not going to leave him without a backup, Langston. I've asked my cousin Sutton Reed to take over for me."

Langston leaned forward. "Has he agreed?"

This time she did laugh when she saw excitement light up his eyes. "Yes."

"Hot damn! Your father better get prepared for the groupies hanging around just to get a glimpse of Sutton."

Maybe because he was her cousin Georgina did not see Sutton like that. Yes, he was gorgeous, a baseball phenom who'd become rookie of the year, won several gold gloves and a batting crown title, World Series ring and two homerun derbies. His image had also appeared on several sports magazines during his celebrated career. He'd married his college sweetheart, but the union ended due to irreconcilable differences after eight years.

"I'm certain Dad won't mind more traffic if it translates into higher sales."

Langston smiled. "Whatever works. Maybe after he's settled in, can you ask him if he's amenable for me to interview him for the 'Who's Who' column?"

Georgina nodded, smiling. The media loved Sutton because not only did he make himself available to them, but he was also extremely photogenic and articulate. "Of course."

"When do you expect him to come back?"

"Not for another month. He's waiting to close on his Atlanta condo." Whenever Sutton returned to the Falls to visit with his aunt Evelyn, her mother came alive, lavishing him with attention.

Several minutes of silence passed before Langston said, "If you didn't work here, would you have left the Falls like so many other kids when they graduate high school?"

"Like yourself?"

He stared at his plate. "Yes, like myself." His head popped up. "Once I was hired as an intern at the news station, I couldn't come back because there was no way I could compare working for a local paper to an award-winning all-news cable network."

Georgina took a sip of water, meeting Langston's

eyes over the top of the bottle. "If I'd had a choice I would've left to go to art school."

His eyebrows lifted. "You wanted to be an artist?"

"An illustrator," she corrected. "I wanted to go into animation. The other alternative was to become a court artist."

"Why didn't you?"

"My brother died."

Langston sat straight. "How did that stop you from going to art school?"

She took another sip of water, and then told him about how Kevin's passing had impacted her family, watching intently as myriad expressions crossed his features. "My mother agreeing to go to Hawaii for a couple of weeks shocked me and Dad. I'm certain my decision to move out temporarily jolted her out of her malaise, but knowing Mom it may not last long. She has good and bad days."

"Do you believe she'll come back to work here?"

"I don't know," Georgina said. "I suppose we're going to take it one day at a time. I never had a child, so I don't know what it is to lose one, but I'd believed my mother would eventually accept the fact that Kevin was gone and never coming back."

"Grief affects everyone differently. Whether it's losing a loved one, or a divorce, those who are involved will never be the same."

"Please don't get me wrong, Langston. I miss my brother and there isn't a day when I don't think about him, and while it took me a long time, I had to re-sign myself to the fact that he wasn't coming back." Georgina didn't want to talk about her brother or the impact of his death on her family, when it appeared as if a modicum of healing had begun with her pronouncement that she was moving out. Now Evelyn would be forced to lean on her husband for companionship and emotional support rather than her daughter.

"Do you still draw?"

She didn't know why, but Georgina felt as if Langston was interviewing her for his "Who's Who" column as he continued with his questioning. However, he'd promised everything she told him was off the record—none of which would appear in the bi-weekly.

"No. It's been years since I've picked up a sketch pad. I did a lot of sketching when I was on the high school's newspaper committee. If you search the archives, you will see some of my caricatures."

"You must have joined the newspaper club after I'd graduated."

"I did," she confirmed. "I waited until my junior year to get involved. But I must admit as the former editor of *The Mountaineer* you were a tough act to follow. Mr. Murray reminded us constantly that you had set a high bar when you were the editor, and that some of our articles were so sophomoric that he was ashamed to put out the issue."

"Murray fashioned himself a slave driver. He said the same thing to me and the others in the newspaper club, and it wasn't until I got into journalism school that I realized he was a pussycat compared to some of my professors."

Propping her elbow on the table, Georgina rested her chin on the heel of her hand. "Don't be so modest, Langston. I'd read some of your articles and they were exceptional. Just accept that you're a gifted writer. And when news of your first book was published, Dad ordered several cartons and convinced everyone who came into the store to buy a copy."

"I'd heard he was offering a fifteen percent discount on their total purchases if they bought the book."

Georgina made a sucking sound with her tongue and teeth. "Whatever works. I'm certain we sold enough copies to boost your sales, so you were able to make a bestseller list. You can't say the Falls' folks don't stick together."

"That was one of the several reasons why I'd decided to come back here to live."

"Why did you come back?" Georgina asked him.

Langston chose his words carefully when he said, "I wanted to go to bed and not wake up to the sounds of honking horns, the wailing sirens from emergency vehicles, explosions or the exchange of gunfire. I believed I'd gotten used to the noise and hustle of New

York City when I went to college, but it was nothing compared to covering a war as a correspondent."

Georgina lowered her arm. "How long were your assignments?"

"Too long, Georgi. Now I know how soldiers feel when they're deployed. The only thing you look forward to is the next sunrise."

She blinked slowly. "Do you have PTSD?"

Langston stared over her shoulder at the countertop with a microwave, single-serve coffeemaker and toaster oven. "Yes."

"Have you seen a therapist?"

"Yes," he repeated. "The flashbacks don't occur as often as they had in the past. I've had only two since I've been back."

"Hopefully, one day they'll disappear completely." There was a hint of wistfulness in her voice.

"That's what I'm hoping," he said, although he doubted whether certain atrocities he'd witnessed he would ever forget.

"You stay and finish your dinner while I pull up an ad for you."

"Do you need my assistance?"

She stood. "I don't think so. I save all of our ads on the computer so I just have to find a file with Easter items and revise or update it."

Langston rose with her. "If you don't mind, I'll clean up here."

"I don't mind. Just scrape and rinse the dishes before you put them in the dishwasher."

"Yes, ma'am."

He waited for Georgina to leave to clear the table. It was the second time they'd spent time together and just her presence reminded him how long it had been since he was able to have an intelligent conversation with a woman with whom he'd found himself interested.

When she'd suggested he get a girlfriend his intent was to tell her she would be his first choice. Langston told her a woman's looks did not matter because he didn't want her to think of him as shallow.

He was transfixed by Georgina's bare face with a sprinkling of freckles across her nose and her hair fashioned in a single braid, and equally enthralled with the transformation with a subtle cover of makeup and the absence of curls in a sophisticated twist.

She'd shocked him when she'd revealed she was opening a business in the Falls. Georgina would become the second woman in less than six months who would become a business owner, of which there were too few in a town of more than four thousand residents.

Dr. Henry Franklin retired from his family practice and it was now run by Philadelphia transplant Dr. Natalia Hawkins-Collier. Pastry chef Sasha Manning had returned home to open Sasha's Sweet

Shoppe to much success. Bessie Daniels owned Perfect Tresses, and now Georgina would be added to the list of women business owners when she opened her craft shop.

He'd left Wickham Falls at eighteen to attend college and had returned at thirty-six and only a few things had changed during his absence. His parents retired, sold the pharmacy and moved permanently to their Key West vacation home.

His parents said repeatedly that they had the best boss in the world—themselves. After graduating with degrees in pharmacology, his father went to work in a hospital pharmacy, while his mother got a position with a chain store pharmacy. After several years they'd decided to go into business for themselves, which allowed them to make their own hours and control their future. It had taken Langston many more years than his parents had, but he was now his own boss. Jacklyn had also followed in their parents' footsteps when she left teaching to become a writer. He had finished cleaning up the break room at the same time Georgina returned.

She handed him a printout of the ad. "I just downloaded a copy to the paper."

A chuckle rumbled in his chest before it exploded in an unrestrained laugh. "This is incredibly cute." The ad had tiny bunnies, and baby chicks spelling out the department store's logo and bold lettering advertising pre-Easter discounts on candy and decorations.

Georgina flashed a smug grin. "I'm glad you like it."

"Did you design this?"

"Yes."

He gave her a sidelong glance. "I thought you said you didn't sketch anymore."

"I don't. I'm sorry to disappoint you, but I have templates of all kinds of images and I highlight what I want and then transfer them to an ad or flier."

Langston wanted to ask Georgina who was being modest now. Not only did she have an exceptionally creative mind, but she also had an incredible eye for detail. "This is the most eye-catching ad you've sent us."

"Thank you."

"No, Georgi, thank you. You're very talented."

She exhibited what passed for a smile. "Well, this very talented tired shopkeeper is about to head home so she can get some sleep before getting up to come back to this rodeo." Georgina pointed to the containers on the table. "Please take those with you."

"What if I leave them for your employees?"

"What if you don't?" she countered. "The ladies are on restricted diets and I don't want them to accuse me of trying to sabotage them."

"I can't eat all of this food."

"Now you sound like me. What if I come to your

house tomorrow after I close, and I'll help you put a dent in this mini banquet?"

Langston felt as if he'd won a small victory. He hadn't invited Georgina to his house to come on to her but to prove to himself that he could regain a sense of normalcy that had evaded him far too long. Before moving back to the Falls he'd closed himself off from friends and former colleagues who he'd meet after work for happy hour or invite to his condo during football season.

His therapist had recommended he get out of his apartment or invite some of the guys who worked for the station over to watch a game, but he had resisted because he feared having them witness a flashback. None of them were aware he was afflicted with PTSD. Inviting employees to his home was not an option, but Georgina wasn't his employee but someone with whom he felt comfortable enough to be forthcoming.

"Text me and let me know when I should expect you. Now, I'll wait for you to lock up and then we'll leave together."

Georgina did not want to think of going to Langston's house to eat as a date, but based on her experience with men it was to her. She couldn't keep a steady boyfriend once they discovered she still lived with her parents. Her relationship with Sean was the exception because she always drove to Beckley to see him. Perhaps she'd been naive when she had overlooked the signs that told her Sean wasn't what he presented. Most times he paid for their dates, but occasionally, he'd claim he'd overspent and asked her to cover the check. However annoying, it hadn't happened so often that alarm bells went off in her head that her boyfriend had a problem managing his finances. She'd continued to see him because he'd charmed her parents, and her father liked the fact that she was dating a man whose family was also successful business owners.

They'd even talked about marriage and debating where they would live while both continued to oversee their respective family enterprises; her so-called fairy-tale romance ended abruptly when Sean called her in a panic, begging her to meet him at his house later that night.

She'd driven to Beckley, her pulse pounding an accelerated rhythm as she tried imagining what had upset him. Once he revealed his dilemma Georgina felt as if she'd been stabbed through her heart. The man with whom she'd fallen in love and contemplated marriage was addicted to gambling. He'd pleaded with her to lend him the money because not only did he need to cover the fifteen thousand he'd embezzled from the dealership, but he also owed his bookie more than five thousand dollars. She'd experienced twin emotions of shock and disappointment. Shocked that she'd fallen in love with a gambler, and disappointed that yet again a man was only interested in her bank balance.

Although she did not regard herself as wealthy, she was far from being labeled a pauper. She lived at home, and therefore she did not have to pay for housing; her closet wasn't filled with designer labels because her social life was nonexistent. And her only big-ticket item was an automobile, which she never financed. Georgina knew it was the future possibility of her assuming complete control of Powell's that had folks viewing her as the golden goose.

She'd shown no emotion when she wished Sean luck and if his bookie followed through with his threat then she was certain his mother would let her know where to send flowers: to the hospital or funeral home. However, she did promise him that she wouldn't tell anyone about his addiction. Georgina returned to Wickham Falls devastated and told her mother why she'd decided to break up with Sean. Evelyn claimed it was all for the best, and that she would get over his duplicity faster by throwing all her energies into Powell's.

Georgina removed her smock, leaving it on a coatrack, and left her office. She approached longtime employee Diana Kelly. "Mrs. Kelly, I have to leave for a while, so I'd like you to cover the front for me."

The middle-aged grandmother's quick smile and friendly greeting to everyone who came into Powell's had made her a favorite go-to clerk and an invaluable employee. "Of course, sweetie." Everyone was *sweetie* to the petite, dark-skinned woman with short, natural hair.

Georgina chided herself for not putting on a jacket over her long-sleeve tee when she left the store and walked along Main Street to Sasha's Sweet Shoppe. The rain had finally stopped but not even the bright spring sunlight could dispel the unseasonal chill in the air. She quickened her pace and opened the door to the bakeshop, the bell chiming and announcing someone had come in. Within seconds Charlotte Manning came from the rear of the store. Charlotte had stepped in to help her daughter when she volunteered to manage the bakeshop for the morning shift, while Kiera Adams, the dentist's teenage daughter, worked the afternoons.

"What brings you in so early?" Charlotte Manning asked, smiling. The widowed, fifty-something woman with silvered blond hair and brilliant blue eyes hadn't lost any of her youthful beauty.

"I came to ask Sasha for advice about what type of dessert I could bring to someone's home for dinner."

"Go on back. Right now Sasha is decorating cupcakes."

Although she and Sasha shared many classes in high school, their friendship did not extend to sleepovers. Sasha had confided to her that her parents argued constantly, and she wanted what went on in the Manning household to remain behind closed doors; all three Manning kids left home within weeks of graduating.

"Hey, friend," Georgina crooned when Sasha's net-covered head popped up. "Oh, my word! Those decorations are awesome!"

Sasha set down the piping bag and removed a pair of disposable gloves. "I use Russian piping tips to create leaves and colorful flowers. I'm able to decorate dozens in less than a half hour."

"They look too pretty to eat." Delicate green leaves surrounded circles of vibrant pink and red roses.

"I try to take them to the next level."

"You more than try, Sasha. Everyone's talking about the deliciousness coming out of this shop and I can see why. It's like Willie Wonka's. Instead of chocolate it's cupcakes and cookies."

Sasha sat on a stool and patted the one next to her. "Sit down, Georgi, and tell me what you want."

She stared at the naturally curly strawberry-blond woman with emerald-green eyes, silently admiring her friend who'd turned heads at the Chamber fund-raiser. Georgina knew it wasn't only from what she'd been wearing but also because she'd attended as Dwight Adams's date.

"I know this is short notice, but I'm going to someone's home for dinner tonight, and I'd like a suggestion what I can bring as dessert."

Sasha pushed her hands into the pockets of the pink smock. "How many people will be at the dinner?"

"Just two."

A smile played at the corners of the chef's mouth. "Should I assume the other person is a man?"

Georgina smiled. "Yes. It's Langston Cooper."

Throwing back her head, Sasha laughed loudly. "When I saw you two together at the fund-raiser, I told Dwight that Langston was—what's the word they use in romance novels when the hero falls hard for the heroine?"

"Besotted."

Sasha snapped her fingers. "Yes, that's it. He was totally besotted with you."

Georgina wanted to tell her friend she was wrong. Although he'd given her a chaste kiss and alluded to her becoming his possible girlfriend, she didn't get the vibe that he was serious. "And Dr. Adams isn't besotted with you?" she countered.

"No. Our only connection is that his daughter works for me."

"If you say so, Sasha."

"You don't believe me?"

"No, I don't. You haven't been back long enough to know that a lot of women are willing to give up their eyeteeth to get Dwight Adams to notice them."

Sasha laughed again. "I can't believe you have dentist jokes." She sobered. "Now, back to you and Langston. What are you looking for?"

"Something that is not too sweet."

"I can put together a box of miniature red velvet brownies and petit fours."

Georgina passed her palms together. "That sounds perfect. How much do I owe you?"

"Nothing," Sasha said as she slipped off the stool. "I don't charge my friends for their first order. The exception is a wedding cake."

"Bite your tongue, my friend. You know I'm no-where ready to become someone's wife. Thanks to you, I'm planning to move into my own place, and it will be the first time in my life that I'll be totally on my own." Smiling, she stood. "And right now I'm a little too selfish to share me with anyone on a permanent basis."

"You don't have to thank me, Georgi. Don't forget I cried on your shoulder every week about what was going on in my home when we were in school together. You were the one who told me that I had options. That I could enlist in the military or find a position in another city or state."

Sasha had taken her advice and left Wickham Falls; she'd enrolled in culinary school, becoming a pastry chef, then a contestant in a televised baking competition, which set the stage for her baking for celebrities, and she'd also married A-list country superstar Grant Richards. Now Sasha had come full circle. She'd relocated from Nashville after divorcing her husband to start over in Wickham Falls.

"I'll come over later to pick it up."

"Don't bother, Georgi. I'll have my mother drop it off at the end of her shift."

Georgina hugged Sasha. "We have to get together whenever I'm settled in my new digs."

Sasha pressed her cheek to Georgina's. "That's a bet."

She returned to Powell's, thanked Mrs. Kelly for filling in for her and answered a customer's question about which mandolin was best for zesting. Aside from the arts and crafts section, she liked housewares best, and Georgina was looking forward to the time when she would be able to prepare her own meals in the guesthouse kitchen.

The morning and afternoon passed quickly and when the programmed recorded announcement echoed through the store it would be closing in ten minutes, Georgina knew she had to get home, shower and dress for her dinner date with Langston.

Chapter Six

Langston stood on the porch, waiting for Georgina's arrival. She'd sent him a text indicating she was on her way. Although they lived within walking distance, he rarely got to see Georgina when they were growing up, and he attributed that to the four-year difference in their ages. She and his sister shared several classes, however they never connected to become more than classmates.

Headlights swept over other cars parked in the cul-de-sac and he smiled when her off-white SUV came closer. Coming down off the porch, Langston motioned for Georgina to park behind the classic Mustang that had once belonged to his father. Over the years, Annette Cooper had accused her husband of loving the muscle car more than her and any of their children and had convinced him to gift it to Langston rather than transport the vehicle to Florida. Langston had contacted Jesse Austen, who owned and operated the only auto repair shop in Wickham Falls for decades, to tow the car to his garage for a complete overhaul. And the result was the forty-year-old vehicle ran like new.

He opened the driver's-side door after Georgina came to a complete stop and cut off the engine. A smile softened his features when she placed her palm on his as he assisted her down. A ponytail had replaced the ubiquitous braid, a cascade of curls floating halfway down her back over a ruffled white silk blouse. He thought she looked incredibly feminine in the blouse she'd paired with stretchy black slacks and matching ballet flats. Langston inhaled her perfume, a scent that had lingered with him hours after the fund-raiser ended, and he'd found the fragrance as unique as its wearer. It wasn't flowery, but slightly woodsy with notes of patchouli and vanilla.

He dipped his head and pressed a kiss to her cheek. "Thank you for coming."

"Thank you for the invite."

Georgina's smoky voice caressed his ear, reminding him why he liked talking with her. The timbre was low, hypnotic and controlled. Even when annoyed, her tone did not change.

"I decided to change the menu."

"To what?" she asked.

"Come inside and you'll see."

"I brought dessert. It's on the passenger seat."

Langston rested a hand at the small of her back. "I'll get it. Please go inside, Georgi. I've got this."

Georgina walked up the porch steps and into the house where Langston and his sister Jacklyn had grown up. The farmhouse style was like hers and others in the upscale neighborhood designed by the same architect/builder nearly fifty years ago. All two-story structures were advertised with four bedrooms, three baths, formal living and dining rooms, full basement, two-car garages and wraparound porches. Unlike her house, the Cooper property was in a cul-de-sac with no access for through traffic.

Growing up she'd found it odd that the residents in the enclave usually kept to themselves. The exception was when someone passed away, then they all came together to support the survivors. They preferred joining local civic organizations when it came to socializing with one another. Georgina's mother had participated in the church's semiannual food drive, Toys for Tots and had been an active member in the Chamber of Commerce. After burying Kevin, she rarely left the house, and when she did it was to sporadically attend church services or drop by the store. Georgina wished her father had told her sooner, rather than later, about her mother's inability to have more children, which would've made Evelyn's behavior much more tolerable.

The entryway appeared to be a desert oasis with tables of varying heights cradling decorative pots filled with a variety of succulents. Bright red flowers sprouted from the saguaro in a large copper planter. She felt the heat from Langston's body as he came up behind her.

"How often do you water these beauties?"

"Once a month. These were my mother's pride and joy and she wanted to take them with her to Florida, but Dad talked her out of it because the bungalow is very small. It's no bigger than a studio apartment I'd once rented in New York City. By the way, you didn't need to bring dessert, but I'm not going to refuse anything that comes from Sasha's patisserie."

Georgina smiled at Langston over her shoulder. "Did you know she wanted to call the bakeshop Sasha's Patisserie, but decided against it because she thought most folks wouldn't understand what the word meant?"

"We mountaineers aren't that uninformed," Langston said defensively.

"Please, don't get me wrong, Langston, because as a fellow mountaineer we definitely aren't ignorant. You know what patisserie means because you've spent at least half your life traveling to different countries, while many from the Falls have barely left the state."

Langston reached for her hand. "One of these days I'll tell you about some of the countries I've visited."

"Was it for work?"

"Not all of them. There were some countries I always wanted to see, and being stationed abroad made it easier to take side trips."

Georgina entered the living room and saw first-hand why the Coopers had decided to retire to Key West, Florida. As a student of art, she recognized Caribbean island influences with rich mahogany carved pieces, a mixing of rattan and woven furniture, with an emphasis on plants. The influence stemming from France, Spain, Holland and Demark, all vying for control of the many islands, was apparent in the furnishings in the formal dining room with a Regency-style table with Jamaican rope-style legs. The table was set for two with plates, silver and crystal.

"Your home is beautiful." She couldn't hide the awe in her voice.

"I'll let Mom know you admire her decorating skill."

Georgina wanted to tell Langston that his mother's decorating skill went beyond someone who knew what she liked. The items she'd chosen to decorate her home were comparable to those selected by professional interior decorators. "Did it bother her that she had to leave all this when she relocated?"

Langston nodded. "Yes. Dad used to call me several times a week complaining that Mom wanted to sell the Key West bungalow and buy a larger house so she could transport the furniture in this place to their new residence. There was no way Dad was going to trade one four-bedroom house for another at his age. The impasse ended when I told him once I sold my DC condo I'd buy this house and with the furnishings, which pacified Mom. Decorating the rooms in this house had become her passion, and whenever she had time off she would call antiques shops to ask if they had a particular lamp, table or bed."

"With her eye for detail, she definitely could have a second career as a decorator."

Langston laughed softly. "After forty years as a pharmacist, all my mother wants to do is kick back and relax. She and Dad are so laidback that they don't have any clocks in the house. They even turned off the one on the microwave."

"Do you intend to follow in their footsteps once you retire, Langston?"

"I don't know. I'm thirty-six, so I have at least another thirty years before I can plan for my retirement. What about you, Georgi? Have you thought about what you'd like to do once you retire?"

Turning, Georgina looked up at Langston staring down at her. Wearing flats made her aware of the differences in their heights. She stood five six in bare feet, and he towered over her by at least another six inches. "After coming back from vacationing in some exotic locale where the only strenuous thing I'd have to do is raise my hand for a waiter to bring me more food and drink, I'd sit on the porch knitting sweaters and hats for my grandchildren."

Throwing back his head, Langston laughed with abandon. "Now that sounds as if you're not going to exert much energy whether on vacation or sitting on the porch," he teased.

"That's because I'm going to put all of my energy into running my business, where I will be entitled to take it easy once I decide to retire."

"Should I assume marriage and children will figure into your equation?"

Georgina shrugged her shoulders under the frilly blouse. "If it happens, Langston. And if it doesn't, then it's not going to be the end of the world for me. A lot of women go through life unmarried and childless and live wonderful, fulfilled lives."

"You're right about that," he said in agreement. "I've worked with a lot of women who prefer career to marriage and motherhood."

"Do you admire them for that?" Georgina questioned.

"Whether I do or don't is irrelevant. I believe because we all have an expiration date, folks should do whatever they want, because life can be totally unpredictable and to wait may not be best for them."

"Do you want to get married again, and maybe this time have children?"

His mother had asked him the same question and he'd told her no, because at the time his head was so mixed up, he hadn't known what he wanted to do at that moment or even the next day. But Georgina wasn't his mother and he was now in a better place mentally and emotionally.

"I've been thinking about it."

"How long do you plan to think about, Langston? Either you do or you don't."

Suddenly, he felt as if he was being cross-examined about something of which he had no knowledge. "I do." The two words came out unbidden.

Georgina patted his shoulder. "There you go. That wasn't so difficult to admit."

His eyebrows lifted slightly. "Are you in the running to become Mrs. Langston Wayne Cooper?"

"Surely you jest, Langston. I told you before I don't have time for a boyfriend and even less for a husband."

"But you're not opposed to marriage?"

She frowned. "I never said I didn't want to get married. Just not now."

Langston realized now that she was taking control of her life she would be more amenable to the things women her age wanted and looked forward to experiencing. He put his arm around her waist. "Come with me to the kitchen and I'll show you what I've prepared for dinner."

"What about the food from Ruthie's?" she asked.

"It will keep. I put them in vacuum-sealed bags that will go from the freezer to boiling water."

"You're really domesticated, aren't you?"

He winked at her. "You don't know the half."

Georgina let out an audible gasp when she saw the tray of ravioli on a parchment-covered cookie sheet. "You made ravioli."

Langston set the small white box stamped with tiny cupcakes on the countertop. "You said you like them, so I decided they would be better than eating leftovers."

Going on tiptoe, Georgina brushed a kiss over his mouth. "Thank you."

"You're most welcome."

"Where did you learn to make them?"

"That's a long story, Georgi."

"Well, we have until midnight before I have to leave, so I'm all ears."

Langston dropped a kiss on her curly hair when he wanted to kiss her mouth, if only to let her know of his deepening feelings for her. He'd told himself that he liked Georgina Powell, when in truth what he was beginning to experience went beyond a liking to wanting to spend uninterrupted hours with her, telling her things he had never told any other woman, including his ex-wife, because she'd proven not to be judgmental. When he'd admitted to experiencing PTSD, she hadn't asked him about his flashbacks but whether he had sought a therapist. He'd encountered worldly women, from every walk of life, some who interested him and others he couldn't wait to get away from. What he'd found ironic was he had to come back to his hometown to find himself attracted to one who appealed to something deep inside him. Under the veneer of being a world traveler and bestselling author, he was still a small-town dude who needed a woman similar to him in which to live his best life.

"I'll tell you everything over dinner."

Georgina sat across the table from Langston as she ate melt-in-the mouth little pockets of homemade pasta filled with butternut squash, Asian-infused shrimp, pork and spinach with feta in a delicious vodka sauce. He'd grilled marinated rib lamb chops and the seasonings of finely minced garlic and mint tantalized her palate. A mixed green salad with a ginger balsamic vinaigrette complemented the meat and pasta dishes. She'd drunk sparkling water in lieu of wine because she feared sleeping past the time when she had to get up in time to open the store.

"You missed your calling, Langston. You should've become a chef rather than a journalist."

Light from an overhead chandelier reflected off the sprinkling of gray in his cropped hair. "It was because I wanted to become a journalist that I learned to cook, not the other way around."

"I noticed a lot of Asian spices in the ravioli."

"That's because one of my college roommates came from China."

"How many roommates did you have?" she asked.

"Two. We'd rented a three-bedroom apartment in a walkway about five blocks from Columbia University. Joe Chen and Nicolas Rossi were exchange students from China and Italy who were also majoring in journalism. We didn't have a lot of money, so we'd pool our money and cook for ourselves. What was ironic was that Joe's and Nicolas's grandmothers had given them recipes of dishes they could make themselves, while my mother gifted me with a cookbook of recipes written by Southern church ladies.

"Nicolas had an aversion to store-bought pasta, so he made his own. And when Joe couldn't find the ingredients he needed for his dishes, we'd all hop on the subway and go downtown to Chinatown. Once I introduced them to Southern cuisine it was all she wrote. The apartment would smell like fried chicken and collard greens, or fried fish and grits for days until we were forced to open the windows when cooking even in the dead of winter."

Georgina smiled at him over the rim of her water glass. "It sounds as if you had a lot of fun."

"At the time I didn't know it would be one of the best times in my life. We were serious students, which meant there wasn't a steady stream of women coming and going at odd hours. Dad would deposit money in my checking account at the end of each month and if I didn't stick to my budget and ran out of money before the next deposit, then I was what you would call assed-out. I did get a part-time job at a Harlem restaurant waiting tables on the weekends and when I affected my best Southern accent the ladies suddenly would become very generous tippers. After a while I had regulars who'd ask for Country's table."

Georgina gave him an incredulous stare. "They called you *Country*?"

"Yes, ma'am."

"Were you flirting with them?"

"I plead the Fifth."

"Langston!"

He laughed. "Don't look so put out."

"Please don't tell me you were a naughty boy."

"The only thing I'm going to admit is that I was just naughty enough to make enough spare change to buy a ticket to a Broadway play or pay the cover charge at a jazz club."

Langston had no idea he'd gone up several points on Georgina's approval scale, because he was willing to work for what he wanted. Although his parents paid his college tuition, his portion of the rent on his Manhattan apartment and extra money for living expenses, he'd wanted more and worked as a waiter to subsidize the more.

"Did you enjoy living in New York?" Georgina asked as she cut into a piece of tender lamb, and then popped it into her mouth. Langston wasn't just good; he was an exceptional cook. It was apparent he and his college roommates ate very well.

"It took some getting used to. Even though we lived on the fourth floor I could still hear traffic and the wail of sirens from emergency vehicles. I was rest broken for the first few weeks before the noise lulled me to sleep. What I really enjoyed was spending the Christmas holiday in the city with all the lights and decorations."

"Do you think you could live there again?"

"No," Langston said without hesitating.

"What about DC?"

His expression changed, becoming a mask of stone. "I don't think I'll ever be able to live in a cosmopolitan city again."

Georgina knew it was time for her to stop probing into Langston's life when she saw hardness settle into his handsome features. It was obvious she'd asked him about something he'd rather not talk about or even forget. "It is apparent you haven't lost any of your cooking skills because dinner is delicious."

Langston inclined his head. "I'm glad you enjoyed it."

"I doubt whatever I'll make can come close to this."

"Why don't you let me be the judge of that?" he countered.

"I hope whenever I invite you over that you won't judge me too harshly."

He stared at her across the space under lowered lids. "If you hung out with your grandmother who taught you to knit and crochet, I'm certain she also taught you to cook."

Georgina touched the napkin to the corners of her mouth. "You're right about that. I loved going to Grandma Dot's house because she always had something simmering on the stove. She believed in making one-pot meals and whenever she made beef stew, pot roast, oxtails with ham hocks, fresh or smoked neck bones, she could count on me staying for dinner. My personal favorite of hers was smothered pork chops."

Langston groaned as if in pain. "Oh no, you didn't say smothered pork chops."

She smiled as he licked lips. "Yes, I did."

Placing a hand over his heart, Langston shook his head. "I haven't had them in *years-s-s*." The last word came out in several syllables. "I've tried to eat healthy, but diet be damned for pork chops with gravy."

"When was the last time you had them?" Georgina asked.

Langston appeared deep in thought. "I can't re-member."

"Are you ready to indulge for old times' sake?"

He narrowed one eye. "What are you hatching in that beautiful head of yours?"

Georgina did not visibly react to his calling her beautiful, because she didn't want to read more into the adjective than necessary. He hadn't only admitted it, but she was able to read between the lines when he'd revealed his intent to turn on the charm with women to earn tips.

"One of these days when I make smothered pork chops, you're welcome to come over and eat to your fill."

Langston pressed his palms together in a prayer-ful gesture. "Thank you."

Georgina had just made it easy for him to see her again. He did not want to come on too strong, turn her off, or pressure her to feel obligated to date him. He still wasn't certain what it was about Georgina, other than her overall physicality, that had drawn him to her, and he could not believe he'd traveled the world, encountered countless beautiful women from all races and ethnic backgrounds, yet he had come home to discover one who'd grown up and still lived literally in his backyard. Langston was aware that he did not have a type when it came to women. The only requisite was the ability to talk to each other.

He and his ex-wife had connected immediately because of her outspokenness. She'd let him know what she thought and felt and that if she hadn't been involved with another man she would've slept with him. Langston was shocked and flattered by her aggressiveness when she asked for his number with a promise that she would contact him once she broke up with her current boyfriend.

He'd forgotten about the aspiring off-Broadway actress until she called him a year later to let him know she was no longer in a relationship. He and Ayanna had been dating for three months when he received an assignment to travel to an African country to cover an upcoming election between a long-time president and a London-educated lawyer who'd returned after being exiled for six years. Langston had proposed marriage, Ayanna accepted and a week later they exchanged vows at a Bronx courthouse with one of her cast mates and his colleague as witnesses.

Covering the election was the first of many overseas assignments once the chief of the cable station's foreign news bureau recalled Langston's facility with languages. He had minored in Middle Eastern languages and had become fluent in Arabic, Farsi, Persian, Urdu, Hebrew and Dari—the most spoken language in Afghanistan. He'd also picked up Mandarin and Italian from his college roommates. When people asked him how he'd become a polyglot, Langston explained that something in his brain switched on when hearing another language other than English and after a while he had the ability to recall enough words and phrases to communicate with the locals. The gift had become a blessing and a curse after he'd published his second novel.

Divorcing Ayanna, resigning his position at the news station, selling his condo and severing ties with his literary agent were now a part of his past. He'd returned to Wickham Falls after a sixteen-year absence, purchased his parents' home, bought the failing biweekly, all with the intent of starting over. And Langston hadn't thought when he was assigned to a table at the Chamber's fund-raiser he would encounter someone with whom he'd rarely exchanged a word and that she would enthrall him as no other woman had, including his ex.

When he'd asked Georgina where she planned to open her shop she seemed almost shocked that he believed she would consider anyplace else. In that instant Langston knew they were kindred spirits. She'd spent her entire life in the Falls, and she did not plan to abandon it when starting up a new business.

He'd come back not to work for a local daily or television station but to attempt to resurrect a biweekly that had been the voice for Wickham Falls for generations. Editors had come and gone; some willing to challenge local government to do their elected duty to right the wrongs, while others pocketed money to circumvent the truth. As the current editor for *The Sentinel*, he owed it to his hometown to only print the truth.

"How much would you charge me if I commissioned you to knit a pullover sweater for my five-year-old nephew?" Langston asked after a comfortable silence.

"It would depend on the type of yarn and how long it would take me to knit it."

"Give me an example."

"If the instructions call for three skeins of bulky yarn at eight dollars per skein, and would take ten hours to knit and complete the garment, then I would charge you two hundred forty dollars."

Langston quickly did the math. "You're saying you'd multiply the cost of the materials by the number of hours to finish the sweater to arrive at the final figure?"

"Yes. The number of hours could vary appreciably if the instructions have a particular pattern with different colors, then of course this would increase the time spent and affect the total fee."

"How much time in advance do you need to knit a garment?"

Georgina's eyes studied him with curious intensity. "Do you want me to knit something for your nephew?"

"I'm thinking about it."

"Don't think too long, Country, because once I

have my grand opening I'm not going to have much free time for private customers."

Biting his lip, Langston slowly shook his head. "Something told me not to tell you about that."

"But you are country, Langston."

"And you're not?" he countered, grinning.

"Heck, yeah," Georgina admitted. "I'm a country girl down to the marrow in my bones, and I'm not ashamed to admit it."

"Well, Miss Country, my nephew will turn six on Halloween and I think he'd love to wear a holiday-themed sweater to school on his birthday."

"You're in luck because I have a book of children's holiday sweaters and I may be able to find one with Halloween. If not, then I'll make up a pattern."

"How would you do that?"

"I use graph paper and color in the boxes to correspond with the different color yarns. I prefer knitting the designs in the garment than appliquéing it. I could also crochet the sweater, which takes less time than knitting, but the flipside is that in crocheting I'll use much more yarn."

Suddenly, Langston saw Georgina's needlework skills in a whole new light. It was a lot more complicated than he thought. "I'll ask my sister what he likes about Halloween and then I'll let you know what she says."

Georgina looked back at him for a long moment and then said, "You're very special, because you'll become my first customer even before I open the front door."

Langston wanted to be special to her for a reason other than he'd asked her to make a handmade sweater. "Do you have a name for your shop?"

Her smile was dazzling. "Yes. It's A Stitch at a Time."

Reaching across the table he extended his fist, and he wasn't disappointed when Georgina gave him a fist bump. "Girl, you're on fire!" Leaning back in her chair, Georgina flashed a smile he interpreted as supreme confidence. She may have been denied going to art school, but with her patience and determination Langston knew instinctually that she was going to become a successful businesswoman.

It was close to ten when Langston walked Georgina to her car and waited for her to drive away. He'd spent more than two delightful hours with her, and again it wasn't enough. He had waited a year before welcoming a woman into what had become his sanctuary and the wait was worth it, because Wickham Falls was too small, and he too recognizable for him to have women coming and going like Union Station.

And once this week's paper was delivered to subscribers the photographs from the fund-raiser would take up the entire centerfold, and he knew tongues would start wagging with the candid photos of his interaction with Georgina. And judging from their smiles and body language they were into each other.

Although he'd told Jonas he did not care if folks talked about him, he did wonder how Georgina would react to the images of them together as what could be interpreted as a romantic couple. Langston couldn't stop people from drawing their own conclusions, yet he didn't want to place Georgina in a position where she would be forced to explain or defend her actions.

He decided to wait until the paper was out and then wait for her to contact him. If she didn't, then neither would he broach the subject.

Chapter Seven

Georgina walked into the kitchen Sunday morning to find her parents sitting in the breakfast nook flipping through back issues of *The Sentinel*. Their flight had landed Friday evening; they complained about experiencing jet lag and went directly to bed and slept through the night and into the following afternoon. It was apparent her father had gotten too much sun as evidenced by the peeling skin on his face and head, while her mother looked rested and content.

"I thought you guys would still be napping," she said, cheerfully.

Bruce smiled at her. "I decided to get up and go into the store today."

"Are you sure that's what you want to do, Dad?" Georgina asked him. Although it was his Sunday to work, she'd decided to step in and give him time to recover from his vacation.

"Yes. It's only six hours and if I hang around the house, I'll go stir-crazy."

Evelyn glanced up over her reading glasses. "Bruce, the store is not going to fall down if you don't go in."

"You tell him, Mom. It didn't fall apart when you guys were gone."

"I'm still going in," Bruce said under his breath as he walked out of the kitchen.

Georgina threw up a hand. "Mom, please talk to your husband."

Evelyn took off her glasses. "I'm going to do better than that. I'm going in with him and when he falls and hits his hard head, I'm going to call the EMTs and tell them to take him to the county hospital for observation. Your daddy doesn't know how to slow down and relax."

She had to agree with Evelyn. Her father ate, slept and breathed Powell's, and he did believe it would fall apart if he wasn't there to oversee it. And Georgina did not want to believe her mother had planned to go into the store. Perhaps going away had given Evelyn time to reflect on how she'd been living her life, cut off from the outside world, while she'd continued to dwell on the past.

"Do you want me to cook something that will last you for a few days?"

Evelyn shook her head. "No. It's been a while since your father and I have gone out for dinner. You've done enough while we were gone, and now it's time for you to relax."

Georgina smiled. "Thanks, Mom."

Now that she didn't have to go to work, she planned to go to the supermarket and shop for groceries to take to the guesthouse. She'd also bought a set of cookware and kitchen utensils she wanted to use when preparing her meals.

Evelyn returned her smile. "I see from the photographs in *The Sentinel* that you and Langston look like a real couple. I'm sorry I didn't get to see you before you left the house, but you are absolutely beautiful in the photos."

"Thank you, Mom," she repeated. "I must say we had a lot of fun."

"Langston has always been a nice boy."

Georgina wanted to remind Evelyn that Langston was no longer a boy, but a man. Albeit a man she'd found extremely attractive. "Yes, he is," she said.

She did not know what had occurred between her parents in Hawaii to elicit a change in her mother's temperament where she had become the woman with whom Georgina was familiar when she was a child, but she had no intention of asking either of them. She would wait and see for them to tell her where they'd gone, what they'd seen and if they planned to return soon.

"I brought you something back that I think you'll like, but you're going to have to wait for me to unpack," Evelyn said.

"You didn't have to do that, Mom."

"Yes, I did."

Georgina wasn't about to argue with her mother now that they seemed to have called a truce. "Take your time unpacking. I need to do several loads of laundry, so if you have something that needs to go in the wash, then leave it the laundry room."

Evelyn closed the newspaper. "When are you moving into your new place?"

"Tomorrow. After I leave the store I'm going directly to the house."

"Why don't you take off tomorrow and take the day to settle in?"

Georgina went completely still; she could not believe her mother was urging her to take a day off. "Who's going to help Dad?"

"I will. Things haven't changed so much that I don't know how to run the store. In fact, I'm going in for a few hours this afternoon to look after your father. There were times when he really overdid it when we were in Hawaii. I'd tried to convince him to slow down, but he wanted to hike trails to see volcanos, pineapple plantations and waterfalls. The first few days he was so sunburned that I suspected he had second degree burns, but you know he's stubborn as a mule and when he sets his mind on something it's almost impossible to get him to change it."

"You knew that, Mom, even before you married him."

Evelyn lowered her eyes. "You're right, and I suppose I have to accept what cannot be changed."

"We all have to accept what we cannot change," Georgina said in a quiet tone.

Evelyn slipped off the bench seat and approached her. If her mother's attitude had changed, so had her overall appearance. She'd gained weight, her face had filled out and the permanent frown that had settled into her features was no longer evident. It had taken more than a week and six thousand miles away from Wickham Falls for grief to release its relentless grip on Evelyn Powell.

"If you need my help setting up things, just let me know."

Georgina hugged her mother, and then pressed a kiss to her hair. "Thanks for offering, but I've been going over to the house every few days to put things away."

Evelyn wrapped her arms around Georgina's waist. "I know I've haven't told you, but I am so proud of you, baby. It probably wasn't easy for you to accept that you weren't going to go to art school, yet you stepped up to help your father run the store. He never would've been able to do it without you."

She wanted to tell her mother that her husband could have done it with his wife but did not want to ruin the fragile truce forming between them. That if Evelyn had gone back to work after a period of mourning, Georgina knew she would not be planning to move into a guesthouse on the Remington property. But unlike her mother, who'd allowed herself to wallow in the past, she was looking forward.

Once she'd made the decision to open A Stitch at a Time, Georgina was forced to admit to herself that attending art school may not have been best for her future, because she would have to work for someone else. Opening a business in her hometown where she could be her own boss was heady indeed. It would become a one-woman operation and she looked forward to reconnecting with the loyal customers who'd patronized Powell's arts and crafts department.

"We're family and because of that we'll always stick together," Georgina said instead.

Evelyn eased back. "Speaking of family, I spoke to my sister yesterday and she said she's thinking about selling her house and buying a one-bedroom condo. Michelle claims she doesn't need a house with three bedrooms when she's the only one living there. She never would admit it, but I think she's trying to get rid of some of her deadbeat friends who like to hang out at her place."

"That's because Aunt Michelle is a lightning rod for the downtrodden."

"Like Sutton's father," Evelyn spat out, twisting her mouth as if she'd tasted something too salty or acidic. "I'd tried to tell her he was no good, but she refused to listen until she discovered she was pregnant, and then he took off like an antelope being chased by a cheetah."

Georgina smiled. "She's lucky because Sutton is a wonderful son."

"You're right," Evelyn agreed. "When I asked Michelle what Sutton's going to do now that he's done playing ball, she said she didn't know."

I know, Georgina thought. Sutton has sworn her to secrecy because he wanted to return to life as a private citizen with as little fanfare as possible. "You know Sutton never really liked the spotlight."

"That's because he's always been a very private person. When was the last time you spoke to him?" Evelyn asked her.

"Several weeks ago," she answered truthfully. Not only was Sutton her first cousin, but he was also the closest thing she had to an older brother. And he'd always made himself available to her whenever she needed to vent. She'd leave a message on his voice mail, and even when traveling to another city for a game he would get back to her, offering words of encouragement while volunteering to intervene on her behalf to convince his aunt to allow her to follow her dream. Georgina had declined because she didn't want to start a rift between Sutton and Evelyn.

"Did he say anything about staying in Atlanta?"

"No." She hadn't lied to her mother because Sutton did not talk about staying but leaving Atlanta.

"I'm going upstairs to get dressed, because I don't want your father to leave without me."

Georgina stared at her mother's back as she walked out of the kitchen. It would take time for her to get used to Evelyn agreeing to help her husband at the store when she'd balked at it for years. She would arbitrarily walk into Powell's to pick up something she needed, and then walk out without interacting with any of the employees, who'd gotten used to her appearing and disappearing like an apparition. Not working Sunday and Monday would free Georgina up to move in and adjust to her new home.

A shiver of excitement swept over her as she experienced a fathomless peace and satisfaction that all was right with her life.

Langston printed a copy of the town hall agenda for the first Wednesday in the month meeting that was open to the public. The mayor and deputy mayor would begin with opening remarks, followed with reports from commissioners overseeing the highway, fire department, power and light/emergency management, police and the building inspector. The meeting was scheduled to begin at 8:00 p.m. at the town hall, and usually ended before ten. Residents were always encouraged to attend and get involved in important community gatherings that directly affected them. The mayor had instituted an open-door policy where locals were welcomed to voice their concerns.

A light knock on the door garnered his attention. Swiveling on the executive chair, he saw the office manager standing in the doorway. "Yes, Sharon."

Sharon Williams walked into the office, closing the door behind her. "I need to talk to you about something that I'd like to stay between us."

Langston rose slightly, staring at the woman in her early fifties who always looked as if she'd stepped off the glossy pages of a fashion magazine. She favored suits, either with skirts or slacks, tailored blouses and her favored Ferragamo pumps. Her jewelry of a single strand of pearls and matching studs never varied from one day to the next. And no one knew the length of the brunette hair she always wore in a twist on the nape of her neck.

"Please sit down. And whatever you tell me will stay between us."

Sharon sat, nervously clasping and unclasping her fingers. She lowered hazel eyes before meeting Langston's steady gaze. "I wanted to wait until everyone left to give you notice that I will be leaving the paper in three weeks."

Langston slumped in his chair, replaying her words in his head and not realizing he'd been holding his breath until he felt restriction in his chest. "Why?"

"I'm getting married."

He was certain Sharon heard his exhalation of relief. "Congratulations!"

"Thank you, Langston. Not only am I getting married, but I will be moving to Ohio for a year."

Her mentioning Ohio reminded him why she'd informed that she was leaving the paper. He ran a hand over his face. "To say I'm shocked is putting it mildly."

Sharon smiled. "So was I when John asked me to marry him."

Langston recalled Sharon telling him that she'd reconnected with an ex-college boyfriend on Facebook and had driven to Ohio for Christmas to reunite with him. Now, five months later, she'd accepted his marriage proposal. "But why a year?"

Sharon's lids fluttered. "I tried to convince him to come here to live, but he has one more year before he can retire after thirty years of teaching."

"What aren't you telling me?" he asked when she nervously chewed her lip.

"I'd like you to approve a leave of absence for a year for me, because once John retires, we plan to move to the Falls."

Langston blew out his cheeks. Sharon was too valuable an employee to deny her request. He also planned to ask one of the part-timers if they were willing to come on full-time during Sharon's absence. "Take the year and make certain you don't forget to come back," he teased.

"Thank you, Langston. I promise we'll be back as soon as his school term ends. Meanwhile, I'm going to tell Mrs. Reilly to list my house as a rental until I return."

"Even though I'm happy for you, you have to know I don't want to see you go."

"And I really don't want to go, but I don't want to miss a chance to have my happily-ever-after."

Langston smiled despite his disappointment, because he had come to depend on Sharon from overseeing the office staff to maintaining the books. Once he assumed ownership of the paper, Sharon had become his mentor, shepherding him through every column of the biweekly for the past year, while they brainstormed how to make the periodical more reader friendly. Working as a foreign correspondent was not the same as running a newspaper, and *The Sentinel's* office manager had proved to be invaluable to and for him.

"Should I assume you don't want the staff to know you're leaving?"

"Yes, because I don't like saying goodbye. Can you tell everyone that I had to go away for a while to take care of personal business?"

"I'll tell them whatever you want, Sharon. After all, you are entitled to your privacy."

Sharon pushed to her feet. "Thank you, Langston. I'm sorry—"

"Don't you dare apologize," Langston said, interrupting her. "Do what you have to do to live your happily-ever-after." Moisture shimmered in Sharon's eyes and she raced out of the office before the tears fell.

Swiveling and leaning back in his chair, he stared out the window. Sharon talking about a happily-ever-after reminded him of the fairy tales he and Georgina had discussed. It had been more than two weeks since she'd come to his home for dinner, and he wondered if she'd finally moved into her guesthouse.

His cell phone rang and he turned to glance at the screen and smiled. It was as if thinking about Georgina had conjured her up. "Hello, princess."

"Hello, Langston. I'm calling to ask if you have plans for Sunday?"

He sat straight. "As a matter of fact, I don't. Why?"

"I'd like to invite you over to my place for dinner."

He smiled. "I'd love to come. What time and do you want me to bring anything?"

"How's three?"

"Three is okay."

"I don't want you to bring anything, Langston."

"You know we've been raised never to go to someone's house empty-handed. Didn't you bring dessert when you came to my place?"

"Yes, because you didn't mention anything about dessert. I have a fully stocked bar, and I plan to make dessert."

"Okay, Georgi. I won't bring anything." Langston knew he had to come up with something in which to celebrate her housewarming.

"I guess that settles it. I'll expect you Sunday at three."

"You've got it."

Langston ended the call. Despite what Georgina said, he had no intention of going to her home the first time without bringing something. However, he did not want to clutter his mind with the possibilities when he had to read a stack of emails for the "Sound Off" column. Once he added the column the emails began to pour in, with the proviso if printed, the complainant would remain anonymous. Although he read every one of them, there were very few that were fit to print. Complaints about abandoned cars, barking dogs or noisy neighbors were quality-of-life complaints that should've been reported to town hall.

The advantage of printing a biweekly allowed him time to read every column, the proofreader's corrections and double-check all photo captions. He was responsible for every printed word in the publication and loathed having to print corrections.

Langston read the first email and then typed it in the column's template:

We are required to bag our garbage and put it in plastic containers. Why, then, if the garbage man drops the bag and garbage spills out, can't they pick it up? The neighbors on my street have been complaining about seeing critters around looking for scraps of food.

Concerned citizens on Mayflower Drive

He decided it was a legitimate complaint and decided to include it in the column, because it was the third complaint from a different neighborhood about garbage men not picking up after themselves. Langston read another email and typed it:

I thought there was a town regulation about not owning more than three dogs per household. And if outside, they must be secured in a fenced-in yard. There is a family on Harrison Lane with five dogs and no fence. How can you allow this to go on?

Langston perused a few more emails. He had no idea when he'd created the column that it would lead to neighbors snitching on one another. However, the results were more positive than negative because it alerted town officials of incidents and infractions needed to be addressed and hopefully resolved in a reasonable amount of time. He selected one more to print:

Thank you "Sound Off." After I wrote about the un-
usual activity at a house on Manchester Court the
sheriff's office posted a deputy in the area result-
ing in the arrest of the homeowner for selling drugs.

He saved the column and then forwarded it to the
proofreader. Since assuming ownership of the paper,
Langston scheduled staff breakfast meetings Monday mornings to discuss the tone of the upcoming
issue. Unlike Eddie Miller, who always decided on
the headlines and which articles would appear on the
front page, Langston solicited the input of everyone
on the editorial staff, reminding them they weren't
a tabloid, and their focus should be on truth. It was a
hometown newspaper and except for the Op-ed page,
the articles steered clear of politics. As the editor, he
refused to endorse any candidate, but was not opposed to them taking out ads or writing Op-eds to
reach out to their constituents.

The afternoon passed slowly as he read over the
article written by the reporter who'd interviewed the
public school superintendent to address the issue of
a potential teacher's strike because they had been
working without a contract for the past three years.
The teachers wanted more than a six percent salary
increase over the next three years, while refusing to
give up any of their hard-won benefits.

Georgina's invitation played around the fringes
of his mind as he struggled to concentrate on the

words filling the computer screen. Massaging his forehead with fingertips, Langston knew reviewing the article with an open mind was futile and decided to quit for the day. It was after five and everyone had gone home.

Although she had insisted he not bring anything, Langston still did not feel comfortable showing up empty-handed. He had several days in which to come up with something generic that would demonstrate his appreciation for her invitation.

It was Sunday, and after attending the early service, Georgina returned home to prepare dinner for her first and very special guest. And that was how she'd begun to think of Langston. He was special. She'd debated whether to make lamb or pork chops, and finally decided on the latter, because Langston had broiled lamb chops for her when he'd invited her to his home. But then again, she'd promised to make smothered pork chops for him.

She'd cooked for Sean, but this was different. They'd slept together, while she did not plan to sleep with Langston because it would ruin their budding friendship. She found it so easy to talk with Langston, while there were occasions when she had to struggle to make Sean open up to her. He would ask to see her, and she would drive to Beckley only to sit in his apartment waiting for him to open his mouth to say something. She'd give him fifteen minutes, then she would get into her car to reverse the trip. It would be several days before he'd call her again, and that was when she'd warn him she did not intend to drive to see him only to encounter a mute. And little did she know that he was struggling with the dilemma of how to repay his gambling debts. Although devastated when he'd asked her for money, Georgina realized Sean had done her a favor because if she'd married him or even had a child with him, her future would have been filled with not only heartache but also stress from Sean's financial irresponsibility.

Georgina had planned her menu to include a spinach salad, sautéed red cabbage with slivers of apple, a sweet potato casserole and mini apple crisps to accompany the smothered pork chops. She'd also purchased a bouquet of flowers from the local florist and votives from Powell's as a centerpiece for the table. After dusting and vacuuming and cleaning the bathroom, she felt the house was presentable for her first guest.

Georgina had settled into the guesthouse and within minutes of closing the door she believed that she'd finally come home. She felt free, freer than she ever had in her life, and chided herself for not moving out of her parents' home much sooner.

She rose at the same time each morning, lingered long enough to eat breakfast and then drove to the downtown business district to meet her father at the store. She had also continued the ritual of cooking various dishes on Sunday to last her for several days, with leftovers for lunch. It had taken Georgina less than a week to find people coming to her home to clean and vacuum when she wasn't there invasive, and informed Viviana that she wasn't going to avail herself of the housekeeping services. The owner of the B and B delivered a supply of towels and bed linens when Georgina informed her she would do her own laundry. Once she opened the door, walked in and closed it behind her, she didn't want to see evidence that someone else had been there before her.

She realized a bed-and-breakfast and hotels were run on the same model, but she wasn't spending a few days in a hotel or motel; the guesthouse had become her home—a place that had become her safe haven where she could unwind at the end of the day without interruptions or interacting with anyone.

If she'd changed, so had her mother. Evelyn had shocked her when she came into the store one afternoon and asked if she would show her the software program she had set up to keep track of the inventory. One day became two, and after a week the murmurings about seeing Evelyn in Powell's ceased altogether. When she'd asked her parents what they were doing Sunday, Bruce informed her he wanted to surprise Evelyn by driving up to Charleston after closing the store, checking in to their favorite hotel overnight and ordering room service. He appeared slightly embarrassed when he confessed that he felt as if they were newlyweds, rediscovering a passion that had been missing for far too long.

Georgina tried imagining what it would feel like to marry and even after thirty-plus years of marriage still enjoy making love with her husband. She'd convinced herself she didn't have time for a romantic liaison when it was exactly what she needed, if only to allow her to trust a man enough to believe he did not have an ulterior motive for wanting to be with her.

She opened the refrigerator and removed a bag of freshly washed spinach, a carton of mushrooms, red onion and several strips of bacon. Once she boiled an egg and let it cool, then she'd slice it for the salad along with crisp bacon.

Georgina turned on the radio on the kitchen countertop and selected a station that featured upbeat dance tunes. She'd only shared one dance with Langston, albeit a slow one. Sean had loved to dance, and he would take her to different clubs where she'd spent so many hours on the dance floor that she'd occasionally arrive home holding instead of wearing her shoes.

She lit several scented candles to offset the cooking aromas as she chopped, minced and sautéed the ingredients for dinner, stopping to shower again and change into a hot-pink sleeveless sheath dress, ending at her knee. She'd just slipped her bare feet into a pair of espadrilles with matching pink ties when the doorbell rang. Not bothering to take a last glance at her reflection in the Cheval mirror, Georgina walked out of the bedroom and to the front door.

Peering through the security eye, she saw Langston staring back at her. She opened the door and sucked in a breath at the same time her heart pumped wildly in her chest. He wore a royal blue tailored suit with a white shirt and silk tie that was the perfect match for her dress.

Her delight in seeing him again was reflected in her eyes and smile. "Welcome."

Langston extended the hand behind his back, handing her a cellophane-wrapped jade plant in a white glazed pot with black Asian lettering. "This is a little housewarming gift."

Chapter Eight

Langston knew Georgina wasn't expecting him to bring anything, but the smile softening her delicate features grew wider when she stared at the plant. "Oh, it's beautiful! Thank you so much, Langston."

"You're welcome. And may I come in?"

Georgina stepped aside. "Yes. Do please come in."

He walked into the house and glanced over Georgina's head to examine her new home. It was as charming as the woman occupying it. The ubiquitous hotel/motel vibe was missing, and in its place was a space designed for family living. A bundle of dried herbs lay on the grate in a faux fireplace and the scent of lemon from several jars of lighted candles wafted in the air. A table in the living/dining area was set for two. His gaze lingered on a vase of deep rose-pink roses and tulips.

"Lovely," he whispered. Langston shifted his gaze from the table to Georgina. "Lovely," he repeated, staring directly at her. And that she was. She had blown out her hair and pinned it up in what he recognized as a messy bun. She lowered her eyes in a demure gesture that never failed to turn him on. Everything about her was a visual feast.

"Even though I told you not to bring anything, I love the plant. Thank you so much."

"You're not going to hold it against me?" he asked.

"Of course not. I was thinking about buying a few potted plants to liven up the place. Now I'm forced to so this little guy can have some friends. What does the lettering say?"

"Love, peace and eternal happiness."

"So you also read Chinese?"

Langston laughed. "No. There was a note card attached, translating the words. This place is very nice. How many rooms do you have here?"

"Two bedrooms, galley kitchen a full bath, living/dining area and there's a king-size bed in the loft with a wall-mounted television."

Langston walked over to the window. "I've driven past the Falls House countless times and never knew these guesthouses were here." They overlooked a grassy pasture with a copse of trees and wildflowers growing in abandon.

Georgina removed the cellophane from the plant and set it on a side table. "Neither did I. Remember, the Remington kids didn't go to the public school with the rest of us, and I doubt if they had sleepovers like the rest of us."

Langston was aware that Viviana graduated from a private boarding school, while her brother Leland transferred to the high school where he hadn't made many friends. "Are your parents going to join us?"

"No. My folks are going up to Charleston later this evening to eat at their favorite restaurant." She didn't want to tell him that her parents had planned to check into a hotel for the night.

Langston smiled. "That's nice."

Georgina also smiled. "I agree. They've been acting like lovebirds since coming back from Hawaii."

"Good for them, Georgi. Just because couples have been married for a long time doesn't mean the passion gets old. My folks act like teenagers when they decide to make out in front of me and my sister."

"Aren't they embarrassed for you to see them like that?"

"Heck, no. The one time I said something to Dad, he told me in no uncertain terms that it was his house and therefore he could do anything he wanted. And when I get my own place, then, as king of my castle, I could do whatever I want. Of course, my mother differed with him because she said she didn't want her son to have a revolving door of women coming and going, because what I did in the dark was certain to come out in the light. And she said that before social media blew up."

Georgina nodded. "Your mother is right. You can have one mishap in college, and it can follow you for life."

"I'm no monk, but I've tried to be selective when it comes to who I've been involved with."

"You know there's talk about us being photographed together at the Chamber dinner-dance."

Langston's expression did not change with her mention of them possibly being linked as a couple. Jonas had mentioned it, and so had a few people he'd run into when at the supermarket. He'd been noncommittal about their so-called relationship when they'd asked if he and Georgina were dating, while he'd wanted it to become a reality.

"I know," he said truthfully. "Does that bother you?"

"No," Georgina said quickly. "I learned a long time ago not to be swayed by what folks say, because they're going to believe whatever they want regardless of how you try and convince them it's not that way."

Crossing his arms over his chest, he gave her a lengthy stare. "Are you saying you don't mind us being seen together in public?"

She laughed softly. "We were already seen together in public."

"That's not what I mean."

"I know exactly what you mean, Langston. You're asking if I would be willing to date you."

He blinked slowly. "Yes."

"Yes, but only when I have some free time."

His smile was one of supreme confidence and victory. Getting Georgina to agree to go out with him was easier than he'd anticipated. Langston did not know why but he'd expected her to turn him down.

"I promise not to get into a huff when you say you can't see me."

"Thank you, because I don't do well with bad attitudes."

His eyebrows lifted slightly. "I'll try and remember that."

"You can lose the jacket and tie, because dinner is going to be casual and relaxing," Georgina said.

Langston wanted to tell her that flowers and candles were a step above casual, but decided not to say anything. "Is there anything I can help you with?"

"You can open the wine and allow it to breathe. I've made the salad and dressing, cooked the cabbage, and the sweet potato casserole is in the oven along with apple crisps. I've seasoned and stuffed the chops, and I wanted to wait until you got here to cook them."

He shrugged off his jacket, leaving it on a chair,

loosened his tie and rolled back the cuffs on his shirt. "Do you mind if I watch you make the chops and gravy?"

"Of course not. I'm going to get you an apron, so you won't get food on your shirt."

Langston pressed his hands to his belly. He realized he'd eaten too much, but he couldn't stop himself when he had second helpings of the sweet and sour cabbage, sweet potato casserole with a topping of finely crushed sugared pecans and the fork-tender double-cut stuffed pork chops with an onion and pepper gravy that literally melted on his tongue.

"If I eat like this every day I'd end up gaining at least fifty pounds," he said, smiling across the table at Georgina. Where did you learn to cook like this?"

She smiled. "My grandmama taught me."

Langston raised his glass of rosé. "Here's to grandmothers all over the world who taught their grandbaby girls how to cook."

"Grandma Dot was old school and she told me no young woman should marry unless she knew how to cook because she didn't much believe in eating in restaurants, or husbands being able to cook."

Langston partially agreed with Georgina's grandmother. "Restaurants are necessary at times, but I personally would rather a home-cooked meal anytime to eating out. Is your mother a good cook?"

"The only thing I'm going to say is that she's better than my aunt Michelle. My grandmother gave up on them when they claimed they didn't want to be chained to a stove, which meant I was her next pupil. I loved going to my grandmother's house because whatever she made was delicious. And she was in seventh heaven whenever I asked her to teach me how to cook something I really liked. She'd sit me on a stool near the table or stove and patiently show me step by step how make perfect fried chicken or ribs."

A slight frown furrowed Langston's forehead. "She fried ribs?"

"Yes. She'd cut up ribs, wash and season them with kosher salt and lots of black and white pepper. Then she would put flour in a paper or plastic bag and coat them well. And like with chicken, she'd shake off the excess flour and fry them in oil until they're brown all over. They would take only about two to three minutes to cook. I varied the cooking method with spraying them with canola oil and oven-fry them. They come out just as crispy but with less oil."

"Wow! One of these days I want you to come over so I can watch you make them."

Nodding, Georgina smiled. "Okay."

"I'll buy the ribs from the butcher at the supermarket and have him chop them into bite-size pieces."

"What else do you plan to serve with the ribs?" she asked.

Langston searched his memory for what he'd

eaten when visiting his grandmother in South Carolina. "Potato salad and cole slaw."

Georgina's eyebrows lifted. "You're going to make potato salad?"

Langston winked at her. "You're not the only one with a grandma who could burn some pots. She did teach her grandbaby boy and girl how to cook."

Propping her elbow on the table, Georgina rested her chin on the palm of her hand. "And she taught you well, because you are quite good."

He inclined his head. "Thank you. But what I'm looking forward to is us cooking together so I can pick up some pointers from you for our next encounter."

"Are you talking about a cook-off?"

Langston winked at her again. "So I see you catch my drift," he drawled.

"Do you have any idea what you are proposing?" Georgina asked as she lowered her arm. "You have to know that Dorothea Reed won first prize for her dishes whenever she competed in the Fourth of July cook-off. Folks would always ask for her recipes, but rather than say anything she'd pretend she didn't hear them. Only her granddaughter is her recipe secret keeper."

"So it's like that, princess?"

"Yes, sweet prince. It's like that. There's a hard and fast rule that only someone related to a Powell can become management at the department store. It's the same with family recipes that have been passed down from one generation to the next. So," she said, pantomiming zipping her lips, "no can do."

Langston switched chairs, sitting next to Georgina, and took her hand, cradling it gently in his larger one before bringing it to his mouth and kissing her knuckles. "What if we were married? Would I still be exempt?"

Georgina froze. Nothing moved. Not even her eyes. It was the second time Langston referred to her marrying him. She searched his face for a hint of guile but found it impossible to read his impassive expression.

"No, you wouldn't be exempt even though that's not going to happen."

"What isn't?"

"Marriage. Several years ago I dated someone, believing I was in love with him and if he had proposed marriage I would have jumped at the opportunity to become his wife. But when I discovered he was hiding something from me I realized I had to walk away."

Langston tightened his hold on her hand. "Everyone has secrets."

She closed her eyes for several seconds. "I know that, Langston. But his secret was one that wouldn't allow me to ever trust him. And for me, trust is more important than love."

"You are preaching to the choir, babe."

A small smile trembled over her lips. "The difference between you and me is that everyone in the Falls knew about your breakup because you'd married a celebrity, while few folks in the Falls were aware that I was seeing someone."

"Was that by design?"

"Not really. He lived in Beckley and most times I'd drive down to see him."

Langston released her hand and settled back in his chair. "I found out Ayanna was cheating on me when someone at the station sent me a photo of my wife and her costar splashed across the front page of a supermarket tabloid locking lips at a Mexican resort."

"Where were you at the time?"

"Afghanistan."

Georgina gasped. She did not want to believe a woman could cheat on her husband while he'd faced impending death every second of the day. "How selfish."

"Yes and no."

She gave him an incredulous stare. "Are you saying that you gave her a pass for cheating on you?"

"No. Our relationship was very complicated. When I married Ayanna, I was more than aware of her dealing with issues of abandonment. She was twelve when her father went to the store and never came back, leaving her mother to raise her and her younger sisters on her own. When I told her about my overseas assignment we got married a week later, and our wedding night was spent with her crying and begging me not to go. I manage to convince her that it would be for less than a year, which seemed to belie some of her insecurity."

"You deceived her, Langston, because you were abroad for more than a year."

"That's where you're wrong. When I told her I was coming home, she said I could stay because she'd gotten a role in a popular Broadway play and with rehearsals and six performances a week we'd rarely get to see each other."

Georgina felt heat from embarrassment suffuse her face. She'd spoken too quickly and misjudged Langston. "I'm sorry," she said in apology. "I didn't know."

He managed what passed for a smile. "Very few people know. When I confronted her, she claimed she didn't want a divorce but there was no way I was going to remain married to a woman who didn't attempt to hide her affairs."

"Affairs?"

"Yes, Georgi. Ayanna had had several affairs during our marriage."

"But why?"

Langston pressed a fist to his mouth as he appeared to be deep in thought. "I don't know the answer to that. Some men and women need constant attention and when they don't get it at home they seek it with others."

"Do you ever hear from her?"

"She called me a couple of months before I left Washington to invite me to her wedding. But I declined and wished her the best."

"Did she marry the man with whom she was photographed in Mexico?"

"No. Her new husband is much older than she is."

Georgina wondered if Langston's ex was marrying an older man to replace her absentee father. "I hope she finds what she has been looking for in her new husband."

"So do I. Enough talk about exes. Do you have your sketches with you?"

"Yes. Why?"

"Do you mind if I see them?"

She gave him a sidelong glance. "Do you intend to grade me?"

Langston chuckled under his breath. "No. I researched the high school archives and saw old newspapers with your illustrations. I have to admit that you were very good."

Georgina stared at the tablecloth. "I'm certain I would've been a lot better if I'd gone to art school."

"That is debatable, Georgi. Some people are born with a natural talent without professional training or instruction. I've seen phenomenal work by graffiti artists who go from spray painting buildings to having their work hang in museums."

"Are you referring to Jean-Michel Basquiat?"

"Exactly. I saw an exhibition of his work in a museum and I was blown away that he used social commentary in his paintings to get his message out about colonialism and class struggles."

"Basquiat is the exception for a graffiti artist, Langston, because he did attend art school. He is what I think of as an artistic genius who was destined for fame. Unfortunately, he couldn't deal with his artistic success, and the pressures put upon him of being a black man in the white-dominated art world and he turned to drugs to cope. I admire him because he was so prolific during his short life and career, leaving the art world more than fifteen hundred drawings and around six hundred paintings."

"Imagine, Georgi, you're only twenty and meanwhile you're homeless and unemployed and you've been supporting yourself selling T-shirts and homemade post cards when suddenly a single painting sells for twenty-five thousand dollars. That's a lot for someone his age to accept."

Georgina had taken three art history courses in high school and totally immersed herself in the lives and works of artists, many of whom didn't achieve fame until after their deaths. "It is. How many artists do you know who were able to sell their work and become über wealthy during their lifetime?"

Leaning closer until their shoulders touched, Langston pressed a kiss on her hair. "Times have changed from struggling artists painting in unheated garrets while subsisting on bread, cheese and wine. And the ones who had a patron were luckier than the others. Artists today have a lot more options when they can exhibit their work at galleries or even on street corners."

"True. But as an illustrator it wasn't about becoming wealthy. I just wanted to be known as a professional artist."

"Have you thought of sketching in your spare time?" Langston questioned.

"What spare time? Right now I'm working an average of ten or more hours a day, with every other Sunday off. Then once I open my shop I will spend most of my time knitting and crocheting sale samples."

"Do you plan to open seven days a week?"

Georgina shook her head. "No way. I'm going to close Sundays and Mondays. I plan to open at ten and close at six Tuesdays through Saturdays."

"Good for you. Now, are you going to show me your sketch pad?"

"Sketch *pads*," she said, correcting him. "I have at least a half dozen pads."

"Then I'd like to see all of them."

"And what do you intend to do with them, Langston?"

"I want to observe your artistic talent before I interview you for the paper's 'Who's Who' column after you have your grand opening."

Georgina hesitated as she pondered Langston's reason for wanting to see her sketches. Pushing back her chair, she stood. "Okay. I'll get them for you."

Langston waited for Georgina to leave the kitchen before he began clearing the table. Sharing dinner with her was enlightening. It wasn't until Georgina revealed she had been involved with a man that something had communicated to him that she was a virgin. There was something in her body language that had led him to believe she hadn't had much experience with the opposite sex. She didn't shrink away whenever he touched her, but he'd detected an uneasiness in her which would not allow her to completely relax.

She'd proudly announced that she was a country girl down to the marrow in her bones, and that was what he'd found so refreshing. Georgina was open and wholesome, while not flirtatious or overly provocative, He thought of her as an enigma when she went from a bare, freckled-face woman with braided curly hair to a drop-dead gorgeous sophisticate with a subtle cover of makeup highlighting her best features. He much preferred her natural curly hair to the straightened strands. And his libido always went into overdrive whenever she wore a dress to reveal her legs. Some men liked breasts, and others were drawn to hair and hips, but for Langston it was legs.

Georgina Powell was an unpretentious small-town woman who appealed to his need to settle down and begin a life far from the glare of cameras or adoring fans who'd come to bookstores for him to sign their books. She was a reminder of how life was and could be again after the constant fear and threat of losing his life in some foreign war-torn country.

When first assigned as a foreign correspondent Langston felt as if he was on top of the world. He had recently celebrated his twenty-sixth birthday when he found himself on a jet flying to Africa and a tiny country on the continent that had gone through decades of war and genocide. He was optimistic and fearless, believing himself invincible. The first time he saw a dead body on a street that had been there so long it was bloated from the heat, he'd nearly lost the contents of his stomach. His guide laughed and told him to get used to it.

Langston never got used to seeing death and dying in all the years he remained abroad, and whenever he was granted a vacation he'd book a flight to someplace he deemed relatively safe for tourists. He'd check into hotels off the beaten track and sleep until hunger or nature forced him to get up. His facility with languages proved invaluable whenever he asked locals for places he should visit or restaurants serving the best food in town.

He fell in love with Venice, Paris, Córdoba and Granada, the Moorish cities in Spain and the tranquility of several Greek islands. The respite allowed him to regroup and refuel to return to his assignments and view them differently with the realization that it was his chosen career and he had the option of staying in or getting out.

And when his mother questioned him about not coming back to the States he told her if he had then he would not have returned. But after eight years he had decided to call it quits once he realized he was experiencing PTSD. The nightmares had kept him from a restful night's sleep. He never regretted handing in his resignation and knew he had to see a therapist to deal with the flashbacks. It took a year before he felt able to cope with his past in order to move forward.

He'd cut himself off from friends and colleagues. The exception was his sister and her family. She lived in a DC suburb and whenever he went to visit with her he was able to experience a modicum of normalcy as Uncle Lang.

Georgina returned with the sketch pads and handed them to him. "At what age did you begin drawing?"

"I had to be about six or seven."

"Do you mind if I take these home with me? I promise to give them back after I go through them."

A beat passed before she nodded. "Okay."

Langston exhaled an audible breath. At first, he thought she was going to refuse him. "I also promise not to eat or drink anything while I look at them."

"I would appreciate that even though I doubt if I'll ever do anything with them." She paused. "Are you ready for coffee and dessert?"

He set the pads on the chair at the table. "Yes, ma'am."

It wasn't until Langston drove home, changed into a pair of sweats, sat in the family room and opened the first sketch pad that he immediately recognized talent even at the age of six or seven. She'd sketched a cat asleep and stretched out on the driveway of her house. There was nothing childish or amateurish in the pencil drawing. He lost track of time as he turned page after page in each of the books, seeing the growth and confidence in the drawings as she matured.

He was transfixed with one of two little girls jumping rope. The expressions on their faces radiated joy, matching those of the ones turning the rope. Langston noticed she'd change themes from people to flowers, animals and landscapes. He went back to the ones of young children and stared at them for an interminable length of time. Then something in his head clicked when he reached for his cell phone and called his sister.

"Now, what did I do to have the honor of my favorite brother calling me?"

Langston smiled. "I'm your favorite brother, Jackie, because I'm your only brother."

"True. What's up?"

"I think I have something you should look at for your next book."

"Do you want to give me a hint?"

"No. I'm going to photograph them and send them to you. I'll text you before I send them, so Mrs. Lindemann, please don't forget to check your email." His sister claimed she had thousands of emails but loathed reading and deleting old ones.

"Now I'm really curious."

"By the way, what size sweater does Brett wear?"

"I usually go by his chest size, which is now twenty-six inches. But if you're going to buy him a pullover, then it should be at least twenty-six inches, because I always have him wear a shirt under it. And don't forget he's sensitive to wool, so it has to be acrylic."

"I forgot about that. How's Sophia?"

"Please don't talk about Miss Grown. She's all of three and trying her best to work my last nerve. I told her father that one day he's going to come home and find him with one less dependent to claim because I'm going to send her down to her grandparents to live, and you know Mama refuses to put up with a sassy girl."

"Like mother, like daughter," Langston teased. His sister did not know when to stop talking whenever Annette warned her the conversation was over, and it always ended with Jackie being grounded for weeks at a time.

"That's not funny, Langston. Just wait until you have some kids."

"And I'm willing to believe the children I hope to have will be perfect."

"Yeah, right. I hate to end this call, but Chris just walked in and I want to make certain he eats something before he goes to bed."

"Give him my best, and I'll be in touch again." His brother-in-law, assigned to the FBI's CIRG— Critical Incident Response Group, was on call 24/7.

"Love you, Lang."

"Love you, too, sis."

Langston rang off and continued to stare at the images of the children before he rose to his feet to get a camera. He had to use a wide-angle lens in which to capture the entire sketch on each page. It was close to midnight when he finally finished what he wanted to send to his sister. Jacklyn had taught school for several years before deciding she wanted to stay home with her children until her youngest was at least five. In the interim she'd fulfilled her wish to write a children's picture book. After several rejections, she finally found a publisher willing to accept it. She'd published it under a pseudonym and then bragged to him that he wasn't the only published writer in the family.

Her first two books proved to be successful, which gave her confidence to begin a series focusing on diversity and inclusion for elementary school-age children, and Langston believed Georgina's sketches of children would be the perfect illustrations for Jacklyn's books.

He didn't want to say anything to Georgina until after he got feedback from his sister. However, he planned to return her sketch pads in a couple of days. Hopefully, Jackie would like what she saw and would recommend the illustrator to her editor and thus fulfill Georgina's wish to become a professional artist.

Langston knew he wasn't being completely altruistic in wanting to help Georgina realize her deferred dream. He liked her a lot and those feelings deepened whenever he spent time with her.

Although he'd been married, Langston hadn't been given the opportunity to feel like a husband when he was thousands of miles away from his wife. Now he craved stability that let him come home every night to his wife and children. He wanted to have family vacations and he wanted to grow old with his wife, and the biggest concern was where they would retire so they would have time to spoil their grandchildren.

To others he probably would sound naive. But if they'd witnessed what he'd experienced in his former career they would want the same.

Chapter Nine

Georgina covered her mouth with her hand to keep from screaming. Her permit to open A Stitch at a Time was approved and she could officially occupy the space in July.

After reaching for her cell phone, she punched in Sasha's number. "I got it," she said when her friend answered.

"They approved you?"

"Yes! Right now I'm doing the happy dance. I can officially open next month. I'm going to arrange for the shelving and the furniture to be delivered."

"Oh, Georgi, I'm so happy for you. I'm going to

make a batch of cupcakes and other goodies for your grand opening."

"You don't have to do that, Sasha."

"Yes, I do, so please act gracious and accept my gift."

"I can't be gracious when I'm delirious."

"I hear you, girlfriend," Sasha drawled. "And with your artistic ability, I know your shop is going to be beautiful."

"I'm going to try. You're the first one I called, so don't say anything until I go public."

"Girl, please. Your secret is safe with me. Speaking of secrets, Dwight and I were seeing each other on the down low, but now I'm ready to go public."

"I knew it! I saw the way you two were looking at each other. And you denied everything when I asked you about him."

"That was then, and this is now. I did not want to say anything because I didn't want to jinx myself. Georgi, he's wonderful. I was so turned off men after marrying that pompous, egotistical cretin that I refused to look at another one."

Georgina smiled even though Sasha couldn't see her. "It's real hard not to stare at Dwight Adams. The man's beautiful." The town's resident dentist was the epitome of tall, dark and very handsome.

Sasha laughed. "I could add a few more adjectives to describe him, but it would be too much information."

"I get the picture. I'm going to hang up now because I have to call my cousin."

"Congratulations again."

"Thanks."

Georgina had managed to calm down by the time she dialed Sutton's number. He picked up after the third ring. "Hello."

He sounded sleepy. "Did I wake you?"

"No. I was just…" His words trailed off.

"Look, Sutton. Call me when you have time." Something told Georgina she'd interrupted something she didn't need to know about.

"It's okay, Georgi. What's up?"

"My certificate of occupancy was approved, and I can officially open for business July first. I haven't told my folks because I want to know when you can come up to help out in the store."

"I can be there in a week. I closed on the condo yesterday and right now I'm staying with a friend while the movers pack up my stuff and put it in storage. I'm going to call Aunt Evelyn after I get off the phone with you and let her know I plan to stay with her until I find a house."

"Thanks, Sutton. You know I owe you."

"No, you don't. After all, we're family and that means we have to look out for one another."

"What about your mother? Does she plan to stay in Atlanta?"

"Right now, she's on the fence whether she wants

to stay or leave. She claims she's coming up for the Fourth of July celebration because it will give her a chance to reconnect with folks in the Falls."

"How long does she plan to stay?"

"I'm not sure. She claims she needs a break from her what she calls her so-call friends."

"What's wrong with them, Sutton?"

"I told her the sooner she gets rid of her entourage, the better her life will be. Once folks found out that she was my mother they began swarming around her like flies on fish guts. I told her over and over that they were using her, but Mom told me I was jealous because I didn't have any friends. What she fails to realize is that I don't need friends who are nothing more than parasites. That's where a lot of dudes go wrong because when the money runs out their homeboys find other places to park their dusty butts. I refuse to have folks laying up in my house when I'm on the road. And whenever someone asks to come over I politely give them a time to leave. I tell them I'm not running a hotel or motel, so there's no checking in."

"Wow! What do they say?"

"There's not much they can say. My house, my rules. And those who drink too much and can't drive, I arrange for a car service to take them home."

Georgina knew very few men were willing to challenge her six-four, two-hundred-thirty-five-pound cousin who could hit a baseball into the upper deck and occasionally out of a ballpark. She knew Sutton's aversion to having people lounging around his house was the result of his ex-wife's constant need to entertain her family and friends. He'd finally had enough and filed for divorce. He gave her the house and a generous settlement and moved into a three-bedroom condo in a gated community.

"I'm going to let you go back to whatever you were doing before I interrupted you," she teased him. "Let me know when you arrive."

"FYI, I'd just finished."

"Bye, Sutton."

"Bye, Georgi."

I knew it, she thought. It was obvious he was in bed with a woman. She hadn't known Sutton to be a love-them-and-leave-them type of guy; however, she knew for certain that whomever he'd been seeing in Atlanta, wasn't going to be returning with him to Wickham Falls. At least not until he purchased his own home.

Georgina smiled when she realized she had to make one more phone call. Langston had come by Powell's a couple of days ago to return her sketch pads and he'd picked the right time because Evelyn had left early to prepare dinner for her husband at home.

"I got it," she said when he answered her call. "I can open A Stitch at a Time in early July."

"Congratulations, sweetheart. Are you ready to celebrate?"

"Not yet. I'm going to wait for my grand opening."

"Have you eaten?"

"No. Why?"

"I know I can't keep you out too late, so I'm coming over to take you to the Den. Once you're up and running, I'll take you someplace real fancy so we can celebrate on a grand scale."

Georgina wanted to tell Langston that she didn't need a fancy restaurant to commemorate what she'd planned and patiently waited for. The fact that her shop was going to become a reality was enough. However, it had been a while since she'd gone to the sports bar. The last was when Sutton had come up from Atlanta during the All Star break. When they'd walked in together he was given the rock-star treatment with fist bumps, slaps on the back and some had even asked for his autograph.

"Give me time to shower and change my clothes."

"Can you be ready in thirty minutes?"

She glanced at the clock on the microwave. It was seven-thirty. "Yes."

"I'll be there at eight."

Langston felt as if he'd been punched in the gut when Georgina opened the door. A mane of reddish-brown hair framing her face flowed over her shoulders and down her back like loose ribbons. At that moment he wanted her in his bed, the curls spilling over the pillow under her head.

He swallowed an expletive when he felt the growing bulge in his groin. "You look incredible," he said in a hoarse whisper. And she did in body-hugging black jeans and cotton black long-sleeved tee. A pair of high-heeled booties put her head level with his nose. She smiled, bringing his gaze to linger on the vibrant red color on her lips.

"Thank you. It looks as if great minds think alike because we're both wearing black."

Langston glanced down at his untucked black shirt, jeans and Doc Martens, grateful that his erection was going down. "You're right about that. By the way, I called ahead and asked Aiden to save us a table."

"You have juice like that?" she said, teasingly. Retired navy SEAL Aiden Gibson returned to Wickham Falls to assist his uncle and was now the official pit master for the popular barbecue sports bar.

"You didn't know?"

Her smile grew wider. "Should I take you with me whenever I decide to go to the Den?"

Reaching up, Langston brushed a curl away from her cheek. "Of course." He wanted so much to kiss her but knew if he did he wouldn't stop. "Let's go, Cinderella."

Georgina scooped up her wristlet with her cell

phone and key card and closed the door. "Oh, my goodness. You have your father's Mustang."

Cradling her elbow, Langston led her over to the classic car. "Dad gave it to me, and I always keep in the garage."

"It looks brand-new."

He opened the passenger-side door. "That's because I had a body shop restore the outside, and Jesse Austen took care of what was needed to be replaced under the hood."

Langston waited until Georgina was seated and belted in before rounding the car and slipping behind the wheel. He found it hard to concentrate on driving with her sitting less than a foot away. The warmth of her body, the tantalizing fragrance of her perfume and knowing she was the first woman who would accompany him to the Wolf Den made the occasion even more special.

He tapped a button on the dash, turning on the satellite radio that had replaced the one that had originally come with the car. The distinctive voice of Lionel Richie singing "Out of My Head" filled the interior of the vehicle. Langston was familiar with the song, but it was the first time he concentrated on the lyrics. It was about a man who'd lost the love of his life and couldn't get her out of his head because he'd believed their love would never die. He was tempted to change the station when he heard Georgina mouthing the words under her breath.

"You know this song?" he asked her.

She turned to meet his eyes for a brief second. "Yes. I have everything Lionel Richie has recorded, including the time when he sang with the Commodores."

"What type of music do you like?"

"I'm not partial to any genre. It doesn't matter whether it's pop, R&B, rap, hip-hop or country. I usually download music of the artists I like."

"Name some."

"Rihanna. Anthony Hamilton. Anything by Whitney Houston or Aretha Franklin. Adele and Sam Smith are my favorite British singers. And last, but certainly not the least, is Tina Turner."

Langston smiled. "I flew to Montreal to see Tina in concert during my second year in grad school for her Fiftieth Anniversary Tour, and I can honestly say it was the best live performance I've ever witnessed."

"I've seen videos of her performances, but they probably can't come close to seeing her live."

"You're right about that. I have a confession to make."

Georgina rested her hand on his, which was gripping the steering wheel. "What?"

He came to a complete stop at a four-way intersection, looking both ways for oncoming traffic before driving across the roadway. "I went to see her again three months later in London."

"No, you didn't!"

Langston's laughter floating up from his throat filled the interior of the car. "Yes, I did. I'd saved all of my tips waiting tables, so I told my professor that I had to take a few days off for some personal business, not telling him I was flying to London to see Tina because I had a mad fan crush on her."

"You really had it bad."

He shook his head. "You just don't know the half of it. I was twenty-four and young enough to be her son or even grandson, but that didn't matter because I was obsessed with her."

"How long did you stay in London?"

"Two nights. I came back so jet-lagged that it took me a while to get my circadian rhythm back to normal. I still waited tables on the weekends and the manager sent me home after I dropped one too many orders. I lied and told him that I was coming down with something and he yelled at me never to step foot in his restaurant again if I was feeling sick. I went back to my apartment and slept for sixteen hours straight and when I woke up I realized it was impossible for me to attend classes, wait tables and jaunt off on a whim to attend a concert I'd seen before."

"You were young and had the hots for Tina."

"What man wouldn't, Georgi, regardless of his age? The woman is as beautiful as she is talented." *Just like you*, he thought. Georgina's sketches, even to the untrained eye, were impressive, and he knew if she had attended art school there was no doubt she would've been a very successful illustrator. "Did you ever have a crush on a singer or movie star?"

"Yes, and too many to name. It was as if I fell in love with every leading man. He didn't have to be drop-dead gorgeous. I think it was the acting that captivated me."

"So it was the art?" Langston asked.

"Yes, because acting is an art form. But there is a distinct difference between an actor and a movie star."

"Who are some of your favorite actors?"

A beat passed. "Viola Davis, Benicio del Toro, Taraji P. Henson, Denzel Washington, Will Patton, Mahershala Ali, Meryl Streep, Angela Bassett and Michael B. Jordan to name a few."

"You really like traditional actors who are not pigeonholed into playing a particular character."

"What I like, Langston, is their versatility and their ability to morph into whatever character they've been selected to play."

He smiled. "You should've been a movie critic."

"No, Langston. I'm going to be what I always wanted to be. Someone who will be successful and in control of her own destiny."

He had wanted to tell Georgina her permit had been approved after hearing the decision while covering the meeting for the paper but decided to wait until she'd received written notification. Langston did not know why, but her joy had become his, because he realized his feelings for her surpassed friendship. Although it wasn't love yet, he knew he was falling in love with her. And when she talked about being successful, he had no doubt she would be.

Even her choice in actors and music revealed she wasn't ready to embrace the latest fads. It had taken him a while to realize he, too, was a small-town guy who, despite his worldwide travels, never felt more at home than he did in Wickham Falls. He was certain his colleagues and the friends he'd made over the years would either laugh or look at him sideways if he invited them to the Falls, while wondering what was there to lure him back into a lifestyle they probably would've said was not only boring but also predictable. But it was the predictability that Langston craved because he did not have to go to sleep or wake to the sounds of bombs and gunfire.

Georgina had spent her entire life in the Falls, while he'd spent half his life away from it. Well, he was back, and this time to stay. To stay, start over and put down roots as his father's family had done generations ago.

She had asked him whether he'd wanted to remarry and have children and he could honestly say that he did. And this time he would be there for his wife and the children he hoped to share with her.

"It's now early-June and do you think you'll be able to have your grand opening the first week in

July?" Langston asked after what had become a comfortable silence.

"I'm not sure, because a lot has to happen in a month. I must call several companies to deliver the shelving, furniture and other equipment that I've placed on order. And even before that I'm going to give the space a good cleaning."

He gave her a quick glance. "What about your stock?"

"It's in the spare bedroom. I've spent hours scanning the barcodes into a computer program to keep track of the inventory."

"Have you finished?"

"No. You'd be surprised how many shades of white there are. I began with embroidery thread and ended with bulky knit for each color."

Langston shook his head. "That definitely must be time-consuming."

"It's more like laborious but once it's done, I won't have to repeat it," Georgina said.

"Which color are you up to now?"

"Red."

"I want you to let me know when you have your grand opening because I'll make certain one of the staff reporters will be on hand to cover the event. Even before that I'd like to interview you for the 'Who's Who' column, but I won't run that until you've been open for at least a month."

"The week before I open I'd like to place an ad in

The Sentinel, offering discounts to customers who sign up for knitting, crocheting or quilting workshops."

"I'll have Randall Stone contact you for the ad. Of course, as a first-time advertiser you'll be given a generous discount with the hope that you will become a repeater in the classified section."

Reaching over, Georgina covered his right hand on the steering wheel with her left. "How much of a discount, Langston?"

He registered the teasing tone in her voice. "That all depends."

She leaned closer. "On what?"

"I don't know. You have to let me think about it."

Georgina laughed, the throaty sound echoing in the closeness of the vehicle. "You don't have to think about it, Langston. Even though I'm dating the owner of the newspaper I'm not going to ask for any special favors. After all, you are in business to make money."

"Yes, I am. But are you saying because we're dating each other that our businesses shouldn't factor into our personal relationship?"

"That's exactly what I'm saying. I want you to treat me like you would your other advertisers, and if not then you can consider this the last time I'll go out with you."

Langston did not want to believe she would stop seeing him because he'd wanted to help with her new startup. "Don't you believe in compromise, Georgi?"

"What do you think I've been doing my entire life, Langston? I've compromised not going to art school because I had to help my parents at the store. And I've compromised not having a love life because I've had to work 24/7 to help keep Powell's afloat. But that's over, because it's time for Georgina Mavis Powell to go it alone. And that means we cannot mix business with pleasure."

He'd wanted to tell her that his parents had married and worked together for more than thirty years and were now enjoying in retirement doing exactly what they wanted. And it didn't have to be any different between him and Georgina; he knew he had to understand where she was coming from, and although he'd found himself falling in love with her, he had to allow her the independence she needed to succeed or hopefully not fail.

"Okay, babe. I promise not to interfere."

Georgina gave his hand a gentle squeeze. "Thank you."

Langston wanted to tell her there was no need to thank him, because he was willing to agree to anything if it meant their continuing to date each other. Georgina was so different from the other women with whom he'd been involved that he'd almost forgotten they'd existed. There weren't so many he couldn't remember their names or faces, but when he looked back, he realized some he should have never engaged in conversation, because at the time he'd experienced a restlessness that wouldn't permit him to stay in one place for any extended length of time. And that meant he hadn't been willing to commit to a woman.

Langston was just beginning to acknowledge what had drawn him to Georgina other than her overall physical appearance. It was confidence and a resolute belief that she could accomplish whatever she wanted. She was loyal almost to a fault, because a lot of young women would've left town to seek their own fortunes rather than work for their family. She'd mentioned sacrificing a love life because she'd had to work long hours but once she became the proprietress of A Stitch at a Time she planned to close two days a week.

Yes, he thought. He was lucky because she'd agreed to see him rather than some other man and knowing this, he did not want to do anything to sabotage their fragile relationship. He drove down the road leading to the Wolf Den and maneuvered into an empty space at the rear of the restaurant. It was Saturday night, and the parking lot was nearly filled.

"It looks as if there's a full house," he said, unbuckling his belt.

"Is it always this crowded on Saturdays?" Georgina asked.

"I don't know. I usually drop by during weeknights. I try and stay away on Mondays because that's when everyone who's past and present military comes by. A lot of dudes stop by on Wednesdays for Ladies Night, with the hope that they can meet someone."

She smiled. "Don't you mean hook up?"

Langston held up both hands. "No comment."

He got out, rounded the car and helped Georgina to stand. Threading their fingers together, he led her to the front door. Other than when they'd danced together at the Chamber dinner dance, this would be the first time they would be out in public together. Langston knew being seen with the Powell girl, as many of the locals referred to her, would generate a lot of talk but it was something he was more than prepared for.

He opened the door and allowed her to precede him into the noisy, crowded sports bar. Music blared from speakers, making it almost impossible for someone to be heard unless they were standing only feet apart, while a dozen televisions were muted and tuned to various sporting events. The line at the bar was two-deep as a trio of bartenders was shaking, mixing and pouring drinks. Icy pitchers and mugs of beer lined the mahogany bar as the waitstaff shouldered their way through the throng carrying trays. Langston preferred coming to the Den for lunch when he did not have to shoulder his way through diners to find a table.

He tapped the arm of a passing waiter to get his

attention. "I reserved a table for two with Aiden. The name is Cooper."

The young man, who didn't look old enough to shave, smiled. "Come with me. Your table is in the back."

Resting his hand at the small of Georgina's back, Langston followed the waiter, stopping short when he realized they would be seated close to Dwight Adams and Sasha Manning. "What's up, Doc?"

Dwight pushed back his chair, coming to his feet. "I should be asking you the same thing, Cooper." The two men shook hands.

Sasha sprang to her feet and hugged Georgina before Langston was able to respond to Dwight. The two women were talking at the same time and he shrugged his shoulders when the dentist nodded and smiled. Langston and Sasha's brother Stephen were best friends.

Georgina turned and smiled up at him. "Langston, would you mind if we pushed the tables together so Sasha and I can sit next to each other without having to shout to be overheard."

He stared at Sasha's date. "Dwight, are you all right with us sitting together?"

"The more, the merrier," the retired army major quipped.

Langston removed the Reserved sign and he and Dwight pushed the tables together. He seated Georgina and lingered over her head. "Can I get you anything from the bar before we order?"

She met his eyes. "If I'm going to eat barbecue, then I'll have a beer."

"Wait for me, Cooper," Dwight said. "I'm also going to the bar." When they were out of earshot of the two women, Dwight asked, "Is it serious between you and Georgina?"

Langston chuckled. "A little, but definitely not as serious as it is between you and Sasha Manning."

It was Dwight's turn to laugh. "So you noticed?"

"It's as plain as the nose on your face that there's something going on between you and the town's pastry chef," Langston said, smiling.

Dwight flashed a wide grin. "I really enjoy being with her."

"Good for you."

Langston wanted to tell the dentist that he also enjoyed dating Georgina, because she was a constant reminder of the normalcy that had been missing for more than half his life. He'd convinced himself that he didn't need a woman in his life after his divorce; that he was content to remain a bachelor and not commit to any woman. Until now. Unknowingly, Georgina had changed him where he did want to remarry, become a father and raise his children in Wickham Falls, West Virginia.

Chapter Ten

"I had no idea when we spoke earlier that I'd be seeing you here with Langston," Sasha said in Georgina's ear.

She leaned closer to her friend, their shoulders touching. "He wanted to celebrate the council approving my application to open a business."

Sasha gave her a *you've got to be kidding me* look. "Do you really believe that, Georgi?"

A slight frown appeared between Georgina's eyes. "What are you talking about?"

"Open your eyes, girl. Langston Cooper will concoct any story he can to see you, and includes celebrating your new business." She held up her hand when Georgina opened her mouth to refute her. "Please let me finish." Georgina nodded. "I suspect I've had a lot more experience with men than you have, so please believe me when I say that Langston looks at you the same way Grant Richards looked at me when I met him for the first time. And that translates into I like and want what I see."

"Langston and I are friends, Sasha."

"Like Dwight and I went from friends to lovers. No one was more surprised than I was once I realized that Kiera's father was nothing like any other man I'd ever known or met. He was the first man who has allowed me to be me. My ex tried to control my career because he had to be the superstar in the family, while Dwight supports and respects the decisions I've made when it comes to the bakeshop."

"Why shouldn't he?" Georgina asked. "After all, the bakeshop is yours, and not his."

"True, Georgi. But I've been around enough successful couples to discover that men have very fragile egos, and once they realized their wives' or girlfriends' popularity begins to eclipse theirs, they do whatever they can to tear them down. My relationship with Dwight works because we don't have to professionally compete with each other."

Georgina wanted to tell Sasha that she couldn't compare and base everyone's relationship on her failed marriage. That couples broke up for myriad reasons and that envy could be added to the list of irreconcilable differences. And there was no way her enterprise would conflict with Langston's. He was a journalist and she a needle worker, which meant there would never be any competition between them.

"Are you ladies looking for company?"

Georgina's and Sasha's heads popped up at the same time, both recognizing boys with whom they'd attended school. "No!" they said in unison.

"That's enough, fellas," Langston said as he approached the table. "Go and annoy someone else."

"Now, gentlemen!" Dwight commanded when the two men lingered longer than necessary.

They saluted Dwight, backpedaled and made their way to the front of the restaurant. Georgina hid a smile. As a retired major, Dwight was the Falls' highest-ranking officer, and was well respected by the community. The divorced single father had become a very eligible bachelor; women were drawn to his lean, sable-brown sculpted face, and his large, dark, penetrating eyes and dimpled smile were mesmerizing, while his buzz-cut salt-and-pepper hair was a shocking contrast to his unlined face. Georgina shared a look with Sasha before both dissolved into hysterical laughter.

Langston set a pitcher of beer and two frosty mugs on the table, while Dwight set another pitcher filled with pop on the table with two mugs. "What's so funny?" he asked, sitting opposite Georgina.

"Those guys were our prom dates," she volunteered.

Dwight took his chair, staring across the table at Sasha. "Y'all went to prom with the MacDonald cousins?"

"It's not as if Liam and Chris Hemsworth were available to ask me," Sasha retorted.

"Or Michael B. Jordan for me," Georgina added, staring directly at Langston.

"Damn, brother Cooper," Dwight said under his breath. "I suppose we'll never be able to compete with their Hollywood heartthrobs."

Langston smiled. "I wouldn't worry too much, Major Adams. Those dudes have nothing on us."

Georgina and Sasha shared a smile. Langston was right. She wanted nothing to do with anyone who lived their life in the spotlight. But then she had to remind herself that Langston had become a celebrity in his own right with a bestselling book that had garnered the attention of Congress.

All conversation ended when a waitress approached the table to take their food order. They all agreed to order the newest item on the menu—Korean barbecue short ribs. Georgina had finished half her beer when the food arrived, and she sampled perfectly smoked chicken, fall-off-the-bone spareribs and melt-in-the-mouth brisket, but also sides of potato salad, collard greens, cole slaw and mac and cheese.

I was a carnivore tonight, she thought, touching the napkin to the corners of her mouth. Not only had she eaten more meat in one sitting than she'd had in a long time, she had also loaded up on carbs.

Georgina also knew the answer immediately when she'd asked herself why it had taken so long for her to come to the Wolf Den. She hadn't wanted to dine alone. If Sasha hadn't left the Falls, she was certain they would've hung out together. And inviting Sean to the Den had not been an option. They always dined in Beckley where he would occasionally run a tab with several restaurants, and not once had she questioned why he didn't have a credit card, or rarely carried cash.

Dwight placed his napkin next to his plate. "Now that the weather is warmer, I'm spending more time at my lake house, where the rainbow trout and small-mouth bass are literally jumping out of the water. You guys are welcome to come and hang out with us whenever you need to kick back and relax."

Georgina met Langston's eyes, wondering if Dwight was extending the invitation to him or to them. Had he thought of them as a committed couple because they'd danced together at the fund-raiser and had come to the Den together?

"I'm afraid that's not going to be possible," she said, "until later in the year."

"How much later?" Dwight questioned.

Georgina knew it was time to tell Dwight what

she'd revealed to Sasha and Langston, because once the next issue of *The Sentinel* was published, everyone in Wickham Falls would know another Powell planned to open a business in town.

"I'm going into business for myself." She told Dwight everything, watching as a smile parted his lips.

"It's about time the Falls got another businesswoman."

"I agree," Langston said.

"The invitation is still open if and when you get a break, Georgi," Dwight continued. "The same goes for you, too, Cooper."

Reaching across the table, Langston took Georgina's hand and threaded their fingers together. "We accept your rain check."

The drive from the Den back to her home was accomplished in complete silence as Georgina closed her eyes and chided herself for eating and drinking much too much. The time she'd spent with Sasha, Dwight and Langston had passed quickly and when she glanced up at the wall clock, she realized she'd lost track of time. It was close to eleven when they'd finally left the restaurant.

"We accept your rain check," Georgina said, repeating what Langston had said once they stood in the middle of her living room. "Do you realize you

gave him the impression that we are sleeping to-gether?"

Langston pushed his hands into the pockets of his jeans. "No, I didn't, babe. People see what they want to see and draw their own conclusions. If he believes we *are* sleeping together then do you want me to tell him that we're not?"

"No, but—"

"If it's no, then you have nothing to worry about, Georgi," he said, cutting her off. "Now, if you were to ask me whether I want us to sleep together, then the answer is a resounding yes."

Georgina went completely still. She hadn't ex-pected Langston to be that candid. He wanted to sleep with her, and she'd convinced herself that she did not want or need passion in her life; that becom-ing an independent business owner was enough. But even before opening the doors to A Stitch at a Time, she knew she needed more cutouts to complete the puzzle that had become her life. She'd known she wanted to live on her own and start up a business, but not falling in love, marrying and starting a fam-ily after she'd broken up with Sean, and looking back she wondered how she had allowed distrust to turn her off love.

"At least I know where you're coming from."

Langston angled his head. "And where are you coming from?"

She chewed her lip. "I like you, Langston. A lot,"

she added. "But I need time to sort out my feelings for you."

Taking two steps, he cradled her face in his hands. "And you can have all of the time you need because neither of us is going anywhere. I know where to find you and you know where to find me."

Georgina rested a hand alongside his lean jaw, went on tiptoe and brushed her mouth over his. "I promise not to run away."

"You better not," he whispered against her parted lips.

She lowered her hand. "Thank you for tonight. I really had a fun time."

Langston lowered his hands and dropped a kiss on the bridge of her nose. "It's only the first of many more to come."

He kissed her again, this time on the mouth, increasing the pressure until her lips parted, while Georgina's stomach muscles clenched and unclenched before trembling like frozen gelatin. Every nerve and muscle in her body screamed from the sensations holding her captive and reminding her of how long it had been since her self-induced celibacy. Langston kissing her, feeling the strong beating of his heart against her breasts, the pulsing between her thighs, forced her to acknowledge that she was a woman who'd denied the strong passions within her for far too long.

Pushing against his shoulder, she managed to extricate herself. "Please go, Langston, before I beg you to stay and make love to me."

He buried his face in the wealth of curls cascading down her back. "You'll never have to beg me, sweets. All you have to do is tell me what you want me to do with you."

Georgina nodded and pulled her lip between her teeth. She was unable to speak because of the pleasurable throbbing drowning her in a maelstrom that threatened to tear her apart. She'd just opened her mouth to plead with Langston to leave when he turned on his heel and walked out. Muffling a sob, she walked on shaky legs to the bedroom, fell across the bed and waited for the sensations gripping her traitorous body to ease.

She lay facedown on the quilt, eyes closed as she thought about what she'd shared with Langston since sitting next to him at the fund-raiser, and she could not believe the months had passed so quickly. He'd cooked for her, and she in turn had cooked for him, and tonight was the first time they'd appeared in public as a couple. Wickham Falls was a small town and gossip spread quickly, which meant she had to be prepared for the fallout.

Although Sasha had admitted to seeing Dwight in secret, it was apparent she was either tired of hiding or did not care who knew it, but her being seen with him at the Wolf Den spoke volumes.

Turning over, Georgina stared up at the ceiling,

wondering why it had taken her so long to come into her own. She was thirty-two, unmarried, childless, solvent and only recently had become emancipated. She'd dated a man for nearly eight months and hadn't been willing to introduce him to her parents until wearing his engagement ring. However, in her naiveté, she'd believed having a fiancé was necessary for her to ensure a modicum of independence. Combing her fingers through her hair, she held it off her face.

Circumstances beyond her control hadn't only affected her, but were also the impetus that changed her life once her father made the decision to eliminate Powell's crafts section. Rather than putting the items on sale with deep discounts, she'd boxed and stored them for what would become the next phase in the journey to control her destiny. And when she'd used Sasha as a sounding board about how stagnant her life had become, Georgina's friend confirmed what she'd already visualized.

And like Cinderella she was no longer the stepsister, existing behind the scenes, and after attending the ball and encountering her prince, she had no intention of hiding her relationship with Langston from her parents or anyone else. He was her man and she was proud of it.

Georgina smiled at her father when he rapped lightly on the door. "Good morning."

Bruce walked into the office, leaned over and kissed her cheek. "How's it going, baby girl?"

She rolled her eyes upward and wanted to remind her father that she was no longer a little girl. "Everything's good. Please sit down, Dad. I have something to tell you."

Crossing his arms over a crisp, white, short-sleeve shirt, Bruce met her eyes. "I think I know what you're going to say."

"Since when did you become a mind reader?" she teased, smiling.

Bruce took a chair opposite Georgina, leaning back and tenting his fingers. "Sutton called last night to tell me he's moving back to the Falls to help manage this place. His timing is impeccable now that you'll be opening your own shop."

Completely shocked, Georgina couldn't stop the gasp escaping her parted lips. "How did you know?"

Bruce lowered his eyes. "There are very few things that go on in this town that I don't know about." He glanced up, giving her a long, penetrating stare. "What bothers me is that you did not trust me enough to tell me what you'd planned."

She squared her shoulders while refusing to accept guilt for her actions. "What I didn't trust was for you not to attempt to sabotage my plans, Dad. If you'd made a phone call to someone at the town council to alert the landlord that I wanted the storefront I never would've been able to rent the space on Sheridan Street."

"I wouldn't have done that," Bruce said in a quiet tone.

"Wouldn't you, Dad? All you had to do was mention it to Mom and even if you did want to support me you would've caved like a deflated balloon and gone along with her."

Bruce's dark blue eyes grew hard. "That's where you're wrong, Georgina. I went along with your mother to keep peace in my home because I remember my mother constantly arguing with my father about absolutely nothing. If he said the sky was blue, then my mother would try and convince him it was lavender. It was one of the reasons why my brother and sister moved so far away. My folks were the perfect couple in public but hell-raisers behind closed doors."

Georgina never met her paternal grandparents who'd passed away within months of each other the year she'd celebrated her second birthday. They weren't the only couple in the Falls who'd attempted to conceal their volatile union. Sasha had confided to her about her parents' never-ending verbal encounters, which was why she never had sleepovers and it was the reason her brothers enlisted in the military within days of graduating high school.

And it was apparent Georgina had misjudged her father. "I'm sorry, Dad," she said in apology.

"There's no need to apologize, baby girl. I…" His words trailed off as a flush darkened his tanned face. "I need to stop calling you that. After all, you are over thirty."

She rested her hand atop his larger one. "You can call me that, but only in private." A beat passed. "Does Mom know?"

Bruce's red eyebrows flickered slightly. "Yes. I told her when we were in Hawaii. She started to go off on a tirade, but I stopped her, saying a few things I'm now ashamed to repeat. I must have gotten through to her when she finally calmed down enough for me to convince her she'd mourned Kevin long enough and it was time for her to help me run this place as she'd promised before we married."

"So that's why Mom came back so different."

"That wasn't the only reason. Getting her away from Wickham Falls was akin to shock therapy. She was trying hard to once again become the woman with whom I'd fallen in love and married. Every night was date night with intimate dinners, long walks and even longer talks. I told her she had to let you go before losing you completely. It hasn't been easy for her but she's finally seeing things my way, which, now that I look back, benefited all of us."

Georgina felt as if she had shed a lead suit with her father's disclosure. Now she didn't have to conduct her life like a covert agent, operating clandestinely to establish her business. Her parents knew and it was just a matter of time before all of Wickham Falls would know.

"Thank you, Dad, for your support."

"There's no need to thank me, Georgina. You're my daughter, my flesh and blood, and there isn't anything I wouldn't do to help you succeed. Would you mind if I invest in your new business?"

She knew her father was offering to give her money. "Yes, I would mind, because I don't need investors. Not even my father," she said, smiling.

"Promise me you'll let me know if you have a cash-flow problem."

"I will."

Georgina didn't tell him that she doubted whether she would have a cash-flow problem because she'd deposited enough money in her business's operating account to cover the rent and utilities for the next two years. She didn't plan to hire an employee and had projected she had enough inventory on hand to sustain her for at least six months, even with brisk sales. She had purchased furniture and equipment and as soon as they were delivered and set up, Georgina would alert town officials as to the date and time of her grand opening. The approved certificate of occupancy allowed her time to become operational, but now that it had become a reality, Georgina felt less anxious than she had before. It was now early June and she projected opening within a month.

"Did Sutton tell you when to expect him?"

Bruce nodded. "Sometime next weekend. Meanwhile, your mother has volunteered to work Saturdays and Sundays."

"It's good for her to get out of the house if only for a few days a week."

"That's what I told her. By the way, how much more do you have to do before you open?"

"Not too much, Dad. I emailed the vendors to confirm the date and time when I want them to deliver what I need to furnish the shop. And I'm still working on computerizing my inventory, and project completing that sometime this week."

Bruce narrowed his eyes, appearing deep in thought. "Today will be your last day working at Powell's."

Georgina's jaw dropped. "You're firing me?"

"Yes, Georgina, I am firing you, because I don't want you stressed out working here and then trying to finish what you need to open your shop. I'm going to give you a generous severance package and continue to pay your health insurance, so that's something you don't have to concern yourself with."

She didn't want to believe her father was letting her go, but she understood that he wanted her to succeed in her new venture. "Thank you, Dad."

"I should be the one thanking you," Bruce countered. "You've gone above and beyond being the good daughter when you stepped up and helped me out, and for that I'll be eternally grateful."

"Gratitude has nothing to do with it because we're family."

Bruce smiled. "You know that's what Sutton said when I thanked him for coming on board."

Georgina smiled. "I'm certain he's going to enjoy being away from the glare of cameras and reporters delving into his personal life."

"I admit he's handled being a celebrity well because he never let money or the spotlight change him like some young kids who can't handle the fame and act like a complete fool."

She wanted to tell Bruce that Sutton had confided to her that he'd seen firsthand how some of his college buddies who were signed to professional sports teams self-destructed when they either dabbled in banned substances or were embroiled in baby-mama drama, and he'd wanted none of it. Sutton had at one time stopped talking to his mother when he'd shown up unexpectedly to find his father staying with her. It was only when Michelle Reed finally cut off all communication with her son's father that Michelle and Sutton had renewed their close relationship.

"Dad, you have to know you're going to get more than normal foot traffic once the word gets out that Sutton Reed will be working at Powell's."

Bruce flashed a wide grin. "That's something I'm not going to complain about. And he's coming back at the right time. You know I usually close for the Fourth Of July celebration festival, but I'm thinking about opening one of the three days to bring folks into the store to meet Sutton."

"That's something you should give some serious thought, Dad, because you know Sutton really doesn't like being put on the spot."

Bruce paused. "He should've gotten used to that while playing ball. He was a baseball phenom and a role model for kids, and now that he's retired, he will have to contend with folks asking for autographs and if they can be photographed with him."

"Celebrity or not, he is entitled to a modicum of privacy," Georgina said in defense of her cousin. "Even though I won't be working for you, do you still want me to design the ads for the store?" she asked, changing the topic of conversation. "I promise not to charge you."

"Of course you can still design the ads, but we will have to talk about you charging me. Remember, Georgina, you're now going to be a businesswoman in your own right, and folks pay for goods and services. Although we're family you still have to be paid for what you do."

She knew her father was right. She'd come on as a full-time employee at eighteen, and in the ensuing years earned raises and bonuses commensurate with her responsibilities. Living at home was a perk because she didn't have to pay rent or buy food and was able to save an appreciable portion of her salary. The year she celebrated her twenty-fifth birthday she'd contacted a financial manager to set up a retirement account for herself, given she'd planned to work for another forty years. Little did she know at the time that she would be working for herself and that meant she would have to modify her plans.

Bruce pushed to his feet. "It's almost time to open up, so I want to give you something to think about."

Georgina stared up at him. "What is it, Dad?"

"Take time to enjoy life, because tomorrow isn't promised to any of us."

She froze. What was her father not telling her? "Is there something wrong with you?"

He nodded. "Yes. I'm a workaholic, and that's something I inherited from a long line of Powells. And because this store has earned the reputation of being the oldest family-owned business in Wickham Falls, I didn't want to lose that distinction. My fourth great-granddaddy started out selling feed to farmers before graduating to a general store and now into a department store able to compete with the big-box chains because we never cheated local folks. Even the Wolfes couldn't put us out of business when they set up a company store because we were willing to extend credit to the miners until they got paid. A few times when they'd sent their goons here to try and intimidate us, they were sent packing after we'd armed every employee with a shotgun ready to blast them to smithereens. Don't be a workaholic, baby girl. Close for vacation and holidays. And there's no need for you to work every day if you plan to have a family. I'm saying all of this because one of these days I would like to become a grandpapa."

Georgina stood up and hugged him. "I don't know about making you a grandfather in the very near future, but I do plan to open five days a week and close for the major holidays."

Bruce kissed her cheek. "That's my girl."

She sat down again once her father left the office to open the store. A smile stole its way over her features before becoming a wide grin. Georgina did not want to believe her parents knew about her future business venture but hadn't said a word to her.

It was obvious she wasn't the only one who had been hiding a secret. Leaning back in the chair, she kicked her legs in the air as if riding a bicycle. She'd planned to open A Stitch at a Time with or without her parents' approval, but knowing they wanted her to succeed filled her with an indescribable joy.

Chapter Eleven

Langston found his thoughts drifting from the agenda during the regularly scheduled Monday editorial meeting. When he'd first assumed ownership of the paper, he'd decided to switch the weekly meetings from Wednesdays to Mondays. He'd discovered the week the paper was to go to the printer, some of the reporters wanted to make last-minute changes or corrections, which had become a pet peeve for Langston.

He'd slept fitfully and once awake he found himself unable to go back to sleep. It had been the first time in more than a year since he'd had a nightmare that was a flashback of an incident he'd witnessed in Angola hours before he'd been airlifted out of the country. His therapist had warned him he would occasionally experience them because it was impossible for him to erase his memory like striking the backspace or delete key on a keyboard.

Langston forced his attention back to the reporter who was responsible for covering reporting on all school events, and that included sports. "Are you saying that the president of the teachers' union is talking about going on strike at the beginning of the next school year?"

Mitchell Garner blinked slowly behind a pair of black horn-rims. "Not really. She spoke to me off the record."

Langston's eyebrows lifted questioningly. "Off the record?" he asked. "Are you saying she wants you to mention it in the column?"

Mitchell shook his head. "No. She claims she's just giving me a heads-up of what's to come."

"If that's the case, then we won't print it," Langston said. He nodded to Randall. "You're next."

"I'm glad to report that advertising revenue is up again. I met with the developer over the weekend who's building on the Remington property, and he says he wants us to run a series of full- and half-page ads beginning with the August issue advertising the newly constructed homes." A smattering of applause followed his announcement.

"Good work," Langston said, smiling and complimenting the advertising salesman. "I..." His words trailed off when his cell phone vibrated; he glanced at the screen. His sister was calling him. He found it odd that Jacklyn would call him during the day when they usually spoke to each other in the evening. Standing, he picked up the phone. "Please hold on." He glanced at those sitting at the table in the conference room staring back at him. "Excuse me, but I have to take this call. What's wrong, Jackie?" he asked as he walked into his office and shut the door behind him.

"There's nothing wrong, Lang."

"If there's nothing wrong, then why are you calling me in the middle of the day?"

"I didn't think I needed permission to call my brother before the sun went down."

He smiled for the first time since answering the phone. "You don't. But you're so regimented that I thought something had happened."

"It's called being disciplined, Lang. And if I wasn't then I would never get anything done with two young children and a husband who has a go-bag sitting at the door because he never knows when he's going to be called to leave at a moment's notice. Now, back to why I called you, and I promise not to take up too much of your time. Remember the sketches you sent me?"

"Of course."

"Well, after looking them over I decided to write

another book based on the drawings of kids. I submitted it to my agent, who in turn sent it to my editor. I'm telling you all of this to let you know they want to publish the book with the illustrations. But first you have to let me know who the illustrator is so the publisher can contact him or her to offer them a contract."

Langston sat down heavily in his chair. He knew Jacklyn's contract with her publisher had given her the option of choosing the illustrator for her bestselling series of children's books based on diversity; however, when he'd downloaded photos of Georgina's sketches of children, he had deliberately not revealed the identity of the artist.

"Are you sitting down, Jackie?"

"Yes. Why?"

"She's someone you are familiar with."

"Langston Wayne Cooper, I don't have time to play guessing games with you. Just tell me her name!"

"Damn, sis. Why did you have to go and blurt out my whole government name?"

"I did it to get your attention."

"Well, you did. The artist is Georgina Powell." There was complete silence for nearly thirty seconds. "Jackie, are you still there?"

"Yes, I'm here. I… I'm just trying to process that someone I'd graduated with is going to be the illustrator for one of my books."

Langston wanted to warn his sister not to get ahead of herself, because Georgina was totally unaware that he'd sent her sketches to Jackie. "You're going to have to wait to celebrate because Georgi doesn't know I sent you her drawings."

"What! Have you gone and lost your mind, Langston? When you sent me the sketches the only thing you said was that they belonged to a friend and that you wanted me to look at them for some of my books. And now you tell me that Georgi has no idea her illustrations will appear in a book? I don't know what's going on between you and the Powell girl, but whatever it is I want and need you to convince her that I want those illustrations and that I'm going to tell my agent to get as much money for her that the publisher is willing to part with."

Langston knew his sister was angry, and he didn't blame her; he'd always been able to deal with Jacklyn's quick temper. He didn't know Georgina well enough to gauge her reaction to the news that she was about to become a professional illustrator. "I had no idea you were going to send them to your agent and editor. And that means I'm going to have to talk to her."

"Do more than talk, brother, because I want those illustrations. Better yet, why don't you convince her to come to DC so *we* can talk? Georgi and I weren't close like her and Sasha Manning, but we did speak to each other. After you talk to her I'd like you to give her my number. If she's going to turn me down, then I want to hear it directly from her."

Langston glanced at the clock on his desk. It was time he got back to his meeting. "I'll be in touch, Jackie."

"You do that, brother love."

"Yeah, right. Now it's brother love." He ended the call not giving her chance to come back at him. He loved his sister unconditionally, but there were times when she irked him because either it had to be her way or no way, and he didn't envy his brother-in-law who appeared unfazed by his wife's mercurial moods, claiming most artists were temperamental. Not only was Jacklyn an incredibly talented teacher and writer, but she was a whiz when it came to financial investments. So much so, that Langston had trusted her to handle his finances. She'd set up an account for his retirement and another that he could access without incurring a penalty for early withdrawals. It was this account he'd used for midyear and Christmas bonuses for the newspaper's staff.

"Sorry about that," he said in apology when he walked back into the conference room.

The meeting continued when the reporter who covered all social and civic events gave her report. Once everyone with a byline finished, the session adjourned minutes before a delivery person from Ruthie's arrived with lunch. Langston had begun the practice of ordering lunch for everyone after the editorial meeting and it was the least he could do for a staff who had been willing to take pay cuts while he worked tirelessly to ensure the paper's viability. After the first six months he was able to restore some of the salaries, and he projected with the increasing revenue he hoped to offer more raises and larger bonuses.

The most important thing on his mind now wasn't the newspaper, but how to tell Georgina that she could possibly become a professional illustrator with the publication of his sister's next children's book.

The ringing of the phone on the bedside table penetrated Georgina's much-needed sleep. She'd spent every waking hour preparing for the grand opening. She'd completed scanning and cataloging every piece of merchandise, including thimbles and sewing needles.

There had been a delay in shipping the reception-area furniture, and delivery and installation of the shelving was also pushed back several weeks. The warehouse foreman hadn't been able to give her a tentative date; he promised to call her the first week in July to give her an update. She'd given up projecting a date when she would open and had resigned herself that it would eventually happen.

Opening one eye, she reached for the phone and tapped the phone app. "Good morning, Langston."

"It's afternoon, babe."

She sat up. "I decided to lie down, but I must have fallen asleep."

"Are you all right?"

"Yes. Why?"

"What are you doing sleeping in the middle of the afternoon? And, where are you?"

Reaching around her, Georgina adjusted the pillows cradling her shoulders. "I'm home."

"Why aren't you at the store?"

"I no longer work at Powell's because my father fired me yesterday."

"What!"

Covering her mouth, she smothered a laugh. Georgina was surprised that the news hadn't gotten out that she no longer worked at the department store. The employees probably thought either she'd taken vacation time or wasn't feeling well.

"He let me go so that I could concentrate on what I need to do to open my shop."

"I thought the two of you had a falling out!"

Georgina smiled. "That's not going to happen. Dad and I don't agree on everything, but there's no way he's going to turn his back on me. Now, sweet prince, why are you calling me in the middle of the day?"

"I have something to tell you, but I'd rather say it in person."

She paused. There was something in Langston's

voice that made the hair on the back of her neck stand up. "Is it something that's going to upset me?"

"I don't believe it will."

"If that's the case, then why don't you tell me now?"

"It's somewhat of a surprise."

"Can't you give me a hint, Langston?"

"No, then it wouldn't be a surprise. Can you come to my place tonight?"

"I suppose I can. What time do you want me to be there?"

"Seven. We can have dinner and then watch a movie."

Georgina smiled. "I like the sound of that."

"I'll see you later."

She hung up, wondering what sort of surprise Langston was planning. She knew she'd shocked him once she told him she'd been fired. When her father had decided to let her go it was the best thing that could've happened to her, because it freed her up to do whatever she wanted and needed to do for the eventual opening of A Stitch at a Time.

She had gone online to order framed prints of anything resembling needlecrafts, and she'd also contacted someone to paint the name of the shop on the plate-glass window. Meanwhile, she'd designed her own logo for letterhead and note pads. It had taken several hours before she'd decided on a square with underground railroad quilt codes. The codes were special for her because she'd inherited a collection of quilts from her third great-grandmother who'd been a conductor in assisting blacks escaping the bonds of slavery to seek freedom in the North and Canada. The logo was the perfect complement for the shop's name because there was a time when quilts were made a stitch at a time; it was a process she enjoyed more than machine stitching because she'd found it more relaxing.

Georgina decided to stay in bed because she'd been up most of the night printing sticker prices for every item in the inventory. The task was time-consuming and laborious, but when she'd finally finished the sun had come to signal the beginning of a new day. Blurry-eyed and stiff-limbed, she'd managed to shower without falling over from sheer exhaustion and had stumbled to the bed and fallen asleep within seconds of her head touching the pillow. She set the alarm on her phone for five, turned on her side and went back to sleep.

Langston came down off the porch when Georgina pulled into the driveway and came to a stop alongside his Jeep Wrangler. He opened the driver's-side door, waited for her to scoop a decorative bag off the console and then helped her down.

He resisted the urge to kiss her when he spied a couple coming out of their house. He waved to them, and both returned his wave. Mr. and Mrs. Daniel

Howard sat on their porch every night regardless of the weather, listening to their favorite radio station. His house and the Howards' were the only two homes in the cul-de-sac. They'd moved to the Falls nearly twenty years ago and normally kept to themselves. The rumors they were in the witness protection program proved unfounded when the truth was revealed that they'd sued a hospital for the wrongful death of Mrs. Howard's identical twin sister.

"You look incredible." And she did, in a pair of white cropped slacks, a zebra-striped off-the-shoulder top and black flats. She'd styled her curly hair in a single braid.

Georgina smiled up at him. "Thank you. I brought red and white wine."

He took the bag from her grasp and led her around to the rear of the house. "Do you mind if we eat outdoors tonight?"

"Of course not. The weather's perfect for a cookout."

Langston had made it a practice to cook outdoors during the warmer weather. After his parents installed the outdoor kitchen and gazebo, they'd enclosed the rear of the property with a fence high enough to ensure a degree of privacy from their nearest neighbors. He'd lit a few citronella candles to warn off insects and covered platters with mesh domes to keep them off the food.

He seated Georgina on a cushioned chaise. "I decided to go with seafood tonight after all of the meat we ate the other night."

"Good, because I'd truly earned my carnivore badge that night."

Cradling the back of her head, he leaned down and brushed a kiss over her mouth. "I didn't want to do that with someone eyeballing us."

Georgina stared at him, completely confused. "You invite me to your home, and now you're concerned whether someone will see you kissing me?"

Langston hunkered down in front of her. "I don't have a problem with folks seeing you here, but what I'm not comfortable with is public displays of affection. I know what it is to be the object of gossip because my ex flaunted her affair for the world to see. I refuse to put you in a category where folks talk about my putting you in a compromising position. In other words, what goes on behind the doors and fence of the Cooper house, stays here."

Cradling his face between her hands, Georgina leaned closer and pressed her mouth to his. "Thank you."

He smiled. "There's no need to thank me, Georgi. There's only one thing I want from you."

She felt her heart stop and then start up again in a rapid beating that made her feel slightly lightheaded. "What is it?" The query had come out in a breathless whisper.

"Please don't change."

Georgina was certain Langston had registered her exhalation of relief. She didn't know why, but she'd expected him to ask her to sleep with him. It's not that she didn't want to share his bed, but it had to be by mutual agreement.

"I won't because I can't. What you see is what you get."

"I happen to like what I see, babe."

"Ditto," she countered.

There wasn't anything about Langston Cooper that she did not like. Aside from his overall masculine attractiveness, he was intelligent, artistic and modest. He'd won awards as a war correspondent, become a *New York Times* bestselling author, survived long, grueling sessions when appearing before a congressional committee and had managed to put to rest the gossip surrounding his failed marriage once he refused to vilify his estranged wife for her infidelity.

"I'm going to feed you first before I let you in on my secret."

"Do you need help?"

Langston ran a finger down the length of her nose before standing straight. "No. Just sit and relax. I've prepped everything. The only thing that's left is heating up the grill."

Georgina stared at his retreating back as he walked to the six-burner grill. The Coopers, like so many in their enclave with their homes set on quarter-acre lots, had installed outdoor kitchens. Cooking outside offset heating up their homes during the summer months and provided space to entertain friends and family. There had been a time when her mother had become the consummate socialite when she hosted meet-and-greets for candidates running for public office, or for a contingent of women's groups seeking for more representation in local government. Everyone waited for her period of mourning to end where she would emerge once again as the Falls' social doyenne, but they gave up once one year stretched into two and beyond, and Georgina doubted if Evelyn would return to the life before losing Kevin, because she seemed very content working in the store where she greeted customers and employees alike with a kind word and friendly smile. Bruce had gotten his wife back, and she had gotten her mother back.

Smiling, she closed her eyes and let her senses take over. Georgina found the scent of citronella mingling with those of newly opened blood-red roses intoxicating. The distinctive hoot of an owl could be heard over the twittering of birds hopping nimbly from branch to branch. It was dusk, her favorite time of the day, when everything appeared to slow down in preparation for nightfall and sleep. Inground solar lights came on, illuminating the area in a soft golden glow.

Her thoughts drifted off when she tried to imagine what it would feel like if she and Langston were married and they ended their day together relaxing outdoors. And starting a family would not negatively affect her business, because she would set up a nursery in an area of the shop's storeroom with a monitor to keep an eye on her son or daughter.

"Georgi, it's time to eat."

She opened her eyes and placed her hand on Langston's outstretched palm. Pinpoints of heat stung her cheeks when she realized where her thoughts had gone. She'd fantasized being married to Langston and having his child when they'd admitted to liking each other. And liking was a far cry from love or even falling in love. But then she had to ask herself if she was falling in love with him and she had to admit she was.

Georgina had believed herself in love with Sean yet when she compared her feelings for him to Langston, they did not come close. It wasn't until she walked away from him that she was forced to acknowledge that their relationship was wholly physical. He was the first man with whom she'd slept and had confused sex for love.

"Something smells wonderful."

"I hope you'll like what I made."

Resting a hand at her waist, Langston directed her to the gazebo where he'd set a table for two, along with a bottle of champagne in an ice bucket and a couple of flutes. A trio of lights hung from the ceiling. Mouth-watering aromas wafted from a large platter with grilled fish and vegetables.

Smiling, she sat on a cushioned bench seat. "You're incredible. I think I'm going to keep you." He'd grilled shrimp, lobster tails, scallops and pinwheels of sole stuffed with crabmeat.

Langston sat opposite her, filled the flutes with champagne and handed one to her. "It's not going to be that easy to get rid of me."

She took the flute. "What are we celebrating?"

He stared at her over the rim of his glass. "The possibility of you becoming a professional illustrator."

Georgina looked at him as if he had taken leave of his senses. "What are you talking about?" She listened in complete shock when he revealed he'd sent her sketches to his sister, who'd given up teaching to become a children's book writer.

"Jackie wrote a picture book based on some of your sketches and sold it to her publisher. What she needs is your approval to publish the book with your illustrations. She publishes under a pseudonym as Laila Lucien."

Georgina hadn't realized her hands were shaking when she put the flute to her mouth and drained it. She was familiar with the pseudonym because the author's books had won several awards, and it was obvious Langston wasn't the only award-winning writer in his family.

"Why, Langston? Why did you do it?"

"I'm surprised you've asked me that. Don't you know I'm falling in love with you, and I would do whatever I can to make you happy?"

She held out her flute for him to refill it. Everything was coming at her so fast that she found it hard to process any of it. Langston had just admitted to being in love with her while his sister wanted her as an illustrator for one of her books.

A weak smile trembled over her lips and she forced herself not to break down completely as twin emotions of shock and wonder eddied through her. "I don't know what to say. I… I had no idea you loved me."

"Remember when I asked you if you believed you were unworthy for a man to care about you and you said *of course not*? Which is it, Georgi?"

She lowered her eyes. "I am worthy."

"Yes, you are. And one of these days I'm going to prove to you just how worthy you are."

"I have a confession to make," Georgina said after a pregnant pause."

Langston gave her a lengthy stare. "What is it?"

"I love you, too." Admitting to him what lay in her heart felt as if a weight had been lifted, that what she'd been fighting for weeks had ended in a glorious victory.

Rising, Langston rounded the table and kissed her, this kiss so different from the others they'd exchanged. It was as gentle as a caress, and she was overcome with emotion she felt like crying tears of joy. He ended the kiss and retook his seat, smiling.

"To be continued," he promised. "After we eat, I'm going to call my sister because she wants to talk to you."

Georgina picked up a pair of tongs to serve herself, eating but not really tasting any of the deliciously prepared fish and vegetables, but found herself drinking more wine than she normally would under another set of circumstances.

Everything was falling into place and all was right in her world. She had always wanted to become a professional illustrator and that could possibly happen if she agreed to the terms in a publishing contract, and she'd fallen in love with a man who hadn't asked anything from her, unlike other men she'd met or known.

"What are you thinking about?" Langston asked, when the corners of her mouth lifted in a smile.

"I do love you, Langston. You're so different from other men I've known that there are times when I'm just waiting for the other proverbial shoe to drop where I'll stop trusting you."

Langston speared a shrimp but halted putting it into his mouth. "I will never cheat on you."

Georgina doubted whether he would cheat on her

because of what he'd gone through with his ex-wife. "I'm not referring to infidelity."

A slight frown furrowed his smooth forehead. "If it's not infidelity, then what is it?"

"Money."

Langston gave her a look mirroring his disbelief. "Money?"

"Yes."

He listened, appearing stunned by her revelation that boys wanted to date her because they saw her as a good catch, and her last serious boyfriend had asked her for money to cover his gambling debts. "I don't need your money, Georgi. Not today, tomorrow or fifty years from now."

A beat passed as they stared at each other, and then she said, "I believe you."

Langston smiled. "Now that we've settled that, I'm going to call my sister so we can FaceTime her." He came around to sit next to Georgina. Picking up his phone, he tapped Jacklyn's number. "Hey, Jackie. I'm here with Georgina," he said when her face appeared on the screen.

"Hi, Georgi. Long time no see."

"I could say the same about you. Your brother told me that you're now an award-winning children's book writer." She had to admit time had been more than kind to the woman with whom she'd shared several classes in high school. Jacklyn had left the Falls to attend Howard University while she had stayed behind in their hometown. Shoulder-length twists framed a dark brown complexion that glowed with good health.

"That's something I don't advertise as Jacklyn Lindemann. As the wife of an FBI special agent I like to keep a low profile."

Georgina nodded. "I understand. It appears as if your brother went behind my back to send you some of my sketches."

Jacklyn laughed. "That he did. If he'd told you in advance what he was going to do would you have agreed to it?"

Her question gave Georgina pause. "I doubt it," she said truthfully. "I'd given up the dream of becoming a professional illustrator a long time ago."

"Well, get ready for your dream to become a reality because I love your sketches and I'd like for you to come to Alexandria whenever you have time to meet with me and my agent to go over some legal work."

"Can't it be done with a conference call?"

"No, because my agent is paranoid about talking on the phone. She once represented a client whose phone was bugged by the government because he apparently was involved with some shady business, and that meant they were taping her conversations with him, as well. When they gathered enough evidence he was charged with trafficking in illegal substances."

Suddenly, Georgina felt as if she was caught in

the crosshairs of a situation with people who used fake names and were suspicious of conducting business on the telephone. "How long do you think it will take?" Although Alexandria, a suburb of Washington, DC, wasn't far from Wickham Falls, Georgina did not want to be away that long because she wanted to be available once she got the call confirming the furniture delivery.

"Probably no more than a day. Why don't you and Lang come during the July Fourth holiday weekend? Amelia can take the train down from New York and stay over, and that way we can discuss business without y'all having to rush back."

When Jacklyn mentioned their staying over at her house, she wondered what Langston had told his sister about their relationship. Even though they hadn't slept together she wanted to be an adult if they were assigned the same bedroom in his sister's house. "I'm free, but you'll have to ask your brother." She smiled when Langston elbowed her gently in the ribs.

"When do you need us to be there?" he asked his sister.

"Either Friday night or Saturday morning. As soon as I get off the phone with you, I'm going to send Amelia a text to let her know you're going to be in town. Once she confirms I'll text you back to let you know what day we're going to meet."

"That sounds good, Jackie."

"Thanks, Georgi, for agreeing to let me use your

illustrations for my new series. I know it's going to do well, and that means you'll become my personal Tomie dePaola."

Georgina laughed. Tomie dePaola had written and illustrated more than two hundred fifty books, many she'd read as a child. "Tomie is definitely an icon."

Jacklyn waved. "I'm going to hang up now and contact Amelia. Lang, look for my text so we can plan the weekend accordingly."

"Okay, sis."

Georgina waited for him to set down the phone and then asked, "What did you tell your sister about us?"

"I didn't tell her anything other than I saw your sketches and thought she should look at them. Why?"

"Okay."

"Just okay, Georgi?"

"Yes."

He shifted closer to her, close enough for her to feel his breath in her ear. "You know I don't like public displays of affection and I'm also not one to kiss and tell. What goes on between you and me is not a topic for discussion. Not even with my family."

Georgina closed her eyes and rested her head on his shoulder. It would take her a while before she would get used to a man mature enough to know who he was and what he wanted. "I like your surprise," she said after a comfortable silence.

"I'm glad you did."

"How will I ever thank you, Langston?"

He chuckled softly. "I'm sure I'll think of something that we both like."

"I'm going to have to hang out here a little longer because I exceeded my two-drink limit." The bubbly wine had temporarily dulled her reflexes and she didn't trust herself to get behind the wheel.

Langston kissed her hair. "You can spend the night if you want. I can put you up in one of the spare bedrooms."

"If that's the case, then I'm going to need a toothbrush and a T-shirt."

"Your wish is my command, princess."

Georgina shifted until their mouths were only inches apart. At that moment not only did she want him to kiss her again but also to make love to her. "I'm also going to need you to give me a raincheck for that movie."

He nuzzled her ear. "Consider it done. What else do you need from me?"

She knew if she didn't say it, then the time would pass, and she would be left chiding herself for being a coward. "I want you to make love to me." The words were out, and she couldn't retract them. Since becoming involved with Langston she'd found herself fantasizing about his making love to her.

Langston blinked slowly. "Is that what you really want, babe?"

"Yes. And please don't make me beg you."

"That's something I don't ever want you to do. And you have no idea how long I've waited for you to say those words."

"How long?"

"Too long. I have to clean up out here, and then I'm going to show you just how much I've come to love you."

Chapter Twelve

Langston didn't want to believe his fantasy was going to become a reality when he reentered the bedroom to find Georgina in his bed. However, he knew making love to her tonight was not a possibility because she'd fallen asleep waiting for him while he'd extinguished candles and put away the remains of their dinner. Light from a bedside lamp provided enough illumination for him to observe the rhythmic rise and fall of firm breasts under his T-shirt. He smiled. It was apparent the clothes she'd chosen to wear had artfully concealed a lithe, lush, very feminine body. She had loosened the braid and a profusion of wayward curls covered her pillow. To say she was sexy was an understatement.

He walked into the bathroom to brush his teeth and when he returned to the bedroom Georgina rolled over on her side, facing away from him. Slipping into bed next to her, Langston reached over and turned off the lamp, plunging the room into darkness. Georgina stirred slightly when he pressed his chest to her back, but did not wake up. Resting an arm over her hip, he closed his eyes and sank into a deep, dreamless slumber.

Georgina woke with a start, eyelids fluttering as she tried focusing on her surroundings. Suddenly, she remembered she was in Langston's bed. She tried sitting up, but the arm on her midsection weighed her down.

"Stop wiggling, babe."

"What time is it?"

"Why?"

"Because I need to know." Georgina was so disoriented that she felt like Alice in Wonderland who'd fallen down the rabbit hole."

Langston removed his arm and reached over to peer at his cell phone. "It's 11:14."

She sighed audibly. "I thought it was much later."

He kissed the nape of her neck. "What's the matter, Cinderella? Do you still have to get home before midnight?" he teased.

Georgina laughed as she shifted into a more comfortable position. "I've transitioned from Cinderella to Sleeping Beauty. I can't believe I drank that champagne."

"You only had two glasses because you didn't finish the third one."

"That's where I went wrong because I never should've accepted the third one. Shame on you, Langston Cooper, for trying to get me tipsy so you could take advantage of me."

"I would never take advantage of you, babe. And I would never do anything to you that you don't want me to do." His hand splayed over her flat belly moved lower to the waistband of her panties, and still lower to cover her mound under the lacy fabric. "Does it bother you if I do this?"

Georgina sucked in her breath. "No," she gasped.

His hand slipped under the waistband and it was flesh against flesh. "What about this?"

She closed her eyes and liquid fire shot through her. "That feels so good."

Langston buried his face in her soft, scented hair, breathing a kiss on the fragrant curls. His mouth moved slowly to the side of her neck, pressing a kiss to the velvety flesh. Using a minimum of effort, he turned her over on her back and moved lower, down to her throat, tasting the sweetness of her skin. Even in the dark, she was a visual feast. He continued his oral exploration when he divested her of the T-shirt and his mouth closed over her breast, suckling until the areola pebbled like tiny seeds. His hands were as busy as his mouth when he relieved her of the scrap of lace that made up her panties.

The moans coming from Georgina's throat were Langston's undoing. He'd hardened so quickly that it made him light-headed. He knew he had to slow down or his making love with her would be over before it began. Taking deep breaths, he flicked his tongue over her nipples, worshipping the flesh covering her perfectly formed full breasts. Langston loved her smell, the way she tasted, and now that he'd openly acknowledged he was in love with her he wanted her to be the last woman in his life.

He wanted to taste every inch of Georgina's fragrant body, but wasn't certain whether she had experienced a full range of lovemaking. She may have had sexual intercourse, but he wondered if she'd ever been made love to. And that was what he wanted to do—make love to her. His touch and kisses became bolder as his tongue dipped into the indentation of her belly button. Attuned to the changes in her breathing, the slight movement of her body, Langston took his time giving and receiving pleasure. Her hands went to his head when he buried his face between her thighs to inhale her distinctive feminine warmth and scent.

Her fingernails bit into his scalp as her hips lifted. "Easy, baby," he crooned softly. "Let me make you feel good." She tried to sit up, but his right hand splayed over her belly stopped her. "Relax, darling. I'm not going to hurt you."

Georgina wanted to tell Langston there was no way she could relax when she was drowning in erotic sensations that heated the blood coursing through her veins, taking her to a place where she had never been. She'd had only one man by whom to judge Langston's lovemaking, and there was no comparison. This was no frantic coupling, but a slow, measured seduction that had her craving his caress, his kiss. Everywhere he touched her ignited a burning passion that grew hotter and hotter until she found herself gasping in the sweetest agony.

The barrier she had erected after she had ended her relationship with Sean was swept away with the onslaught of desire that weakened her defenses, and she opened her heart to welcome the pleasure that had eluded her for years.

He lessened his sensual assault on her flesh when he reached into the drawer of the bedside table and removed a condom. It took only seconds for him to protect her from an unplanned pregnancy. Currently having a baby was certain to short-circuit all her plans.

"It's all right, sweetheart," Langston whispered in her ear, when he positioned his erection at the entrance of her femininity. She grew stiff when he pushed against her long-celibate flesh. "Breathe, baby. Just breathe," he crooned over and over.

Georgina felt the increasing pressure as he finally eased his sex into her body, which flamed with fire one minute, and then she trembled uncontrollably from cold the next. The hot and cold sensations continued until the heat won and love flowed through her like thick, warm, sweet honey. Her arms went around Langston's strong neck, holding him where they'd become heart to heart, flesh to flesh and soul to soul. Establishing a rhythm as if they'd choreographed their dance of desire, she discovered a pleasure that sent shivers of delight up and down her spine. He had promised to make her feel good, and she did.

She felt the contractions. They began slowly, increasing and growing stronger until she was mindless with an ecstasy that shattered her into a million little particles. Georgina screamed! Once, twice, and then lost count as the orgasms kept coming, overlapping one another. She dissolved into an abyss of satisfaction that swallowed her whole. She was too caught up in her own whirling sensations of fulfillment to register the low growl exploding from Langston as they climaxed simultaneously. They lay together, savoring the feeling that made them one with the other.

Georgina moaned in protest when Langston pulled out. Turning over on her side, she lay drowning in a maelstrom of lingering passion that lulled her into a sated sleep reserved for lovers. She was unaware when he had left the bed to discard the condom, or when he returned to the bed, eased her against his body and joined her in a slumber that was a long time coming.

Georgina opened her eyes, her breathing faltering. The slight ache between her legs and the hard body pressed to her back silently communicated she wasn't the same woman who'd awoken the day before.

"Good morning, baby."

"How did you know I was awake?" she asked, because she hadn't moved. A sliver of light came through the drawn drapes.

Langston pressed a kiss to her bare shoulder. "Your breathing changed."

She smiled. "How long have you been awake?"

Rising on an elbow, Langston leaned over and brushed a wealth of curls off her cheek. "Not too long. I was waiting for you to wake up to ask what you'd like for breakfast."

Turning over she smiled at him. The emerging stubble on his lean face only enhanced his overall masculinity. "Surprise me."

"Continental or American?"

"American of course." When given the choice Georgina always preferred a traditional Southern breakfast with bacon, eggs, grits and biscuits, but usually waited for the weekends when she did not have to work Sundays. Now that she no longer worked at Powell's she had a lot more options when it came to her meals. "I need to shower before I eat."

The words were barely off her tongue when Langston scooped her up as if she weighed no more than a small child. "We'll shower together so I can wash your back."

She buried her face against the column of his neck, pressing a kiss under his ear. "Be careful, because I spoil easily."

"Princesses are born to be spoiled. And the next time we have a sleepover, don't forget to bring a few changes of clothes."

"You do the same whenever you stay over at my place."

"It's like that?"

"Yes, Langston, it's like that."

"What do you think about us living together? You give up the guesthouse and move in here with me."

Georgina wanted to scream at him because they'd made love only once and he was ready to shack up with her. Well, that wasn't happening because she'd just moved out of her parents' home and she wasn't about to give up her newfound freedom to cohabitate with a man.

"I can't, Langston."

He stopped at the entrance to the bathroom and met her eyes. "You can't or you won't?"

"Both. I wasn't raised to shack up with a man and

don't forget that I just moved out from my parents' house and it feels good not to answer to anyone but myself as to my whereabouts."

His lids lowered as a wry smile twisted his mouth. "Point taken. Forgive me for bringing it up."

"There's nothing to forgive. Something must have prompted to you ask, so I want you to feel free to say whatever is on your mind."

Georgina felt something had changed between them when Langston set her on her feet. The intimacy they'd shared had vanished quickly, and in its place was a wariness that communicated to her that her lover wasn't happy with her response. What he needed to understand was that she did not move out of her parents' home just to move into a man's. The days when women moved out of their father's house and into their husband's were over.

Perhaps if Langston had become involved with her when he first returned to the Falls she would've jumped at his offer, but now it was too late. Currently she wasn't willing to sacrifice her newfound freedom, not even for love.

Georgina realized she'd misjudged Langston's reaction to turning down his suggestion they live together when he'd send her funny emojis to begin and end her day. He'd called to inform her they would be leaving the Falls to drive to DC late Friday afternoon. The Fourth of July fell on a Monday, which indicated the three-day celebration would begin Saturday morning.

Red, white and blue bunting and American flags were in abundance in the downtown business district. There was an excitement in the air that was almost palpable as a caravan of trunks with carnival rides, games and food vendors arrived to set up in a field that had been left undeveloped to accommodate the number of carnival trailers and the increasing number of vehicles belonging to out-of-towners willing to pay the parking fee.

Georgina was spending more time at the shop when, after several trips, she had transported all the bins from her house to the store. She wanted to be ready when the shelving was finally installed. She'd placed labeled removable adhesive tape on the tiled floor where she wanted the furniture arranged.

The bell rang and she peered through the solar shades. A shriek of excitement escaped her when she unlocked the door and reached for her cousin's hand. "Please come in before folks realize I'm still not open." The words were barely off her tongue when Sutton Reed picked her up and spun her around and around.

Sutton's large, dark eyes were filled with amusement. "I still can't believe that my little cousin is going into business for herself."

She kissed his smooth-shaven cheek. "Believe it. And when did you get in?"

"Less than a half an hour ago. Aunt Evelyn told me I could probably find you here."

Georgina stared at the man who had women waiting at stadium doors and in hotel lobbies to get him to notice them. His brown complexion with shades ranging from rosewood to alizarin, and features, which appeared almost too delicate for a man, were qualifications for Sutton when he'd appeared in People magazine in their most beautiful issue. And seeing him up close and personal was a testament to that description. Whenever he looked at someone, they seemed mesmerized by eyes that gave them his full, undivided attention, and with his towering height and muscled physique he was an imposing figure.

"I can't believe you're no longer on house arrest."

Georgina narrowed her eyes at him. "That's not funny."

Sutton reached for her, but she managed to avoid him. "I'm sorry, Georgi. That was uncalled for. I know how long you've wanted to move out on your own."

She crossed her arms under her breasts. "What's the saying? Better late than never. Enough about me. How's your knee?" He'd shattered his right knee sliding into a base, and was subsequently placed on the injured list. Sutton underwent a serious of surgeries, and then notified his agent that as a free agent he was retiring from the game.

Sutton ran a hand over the stubble on his recently

shaved pate. "It's a barometer. It tells me every time we're going to have inclement weather."

"How long has it been since your last surgery?"

"Seven months followed by countless weeks of rehab. At thirty-six I'm too old for baseball and too young to retire and sit back to do nothing. I'm going to wait a year before I decide what I want to do with the rest of my life. Meanwhile, I plan to do what I can to help out at the store."

"Did your mother come up with you?"

Sutton rolled his eyes upward. "She called at the last minute to tell me she was staying in Atlanta for the holiday. I didn't want to ask because I knew I wouldn't like the answer about who or what is keeping her there."

"Do you think she's still seeing your father?"

"I don't know and don't want to know." He glanced around the space. "You really picked a nice place."

"I was lucky because the landlord completely renovated it after the last tenant. He put in a new floor, updated the electrical system and modernized the bathroom. You can have a look around if you want."

"I'll do that at some other time. I just stopped in to let you know I'm back. Are you going to need help setting up?"

"I don't believe so. The deliverymen will set up the furniture, and those bringing the shelving know they have to anchor them to the wall."

"What about a security system?"

Georgina smiled. It was one of the first things her father had questioned her about once she went over the details of setting up shop. "I'm waiting for him to arrive within the hour." Once she stored her inventory, two flat screens and two sewing machines in the storeroom, she'd scheduled a date for the entire premises to be wired directly to the sheriff's office.

Sutton tugged on the braid falling down her back. "Good for you. I know you're busy, so I'm looking forward to seeing you over the weekend."

"I'm not going to be here for the weekend. I have to go to DC on business." Georgina had decided not to say anything to her family about becoming a children's book illustrator until she'd agreed to the terms in her contract. And she decided not to sign anything until she had her lawyer look it over."

"Well, I suppose I'll see you when you get back."

She looped her arm through Sutton's. "Of course you will. Now that you're staying with your uncle and auntie, I will be certain to drop by and see how you're adjusting to life in a small town."

Since moving out, Georgina stopped in to see her parents once and no more than twice each week, while her mother called every other day to give her an update of the goings-on in the store. She knew Evelyn missed her, and Georgina had to admit she missed seeing her mother, yet decided now that the cord was cut, she did not want to revert to the time when Evelyn depended upon her for constant companionship.

"You forget I came from a small town, and I must admit it feels good to be back."

"Are you saying you got tired of Hot Lanta?"

"Don't get me wrong, Georgi. I loved Atlanta, but there were times when I just wanted to walk out of my house and encounter absolute silence. I didn't need to hear planes flying overhead, car tires on the roadway, or even my closest neighbor's music whenever they were having a party. Wickham Falls isn't Mayberry, but it comes close. I know times have changed where we now have folks addicted to drugs, but it still hasn't reached the stage where it's become an issue."

"That's true. The Falls has changed, but not so much that it has diminished the quality of life," she said in defense of their hometown.

Sutton tugged on her braid again as he lowered his head and kissed her forehead. "I'm proud of you, Georgi, for going out on your own. If you need anything—and I mean anything—just let me know and I'll help you out."

She laughed. "You're no different than my father. Thank you very much, but I don't need any money, Sutton."

He winked at her. "Just asking."

The ringing of the bell chimed throughout the empty space. "That must be the technician."

Sutton walked to the door. "I'll hang out here until he's finished."

"That won't be necessary."

"I'm not going to leave you alone in here with some strange man who may use it as an opportunity to take advantage of you."

"Are you still watching those crime shows?" she asked as he walked to the door. Sutton had admitted to her that his guilty pleasure was watching true-crime programming.

"I wouldn't miss them," he said over his shoulder, and then unlocked the door.

The technician walked in, holding out his ID badge. "Yo, man. You're Sutton Reed. I remember that triple play you made when you caught that fly ball, stepped on first base to double up the runner and then threw home to cut down the player at the plate."

Georgina sat, sighing when Sutton and the technician launched into a discussion about baseball. Her cousin was prepared to leave before she'd mentioned someone coming to wire the store, and now he was deep in conversation with a man whose knowledge of baseball indicated he was an avid fan of the game. West Virginia did not have a professional baseball team, but that didn't keep folks in the Falls from rooting for either the Washington Nationals or the Atlanta Braves. Rather than sit and listen to the two men talk sports, Georgina retreated to the storeroom and opened a large bin with knitted and crocheted babies', toddlers' and children's hats, sweaters and socks. Whenever she sat long enough to relax, she found herself knitting and crocheting handmade garments she anonymously donated to the church's outreach for their clothing drive. She didn't know why, but she always became emotional when seeing a child wearing one of her creations.

Georgina managed to crochet and finish two beanies using lime-green baby yarn by the time the technician completed his task. He'd installed cameras and sensors before instructing her step by step how to arm and disarm the system. He promised to return to hook up a panic button under the reception desk once her furniture was delivered. She waited for Sutton and the technician to leave before punching in her code, arming the system, to leave and return home to pack for her trip to DC.

Georgina stared out the windshield when Langston came to a complete stop in the driveway leading to his sister's home. The three-story house was dark, and she wondered if Jacklyn was still up.

"Maybe we should've waited for tomorrow morning to drive up. It looks as if everyone has gone to bed." They'd left Wickham Falls at nine because Langston wanted to wait for the latest edition of *The Sentinel* to come back from the printer.

Langston undid his seat belt. "Jackie's still up.

She claims she's more creative once everyone goes to bed."

"What if she isn't up?"

"Stop stressing, babe. I called my sister before I came to pick you up, so she knows to expect us."

Georgina undid her seat belt and waited for Langston to come around to help her down. She was looking forward to seeing his sister again, if only to reminiscence about high school. There were times when she regretted not attending college because then her social circle would have expanded beyond the kids with whom she'd gone to high school. Langston had formed friendships with his college roommates and colleagues at the television station, while her day-to-day existence did not venture beyond the environs of Wickham Falls.

Langston had helped her out and gathered their bags from the cargo area when the front door opened. "See. I told you Jackie would still be up."

She walked with Langston up the porch steps, smiling when Jacklyn extended her arms. "Thank you for inviting me to your home."

"There's no need to thank me, Georgi. You're involved with my brother, so that makes you family."

Georgina wanted to tell Jacklyn that she was getting ahead of herself. She and Langston sleeping together did not translate into an engagement or even marriage. "We'd wanted to get here earlier but—"

"Don't you dare apologize," Jacklyn said, cutting

her off. "I rarely get to bed before one in the morning. The exception is when Peter's home."

"Is your husband going to be here this weekend?"

"He came in a couple of hours ago. Whenever Peter is called away, I never know for how long or when he's coming back." Jacklyn looped her arm through Georgina's. "Come inside. I'll show you guys to your room. I'm going to put you in the mother-in-law suite where you will have complete privacy, because it's off-limits for the kids."

"How old are your children, Jackie?"

"Brett is five, and Sophia is three going on thirty-three. Both are really excited because they're going to spend a couple of weeks with my parents on their houseboat."

"Are you going with them?"

"Nope. It isn't often I get a break from my kids, so when Mom and Dad asked to see their grandkids I did not hesitate to say yes. Peter's on vacation, so he's going down with them. Once you have children, you'll discover that a temporary break is needed to maintain your sanity."

Georgina wanted to tell Langston's sister that at thirty-two she still had time before she began thinking about starting a family, because at the present time it wasn't a priority for her.

Jacklyn led them down a hallway off a sitting room. "You guys are here." She opened a door and stood aside while Georgina and Langston walked in. "Sleep well."

Georgina smiled at Langston once Jacklyn had closed the door behind her. The suite to which they'd been assigned had a king-size bed, sitting area, double dresser, en-suite bath and walk-in closets. "This is very nice."

"Jackie thinks of you as special, because whenever I come to visit, I always sleep in one of the third-story bedrooms."

"You're just her brother, while I'm going to be her illustrator."

Langston set their bags on the floor in a corner. "Bragging, princess?"

"Yes." She slipped out of her tennis shoes and then unbuttoned her blouse. "I don't know about you, but I'm ready to go to bed—to *sleep*," she added, when he flashed a wolfish grin.

"Aw, baby. You're not going to give me some?"

"No, and not for the next five days."

He stared at her before realization dawned. "Oh, I see."

Even if she hadn't been on her menses, Georgina had no intention of allowing Langston to make love to her in his sister's home. She wasn't being prudish but felt what they did to and with each other could be done in the privacy of either of their homes.

Bending, she opened her weekender and removed

a nightgown and a cosmetic case. "If you don't mind, I'm going to use the bathroom first."

Fifteen minutes later she reemerged to find Langston in bed, snoring lightly. It was apparent he hadn't waited for her. She slipped into bed next to him and turned off the bedside lamp. Resting an arm over his flat belly, she closed her eyes and fell asleep.

Chapter Thirteen

Georgina sat in the Lindemanns' home office with Amelia Kincaid. The room was more like a living room than an office with a sofa, chairs, wall-mounted flat screen, audio equipment and a wood-burning fire-place with family photographs lining the mantelpiece.

The fifty-something woman had arrived from New York on the noon train, and Peter Lindemann had volunteered to drive to Union Station with his son and daughter to pick up his wife's literary agent. Jacklyn said every time her husband returned home from an assignment his children treated him like Santa on Christmas morning.

When Georgina was introduced as their uncle

Lang's friend, Brett and Sophia had cautiously approached her before Sophia crawled up on Georgina's lap to ask to touch her hair. The toddler appeared transfixed that she had curls like her uncle's friend. Both children had inherited their father's dark-blond hair, and their hazel eyes were a strikingly beautiful contrast to their light brown complexion.

Georgina felt slightly uncomfortable as Amelia continued to stare at her but vowed not to let the other woman see how much she was affected by her. Amelia took off her tinted glasses and pinched the bridge of her pencil-thin, narrow nose. Sunlight coming from the window behind glinted off short, jet-black hair, reminding Georgina of a crow's or raven's feathers.

"You're quite a surprise, Georgina."

She gave the older woman a direct stare. "Why would you say that?"

"When I first saw your illustrations, I thought you would be a lot older."

Georgina's expression did not change. The woman was not only rude but also judgmental. "Are you saying that my age is going to be a factor when it comes to negotiating a contract for me?"

Spots of color dotted Amelia's fair complexion with the jab. "Not at all. I'm just saying that you will probably enjoy a long and celebrated career as a children's book illustrator once I convince Jacklyn's publisher that you should become her personal one."

Georgina lowered her eyes. "I'm sorry. Forgive me for being presumptuous."

Amelia laughed. "Not only are you beautiful, but also modest."

Jacklyn cleared her throat. She'd held her twisted hair off her face with a wide headband. "My brother would definitely agree with you, because he and Georgina are in a serious relationship."

Realization then dawned as to why Amelia had appeared so entranced with her. It was apparent the agent was attracted to women, and it was the first time she'd become conscious of someone of the same sex seemingly coming on to her.

"By the way, where is your brother?" Amelia asked Jacklyn.

"He left to go to the television station where he used to work to reconnect with some of his former colleagues."

Appearing satisfied with Jacklyn's explanation, Amelia opened a leather binder filled with a sheath of papers. "Well, I think it's time we get down to discussing business." She unscrewed the top to a fountain pen and scribbled something. She tore off the page and handed it to Georgina. "This is what I'm going to ask them to give you for the first book in the series."

Georgina stared at the numbers. "Is this your highest, mid or lowest quote?"

Amelia slumped back against the cushion on the armchair and put on her glasses. "Why are you asking?"

"Because it seems quite generous for a first-time illustrator. I know the more they offer me the higher your fee as my agent. What I don't want to do is price myself out of contention when the publisher feels they can get someone for a lot less."

"It is on the higher end of the scale," Amelia admitted.

Although she did not want to minimize the worth of her talent, Georgina also wasn't going to let the agent make it impossible down the road for her to sell her sketches. "What if we start at the middle, then when it comes time to negotiate for a subsequent contract we can ask for a little more than the higher end of the scale?"

Amelia's mouth tightened in frustration. "Your illustrations definitely warrant a little more, Georgina. Do you have any idea of how talented you are? You are truly a gifted artist."

She gave the avaricious agent a long, penetrating stare. "I am aware of my talent because my grandmother told me a long time ago that I have a special gift. So yes, I know that I'm talented." Georgina pointed to Amelia's pad. "Perhaps you can write down another figure that would make it easier for me to agree to have you rep me." The agent scribbled another number and this time Georgina smiled. "That's better. Once the contract is finalized I'd like my attorney to go over it before I sign and send it back to you."

Amelia retuned her smile. "Did you major in business in college?"

"No. I never went to college, but I did have the best teacher when it came to running a business. My father."

"She's right," Jacklyn confirmed. "The Powells have owned and operated the same family business in Wickham Falls, West Virginia, since right after the Civil War, so she's definitely not a novice."

Georgina realized Amelia now saw her differently. If the woman's client had been anyone other than Jacklyn, Georgina would've walked out of the meeting. Greed bred contempt, and she wanted no part of it.

"I will draw up a contract between you and me, outlining my fee and the length of the agreement, which can be terminated in writing with thirty days' prior notice. I hope this meets with your approval?"

Georgina nodded. "It does."

Amelia stood up. "I'm going to go to my room and work on this."

Waiting until the woman left, Jacklyn closed and locked the door behind her and sat on the love seat next to Georgina. "You really pissed her off. There aren't too many who are able to challenge Amelia Kincaid, who has earned a reputation as a piranha. It's true she fights to get the most money out of a publisher for her clients, but she's also in it to make as much for herself. She's never married, doesn't have any kids and lives in a prewar, rent-controlled apartment on the Upper West Side overlooking Central Park that belonged to her parents, and she's also as penny-pinching as they come. Whenever she entertains a client she always orders the cheapest item on the menu."

"Aren't those expenses tax-deductible?"

"Yes, but she still doesn't like to spend money. The one time she came down to meet with me I'd discovered that she'd checked into a flophouse and wound up with bedbug bites. That's why I tell her she can stay here."

"How do you think she would react if you gave her a bill for lodging and food?"

"You know you're bad, Georgina Powell," Jacklyn teased as she flashed a wide grin. "Enough about Miss Tight Wad. Now you have to tell me how you and my brother got together."

Georgina told her everything from the time she and Langston shared a table and a dance at the Chamber fund-raiser, to his being supportive when she decided to move out and start up her own business.

"Are you aware that my brother is in love with you?"

Georgina stared at the pattern on the rug. "I am, because he told me."

"Are we talking about the same Langston Wayne Cooper? Because even when he told me he was going to marry Ayanna, he refused to admit that he was in love with her."

This revelation about the man she had fallen in love with shocked Georgina, because not only was he forthcoming about how he felt about her, but he held nothing back whenever they made love. "Maybe he's changed because of what he'd experienced as a foreign correspondent. Being bombarded daily with the possibility of death can be very sobering."

Jacklyn squeezed her hand. "It's apparent you know my brother better than I do. I promised Peter I would cook out if doesn't rain. He's probably going to invite some of his buddies from the Bureau along with their wives to come over and hang out with us this weekend. So I'm going to warn you in advance that there's going to be a lot of testosterone and concealed weapons in attendance, which I insist they lock up as soon as they arrive."

Georgina laughed and wanted to remind Jacklyn that there probably wasn't a house in the Falls where there wasn't a rifle, shotgun or handgun. Her father had taught her to shoot the year she turned twelve, and the recoil from the powerful automatic nearly knocked her off her feet. It took weeks of practice before she was able to load, unload and hit a target. Then she swore never to pick up a gun again.

Langston felt Georgina's pride as if it was his own. It was her grand opening and A Stitch at a Time was filled with curious and potential customers. Although she had had to wait until the second week in July to open, the wait was more than worth it.

The town council did not meet during the months of July and August; however, several members were on hand to cover the event while Jonas Harper was in attendance to take photos for the newspaper.

Once they'd returned from Washington, DC, Langston did not get to see Georgina as often as he would've liked. And it was as if time had sped up because she was spending more time at the shop waiting for the delivery of furniture and accessories, and then meticulously stocking the Plexiglas shelving with yarns and threads by color and weight. He was in awe when he saw an entire wall of colors from alabaster white to midnight, unaware there were that many colors in the spectrum. He also learned that quilting squares were called fat quarters, crochet hooks were sized by letters and knitting needles by numbers.

She'd arranged the space for ultimate relaxation with love seats and armchairs, where one could opt to watch television or indulge in coffee from a single-serve coffeemaker, an assortment of teas and a cooler with dispensers for hot and cold water. Georgina had ordered an assortment of cupcakes and pastries from Sasha's Sweet Shoppe for the occasion. Framed prints of women knitting, crocheting and quilting adorned the walls covered in a pale wheat-like fabric. There were signs advertising free instructions with purchase of materials, a display case with hats, sweaters, scarves and afghans for sale. Also a corner table with sewing machines and racks from which hung hand- and machine-made quilts. The shop also had a customer-only restroom.

Georgina had designed an ad with a coupon offering escalating discounts for total purchases, and even deeper discounts for the first twenty customers. Her logo, a quilt square along with the shop's address and telephone number, was stamped on white paper shopping bags and business cards.

Langston had interviewed her for the "Who's Who" column and planned to run it in the upcoming edition along with Jonas's photos. When she initially told him she wanted to host her grand opening on a Sunday he'd thought it odd, but when Georgina explained that she wanted people to stroll in and look around and possibly sign up for instruction and then take several days to determine if they wanted to join the scheduled classes she'd set up, he realized it was a brilliant plan, because her first official day of operation wouldn't be until Tuesday.

Georgina's parents and Sutton had also stopped by. Evelyn appeared to be overcome with emotion when she walked in and saw that all the time and hard work her daughter had put into A Stitch at a Time to make it a charming retreat where her customers could come to develop and explore their creativity. He'd found it almost impossible not to stare at Georgina as she exchanged pleasantries or showed someone a pattern from one of the many instruction books on display. Langston had teased her when she'd shown him the black smock with white lettering identifying the business, that she'd turned in Powell's for Stitch's. She'd laughed, and then explained as an artist she had to represent the medium because she remembered having to wear a smock whenever her classes went to art.

There were times when Langston forgot that she was an artist whether sketching her illustrations or piecing a quilt. He'd visited museums where there were exhibits with quilts and other textiles. He had come out to report on her grand opening, but also to support the woman with whom he wanted to spend the rest of his life. The first time he'd asked her to move in with him Langston knew it had been too early in their relationship to make that request. Her comeback that she wasn't raised to shack up with a man spoke volumes. She wouldn't live with him unless they were married.

And he did want to get married again, and hopefully get it right the next time. But he had to remind himself that Georgina wasn't Ayanna. She didn't have abandonment issues and had come into her own as an independent woman and business owner, while he didn't have a career that would take him away from home for extended periods of time. Langston knew he had to wait, wait until Georgina felt confident enough to manage her career, marriage and hopefully children. He'd watched her interact with his niece and nephew, and Sophia clung to her like Velcro. She followed Georgina everywhere and cried when she set her down. Even his sister had mentioned her daughter's fixation with his girlfriend, teasing him that he shouldn't wait too long to make Georgi an auntie for her children.

Waiting until there was a lull in foot traffic, Langston approached Georgina and kissed her cheek. "You are incredible. Congratulations."

Eyes shimmering with excitement, Georgina smiled up at him. "Thank you for helping me set up everything."

"There's no need to thank me, Georgi. I love you and would do whatever I can to make certain you succeed in whatever you set out to do."

She lowered her eyes. "Don't, Langston."

"Don't what? Don't love you?"

Georgina sucked in a breath to compose herself. It wasn't what he'd said, but how it had come out. The passion in his voice made her heart stop for a few seconds before starting up again. All before they were just words, but this time they were more. And for the first time since coming face-to-face with him at the fund-raiser she realized how much he did love her.

"We'll talk about this later. Once I close up, I'll come by your place. I'm not opening until Tuesday, so maybe I can convince my man to take a few hours off on Monday so we can spend some quality time together."

Langston shrugged his shoulders. "I don't know if that's possible. I have to ask my boss if I can take time off."

"You are the boss, Langston."

His expressive black eyebrows lifted. "You're right. I am the boss."

Rising on tiptoe, she brushed a kiss over his mouth. "I'll see you later."

"Okay, sweets."

Georgina watched him walk, unaware her mother was staring at her. "You really like him, don't you?" Evelyn whispered in her ear.

"I love him, Mom."

Evelyn looped their arms. "What are you going to do about it?"

She turned and stared at Evelyn, who looked nothing like the woman she was before she'd gone to Hawaii with her husband. She'd regained some of the weight she'd lost over the years, her hair was fuller, styled in a fashionable bob, the chemically straightened strands ending at her jawline.

"What do you mean?"

"Are you going to marry him, or are you going to drag your feet and let some other woman sink her hooks in him?"

"Mama. Langston and I haven't been dating long enough to even broach the subject of marriage."

"You're not a girl, Georgina, but a grown-ass woman with a ticking biological clock. If not now, then when?"

Georgina could not believe what she was hearing. In the past it had been her father talking about grandchildren, and it was apparent her mother had become his ally. "I'm not going to answer that. I don't intend to fast-forward my relationship with Langston because you want to become a grandmother. However, if things change between us you will be the first one to know."

Evelyn pressed a kiss to her temple. "Thank you, sweetheart. I know I don't say it enough, but I'm so proud of you. This place is beautiful. I know my mother was disappointed that I didn't like knitting or crocheting, but I think it's time I pick it up again. Maybe I'll make Bruce a sweater for Christmas."

"I recommend you begin with an afghan. I have patterns where you can crochet and complete one in forty-eight hours."

Evelyn smiled. "That sounds more like it."

"I know your favorite colors, so I'll pick out the yarn and photocopy a few patterns that will work up quickly."

"Thank you, baby."

Minutes before five, Georgina turned over the sign on the front door from Open to Closed, lowered the solar shades covering the plate-glass windows and dimmed the recessed lights. She cleaned up the coffee station, ran the vacuum cleaner over the floor and carpeted area and rearranged chairs. Potted plants and vases of flowers from well-wishers covered the surface of a table next to the reception area. Her grand opening wasn't about ringing up sales but a welcoming event to introduce townsfolk to their newest local business.

Georgina lay in bed with Langston, holding hands. Within minutes of his opening the door to her ring, he'd swept her up in his embrace and carried her to the bedroom where he'd undressed her and entered her body without saying a word. Words were irrelevant when they allowed their bodies to speak for them.

And she knew at that moment if he'd asked her to live with him, Georgina would've ignored what her mother and grandmother had preached to her about shacking up with a man. She was modern woman who didn't need a promise of marriage to live with a man.

"I think I'm going to ask my boss to take a few hours off tomorrow," Langston teased.

She turned to stare at his profile. "Who will cover the office?"

"Now that Sharon is away, Randall is next in line."

"When did she quit?"

"She didn't quit, princess. She took a leave to deal with some personal business."

"I remember when I used to go the paper's office to hand in an ad or drop off a check, Miss Sharon would give me what I thought of as the stink-eye, because the woman never smiled."

"Sharon is all business and the life's blood backbone of the paper. It would've gone under a long time ago if not for her."

"You've done wonders with *The Sentinel*. It was on life support before you took over and folks were saying it was just a matter of time before it folded completely."

Langston gave her hand a gentle squeeze. "It hasn't been an easy journey, and everyone is on board to keep the presses rolling."

Georgina pressed her face against his muscular shoulder. "You don't have to take off. I'm going to be here all day tomorrow and plan to make a special dinner for you when you come home."

"Be careful because I can be spoiled quite easily with just a few homemade dinners."

Releasing his hand, she straddled his body. "Get used to it, my prince. Because spoiling you makes me very, very happy."

Georgina could not have envisioned the pace in which her business had taken off. She had a steady stream of customers signing up for lessons and more experienced ones who came in to sit and work on their projects, or form new friendships.

The summer was over and with waning daylight hours and the approaching fall and winter holidays, many knitting and crocheting projects were quick sellers. A month following her meeting Amelia, the agent forwarded her the contract from the publisher, which she gave to Nicole Campos-Austen for her perusal. The local attorney gave her a thumbs-up, congratulating her on her new venture. Georgina signed the contract and now awaited an executed copy and payment, which would legally make her a professional illustrator.

Georgina had knitted a birthday sweater for Langston's nephew using a royal blue acrylic yarn. The front of the garment had orange pumpkins, a haystack, scarecrow and cornstalks. She'd resisted knitting witches or other ghoulish images because she felt they weren't appropriate for a child to advertise. Jacklyn had called to tell her Brett did the happy dance when he saw the sweater and refused to take it off even when it was time for him to go to bed.

Georgina leaned over the woman attempting to piece squares using the sewing machine. "You have to control the speed, or your stitches will be uneven."

Mrs. Jefferies shook her head in exasperation. "I just can't use these newfangled machines. I'm so used to quilting by hand."

"Then you should continue to quilt by hand, Mrs.

Jefferies. It may take longer, but you have more control."

The older woman's eyelids fluttered. "I want to finish this crib blanket for my new great-grandbaby for Christmas."

Georgina patted her shoulder. "Don't stress yourself. I'll machine stitch the squares for you, then you can finish it up by hand."

"Really?"

She smiled. "Yes. I'll call you when I'm finished."

The octogenarian gave her a warm smile. "Thank you so much, Georgina. You truly are a blessing."

She thought it was the opposite. Her customers were a blessing for her. They patronized her shop more than they had the crafts section at Powell's. She'd believed she had enough inventory on hand to last at least six months, but swift sales were an indicator she would have to reorder sooner rather than later.

Her relationship with Langston had grown even stronger and there were times when she spent more nights at his house than at hers. Many of the homes in the new development on the Remington property were completed, and Georgina had to decide whether she would continue to rent the guesthouse, move in with Langston, or put in a bid to purchase one of the newly built homes.

She'd lowered the shade in preparation of closing when her cell phone rang. "Hi, Jackie."

"Hi, yourself. Amelia dropped by to leave our executed contracts and checks. I told her to mail yours to you, but I assume she didn't want to pay the postage to overnight it. I can't understand her. She said we live close enough so you can pick it up from me. I just can't get over her obsession with hoarding money."

"It takes all kinds to run the world, Jackie. Maybe she had a partner who took advantage of her generosity where she was left almost penniless, and that's scary for someone who has to depend on themselves to stay afloat."

"I never thought of that. I know I can mail them to you, but the kids have been asking about you."

Georgina smiled. "I miss them, too. I close Sundays and Mondays, so I'll let you know when I'm going to drive up to see them. Don't tell them I'm coming because I want it to be a surprise." Her surprise would be to give both knitted hats and scarves from a supply she had on hand for sale.

It was the first Wednesday in December and Langston was scheduled to attend the monthly town hall meeting, and knowing she would find him at his office, she decided to stop by to give him her good news before going home. She locked up, walked around the corner to Main Street and mounted the staircase to the second story to *The Sentinel's* office.

The door was unlocked, and she walked past the reception area to Langston's private office, stopping short when she heard him talking to someone. Her eyes grew wide when she did not want to believe what she'd overheard.

"Yes, Mom. I do need the money and I'm going to ask her for what I need to cover the year-end salary increases and bonuses. Why are you trying to talk me out of it? I wouldn't ask if I didn't have a problem with cash flow, but this is going to be a one-time request. Yes, I know she's going to go off on me, but she'll get over it because we love each other."

Georgina had heard enough. She retraced her steps and practically ran down the staircase and out into the night. A cool mist feathered over her face like a gossamer spider web and when she brushed her cheek her fingers were moist from the tears flowing down her face.

Not again! screamed the silent voice in her head. For the second time in her life she'd fallen in love with a man who'd used her for his own selfish purposes. She hadn't told Langston how much she was paid for the illustrations; he was aware that she'd set up her shop without taking out a business loan; and he was also cognizant that as a new business, A Stitch at a Time was doing well.

She drove home, filled the bathtub with bath salts and sat in the nearly scalding hot water and willed her mind blank until the water cooled. Then she did something that she'd never done before. She drank several glasses of wine and then crawled into bed and slept until dawn.

Georgina waited until she knew Langston would be up to call him. He answered after the second ring. "Good morning, princess."

"Langston, I've decided I can no longer see you."

"What!"

"Something has come up in life that won't permit me to become involved with a man. Goodbye."

Chapter Fourteen

Langston felt as if he'd been kicked in the head. Georgina's phone call had left him shocked and numb for days. His first impulse was to walk around the corner to her shop and demand she talk to him but didn't want to cause a scene, which no doubt would impact her business.

He spent days and nights searching his memory as to what he may have said to turn her off but could not come up with a plausible explanation for why she'd decided to break up with him.

She's pregnant! It was the only thing he could think of to elicit her abrupt change in behavior. They'd made love once without using protection, and he'd made her promise to tell him if she was pregnant. He didn't want to think she was carrying his child and rather than trap him she'd elected to absolve him of all blame for not using a condom.

Pressing his head against the back of the executive chair, Langston decided to wait and give her time to come around. If they'd had an argument or disagreement, he would've understood her wanting to break off with him. He loved Georgina and knowing she wasn't going anywhere made his decision to wait more satisfying.

Georgina handed Jacklyn her jacket, picked up Sophia and rubbed their noses together. "How big is my favorite girl?" She'd called Jacklyn to let her know she'd planned to come to Alexandria the weekend before Thanksgiving.

Sophia raised her arms above her head. "This big, Auntie Gigi." She looked over the child's head and met Jacklyn's eyes.

"That's what they call you, Georgi. And when are you going to make that a reality?"

She set the child on her feet. "What are you talking about?"

"We need to talk. Sophia, Momma and Auntie Gigi have to talk so I need you to go and play with your dolls."

Sophia stomped her foot. "I don't want to play with my dolls! I want Auntie Gigi."

"What's going on here?" Peter asked as he suddenly appeared out of nowhere. Georgina stared at the tall, imposing agent with a military haircut. His face was deeply tanned, which made his green eyes much more vibrant. "What did I tell you, Sophia, about talking back to your mother?"

"She won't let me stay with Auntie Gigi."

Peter picked up his daughter. "Your mother and auntie have business to discuss that does not include something little girls need to hear."

Jacklyn mouthed a thank you to her husband. She'd told Georgina that she met her future husband when she'd attended Howard University. She was an undergraduate while he was enrolled in Howard Law. He graduated, applied to the FBI and a year later they were married.

"Come into my office where we can have complete privacy."

Georgina sat and glanced around the office. Jacklyn had lit a fire in the fireplace. "I love this room. It's like a warm hug."

Jacklyn smiled. "It's my favorite room in the entire house. I tell Peter that I don't need to go on vacation because this space is my sanctuary."

"You have a wonderful family."

A beat passed. "Thank you. And I hope beyond hope that you would also become part of my family."

Georgina knew it was time for her to open up to Langston's sister as to why she decided to break up with her brother. "Langston and I are no longer seeing each other." Jacklyn's jaw dropped with this disclosure. It was apparent he hadn't told her that they had split up. She continued revealing what she'd overheard Langston talking to his mother about, asking her for money, despite his pronouncement that he did not need it. "I dated a man who had a gambling addiction and strung me along for eight months with the intent of using me to bail him out. Do you realize why I refused to date anyone in high school?" Jacklyn shook her head. "It was because I heard boys talking about going out with me because my father owned the department store and I stood to inherit everything once he retired or passed away."

"You eavesdropped on a conversation where you only heard one side?"

Georgina knew Jacklyn was angry when her hands tightened into fists. "I'd heard enough."

"For someone who's so incredibly talented, you are just as naive. Don't you dare open your mouth to defend yourself until I have my say, Georgina Powell. Langston would never need your money because he has a net worth of seven figures. I minored in finance and he's trusted me with his investments. The advance and royalty payments from Langston's books made him a very wealthy man. He had me run the figures before he bought the newspaper and the house from our parents where we were raised. He was talking to our mother about asking me to withdraw money from one of his accounts to cover year-end raises for his employees. And that should be a lesson to you about jumping to conclusions without hearing both sides of a conversation."

Georgina placed a trembling hand over her mouth. She'd misjudged the only man whom she wanted to marry and have children with. "I'm sorry, Jackie."

"Don't tell me, Georgi. You need to call Lang and apologize to him."

Reaching into the back pocket of her jeans, she took out her phone and tapped his number. "Yes, Georgina."

"I'm sorry."

"Where are you?"

"I'm in Alexandria with your sister."

"How long do you plan to be there?"

"Long enough for you to get here."

"Hang up. I'm on my way."

Georgina sat on a bench at the rear of the Lindemann property, baring her soul to Langston. "I'm sorry I misjudged you. Can you forgive me?"

Reaching for her hand, Langston massaged the back of it with his thumb. "I'll have to think about it but on one condition."

"What's that?"

"Marry me, Georgina Powell. Marry me and make me the happiest man in the world."

Resting her head on his shoulder, she cried without making a sound. "Yes, I will marry you," she whispered. "When?"

Shifting to face her, Langston anchored a hand under her chin and kissed the tears dotting her cheeks. "I'll leave that up to you. I'd like to give you a ring for Christmas, but it's your call when it comes to setting a wedding date."

Georgina placed light kisses at the corners of his strong mouth. "I'd like a Valentine's Day wedding."

"Will it fall on a weekend?"

"I don't care, as long as I become your wife on the day set aside for lovers."

Angling his head, Langston gave her a long, healing kiss, sealing her promise and their future. "Let's go inside and give everyone the good news."

"I'm certain Sophia is going be ecstatic when I try to explain to her that she's going to be Auntie Gigi's flower girl."

Georgina said a silent prayer of gratitude that she'd gotten a second chance at love with a man who'd come back to Wickham Falls to start over and begin a new life with her.

* * * * *

COMING SOON!

We really hope you enjoyed reading this book.
If you're looking for more romance, be sure to
head to the shops when new books are
available on

Thursday 28th May

To see which titles are coming soon, please visit

millsandboon.co.uk/nextmonth

MILLS & BOON

Coming next month

MARRYING HIS RUNAWAY HEIRESS
Therese Beharrie

'It isn't a boat. It's a gondola.'

'My mistake,' she said blandly, and made him smile. She did that a lot. And he was smiling more than he ever had before. That worried him, too. But it didn't stop him from smiling at her. Or from thinking about how different she was now, when she wasn't thinking about the decision she had to make.

What if she didn't have to make it?

He couldn't pay attention to the thought when the gondolier called for them to get in. He did, using the man's help, then gently nudged him aside to help Elena. She smiled brightly, and it became obvious why he'd wanted to help her. Apparently, he would do anything to get that smile. To keep it there, too.

It stuck as they sat down and the gondola began to float down the canal. It was a bright, sunny day, and the blue green of the water around them sparkled as it stretched between buildings. A gentleman began to sing, rich and deep, and Elena sighed at his side. She snuggled closer, not intentionally, he didn't think, but it made him hold his breath.

That might not have been the right description of it. It was more like someone was squeezing his lungs, so he had less capacity to breathe. He'd felt that way the entire day. When they'd been exploring the stores around St Mark's Square. Or when Elena had insisted on feeding the pigeons, then got alarmed when more and more of them came.

'What is it with you and pigeons?' he'd asked. 'I told you this wouldn't end well.'

'I thought you were exaggerating. You exaggerate.'

'You live in Cape Town, Elena. You've been to the Waterfront. You know what pigeons are like.'

'I thought European pigeons would be different.'

He'd laughed, harder when she hid behind him. She'd ended up giving the bag of seeds to a kid before running away, causing the pigeons to scatter. They'd eaten pasta and chocolate crêpes and taken pictures. Once, Elena had photobombed another couple, then apologised profusely and taken about twenty pictures of them alone to make up for it. Now they were here, on the canal, having someone sing to them.

It was a lot to process. Not the experience, but the emotions that accompanied it. And the thoughts. Those insidious thoughts that had popped into his mind all day, then scurried away before he could put his finger on what they were suggesting. They all pooled together now though, growing into an idea that stole his breath.

It was based on never wanting to see Elena as tortured as she had been the night before. To keep her as happy as she was now, as she had been all day. It was built by the memories of how she'd elevated his business banquet that night in Rome because she fitted so perfectly into his world. She went head to head with him when he did something stupid, forced him to think about the way he treated people, and made him feel more like himself than he ever had. If he'd ever encountered his equal, she was it.

She was it.

'This is so nice,' Elena said at that moment, as if sensing his confusing thoughts. And his body, as if confused itself, responding by putting an arm around Elena's shoulders.

He froze. Until she rested her entire body against him. Then he melted.

It was like the hug from the night before. Warm and comfortable. Except there was more now. She was looking up at him, smiling, and he felt himself stumble. Whatever part of him had been standing steady in the face of the onslaught that Elena was unknowingly waging against him broke down. Whatever sanity he had left that told him not to indulge his ridiculous idea fled.

The proposal spilled out of his mouth.

'Marry me.'

Continue reading
MARRYING HIS RUNAWAY HEIRESS
Therese Beharrie

Available next month
www.millsandboon.co.uk

LET'S TALK
Romance

For exclusive extracts, competitions
and special offers, find us online:

 facebook.com/millsandboon

 @MillsandBoon

 @MillsandBoonUK

Get in touch on 01413 063232

For all the latest titles coming soon, visit
millsandboon.co.uk/nextmonth

MILLS & BOON

THE HEART OF ROMANCE

A ROMANCE FOR EVERY KIND OF READER

MODERN

Prepare to be swept off your feet by sophisticated, sexy and seductive heroes, in some of the world's most glamourous and romantic locations, where power and passion collide.
8 stories per month.

HISTORICAL

Escape with historical heroes from time gone by. Whether your passion is for wicked Regency Rakes, muscled Vikings or rugge Highlanders, awaken the romance of the past.
6 stories per month.

MEDICAL

Set your pulse racing with dedicated, delectable doctors in the high-pressure world of medicine, where emotions run high an passion, comfort and love are the best medicine.
6 stories per month.

True Love

Celebrate true love with tender stories of heartfelt romance, fro the rush of falling in love to the joy a new baby can bring, and a focus on the emotional heart of a relationship.
8 stories per month.

Desire

Indulge in secrets and scandal, intense drama and plenty of siz hot action with powerful and passionate heroes who have it all: wealth, status, good looks…everything but the right woman.
6 stories per month.

HEROES

Experience all the excitement of a gripping thriller, with an inte romance at its heart. Resourceful, true-to-life women and stron fearless men face danger and desire - a killer combination!
8 stories per month.

DARE

Sensual love stories featuring smart, sassy heroines you'd want a best friend, and compelling intense heroes who are worthy of th
4 stories per month.

To see which titles are coming soon, please visit

millsandboon.co.uk/nextmonth

t might just be true love...

MILLS & BOON
MEDICAL
Pulse-Racing Passion

Set your pulse racing with dedicated, delectable doctors in the high-pressure world of medicine, where emotions run high and passion, comfort and love are the best medicine.

JOIN THE
MILLS & BOON
BOOKCLUB

* **FREE** delivery direct to your door

* **EXCLUSIVE** offers every month

* **EXCITING** rewards programme

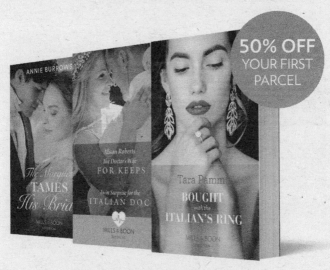

50% OFF
YOUR FIRST
PARCEL

Join today at
Millsandboon.co.uk/Bookclub